THE DERRING-DO CLUB

Volume Two

Also by David Wake

NOVELS
I, Phone
The Derring-Do Club and the Empire of the Dead
Hashtag
The Derring-Do Club and the Invasion of the Grey
Crossing the Bridge
Atcode

NOVELLAS
The Other Christmas Carol

ONE-ACT PLAYS
Hen and Fox
Down the Hole
Flowers
Stockholm
Groom

NON-FICTION
Punk Publishing *(with Andy Conway)*

THE DERRING-DO CLUB

and the

Year of The Chrononauts

DAVID WAKE

WATLEDGE BOOKS

This is a work of fiction. Names, characters, places, and incidents either are the product of the author's imagination or are used fictitiously, and any resemblance to any persons, living or dead, business establishments, events, or locales is entirely coincidental.

First published in Great Britain by
Watledge Books
Copyright © 2014 David Wake
All rights reserved

This paperback edition 2014
1

ISBN-10: 149931695X
ISBN-13: 978-1499316957

The moral right of David Wake to be identified as the author of this work has been asserted by him in accordance with the Copyright, Designs and Patents Act, 1988.

No part of this publication may be reproduced, stored in a retrieval system, or transmitted in any form or by any means, electronic, mechanical, photocopying, recording or otherwise without the prior written permission of the publishers.

This book may not be lent, hired out, resold or otherwise disposed of by any way of trade in any form of binding or cover other than that in which it is published, without the prior consent of the publishers.

Cover art by Smuzz
www.smuzz.org.uk

For
Loncon 3, Worldcon

This adventure of the Deering-Dolittle sisters takes place after the dread business with the Austro-Hungarian **'Empire of the Dead'**.

CHAPTER I

Miss Deering-Dolittle

Thirty four years, eleven months and fifteen days before the End of the World, the men from the future first materialised with plans to change everything, and thus started a chain of events that led inexorably to the death of one of the Derring-Do Club.

The coming of the new century, the Twentieth, promised a new age of hope and opportunity for everyone, except for the three Deering-Dolittle sisters of the Derring-Do Club. Or so it seemed to Miss Earnestine Deering-Dolittle, and, Oh! how she wished Charlotte's silly name for them hadn't stuck. It wasn't their family name! That was spelt 'Deering' for a start. For someone who received letters with the 'a' of her Christian name missing, it was particularly galling. The spelling 'Derring' suggested adventures, which would not do at all.

"Come on," she shouted. "Time's running out!"

Before she left, Mother had given Earnestine strict instructions on the matter: *keep them safe, no exploring, no trouble, no adventures.*

Not that the eventuality was likely, because they were still incarcerated in Zebediah Row, Kensington, utterly unable to mount a rescue expedition to find their lost Uncle, Father and Mother. The members of that ill-fated expedition stared out from the daguerreotypes framed on the wall of the drawing room, each face full of pride and determination, amidst their baggage, bearers and boats. The rest of the Deering-Dolittle family ranged across the wall in mismatched frames, but there was only one picture of the three sisters together: Earnestine, twelve then, already looking stern and important; Georgina seated and already beautiful at ten, and Charlotte, then six, wriggling despite the lollipop bribe.

A year after that picture was taken, Earnestine had become the de facto head of the family – *look after your sisters*, Mother had said as the trunks were loaded onto the ship – and Earnestine had grown up instantly: and yet, she had the responsibility, but none of the rights that came with proper age.

If you were older, they said, if you were married, if... if, *if*... always 'if–'.

Earnestine, the eldest, was not 'of age' and it would be aeons and aeons before her twenty-first birthday in five months' time. In the meantime, Uncle Jeremiah, along with trustees and lawyers, kept them all trapped. It chafed.

"Tighter," she told the maid, as she had her red hair pulled up into a bun, tucked by clips, and yanked upwards. She wanted to stand tall in her fine formal, dark red dress and her best Oxford Street boots.

"Tighter!"

"Miss, I'm doing my best."

"Your best is not good enough."

The maid was such a freckled, clumsy yokel.

"Don't snivel," Earnestine reminded her yet again.

"Sorry, Miss."

Finally satisfied, she felt she gave the correct appearance of a woman in control of her destiny: if only people would take her seriously. And they must, she thought, if she was going to make a life for herself. After all, there was no chance she would find a husband.

Georgina, the middle sister, looked wan after their recent experiences. She'd lost her husband and it had taken its toll on that beautiful round face of hers, framed in dark curls and hidden behind her mourning veil. She was still attractive, of course, and she was young – eighteen was still young – so despite her misfortune she might yet find a suitable match. Earnestine hoped the planned evening would jolly her up. Georgina liked the theatre; she always made the most entertaining of voices, when they'd played with the cardboard actors on the wooden stage of their fine, model theatre. Uncle Jeremiah had made it for them.

Bother it, she thought, he should be here by now.

Also, coming were three eligible bachelors, so perhaps... well, for Georgina's sake, one could certainly hope.

Charlotte was the youngest at fifteen, pretty with long blonde tresses and a tendency to... where was the girl!?

"Charlotte!"

"Coming, Ness."

...tendency to be silly, flouncing around in – oh dear.

"Not that jacket."

"But–"

"A dress, not a military uniform."

"It's a dress jacket."

"Don't be impertinent."

"I was not."

"You are a young lady; you should act like a young lady."

Charlotte, youngest *etcetera*, with long blonde hair that... fell loose around her shoulders.

"Ribbon!"

"Will there be a band?"

"Don't change the subject."

"I'm sure there'll be plenty of variety," said Georgina.

Charlotte wanted to be some sort of female soldier, when really she was an exasperating tomboy flibbertigibbet.

The doorbell jangled and the maid skittered along the hall to answer it.

Major Dan had arranged an evening at the theatre for the *Derring-Do Club* as a belated thank-you and Lieutenant McKendry had sent a note: 'A night out at the theater to put some color back in Georgina's cheeks.' He was another person who had no idea how to spell. The sisters had met the Major's three 'mountaineers', Caruthers,

Merryweather and McKendry, in Switzerland and had thus become embroiled in the adventure... no, not adventure, the *events* of that dreadful Austro-Hungarian business.

Through the bay window, Earnestine could see the waiting carriages looming in front of the house.

The maid bobbed in holding two cards.

"Captain Caruthers, Miss, and Lie... ut..."

"Lieutenant, pronounced with an 'f'."

"To be sure, Miss. Lieutenant McKendry, Miss."

Earnestine stepped into the hall to greet them.

Captain Caruthers stood waiting. The light from the stained glass window around the front door caught his strong features. He was tall with thick brown hair and a matching chevron moustache.

"Major Dan sends his apologies," he said.

"That's a shame," said Earnestine. She saw McKendry waiting outside, easily recognizable because of his thin black handlebar and chin puff, and made a quick calculation: three sisters and only two men wasn't going to work at all.

"We've two four-wheelers ready to whisk us all to the West End," Caruthers pointed out.

"Spiffing!" Charlotte shouted as she raced, ribbon-less, down the stairs.

"Come on girls!" Captain Caruthers called out, holding the door open. "Like the jacket, Lottie."

"Thank you," said Charlotte, ducking beneath his arm in an overly familiar manner.

Georgina gave a little bow and Captain Caruthers stepped aside.

Earnestine waited.

"Come on," said Captain Caruthers, "or you won't get any ice cream."

"But I'm..."

Caruthers sauntered off down the garden path.

...*not a child.*

6

They had ordered two landaus for seven, so it was three per carriage now.

"Oh, Ness," said Captain Caruthers, "your Uncle Jeremiah sent a telegram: he's meeting us at the theatre."

"But..." Earnestine tightened her lips. Their Uncle was supposed to serve as their chaperone (even though he couldn't be in both carriages), but now, three women and two men meant she'd be packed in with her sisters' crinolines for the whole journey.

However, it turned out to be worse!

Lieutenant McKendry had already set off with Georgina and Charlotte in the first carriage, which was fine for a short journey, because Georgina had been married and could act as chaperone for Charlotte, but that left one carriage for Captain Caruthers and herself.

"Facing or back?" Caruthers asked.

It was intolerable.

During the journey, Earnestine had no idea where to look, because the man was sitting directly opposite her. Occasionally, he made to open conversation, or fidgeted with some envelope, taking it out and returning it to his pocket, but the silence just dragged on, particularly when the traffic ground to a halt in Piccadilly.

The four miles seemed more like four hundred.

Captain Caruthers looked over his shoulder: "Seems to be some hold up."

She could see that, she was facing forward.

When they finally arrived in the West End, Uncle Jeremiah was not there to greet them.

Earnestine glanced up and down the street, but there was nothing in the fog, except indistinct shapes looming like phantoms. Any of these ghostly forms could materialise as their Uncle, but they all steadfastly refused to do so.

There was nothing for it, so they all went into the plush entrance hall.

"We'll leave instructions at the Box Office," Earnestine suggested, "that way—"

"There he is!" Charlotte raced forward.

Uncle Jeremiah was on the wide stairs that led to the Circle talking to a lady in a burgundy dress. He'd heard Charlotte's unladylike yelling, so he made his goodbyes, and came down to join them.

"Tell us a story, tell us a story," Charlotte demanded.

"Lottie, little Lottie, stand still so your Uncle can see you," said Uncle Jeremiah, nodding either with approval or because he couldn't decide whether to look through, or over, his half-moon glasses. His sideburns were wild and hairy, his whiskers fine and his white hair was all askew. He was the same old Uncle Jeremiah, who had weaved tales of adventure for them as they grew up. Earnestine, despite her anger at his tardiness, smiled.

"Uncle," she said, "who was that lady to whom you were talking?"

"Captain Caruthers, isn't it?"

Captain Caruthers jolted to attention: "Sir?"

"We met at the... didn't we?"

"Yes, Doctor Deering, at the... yes."

So many conversations these days were frames without a picture. The unmentionable event was the funeral of Georgina's husband, the late Captain Merryweather, whose presence still haunted them with so many pauses.

"This way," Lieutenant McKendry suggested, and he led them up the stairs and along a curving corridor. Much to Earnestine's chagrin, she realised that Major Dan had booked a box. Georgina and Charlotte loved the idea, but to Earnestine's mind it was ostentatious. If they were going to see a show, they should see a show; and not face the rest of the audience as if they were the performers themselves.

"Sit here, my dear," said Uncle Jeremiah guiding Earnestine to the front seat.

"Adults at the back," Earnestine said.

"Yes, dear, and children at the front."

"But–"

"And here are your sweetmeats."

So Earnestine was sat at the front, with her packet of tiny pastries, with her face feeling as red as her dress.

She could hear Uncle Jeremiah, Captain Caruthers and Lieutenant McKendry discussing weighty matters: politics, the troubles in Africa, the recent disappearances and even the cricket with an emphasis on playing by the rules; whereas she had to–

"Do you think there will be elephants?"

"Lottie," Earnestine replied, "how would they get an elephant in here?"

"They might."

"Shhh..."

Where was she? Oh yes, playing by the rules; whereas she had to–

"Ow!"

"Sorry, Ness."

"Don't fidget, Lottie."

Whereas she had to... take her mind off her worries. She'd write it out a hundred times: *I must take my mind...* No, she wasn't a child, so there was no need to write lines any more.

Earnestine looked around the auditorium taking it all in. The curtains were red velvet, plush, and the walls were decorated with curls and patterns picked out in gold leaf. The stalls had the more middle classes, but the Circle and particularly the Boxes held collections of very finely dressed individuals. She could clearly see those in the opposite boxes. Lord and Lady Farthing, some foreign dignitaries with red sashes and, in the third box, a single, elegant woman dressed in a burgundy outfit with a black net veil pushed up to allow her to peer through a pair of powerful opera glasses.

Instinctively, Earnestine glanced over her shoulder: the men were earnestly discussing Grace and Darling, and then she realised they were still going on about whether Australia would win the Ashes. When she looked back, she saw the woman still staring in her direction as if she were studying something. Without doubt, the woman was watching one of them in their box.

But who?

There was only Caruthers, McKendry, Uncle Jeremiah, Georgina, Charlotte or... surely not.

The galvanic lights dimmed and the curtain twitched. An 'ooh' of anticipation gathered in the stalls below and those in the Circle leaned forward.

Instead of feeling excitement, the darkness let Earnestine's recent worries intrude. Simply put, she was too young.

At twenty, she certainly didn't feel like a little girl, but then she had never felt like a little girl. Recently, they'd been thrust into the desperate world of international affairs, vis-à-vis preventing an Austro-Hungarian faction from conquering the British Empire.

This, surely, was an experience that counted over and above the actual number of her birthdays. She had hoped that this service would be rewarded with the funds to mount an expedition to trace their Father and Mother's last known whereabouts.

It didn't and hadn't.

Unfortunately, a twenty year old young lady was not considered responsible enough by the Foreign Office, the Royal Society, the British Archaeological Society or any of the other numerous clubs devoted to exploration. Leave it to the men, they explained patiently: which was all very well, she had no problem with that at all, *except that the men never did anything.*

She was forming the opinion, quite strongly, that all they did all day in those clubs of theirs was sit around talking. Goodness only knew what they spent all that time discussing.

"No, no," said Caruthers, "Darling captained in '99, and he's a left-hander."

"He has a beard though," Uncle Jeremiah replied, "and Grace is right handed."

"Yes, that's all very well," countered Caruthers, "but Grace retired in the series and Archie MacLaren took over."

"Of the English team."

"Yes, my point, and it was the Aussie, who had the moustache."

The other issue, for Earnestine, was money.

The house in Zebediah Row was covered by an annuity put in place by Father and Uncle Edgar before they went exploring, but there was no arrangement for pocket money and they were down to their last shillings. The theatre sold cones of cockles, for example, but, unless one of the men offered, they couldn't even share one between the three of them. (There was the emergency money in the Adventuring Kit, but no! They were not going on another adventure. Mother had been quite explicit: *no exploring, no trouble, no adventures...* so that had to stay there... just in case.)

So, in summary, Earnestine was not happy.

The solution, of course, was for one of them to marry. A man, even some callow youth aged sixteen, could control finances, organise expeditions *and* would be allowed to sit at the back with the adults.

Georgina had married: possibly well, for Merryweather had been a Captain, but now she was a widow. She was the middle sister, so Earnestine had been overstepped and was therefore destined to be a spinster. Without doubt, then, the family's future rested firmly upon Charlotte's shoulders. Earnestine turned to consider Charlotte, who was beautiful in a showy way with her long blonde hair and who was currently *pulling faces at some soldiers down in the stalls.*

"Charlotte!"

11

Charlotte turned a sweet smile in Earnestine's direction: "Ness?"

"Sit back."

"But I won't be able–"

"Sit! Back!"

Earnestine felt the nape of her neck burning. Charlotte was no doubt sticking her tongue out at Earnestine, but Earnestine refused to turn around and give the silly thing the satisfaction of seeing how cross she had made her elder and better. Captain Caruthers and Lieutenant McKendry wouldn't be shocked, they knew Charlotte too well, but it meant that there'd be no bliss in her direction from either man.

Perhaps Major Dan was worth considering? He had, after all, a Major's stipend and hadn't actually met Charlotte.

The auditorium darkened and the galvanic lights came up on the stage. A hush and then applause rippled through the audience as the plump Master of Ceremonies, a jolly dandy in a dress suit, bounded from the wings.

"My Lords, Ladies and Gentlemen," he began. "Tonight, for your entertainment, for your exaltification, your edification and your entreipidation..."

His pause elicited an 'ooh'.

"I don't think those are words," Earnestine said.

"Don't spoil it, Ness," Georgina whispered in reply.

"...your entrapulation."

"See?"

"Ness!"

The Master of Ceremonies established and extended an edifice of excitement and exhilaration before, exhausted, he changed letter: "First, a Maestro of Magic, the Mage of Mañana, the Mephistopheles of Magnificence – do you want to know your future, madam? This man, this prestidigitator of precognition, can *and will*. Lords, Ladies and Gentlemen, all the way from Moscow, the Master Malakov!!!"

Another formally dressed man entered to the Master of Ceremonies beckoning hand.

"Dames, Gospoda! And the spirits, the ethereal conveyors from the beyond, I bid thee welcome."

The magician sported a Russian beard, piercing eyes and some vowels from Hackney, but he had a charisma that demanded attention. He strode across the stage, held his right hand to his forehead and invited the audience closer with his left.

"The spirits," Malakov announced, "they are here, they can see the future. You madam, your name is... Ethel."

"It is, it is," said a woman in pink, turning round to tell everyone behind her row.

"You come from... Harrow."

"I do, I do."

"You – I see it now, clearly as if it were happening this very moment in front of me – you are going to meet a stranger, tall and dark."

"Oh yes."

Everyone in the stalls thought it incredible, but Earnestine was less impressed. I mean, she thought, how would one know if Ethel from Harrow was going to meet a tall, dark stranger? The audience applauded and Ethel was well pleased, but surely such an act should be congratulated only after it was demonstrably true. And men were either tall or short, light or dark, known or unknown, so surely by the law of averages, Ethel was bound to meet at least one tall, dark stranger with every eight men she met.

The Master Malakov turned his attention to the higher realms of the auditorium.

"I feel... is there someone who has lost a dear, dear person to them?"

Georgina stiffened next to Earnestine.

"Well, obviously, one's only got to look at how many people are dressed in black," Earnestine said, rather too

13

loudly. She regretted it as the Master's attention was drawn inexorably towards their box.

"Up here," Malakov said. He pointed and a light from upon high shone in their faces. "Yes, a father... no, a husband... beginning with an eee... jaaa... aahhh."

Georgina cried out: "Arthur!"

"Arthur, he was tall... a military man."

Georgina lent forward: "Yes."

"He's here now."

The audience applauded the arrival of the unseen military man.

"He wants to say something... yes... it's coming through now... 'I love you'."

Georgina breathed out, a gasp of utter rapture: her cheeks shone in the light. She was crying: there was no excuse for such a display, Earnestine thought, and that went for all the women swooning in the stalls as well.

It was simply bad taste to remind those who had lost a loved one of their calamity. Part of the reason they were going out for the evening was to try and jolly Georgina out of the dark humour that had settled upon her, and not to have entertainers turn it into a spectacle for all and sundry.

Now, Georgina would just sink back into her black mood again, all because her husband had been murdered during that business with the Austro-Hungarians, which hadn't been an adventure at all.

It was rotten luck, undoubtedly, but Earnestine had caught Georgina not exactly complaining, but sighing and gazing longingly into the distance and generally carrying on. All this sympathy for Georgina was one thing, but in truth she was jolly lucky to have had a husband at all. Earnestine suspected Georgina was deliberately being sick every morning to engender the appearance of romantically suffering. It came from reading Shelley.

The so-called Russian returned to the stalls and told a man on the third row that he would come into a fortune because of a red crow.

"Running in the two thirty," shouted some wit.

The crowd laughed and the magician made his farewell with a bow.

Earnestine felt guilty: she was being unfair, deplorably so. Her worries were spilling over into meanness and she resolved to stop thinking ill of people and to be kinder.

"Would you like a sweetmeat?" Earnestine asked Georgina.

"Thank you," Georgina replied. She took two: she was eating like a horse these days.

A hand and a military sleeve with frayed cuffs appeared from behind with a handkerchief for Georgina.

One should be more understanding, Earnestine thought. Yes, a little more consideration and a softer voice would be the right tonic for her sister.

"What's the matter with you?" Georgina asked.

"Nothing at all," Earnestine snapped.

Next was a comedy routine about the French Foreign Legion, which was distinctly bloodthirsty. Obviously Charlotte loved that, and jounced up and down braying in a vulgar manner.

This was followed by an equally uncouth turn: a singsong by a cockney lady, whose sharp voice was thankfully drowned out by the massed choir of the stalls.

Another magician showed genuine shimmering ghosts in a large room constructed on stage for the purpose, but their position in the box meant they couldn't see properly. However, they did see an actual apparition clearly present, floating by the magician, which was extraordinary. He finished his act with sword swallowing and Charlotte named all the weapons used.

The crescendo of the cavalcade of coruscation – the Master of Ceremonies didn't approach alliteration alphabetically – was a brass band and another singsong

15

before a collection for Our Boys Across The Sea fighting the wicked Boer.

Eventually, thankfully, the interminable parade of nonsense came to an end.

Captain Caruthers held the door open as everyone made their way out. Earnestine was the last to reach it. Caruthers shifted, blocking her way.

"That magician: conjuring up the dead like that," he said.

"If one believes in that sort of thing," Earnestine said.

"Good old Merry, eh? Talking like that, in front of all those people and without a hint of a stutter."

Earnestine remembered Captain Merryweather's stutter with a smile: "And foretelling the future, but not in a way we can check."

"The future, yes... Miss Deering-Dolittle?"

"Captain?"

He checked they weren't being overheard: "I was wondering... that is to say. Two things. You've done a great service to the Empire over that Austro-Hungarian business. You were jolly brave, admirable in every way, so I thought that... there are other services... duties and wotnot... that is to say, what I mean is..."

"Captain?"

"I understand your situation. A young lady, who has yet to come of age, and therefore not eligible for her trust, is somewhat beholden to other men, so perhaps other men could..." he faltered, and then rallied: "You understand?"

"What are you trying to say?"

If Caruthers was actually bumbling towards a proposal – and it would take all evening at this rate – then everything would follow his suit like cards in Bridge. Georgina would come back into play naturally and Charlotte could be hidden up a sleeve until she was more sensible. This was a truly excellent turn of events.

But shouldn't one feel all aflutter, Earnestine thought, as they did in those books Georgina read?

"I have something for you," said Caruthers.

He dug in his pocket for something, something flat and white, and at any moment he would drop to one knee and present a ring, but instead he thrust an envelope into her hands.

She fumbled with it and, finally, she felt an emotion.

"One cannot accept this," she stated.

"Why ever not?"

"We don't live on charity."

"It's not charity."

"What is it then?"

"It's a letter of introduction for employment."

"Employment!"

"Yes."

"I'm not a domestic."

"No, please... may I start again?"

"If you please – directly."

"Major Dan and I thought, well, your situation prompted us to consider you, and, of course, your sterling service to Her Majesty and the Empire, which must remain secret, so then the secrecy is a qualification. Don't you see?"

"I'm afraid not, you are being obscure."

"It's an administrative position at the Patents Pending Office."

"Patents..."

"Pending Office, yes. On Queensbury Road, it's impossible to miss," Caruthers explained. "You need simply go and announce yourself."

"I see."

"That's a letter of introduction from Major Dan."

Earnestine smoothed out the envelope. It bore a single letter: 'B'.

"I'll give it some thought," she said.

17

"Do," said Caruthers, and then he paused with casual carelessness. "You'd be doing us a great service, of course, and we all have our duties."

He smiled.

Earnestine nodded: she knew when she'd been gulled.

<u>Mrs Arthur Merryweather</u>

The evening had gone so quickly, and for Georgina it had been fleeting and ephemeral. She had laughed, and sung, and actually enjoyed herself. The entertainment had been jolly and diverting certainly, but to have heard from Arthur again had been a true wonder. However, each step now seemed to take her further away from his kindly visitation. Despite the jostling crowd, she felt alone once more.

The show was over.

She missed Arthur. She wanted to check his watch again, to hold that connection with him a little longer, but the crowd bumped into her too many times and she feared dropping it. She'd been without him longer than they'd been together, but time didn't seem to make a difference. He was an ever-present gap next to her.

Outside the theatre, there was the usual bustle and noise. The street was lit by the garish glow of many gas lamps, those of the theatre glaring up at posters of entertainment and advertisement, while the street lamps blazed upon their wrought iron posts. Women sold matches or posies of flowers, boys ran hither and thither with messages and hawkers plied their wares. A Peeler shooed away a beggar. Newspaper men shouted the headlines and waved copies of the evening editions aloft.

"Another disappearance, another disappearance..." they hollered: there being only one story of the day.

That's what she wanted: to disappear, to get away from all the fuss, and well-meaning tea, sympathy and cake. She wanted to be left alone and yet at the same time she wanted to hold on to what she had left. She knew it wasn't the world that was slipping away from her, but she herself who was drifting.

In her bag was a letter, an official document that she had so often hidden, put aside and distracted herself from, so that it had begun to dominate her every thought. Such was its influence that she had got out her luggage and put away her luggage so many times. She'd even taken down her Bradshaw to look up the train times.

Caruthers appeared with an arm to guide her to a quieter area by some stone steps, but even here it was busy.

"Erm..." he said.

A gentleman vendor approached to suggest that they have their picture taken as a souvenir.

Caruthers sidled away leaving Georgina with an opportunity to examine the photographic apparatus, lifting her dark veil to do so. Perched atop a tripod was a teak box. A glass lens protruded from the front held in a brass fitting and at the back, under a cloth, was the bellows used for focussing the inverted image. The man carefully explained the magic of photography and the alchemy of the enchanted plate, while Georgina patiently nodded and examined the ingenious way the silver-coated, copper daguerreotype plate was inserted. She'd read about it and seen figures from 'a' to 'g', but it was fascinating to see one in reality.

The man came to his conclusion: "...and I hide beneath this cloth to perform the conjuring trick."

"I see you are still using the collodion wet plate process," Georgina said sweetly. "I would have thought that the gelatine dry plate would be preferable."

"This is an excellent apparatus and works perfectly satisfactorily."

"But aren't silver halides more sensitive and thus reduce the required exposure time?"

"I have magnesium powder," he said.

The explosive powder of magnesium and potassium chlorate was ready loaded in a metal flash lamp, the dry cells ready to deliver the galvanic ignition charge.

"Gina!"

It was Earnestine, standing between Captain Caruthers and Lieutenant McKendry, and jerking her hand to call her over. Her place was on the lower step between Uncle Jeremiah and Charlotte, so when she joined them, Georgina felt comforted, surrounded as she was. Perhaps, she thought, she should leave a gap to her right, a space for Arthur. She felt like moving away from Uncle Jeremiah to do so.

Charlotte nudged her.

"Lottie, don't crowd so," Georgina said.

Charlotte answered back: "The man says we should move together."

The photographer seemed like a headless monster as he bent down and buried his head under the cloth hood. His arms stuck out and he waved the group together.

They bunched up.

With a shock, Georgina realised that her mourning veil was still raised. She should move it down, but it was too late: the man held the flash upright and lit the magnesium: it burned, crackling loudly and was painfully bright.

"Don't move!" Earnestine commanded in a voice that had clearly been forced between stiff lips.

Georgina gripped Charlotte's hand to avoid any fidgets.

As she felt the others come to attention, she stood erect and proper too, but in the moment of stillness she shivered. It was as if they were all being watched; she fought the impulse to glance around. As the moment stretched, she had a premonition that everything was passing over, disappearing as if the camera wasn't saving the moment, but stealing it away. She held on tight, hoping she could preserve something.

A man walked behind them, but she knew that he would be smeared away by the long exposure.

She thought about the letter in her bag.

The light died away and the man slotted the covering plates into the camera. They could move again.

It was done, the image fixed forever. Or so it seemed to Georgina then.

Miss Charlotte

"Ow!"

Charlotte pulled her hand away from Georgina's clutches, clenched and opened a fist to restore her circulation. Georgina, honestly, she was becoming far too controlling. It used to be Gina and Lottie against Earnestine, but now Georgina was that tiny bit older, it was Earnestine and Georgina ganging up on 'little Lottie'. So unfair.

Earnestine came over, looking all stern and adult.

"Charlotte."

"Yes, Ness."

"Come along here," said Earnestine, "where the others can't hear us."

They moved away, off the steps along the theatre front, until they were a good few yards away.

"Is it a secret?" Charlotte asked, excited.

"You are going to have to get married."

"What!" – this was all too sudden – "But I'm only fifteen, barely fifteen."

"Yes, clearly you have been slacking these last few years. We need to choose someone eligible, not too old, and with a dependable income, something from land."

"I don't want to get married."

"Nonsense. And you are far too young to know what you want. Women have a choice between being an Angel of the Home or a Fallen Women. You don't want to be a fallen woman now, do you?"

21

"Maybe I do?"

"Don't be foolish. You don't know what one is, so how can you have an opinion either way."

"You're not married," Charlotte countered. "Does that make you a fallen woman?"

"Don't be impertinent."

"I wouldn't mind a Captain like Car–"

"He has frayed cuffs and therefore no money. We need to find an Earl or a Lord or a Lancashire industrialist."

"But they're all fat and ninety!"

Earnestine gave Charlotte a glare: "You may tell them you are a Deering-Dolittle, but on no account mention that we are the branch from Kent."

"Our branch saved the Empire."

"Which hardly engenders a reputation as respectable stay-at-home young ladies."

Charlotte wondered how Earnestine could go on about respectable stay-at-home young ladies when she was being utterly horrid: "Stay at home!?"

"Don't whine," Earnestine chided. "You're becoming as bad as Georgina before she was married."

"But she's ill now. She throws up every morning. I don't want to catch Wife Ague."

"There's no such thing, and she does it discreetly, whereas... from now on, you must be seen and not heard, Charlotte."

"But I'm not a child."

"You were complaining earlier that you were too young," Earnestine pointed out. "A child must be quiet, whereas a young lady looking for a husband must be *silent*."

Charlotte went silent, but out of shock.

"So it's decided," Earnestine said, summing up. "A husband."

Earnestine turned away, and Charlotte saw her dictatorial outline, her hawk-like nose and her pointy witch's chin.

That was it then, Charlotte realised; they'd been planning behind her back to farm her off to some old fuddy-duddy. Well, she'd have none of it. First chance she got she'd talk to Uncle Jeremiah: he always understood her, and he'd invite her in to his drawing room, where he always had macaroons in a tin.

Earnestine and Georgina were talking to Caruthers and McKendry. She could hear them comparing this act with the other, preferring the magician or the dancers, and they were all just stupid, because obviously the military brass band had been the best.

Charlotte took a few steps down until she was on street level, wanting to get as far away from Earnestine as possible.

There was still a multitude of finely dressed theatre goers thronging the pavement. The near constant street hawkers and beggars had been pushed aside. Carriages and hansoms came up to collect passengers, but with much trouble as one vehicle remained resolutely parked at the kerb. Its blinds were drawn up, but the inside was dark, a black like pitch or treacle, except for a single, glowing red ember. Smoke drifted out as the occupant exhaled.

Charlotte was drawn closer and closer, a step at a time, curious to see who waited within.

A hand stopped her.

A man had stepped in front. He had a broken nose, tilted to the left, and pugnacious eyes beneath an eyebrow split with scars. Perhaps, Charlotte thought, he was completely bald for, unusually, he had no moustache and he was hairless from the rim of his bowler down.

He'd broken the spell: the bustle of the street crowded in on her like the school bell fills the corridors with commotion.

23

"Excuse me, Miss," he said, sternly in that self-important manner that only butlers or batmen seemed to possess. "That's far enough."

"Oh, I just..." but Charlotte couldn't think of an excuse. Usually, when she was breaking some school rule or other, she had one prepared.

"Jones!" The voice, a woman's, came from the dark interior of the carriage. "Who is it?"

"I don't know, Ma'am."

The embers waved imperiously casting tiny sparks of glowing ash to the breeze.

The man, Jones, turned to Charlotte: "Who are you?"

"Miss Charlotte Deering-Dolittle, if you please," said Charlotte and she bobbed a curtsey.

A hint of a face shimmered in the evening gas light as the woman leant forward. Charlotte picked out an imperious outline, a regal nose and an elegant chin, a face she felt she had seen before, but couldn't place.

"Little Lottie?"

"Yes, Ma'am."

"Well, well..." the woman sat back, so that her deep chuckling came from the darkness itself.

"Ma'am," said Charlotte, "I don't believe we've been introduced."

Charlotte looked at the servant, but he said nothing.

"Charlotte," said the darkness. "I am Mrs Frasier."

"Pleased to meet you, Mrs Frasier," said Charlotte politely. "May I ask–"

"Charlotte! Charlotte!" It was Earnestine shouting out from the theatre steps. "Where are you?"

Two sharp raps sounded on the ceiling of the carriage: "Driver!" Mrs Frasier commanded.

The driver whipped the horse and the carriage jerked out into the traffic. The man Jones ran, caught a handle and pulled himself up to sit beside the driver.

Charlotte was pulled around by a grip on her elbow.

It was Earnestine: "Where have you been?"

"Here."
"Don't wander off."
"I didn't."
"Who was that?"

Charlotte looked out into the street, but couldn't tell which distant carriage had been the strange woman's.

"I don't know," she said. "Some lady called Mrs Frasier."

CHAPTER II

Miss Deering-Dolittle

How time flew!

Almost a month later and on a Monday morning, Earnestine set off to walk to Queensbury Road. It was a fair distance, but it was a lovely morning, sunny, though chill. A few young ladies shot past her on their bicycles, and a chimney sweep and his lad made rude noises. Earnestine ignored them.

A newspaper vendor shouted and waved his wares: "Temporal Peelers! Temporal Peelers! More arrests."

It was the News of the World, so Earnestine declined.

She stopped briefly at the book shop on the corner. She saw herself hovering ghost-like in the reflection of the street before she focused through the glass to see the atlases, expedition journals and biographies of great explorers. She could go in, she thought, she had plenty of time, but common sense prevailed. Once she was in the shop, she knew, an hour or two could easily fly by. She walked on as she wanted to be early.

She took the route through the park. Children used sticks to knock hoops along and others at the small lake launched toy boats. Ladies strolled in pairs and the occasional gentleman tipped his hat as he passed. It was lovely, green and pleasant, and surely England at its best.

Queensbury Road was a small crescent and hardly the place for such an illustrious establishment as the Patent Pending Office. Captain Caruthers had informed her that the place was impossible to miss, but it turned out to be easily possible. She had to go up and down, up and down again, until, eventually, Earnestine spotted a blue door with a small brass plaque announcing the 'Patent Pending Office'.

She rang the bell, stepped back and linked her hands together in front of her.

Presently the door opened and a bewhiskered old man, his dark hair streaked with grey, appeared, blinking in the sunlight.

"I don't drink," he said sharply.

"You don't?"

"No! So I don't need a lecture and I don't need any literature – good day."

"Good day."

The door closed.

Earnestine rang the bell again.

The door opened once more.

"Yes... I said I don't drink."

"I think there's been a misunderstanding."

"You're not from the temperance movement?"

"No."

"Sally Army?"

"Assuredly not."

"Thank goodness, but, whatever you are selling, I already have plenty."

"I have a letter."

"It's not more of the Chronological Jurisprudence nonsense is it?"

"I have no idea what that is, I'm sure," Earnestine said.

"The Law of Time."

"I'm here promptly, if a little early. It's five before nine," Earnestine replied. "My letter is from Major Dan."

The man blinked, wrinkled his nose and then he glanced up and down the street with his beady eyes.

"Major Dan, eh?"

"Yes, Sir."

"You'd better come in."

"Thank you, most kind."

The passageway beyond was musty and dark, the gas turned very low and it shimmered as the flame stuttered for breath. The old man waved his hand along the corridor and Earnestine made her way to the far end. A heavy door opened into an office, study or library that was utterly packed with papers. There were shelves of them, piles on chairs, stacks on the floor like rectangular stalagmites and in pride of place, a huge conglomeration of documents that might have been supported internally by a stout desk. The only exception was a section of the far wall that had a single, neat row of books and seemed Spartan in comparison.

"My," said Earnestine.

"Yes, yes, welcome... I'd better see this letter."

Earnestine took the envelope from her bag and proffered it to the gentleman.

He examined it – tutting – and when he'd finished reading the contents, he slipped the letter back into the envelope before looking around... this way and that... frowning... until he decided to place the item precariously on top of the nearest stack. At the deepest foundations of this tower was a wooden tray that bore the legend 'sundries'. The tower next to that was called 'miscellaneous' and the next one along had collapsed.

"I suppose you'll be wanting a tour."

"That would be an excellent second step."

"Second step?"

"We haven't been introduced."

The man looked around again, up and down this time, before shrugging.

"There's no-one here to introduce us," he said. "And I know who you are."

"You do?"

"Major Dan was quite efficacious."

"Good."

Earnestine waited patiently as she had been taught, because patience was a virtue, she knew, and–

"Sir," she said. "You are?"

"Boothroyd."

Earnestine offered her hand. Boothroyd looked at it, then glanced around as if he were wondering where to put it. Earnestine took it back just in case.

"I'm looking forward to assisting in the patent application process," Earnestine began. "I think that the work here is important to the Empire as our industry is dependent upon cultivating innovation and invention. Perhaps you could tell me how many patents you award?"

"Patents we award?"

"Per calendar month or whatever is most appropriate."

"We don't award patents here."

"You don't?"

"Not a one." Boothroyd smoothed his white hair, parted upon one side, before continuing: "You're confusing us with the Patents Office."

"I am?"

"Yes, the Patents Office deals with Patent applications, awards and wotnot. We're the Patents *Pending* Office."

"I see," Earnestine said, meaning she didn't.

"Tea?"

"Lovely."

There was a small kitchen area to one side, hidden of course, and Boothroyd brewed some Earl Grey. There were papers here too and none of the cups and saucers matched, but at least they were fine china. He served the tea, swilling the pot before pouring, and added milk for them both. Earnestine almost had to bite her lip to stop herself from correcting him and instead she meekly carried the two cups back into the office.

"I'd better explain," said Boothroyd.

Boothroyd, after looking around, took a stack of papers off a chair and indicated that Earnestine should sit. She did so. He then perched precariously on an edge of the hidden desk to sip his tea.

Earnestine did the same, enjoying the reviving taste.

"Well, my dear," he said. "The Patents Office takes applications, checks that they are original, or at least not patented, and then awards a patent number."

"I see."

"We do none of that. Does that make it clear?"

"I'm afraid not."

"Well, let me try again, certain patents don't progress through the Patent system on account of a lack of continuing application on behalf of the applicant. You see?"

Sadly Earnestine shook her head.

"To put it another way, the applicant doesn't complete their application, so the application comes here and..."

He waved to the stacks of paperwork.

"...it can become jolly useful in certain quarters to certain parties like Major Dan and his other Gentleman Adventurers for.. that is to say, for... erm..."

"For mountaineering?"

"Exactly. And so forth."

"What I don't understand, Mister Boothroyd, is why the applicant doesn't complete their application."

"It's usually because they blow themselves up."

"I see."

"And the War Office is jolly interested in new ways of blowing things up, hence this office. And Major Dan for his little... expeditions. So we sort through it all and select those items that might be of interest."

Earnestine let Boothroyd see that she was looking around the office, before she replied: "Sort?"

"Ah, excellent, precisely our little problem," said Boothroyd beaming. "Dan said you were quick off the mark."

"There doesn't seem to be a system."

"Oh, well, I'm afraid, my dear, that's not the issue."

"It isn't?"

"No."

"What is the issue?"

"We have far too many systems."

Boothroyd stood and held his arm up to encompass the North wall: "This is A to L."

Earnestine shifted so that she could see as far as 'L'.

"Little," said Boothroyd, "Littleton, Littleworth."

"And beyond Littleworth?"

Boothroyd moved around clockwise to the next wall.

"And this is 'Alchemy' to 'Chemistry' and anything in the metric system or Sanskrit."

"I see."

Boothroyd turned south: "Here's everything to do with metals, engineering, steam engines, uses screws, except for brass, of course, which is in the second kitchen cupboard."

Boothroyd stopped, uncertainly, as if he were dizzy from the three-quarter turn.

"Mister Boothroyd?"

"Where was I?"

"Brass."

"The centre of the room is, of course, 'miscellaneous', 'unsorted', 'sundry', and anything in code or on yellow paper."

The old man's face suddenly lit up and he threw his arms wide as if welcoming an old friend or favourite nephew.

"Ah, here's our pride and joy, designed by my predecessor, the Bunton Lodgement Cabinet, Mark II – see, see."

Earnestine obliged, putting down her cup and saucer and stepping up in response to his beckoning. It was a strange contraption, part teak writing desk and part steam engine.

"These drawers go back and then round, twenty four in total – Bunton had no regard for 'C' and 'X', he thought them ostentatious – on both sides, see... marvellous, utterly marvellous."

"May I see it work?" Earnestine asked.

"Of course, of course... as soon as we find the key."

They both looked round, somehow already knowing each other's thoughts on the matter.

"Finally, there's this!" Boothroyd stood with his finger on a novel in the only clean set of shelves.

"I noticed there were no papers on these shelves."

"Of course not, my dear, they'd fall off."

And with that, Boothroyd pulled the leather bound volume sharply. There was a click and the whole section opened inwards to reveal a deep recess.

"My!"

"Yes, my dear, the treasure house."

Mrs Arthur Merryweather

Georgina had waited until Earnestine had left the house, carefully checking Arthur's pocket watch until exactly five minutes had passed, and then, reasonably confident that her sister wasn't going to return, she'd hefted her trunk out from under her bed and packed. She'd felt rushed, but by the time she'd manhandled the heavy item downstairs, there was still plenty of time; although each crash of weight on the step had increased her apprehension that Charlotte, Cook or one of the maids, would appear. She couldn't bear to face them in person considering what she had planned.

Was she really going to go through with it?

But she was packed, wasn't she?

The decision had been made when she'd ordered the cab or earlier, when she'd said 'yes' to become Mrs Arthur Merryweather.

In the hallway, she peered through the red and blue stained glass of the front door to see if the hansom was waiting. She'd inserted far too much safety margin into her schedule. Writing and packing clearly didn't take as long as—

"Letter!"

She ran upstairs and found the envelope on her writing desk. She re-read it, even though she'd double and triple-checked it last night when she'd finally resolved to do this. She sealed it – finally – and went downstairs.

Fifteen minutes.

She put Arthur's watch back in her bag and checked outside again, the red pane for up the road and the blue pane for down.

She became aware of the hallway, its embossed Lincrusta wall covering and the teak table by the coat stand. There was Earnestine's umbrella, almost a family heirloom considering its provenance. She wondered about the rest of the house and when she would be back again, or if... ever.

She didn't want Cook to spot her and ask some awkward questions, so she slipped into the quiet of the drawing room and closed the door behind her. The heavy curtains had been drawn back by one of the maids and, although the lace remained, there was a reasonable view of the street. With the drapery tied back, it made the outside world appear like a stage beneath a proscenium arch: a play awaiting her entrance.

She took a long, lingering look around the room and drank in the ambiance as one might savour the fine whisky or the brandy that graced the sideboard. The pianoforte was silent, the photographs on the wall were still and the dust wasn't even allowed in here to settle. Even so, without any specks in the air, something had lodged in her eye.

She should have said something.

She owed it to Earnestine and to Charlotte, and to the Derring-Do Club.

She felt sick.

Breakfast, even though it was kippers today, had held no appeal for Georgina. Her stomach had been very delicate recently, but that was undoubtedly due to the growing trepidation.

The clock ticked.

The hansom was due any minute now – ten minutes – and London cabbies were never late.

Tick-tock, tick-tock.

Hanging on the wall was a new addition, the daguerreotype taken of them all together at the theatre. From left to right, there was Lieutenant McKendry, Captain Caruthers, Earnestine, Uncle Jeremiah, then herself and finally on the right hand side Charlotte. Charlotte appeared indistinct, caught by the slow exposure in the act of fidgeting. Silly Charlotte! She looked like – Georgina shivered – a ghost. She'd seen photographs of real ghosts, spectre-like figures that were seen in shapes and shadows. Most were probably like this one, an effect of the photographic process, but, despite knowing the mechanics, this example disturbed her.

Death seemed everywhere: the world through her veil was dark, her widow's weeds were black and the sinister troubled her thoughts.

There were other pictures, all neatly framed: Mother and Father; Uncle Jeremiah, who had stayed behind; Uncle Edgar, who had not, and even one taken at the expedition's first camp, that last sighting before they had gone up the river and disappeared. There he was, smudged slightly because this was where they always pointed: Father, standing proudly surrounded by native guides and missionaries with his hunting rifle slung over one shoulder.

The clock ticked.

There was no time.

Five minutes.

It wasn't long enough.

She should have snuck down last night to be all maudlin.

She put the letter in its cream envelope behind the mantelpiece clock – the obvious place. She'd addressed it

35

simply to 'Miss Deering-Dolittle', but inside she'd written 'To My Dearest Sisters, Ness and Lottie'.

She was a Deering-Dolittle, not the soft Surrey branch, but the mad brigade from Kent, and the club code demanded she put her best foot forward on any adventure.

So, without further ado, and leaving the letter tucked behind the tick-tocking timepiece, she was going forth on the long expedition into what she hoped was a fabulous new world, full of surprise and wonder, but she knew she was headed towards an 'X' on the map that was in the middle, the absolute middle, if not the furthest possible edge, of nowhere.

A shadow fell across the window.

The hansom cab pulled up, the black horses shaking their heads in unison.

It was time.

With a sudden impulse, she grabbed a daguerreotype off the wall and slipped it into her travelling bag. She needed a keepsake to remind her of the three of them together. As she went to close the clasp, the ghostly image of Charlotte stared up at her.

Click, case closed.

She left, disappearing.

And then there were two.

The clock ticked on.

Miss Charlotte

Charlotte had got up really early, almost as early as the servants, and she'd skipped breakfast, so that there would be time to visit Uncle Jeremiah before the tortuous prison that was school. She left before either Earnestine or Georgina had finished their morning ablutions, and she felt pleased with this. It proved to them, if they'd known, that she was not lackadaisical.

She had it all worked out: she'd explain over tea and macaroons that Earnestine and Georgina had become monsters, and that it was absolutely unfair that she, Charlotte, had to suffer in school when she'd done nothing wrong, while Earnestine and Georgina, simply because they were bossier, were allowed to stay at home and sew all day if they wanted. Not that Charlotte wanted to sew, Uncle Jeremiah would understand, but it was a question of not being allowed to. She wouldn't, if she was given permission, as she was destined for greater things. She would explain that too, despite its being self-evident, and Uncle Jeremiah was an intelligent man with a Doctorate in Antiquates.

For his part, Uncle Jeremiah would smile, understand and give her a letter to absent herself from the Reverend Long's interminable assemblies and Miss Cooper's pointless lessons. They were all very well, Charlotte would suppose, *if* you wanted to be a lady, but Charlotte, once she had formed the Women's Auxiliary Fusiliers, would not need to carry books on her head, sit upright, keep her elbows off the table, or marry – silently or otherwise.

And that would be that.

Uncle Jeremiah had rooms on the first floor of a well-appointed terrace with iron railings in front and smart black doors with crisp white numbers. Uncle Jeremiah's house had a red door. Uncle Jeremiah was jolly flash.

"'E's not in."

Charlotte glared at the maid, who had opened the door: she was just wrong.

"Uncle Jeremiah Deering?" she repeated.

"'E 'asn't been in for three weeks. Landlady's doing 'er nut."

"Three weeks!"

"'E's disappeared like as not."

"But I saw him last week – month. Have you told the Peelers?"

37

"We 'ave, and them bottles said that a Gentleman wot Doctor Deering is, can like as not do as 'e so pleases and thankin' you kindly."

"Did he leave a note?"

"No, 'e did not leave a note," the maid leaned down before adding: "And 'e dint leave no wages neither. Without push, we'll all be in the spike for sure. Landlady's doing 'er nut, she is."

"Thank you."

This was terrible; surely the worst thing that could possibly happen because now Charlotte had to go to school, and without breakfast or macaroons.

Despite running all the way, Charlotte was late for assembly. This wasn't her fault. To start with there had been plenty of time, but the boys in the next door school had suggested a re-enactment when she'd run past and duty called. Earnestine surely would approve of that.

Unfortunately, the defence of Mafeking had not gone well. The Boers had stormed the ramparts and they had fallen back well into Professor Chadlock's orchard. Charlotte had fired her stick with as many loud explosive noises as she had been able to muster, thrown apple grenades, and then, as the cadets had overrun the position, she'd died. Twice, because no-one had been looking the first time she'd gripped her stomach and keeled over.

After all, what was the point of dying if no-one saw it happen?

The Empire was lost, the boys decided to play some new game about Temporary (or something) Peelers, which involved dragged the snotty, fat kid off to be interrogated. It sounded stupid to Charlotte, so she lay on the bumpy grass and looked up through the mottled leaves and the dangling eaters at the blue sky.

Just as she was mulling over the rule about eating fallen apples, one of the local lads yelled at the top of his voice: "Scarper!"

Charlotte wondered what that was about, because the local lads had won the day and so there was no need for them to retreat. It was—

"Charlotte! Charlotte Deering-Dolittle!"

Charlotte jumped up.

Mistake, she should have stayed low and then the firing aspect of Miss Cooper's disapproval would have been too high.

"Miss?"

"What are you doing?"

Charlotte bit her lip to avoid saying anything about Mafeking and the Boer War.

"Well?"

"Miss, I'm practising my French tenses."

"Which French tenses in particular?"

"Er... well... all of them, Miss."

Miss Cooper, an aged harridan in her late twenties, advanced with an angry stride that had brought her right up to Charlotte. Claw-like nails dug into Charlotte's ear as she was dragged away, bouncing along with awkward strides, to the school house.

"You are. The most. Ungracious. Child—"

"I'm not an ungra— ah, ah, ah..."

The Reverend Mr. Long sighed. The kindly looking clergyman brought his hands together as if in prayer and took a long, deep breath that whistled through the gap in his teeth.

Charlotte stood in the centre of his oak panelled study awaiting his judgement.

"Charlotte," he said, gently, "I know well that your family hasn't exactly... that is to say, you have certain disadvantages, but why can't you be more like, say, the Deering-Dolittles of Surrey?"

"I'm sorry Reverend, it won't happen again," said Charlotte quickly.

39

"It's the dawn of a new age and there's a bright future for girls like you; if only you would play by the rules, then you could marry well."

"I'm sorry Reverend, it won't happen again."

"I'm so desperately disappointed. I feel, and Miss Cooper feels, that we've failed in some way. We have tried our best; the Lord knows we have tried our best."

"I'm sorry Reverend, it won't happen again."

"This is going to hurt me far more than it will hurt you."

"I'm sorry Reverend, it wo– the cane! No."

"Yes, Charlotte, it's for your own good."

"But I was only a little late and–"

"For the fifth time this month."

"But–"

"And it's only the fifteenth."

"But–"

"Miss Cooper had to go looking for you."

"B–"

"Hand."

He grabbed hold of her wrist to prevent her from turning or moving, and swiped.

Charlotte did not give him the satisfaction of crying out, but instead imagined shooting him–

Ah... with a Lee–

Enfield .303 after–

Bayoneting him and–

"O!" Blowing him up–

Blood spurting over his stupid dog collar–

Ow, six! Utterly unfair.

He let go, she snatched her hand back: it really hurt. The kindly clergyman hung the cane up next to his cricket bat.

"There now, just the one over," said the Reverend. "That's better, isn't it?"

"Sorry. Reverend. Won't. Again."

"I hope not. Miss Cooper has a punishment for you too."

Miss Cooper's punishment was worse because she forced Charlotte to write out 'I must not play with boys' *five hundred times* and with her wounded hand.

"We are not struggling for suffrage so that young ladies like yourself – are you listening Charlotte? – can go all doe-eyed at members of the opposite wotnot."

Charlotte sat at a desk with a hard wooden seat and tried to bend her smarting palm to grip the pen. Not only was her handwriting appalling, but the ink ran where the rain, somehow getting indoors, dripped from her face onto the paper.

It was so unfair: she didn't want to play with boys; she wanted to fight with men. And she didn't want to learn French tenses. What possible use were French tenses? Ever?

It was so unfair and it was Earnestine who had sent her to this horrid place.

"Miss, I need more paper."

"Don't write with such big letters! Here."

She would run away.

That was it.

She would run away and join the French Foreign Legion, just like she'd seen in that act at the theatre.

She would disguise herself as a boy and become a soldier, which was, now she thought about it, a truly excellent idea. Although, they'd probably insist that she did know some French tenses.

Well, that was fine. It would only be French tenses and not Latin verbs and Greek conjugations, and at least she'd get to fire guns and kill insurgents.

So, that decided, she finished her 'I must not play with boys', making the loop of the last 'y' fill the whole of the rest of the page, and ran away.

41

Chapter III

Miss Deering-Dolittle

The room beyond the secret door was lit by galvanic charge, bright luminous bulbs and strange glowing tubes, which blinked and pinged as they came on to reveal the cavernous brick interior. Boothroyd stepped away from the ornate brass switches and raised an arm like a showman signifying the entrance of the star act. It was indeed something that would be difficult to follow.

Through this anteroom, they reached a large open space, lit from above by a skylight, criss-crossed with metal framing just like a modern railway station. Around a central courtyard were demarcated areas of various shapes and sizes much like a stable with stalls for anything from ponies to shires. Parked in the middle was a hansom cab standing as if ready for a horse to be attached between its limbers.

Some sections gleamed with care and attention, others were green with age and dust, but all were impressive, be they mechanical, industrial, metal, ceramic or simply beyond comprehension.

It was indeed a treasure house.

"It's full of machines!" said Earnestine in amazement.

"Yes," said Boothroyd. "And some of them don't blow up."

"One is utterly flabbergasted."

"Of course," Boothroyd jumped forwards, prancing like an excited child, his dark, grey streaked hair swishing as he turned this way and that. "This is the Haversham – *whoosh* – and this is a steam engine that works by galvanic power – there's no water in it, not a drop. Let's see, here's the Celluloid Billiard Ball gun – those explode – and the Gutta-Percha Spatial Sculptor, makes anything you want according to Morse code tapped in here or according to a paper roll – see. They're both by P. Harrow, Esquire, of... oh, and here's the Brunel collection, and that's a Tesla – see the... it's all copper – and, oh, another Tesla and you don't want to put this one anywhere near a magnet, and a working model of a Nautilus, through here – the other wing – are the balloons and other vehicles, flying machines too! They don't work. And here's the Depth Suit, it'll protect you to 40 fathoms, and here's the Exosphere. If you were in this, snuggled up all tight and cosy, you could easily survive in the upper reaches of the atmosphere and out beyond in the cosmos itself."

"Extraordinary."

"Well, in theory, obviously we've no way of testing such an apparatus, but Leonardo himself designed a parachute long before the invention of the hot air balloon or the Zeppelin. We've one such descent apparatus that tucks away inside a pack much like the Haversham."

Earnestine tightened her lips as she remembered: "I have experience of descents from Zeppelins with parachutes." Or without, she thought. It was not an experience she wanted to repeat, even if the whole adventure – she shuddered at the thought – had led to her introduction to Major Dan and thence to her appointment in this trove of madness and delights.

"You fell from a Zeppelin?"

"I jumped."

"Heavens, why?"

"It was exploding."

Boothroyd clapped his hands together: "Major Dan was right, you're going to fit in splendidly."

Earnestine felt she ought to change the subject, so she picked the contraption nearest to her: all mechanical struts sticking out from a central column. In the middle was the symbol of a heart.

"What's this item?"

"The Rafe – Ridley's Automatic Fencing Exerciser."

"I beg your pardon?"

"It's a duelling machine."

"Duelling?"

"Yes, these armatures move and prod and sweep and strike and slash with an attachment," said Boothroyd, and he pulled out a collection of sharp looking weapons with pommels on the end. "It takes a foil, sabre, cutlass, grambouchaum and... this one. And here are the cards, Jacquard cards, much like the Babbage thing... sorry, can't talk about that.... and they control the particular school of fencing. Such a promising young man, the inventor, such a wealth of ideas, but alas..."

"Fascinating." Earnestine moved to have a closer look. "What happened to the inventor?"

"He was developing a version that worked with duelling pistols, when... I'm afraid."

"Ah."

"He shouldn't have tested it himself really, but when his third assistant ran away... alas."

Earnestine lowered her gaze in honour of Ridley and his... dedication, she supposed.

Boothroyd moved on: "And this... yes, wonderful device, it must do something, if only we could find the blueprints."

Boothroyd turned a brass cog or two experimentally. The side section rotated and articulated. The whole brass conglomeration was as closed a book to Earnestine as Georgina's recent daguerreotype experiments.

"It must be so frustrating, not knowing," Earnestine said.

"Yes, occasionally one of them becomes interesting and a team arrives to perfect it. That large door there leads to a yard and thence to the street. We don't allow experiments here."

"Oh, why's that?"

"On account of the blowing up, my dear."

Boothroyd pointed at a magnificent shining example of steel and glass and then Earnestine realised he meant the

45

blackened and charred wall behind it. Something had certainly made a dreadful mess there once.

They had been all the way round, so there was only one item left to ask about.

"And the hansom cab?"

"Oh, its driver's number changes with this dial, it releases firecrackers to spook any pursuers' horses and, see this, whatever you do don't press it. You won't believe what it does..."

Boothroyd carried on explaining this, that and the quite astounding other, until Earnestine couldn't widen her eyes any more. When the tour was over, they made their way back to the office.

Earnestine tidied away the cups and saucers.

"Well, my dear?" Boothroyd asked.

"I think we are going to have to start from scratch."

Boothroyd sighed: "Yes, that's what we do every time."

"Where to start?"

Boothroyd shook his head as if this was the great mystery of life.

So, Earnestine rolled up her sleeves as it were and set to. Although this smacked of domestic chores, rather than secretarial duties, Earnestine was not afraid of hard work. The first task, she decided, was to generate some space, so she attacked the massive pile in the centre of the room. Sure enough, she soon revealed a double-sized mahogany desk with a green leather inlay, three drawers on the end of each column making twelve in total. Underneath, she found an upholstered swivelling chair that matched the desk and, around the other side, one in red leather that most certainly didn't. The room boasted many other piles, so perhaps there was a second desk hidden away.

Meanwhile, Boothroyd himself, spurred on by Earnestine's attitude, moved some papers from the kitchen to a pile by the door. When he turned round, he gave a delighted cry of wonderment at the revelation of the desk.

"My dear, what can I say? This is just a perfect place for this stack here."

He picked up the very pile that Earnestine had generated when she'd cleared the desk.

"No, no," she cried. "They came from there... there is something you can do, and only you."

"Yes, my dear?"

"Could you, perhaps, identify what we don't need and dispose of it?"

"Dispose of it!?"

"Yes."

Boothroyd sniggered at the prodigious thought: "We could have a little bonfire."

"Surely we can't let these go outside."

"You are right, of course. Indeed, there are items, here in this pile, that even you should not see – state secrets. I'll put... this knight on top to guard them."

Boothroyd placed a large pewter paperweight, a knight on a horse stabbing a lance into a dragon, on to a small pile by the corner.

"One can move it from there though?"

"Of course, my dear, but no peeking."

"We could denote other piles with various weights like this... flat iron. Why is there a flat iron here?"

"It holds the–"

But the kitchen door had already slammed shut.

"Sorry," said Earnestine, but she left the door closed and put the flat iron down upon – *ah ha* – domestic items, perfect. "And the papers we don't need?"

"We could burn them in the fireplace."

Earnestine stopped, looked around at each wall in turn: "Fireplace?"

"So long ago, my dear, I can't remember."

After dithering, Earnestine looked at the ceiling. There were no papers stacked downwards, Newton's Law of

47

Gravity saw to that, and so the outline of the room was visible. Sure enough, on the East wall, there was a chimney breast and below, hidden between 'Chemistry' and 'Metric', she uncovered a fireplace complete with scuttle, poker, brush, tongs, bellows and stand. The fire dog was already rammed with paper ready to burn.

"We could toast muffins," Boothroyd suggested.

"Have you identified anything that can be burnt?"

"I'm not keen on this."

"But Mister Boothroyd, if we don't–" and then Earnestine bit her tongue as she realised why this place was in such a dreadful state: the man was unable to throw anything away.

So she rolled up her mental shirt sleeves, put on her psychological apron and set to work on that problem too.

Mrs Arthur Merryweather

Georgina was hurtling towards her future and the scene that whizzed past her window was one of utter devastation, a sprawling landscape of brown bogs, jutting rocks and skeletal trees bent over by the incessant wind. Dotted here and there were the remains of stone structures, archaeological sites that harked back to a more primitive and ancient time, perhaps the very era when those fossil skeletons of monsters in the Museum of Natural History were clothed in flesh and roamed the moors looking for prey.

Georgina shuddered.

The train joggled from side to side as it went over some points.

She picked up her copy of the Times as a distraction, but the stories of some future calamity held no interest given that she was plunging back to some semi-prehistoric realm.

She'd chosen this fate simply by embarking on a train at Paddington Station, but it wasn't what she wanted.

She wanted Arthur, her husband, and not some ancient pile in the middle of nowhere, but poor Arthur was lost to her, and, dressed in her widow's weeds, she was rushing further and further from civilisation. It was hateful, but she would bear it.

In her travelling bag, she had her documentation: a letter from the Merryweather solicitors, Tumble, Judd & Babcock, and her marriage certificate. She hadn't been interested in the slightest by the description of the property. There was a stipend to claim too. All this was hers, but only if she came to Magdalene Chase in person.

She cared not a jot, she kept telling herself, but the solicitor, Mister Judd, must have known something of the Deering-Dolittle family curse for he had included an item that simply could not be resisted, something that had to be unfolded and pored over, something that needed to be examined in great detail. In short, he had enclosed a map.

So she had resolved many times to put it aside, while she consulted her reference books, traced the railway lines and made careful plans. She'd not shown it to her sisters, because this was hers and hers alone. She often felt she'd lost everything when Arthur was taken from her, so every item of his was all the more precious.

Arthur's big pocket-watch said half-past four, not long now, but it would be dark when she reached Magdalene Chase. She consulted her *Bradshaw's Monthly Railway Guide* as if somehow the information would have magically changed to let her arrive at Tenning Halt earlier.

It had not.

So much for that sixpence, she thought. She closed the yellow covers and put it back into her travelling bag.

Another reason she hadn't told Earnestine or Charlotte, of course, was to save them from any adventure. Earnestine had her new position in a government department and a chance to further the cause of suffrage by example, and Charlotte was enrolled, after much difficulty because of her references, in a new school and she, above everything else, had to learn.

The landscape around the train darkened and looked even more desolate and uninviting. Zebediah Row was firmly in the past.

"Tickets please."

Georgina dutifully dug out her ticket for the Inspector. The train clattered and swayed at that moment causing the uniformed man to pitch somewhat.

"Tenning Halt," he said, clipping the card and handing it back. "Next stop, Miss."

"Oh..." Georgina started to stand.

"Not for a while yet. Stations hereabouts are much further apart than in London."

"How did you know I was from London?"

"Your ticket Miss."

"Of course, thank you."

He moved on: "Tickets please, tickets please..."

The Inspector came back ten minutes before the time Bradshaw had predicted for their arrival.

"There's no-one to help you, Miss?"

"I'm afraid not."

"On your own then?"

"I am."

"You be careful at Tenning Halt."

"I will, thank you."

When the train came to a stop, the Inspector deftly manhandled her trunk out onto the platform. He had clearly been trained; Georgina, considering her difficulties with the wretched thing, found this ability quite extraordinary.

"Someone meeting you, Miss?"

"I sent a letter."

He looked left and right: "There won't be a porter here now, Miss."

"I shall be fine."

"Don't be tempted to make the journey on your own," he said. "The moors can be treacherous."

"I'll stay here until I'm collected," she assured him with a smile.

He nodded and lifted his finger to his hat: "And keep away from Magdalene Chase."

The comment baffled her for a moment, and then she realised it was pronounced 'maudlin' like the college in Oxford or Cambridge.

"Oh, Magdalene Chase," she said. "Why?"

"It's infested with pixies, Miss."

And with that, he disappeared back into the bright, warm interior of the train carriage.

Georgina glanced around, nervous of the shadows.

The station sign was damaged, half of it ripped away in some storm: all that was left was 'g Halt'. The clock above Platform 1 had stopped, frozen at 11:05 with no hint of whether it had been a morning or a night-time disaster.

The train door was only a few feet in front of her, tempting. She could go on to Exeter, Plymouth or Penzance, and then turn back to London and Kensington. She reached out with her gloved hand to the shining brass handle, but she was made of sterner stuff and resisted.

Finally, the train hissed like an angry serpent and jerked away into the night.

Georgina stood by her trunk, alone.

Miss Charlotte

Charlotte went along some filthy streets and across an area of rough ground. Men leered at her and women cackled from the doorway of a public house. There was a fight going on at one corner, three men attacking a fourth. It was rough and messy, and utterly unlike the heroic deeds of soldiers. The sooner she joined the French Foreign Legion and got out of this hell hole, the better, she thought.

It was dark when she reached the East India Docks. She thought it was probably better to go tomorrow and she thought of returning home, but no! She had run away and that was simply that. She simply had to stay the night somewhere.

As she passed a dark doorway, a sailor spat downwards and then spoke: "Evenin' darlin'"

"Evening, Sir."

"You give me a good time."

"Good time... yes... sorry, but I don't have a watch. I mean, I beg your pardon?"

The sailor made a coarse gesture, holding the front of his trousers.

"I think not, thank you, good day."

Charlotte scuttled away and the sailor attempted to follow, but he was far too worse for wear, and stumbled over in that way that Uncle Edgar used to do when his face had turned all red.

She reached a house called 'El Dorado' which advertised proper beds. This would have to do.

She pulled the doorbell cord.

An elderly woman opened the door.

"Welcome, welcome," she said over Charlotte's head and then she lowered her sights: "What have we here?"

"Please Ma'am, I'm after a room."

"We're not that sort of establishment."

"But it's late and..."

"What about yer own pander?"

"I'm sorry?"

"Gentleman... Man anyway. Did he hit you? You don't look hurt."

Charlotte suddenly had a brainwave and showed the woman her right hand. The vivid red lines were still visible even in the weak gaslight.

"Fair enough. You obey the rules of the house?"

Rules – honestly – they were everywhere: "Of course, Ma'am."

"I'm Madam Waggstaff: this is my gaff, my rules. It's a crown to you a night, if you entertain, enough for gin, and you'll like it. We charge the men three crowns. How old are you?"

Charlotte had money, so she thought she could afford a crown at least and she was glad for once that she wasn't a man, although she didn't understand why they were charged more.

"Fifteen," she said.

"Fifteen!"

"No, I mean sixteen. Or eighteen?"

"That's old."

"Twelve."

"Is that your final offer? Then twelve it is. At least you've got the right attitude," she said, and she opened the door wide. "In you come."

Charlotte bobbed under her outstretched arm and went inside.

"We'll take your bag here," Madam Waggstaff said, and she slipped it off Charlotte's shoulder.

"Oh, but–"

"No buts. The others are in the drawing room."

The drawing room was decorated in dark, red colours, dimly lit, and furnished with a chaise longue against each wall. There were four other girls present, who sat around looking sullen and dejected. They glanced up at the new arrival with some loathing.

"Hello, I'm Charlotte."

"Charlie girl, sit here."

"Charlotte," Charlotte insisted as she sat on the edge of a chaise. It was precarious and uncomfortable.

Now that her eyes had become accustomed to the gloom, she saw that the others were all quite brazenly attired. They were clearly of a lower class. Even so, this was something she'd have to get used to in her new life as a soldier.

"I say," Charlotte said in the way of an opener, "quite a queer sort of a place."

One girl tried to focus on Charlotte: "Here," she said. "Have some gin."

"Jolly good of you," said Charlotte. She took the proffered glass, turning it to drink from the clean side.

"Bottoms up," said the girl.

Charlotte took a swig: it tasted of juniper berries and—

"Ahh!" she spat the burning liquid across the room. "It's cough medicine."

The girls all squawked with joy, coming to life for the first time since Charlotte's arrival.

"Quiet!" It was Madam Waggstaff. "We have a Gentleman Caller."

The girls sat upright, leaning forward and suddenly attentive, as Madam Waggstaff ushered in a portly gentleman with wide whiskers.

"Oh, Madam Waggstaff," he chortled. "You wicked woman. Wicked, wicked, I see you have a new lovely."

"Yes, this is... Desiree."

Charlotte stood and offered her hand: "Charlotte."

"Oh, and so forward and eager, I like that."

There was a general groan from behind Charlotte, but Charlotte was used to other girls in class being stupid.

"Number three," said Madam Waggstaff.

"Oh, perfect," said the Gentleman.

Charlotte wondered what to do until Madam Waggstaff waved her to a door. This led along a passage with other doors on either side, but none of them had numbers. Charlotte had actually been to the Savoy when her sister, Georgina, had married Captain Merryweather, and that had been an altogether different arrangement.

"This one, my lovely," said the Gentleman.

"Thank you," said Charlotte, remembering her Ps and Qs. "Well, that will—"

The man came in too!

"A little entertainment if you will."

54

"Ah, of course," said Charlotte. She understood: clearly Madam Waggstaff's clients were expected to keep one another amused in the evenings. She looked around for the pianoforte, but there was only a bed in the room. This was probably a lucky escape for the Gentleman as Charlotte hadn't practised her scales, or her violin, in simply ages.

The man sat on the bed loosening his cravat as he ogled at Charlotte expectantly.

"I can recite the Henry Vth speech before Agincourt or Queen Elizabeth's before the Armada," Charlotte suggested.

"You can take off your clothes."

"Of course, I... I beg your pardon?"

"No need to be shy with me, my lovely."

He reached across and grabbed hold of her.

Charlotte fought back, but he was a big man and pulled her down upon the covers. The bed creaked and complained, jiggling up and down upon its springs. He was on top of her, fumbling for her undoings. Charlotte jabbed with her elbow, slipped out from under him and fell into an uncomfortable heap on the floor.

"Come now!" the man said, getting high-pitched, "Madam Waggstaff will beat you if you aren't nice to me."

Charlotte's hand brushed against a sturdy handle. She grabbed it, lifted it and swung with all her strength. There was a mighty clang when the heavy metal object connected with the man's pudgy face. He went down. The weapon was full of liquid, which went everywhere, cascading down onto the fallen body.

"Euurghh," said Charlotte. She dropped the pot. "Yuk! Yuk!"

The door burst open: "What's going on?" Madam Waggstaff demanded.

"He attacked me!"

"He did?"

"Yes," said Charlotte, "he tried to take my clothes off."

55

Madam Waggstaff's mouth dropped open. The few teeth she had were rotten and she reeked of Juniper cordial.

"You ungrateful girl, you've killed him!"

The man groaned on the floor to give lie to that statement.

"He attacked me!" Charlotte repeated.

"Of course he attacked you," Madam Waggstaff wailed.

"He came into the room! He attacked me. So I hit him. With the chamber pot."

"We've only your word against his, and our Mister Foxley here is a proper Gentleman, Right Honourable and everything. Wait until Mister Waggstaff hears about this, you wicked girl."

"I'm not doing lines."

"Don't you know what to do with a Gentleman Caller?"

"Of course, I do," said Charlotte, indignantly, because she did know. "You offer whiskey or brandy, instead of sherry."

"You've not been with a man! Oh, heavens protect us. You stupid girl, I could have got twenty five pounds for you, more at auction."

"What are you talking about?" Charlotte was shouting now, partly in panic, but mostly because nobody here seemed to understand what she was saying.

"Where do you think you are?"

"I'm in a bed and breakfast," she answered.

There was a sudden terrible splintering of wood, followed by screams.

"What now!" Madam Waggstaff demanded.

The commotion outside spilled along the corridor. A girl, dressed only in her undergarments, rushed past the open door.

"Odette, Odette!" Madam Waggstaff stormed into the corridor and then immediately backed away.

56

A figure appeared, silhouetted in the doorway: he was tall, dressed in a black frock coat and wearing a tall top hat. He was gaunt, clean shaven and wearing the most peculiar glasses imaginable. They were white and made him look blind, but he could clearly see through the slits that created a lattice or grid across the blank lenses.

Charlotte retreated too.

He stepped into the room, followed by another identically dressed man. They could have been twins.

Another appeared: triplets?

"We keep a clean house," Madam Waggstaff was saying. "We paid the Sergeant at the station his money, always regular."

The lead man replied in a deep voice: "We're not the local constabulary."

"Who are you then?"

"I am Chief Examiner Lombard of the Chronological Division, and this is Checker Rogers."

"I'm sorry, I didn't know you were Temporal Peelers. Is it readies you'll be wanting?"

"No, woman, we're not interested in your bordello," said the Chief Examiner. "Leave us to our business."

Checker Rogers stooped over the prostrate gentleman and felt for a pulse.

"Alive?" asked the first, Lombard.

"Yes," said the second, Rogers, as he sniffed his own fingers suspiciously.

"Then arrest him."

Checker Rogers dragged the body towards the passageway until the third man helped him. Metal clattered as they did so and Charlotte noticed their cavalry swords hanging from belts fixed around their frock coats.

"You can't take him," Madam Waggstaff complained. "He's a Member of Parliament."

"He's covered in piss," the third man complained.

"Excuse me, Sir," Charlotte said.

57

Chief Examiner Lombard loomed over her; the top of his hat nearly scraping the ceiling.

"What?"

"Thank you for coming to my aid."

"We didn't come to help some strumpet."

"Well, even so, I'm grateful... strumpet? No, I'm not a strumpet."

But the man had gone.

Charlotte was not entirely convinced she knew what a 'strumpet' was, but it didn't sound good. It might, she realised, refer to one of those unfortunate fallen women, whom the Reverend Long insisted had brought all their misfortunes down upon themselves and that *you young ladies will certainly go the same way if you don't blah-blah-blah.* He didn't explain what a 'fallen woman' actually was, unless he did so between the middle of his sermon and the inevitable 'Charlotte, sit up' that came before the end.

And, Charlotte realised, she could not be a fallen woman, because, even after being attacked, she was the one still standing and the man they'd just carted away had been the one on the floor.

"What are you doing?" thundered another man's voice.

There were muffled replies.

Charlotte sneaked a look.

"Oh Mister Waggstaff, Mister Waggstaff," Madam Waggstaff wailed.

The brightly waist-coated man ignored her and shouted at the top of his voice: "These are my girls! Mine! Get yer own."

Chief Examiner Lombard levelled a device, a kind of gun ending in a giant two-pronged fork: it buzzed and sparked with a dazzle far brighter than the gaslight. Mister Waggstaff, if it was him, jerked upright, shook as if he were having a fit and specks of spittle formed around his lips, before, all of a sudden, he went rigid and keeled over.

Madam Waggstaff screeched and wailed, and threw herself over his prostrate form.

As the Chief Examiner wrapped up his weapon, the other two Peelers removed the arrested man. This gave Charlotte the opportunity to confront the leader.

"Excuse me, Sir," she said, "but what are you arresting that man for?"

The Chief Examiner paused, looking utterly blank, the white, slatted glasses staring down disconcertingly, before he spoke:

"He destroyed the world."

Chapter IV

Miss Deering-Dolittle

Earnestine arrived home late.

She was tired after work and not one of her sisters had stayed up to thank her. Not that Charlotte should have been allowed, of course, but honestly. Again, she was the one looking after them; again, she was the responsible one and, again, she was unappreciated.

Cook had left her a cold collation.

Their house in Zebediah Row seemed completely quiet as if she were the only one there.

Well, good riddance to them, they could nap all day and all night for all she cared, but as she tried to sleep, she couldn't.

She looked at the evening paper, but it was all full of news about arrests and there was nothing about any expeditions, so she turned out the gas again and lay in the dark with various inventions whirring around in her thoughts and eventually in her dreams, mutating slowly in a mad workshop of mechanical toys.

Mrs Arthur Merryweather

A strange half-voice sounded from the pitch darkness: "Miss?"

"Yes?" Georgina wanted to sound confident, but her enunciation cracked.

The man was short, bent over with wisps of white hair protruding from under his bowler hat. He seemed to look with only one eye.

"Are you the lady we have been expecting?"

"I am Mrs Arthur Merryweather, if that's who you mean?"

"Merryweather, you say?"

"Yes, I say."

"That is to be decided."

"No it isn't, it has been decided already."

"We must examine–"

"I have my certificate."

"And witnesses to–"

"God, and half a regiment of British officers as well as my sister were witnesses."

"We will be asking Arthur."

Georgina was outraged and then realised that the figure was shambling away.

Georgina followed: "Excuse me, but who exactly might you be?"

"I am Fellowes."

"Yes, exactly what?"

"Fellowes, just Fellowes."

They reached a small pony and trap. The man indicated that Georgina should climb aboard.

"My trunk?"

Fellowes considered this a while. He did not appear to be strong enough to pick up her trunk.

"I will send the boy back for it."

"I can't leave it there."

"No-one will take it and it will save time if it is here already for the return train in the morning."

"I need my belongings."

Again, the man considered this and then, with a limp that he hadn't had before, he went back to the platform and scraped the trunk along. Georgina stood with her hands together in front of her as she watched him struggle theatrically.

"Oh, let me help," she said.

She took one end, and the man relinquished his part of the bargain immediately. He shambled back to the trap, leaving Georgina to struggle across the platform and heave the trunk up onto the transport. Perhaps she hadn't needed the spare corset or those lovely shoes or the towel?

When she reached the trap, Fellowes was already sitting in the front with the reins in hand, staring out into the darkness, ready to face with fortitude the eternity that it took for Georgina to lift the trunk onto the back.

It didn't fit exactly, so she had to bump it around until she believed it would stay in place. Finally, she brushed her dress down straight, stood as upright as possible to recover some dignity and then went to the passenger side.

Fellowes sat there without even looking at her.

A lady should not get into a carriage without assistance. She had been brought up properly and she would wait.

However, it was cold and getting darker all the time.

Negotiating raising her skirts, hiding her ankle, getting her foot in the metal step and jumping up required three attempts, but she pulled herself into her seat eventually.

"Now, Fellowes, you—"

They were off!

The pony dithering left until yanked around, and Georgina nearly fell out. Five hundred yards from the station the lane narrowed, so that branches from the stunted trees swiped at them dangerously as they hurtled along. The low moon cast a pale light interrupted by the stone walls and by distant rocky outcrops.

"I know it like the back of my hand," said Fellowes, anticipating a question that hadn't crossed Georgina's mind. She was too busy holding on to the metal rail to think clearly.

They passed through a village complete with a church with a clock tower and a pub with a hanging sign, a painting of a man fighting a monster.

When she thought it would never end, they turned into a wider, more level road and the dry stone walls and bushes no longer hemmed them in on either side. The sudden space gave Georgina a desperate, isolating, agoraphobic panic. It was like the pony and trap were transporting them over a black and calm River Styx.

"Magdalene Chase," said Fellowes.

63

Georgina looked – nothing.

And then she saw a black slab of a building against the dark sky and, to the right and high up, a weak flickering light.

Fellowes pulled the pony to a stop outside the main entrance, a dark door framed by white stone pillars that loomed over them.

Georgina climbed down.

"I'll put the pony away," said Fellowes.

"My trunk!"

"Yes, Miss."

"Mrs... Ma'am!"

"When you've got it down then."

Georgina stormed round to the back and grasped the handle of her trunk. It wasn't so much a case of her pulling it down as of the trap being pulled out from under it when Fellowes whipped the pony forward. The trunk swung down and crunched into the gravel. She dragged it to the front and then hefted it up the three steps.

She yanked the bell pull.

There was a delay and then a distant chime.

"Arthur," she said aloud, mist condensing in front of her, "I can understand why you joined the army."

Once she had some light, she thought, she'd consult the Great Western timetable for the first return journey.

The door opened: a smartly dressed hag blocked the way in.

"I am expected," Georgina announced.

The housekeeper opened the door wide: "This way, Miss."

Georgina held her ground: "Mrs! Ma'am!"

The housekeeper merely looked at her uncomprehendingly.

"This way, Ma'am," Georgina said. "You say, this–"

"This way... Miss."

"Ma'am."

"Mam."

64

"My trunk."

"There's no-one to bring it in."

Georgina remembered a suggestion Fellowes had made at the station: "Get the boy."

"He's asleep."

"Then wake him."

"Very well, Miss."

Georgina tightened her lips, shocked to realise that she was turning into her elder sister: perhaps she should imitate her voice: "Very well, Ma'am... you say..."

"Very well... Ma'am."

Georgina crossed the threshold.

It was a wide entrance way with rooms off both sides and a stone staircase leading up to a landing and the upper storey.

"Please wait here," said the woman. "Fellowes will be along shortly to show you to the temporary guest room."

Georgina was alone again.

A clock ticked, loud in the reverberating silence of the stone hall.

Eventually, Fellowes returned, visibly taken aback that Georgina was still there.

"You are to show me to my room," Georgina said.

"Am I?"

"The woman said."

"Did she?"

"Yes."

Fellowes crossed the flags and ascended the staircase. Georgina followed, pausing every two steps to allow the man some sort of lead. By the time they reached the top, the boy arrived with Georgina's trunk.

"The guest room is along here," said Fellowes.

"Where's the master bedroom?"

"It's not been touched since the Captain–"

"I'm simply curious," Georgina said. "Where is it?"

"Along the landing, Miss, and there... blue door."

"Excellent."

Before Fellowes could do anything, Georgina swept along the landing and through the blue door. Fellowes shuffling stride sped up to try and intercept her, but he was too late.

"It's not been aired," he said.

"Bring me some light."

"Miss?"

"And bedding, I shall sleep here," Georgina said, and when the boy, a youth of ten or eleven, appeared and plonked the trunk down, she added, "Thank you, that will be all."

The boy slunk out, smirking.

Fellowes looked reluctant. His hand moved with indecision making the lantern shift the great path of light that shone into the room to illuminate the corner of a bed. Georgina moved across the room and sat there.

"Miss, I really think..."

Georgina gave a tiny smile, thin, and very like Earnestine's.

Fellowes wavered.

"That would be lovely, thank you. Fellowes, is it?"

"Yes Miss."

He disappeared, scurrying away.

Georgina mouthed 'Ma'am' after him, then she felt rather foolish and very like Charlotte.

The door closed slowly and, sitting still, she realised how cold it was in the room. The wind whistled outside, howling suddenly in the echo chamber of a chimney before returning to a low murmuring, and a tree scraped across the window.

Even the light under the door had vanished.

This was Arthur's room, she thought, and it would have been their room. She could not feel his presence, smell his aftershave or hear his heart beat as she had when he'd held her to him. She seemed to be sitting on a raft adrift on an immense black river, while at the same time the darkness enveloped her as if she were in a tomb.

The light flickered under the door frame and Fellowes knocked.

"Come in."

Fellowes had a pair of candles in brass holders. He set one upon a dresser and the other on a bedside table. The room slowly came to life. There was a military jacket hanging outside the wardrobe, shaving equipment laid out on the dresser, as well as pictures and knick-knacks. She touched his aftershave jar, smelt her fingers and almost conjured up the time they'd met, the long railway journey and that one night together.

The sheets weren't fresh but they weren't musty: "This will be fine."

"Miss... I... really, you can't."

"Goodnight, Fellowes."

She ushered him out, closed the door and leant against it to sigh her utmost. It had been a long day.

She undressed herself; it wouldn't do to call a maid as she might join forces with the butler and she'd be in the guest room.

She snuggled into Arthur's bed.

Arthur's bed, the thought was intoxicating.

There were two books on the bedside table: *Wisden's Cricketers' Almanac* edited by Sydney Pardon and *Bleak House* by Charles Dickens. The latter had a bookmark betraying a lack of progress. She would read it, she thought, but use a different device to keep her place. There was another book, which had a blank cover and also empty within, or at least where Georgina opened it. Flicking to the front, she found Arthur's handwriting. It was a journal. The last entry talked about going to London, called in by Major Dan and looking forward to a possible adventure. She had been part of that adventure.

She felt that familiar lump in her throat again.

She decided then to continue the journal.

There was a fountain pen in the drawer and she fished this out, a couple of shakes and it wrote. She wrote the date, neatly, and then began an entry: 'I, Mrs Arthur Merryweather, continue this journal. Upon arriving at Magdalene Chase, after travelling across country on the 11:23 from Paddington, it was dark and–'

The candle guttered, its flickering light warning her of impending darkness. Georgina capped the pen and closed the journal.

When she returned them to the drawer, she noticed a daguerreotype of a beautiful young woman, almost animated by the flickering light, who smiled with her head tilted alluringly and–

Georgina snatched up the picture: who was this woman, this harlot, this strumpet to so litter Arthur's bedside cabinet?

She replaced it very deliberately with her face looking down at the varnished teak.

The light went out.

She slept, worried, and envious of her sisters, who were still safe at home. 'Bleak House' seemed an appropriate choice for this cold forbidding place.

Miss Charlotte

When the strange men finally left, there was a dreadful silence almost as if they had removed the air's ability to transmit sound, and then, all too suddenly, the wailing began and it just didn't stop. It stayed like that until the gin ran out, and then it became worse.

"Ruination!" cried Madam Waggstaff, flapping her arms above the unconscious Mr Waggstaff.

Three Gentleman Callers were turned away by the... Charlotte realised that these similarly dressed, if 'dressed' was the right word, girls were *strumpets*. The arrested man had thought she was one too. If only Charlotte could figure out what that meant?

"Temporal Peelers!" Madam Waggstaff reminded them. "Here! Ruination!"

When Mr Waggstaff regained consciousness, Madam Waggstaff thanked the Lord, the heavens, and Mary, the Mother of God, and more angels than Charlotte could have named. The big burly man, once his wits were restored, shouted incoherently, using words that Charlotte didn't understand. They sounded coarse and she realised that each could be substituted with the b-word, so he was most likely one of those foul mouthed ne'er-do-wells that the papers were so fond of complaining about. Finally, fed up with the bawling explanations, he struck the nearest girl and retired to his armchair.

Little Dove, one of the strumpets, was sent out with a shilling for more gin and when she returned it all quietened down. Come 'chucking out' time, no Gentlemen Callers even rang the doorbell and so – ruination, ruination – it was all apparently over.

"Word has got around!" Madam Waggstaff explained to the ceiling.

Charlotte made a pot of tea.

Madam Waggstaff took a sip: "There's no gin in this."

Charlotte made a face in reply.

"Gin's horrible," she said.

Charlotte stormed off to find a bedroom with a better perfume than the one with the spilt piss pot. The one she found didn't have a number on the door either. She smelt the sheets, wrinkled her nose up, and then found fresh linen. She remade the bed as if she were a domestic, jammed a chair under the handle and went to sleep.

Or rather she lay under the covers and thought hard.

For the whole of the previous day, she had pretended to understand French tenses. What vexed her now was the phrase the man in the top hat, Chief Examiner Lombard, had used. He had said 'He destroyed the world'. Not something like 'he will destroy' or 'he attempted to destroy' or any of the other multitude of options listed on pages 2-14, 17 and 23-45 of her

69

textbook. He'd used the passé composé or the passé historique or... whatever: the *past tense*.

However, manifestly, the man had not destroyed the world. The world still existed and continued to turn, albeit in a confusing and perplexing manner.

She also realised that she couldn't go and join the French Foreign Legion. Partly because it was French and so all her friends, the cadets, wouldn't talk to her any more, but mostly because she'd only managed to travel seven miles and the desert forts depicted in the penny-dreadfuls were so much further than that. She couldn't go return Zebediah Row because Earnestine would send her back to school, where the Reverend Long would cane her and Miss Cooper would give her lines. Also, having assumed a life of adventure and excitement in the desert, she hadn't bothered to even start her homework.

There were mysteries here too: that horrid man's arrest and the disappearance of Uncle Jeremiah. It would be exciting to solve the puzzle and it could even be an adventure, providing Earnestine didn't find out, forbid it and thus spoil everything.

However, her main worry was that she was really hungry.

Macaroons wouldn't be too much to ask for, surely?

Or Garibaldi's?

Or cake?

CHAPTER V

Miss Deering-Dolittle

And they didn't see her off the next day.

Cook had made bacon and eggs, which she wolfed down.

Earnestine walked to work again.

The newspaper vendors were full of news of a Member of Parliament, who had been arrested.

Earnestine asked one: "What's happened?"

"It's Foxley, Miss. They've only gone and nabbed him."

"Foxley?"

"The Right Honourable, brother of the Earl no less, and his were a safe London seat."

"What for?"

"Crimes, Miss, dreadful crimes. And they act all high and mighty and better than us, going on, he did, about family values, but that's their class for you, begging your pardon, Miss."

She bought a paper, folded it and tucked it under her arm and marched to Queensbury Road feeling quite the important business woman, if such a thing could exist.

When she arrived, she glanced right and left. The street was empty, but she couldn't shake the feeling that she was being watched.

Boothroyd was already making the tea.

"Shall we have biscuits?" he said.

Earnestine wasn't sure he realised that she'd left, been away the night and returned.

"Please."

Her first task was to remove the piles that Boothroyd had moved back onto the desk and generally return things to that state they'd been when she'd finally called it a day yesterday. Next, there being no other plan, she simply picked a place and selected the first application. As she worked through, she found various objects to use as paperweights: a brick, a rather beautiful crystal that had been encased in rock, a trilobite and a piece of metal that looked like an important part of something else.

One sculpture she uncovered was a teak box with a strange removable handle on the top and a dial on the front. It didn't work as a paperweight because it was attached to the wall by a twisted cord.

"Oh, the telephonic apparatus!" said Boothroyd. "At last, I know what that ringing noise was."

Earnestine's system was simple: a place for everything and everything in its place.

After a while the room suggested a gallery displaying sculptures and object d'art, which was quite pleasing.

"Mister Boothroyd, may I suggest the fire for this one?"

"Miss Deering-Dolittle, it may be important."

"One can buy this item at a good hardware store."

"Can you?"

"Indeed, we have a cast iron one ourselves at home."

"The fire then," Boothroyd conceded. "What would I do without you?"

"I've only been here a day, Mister Boothroyd."

"And already you've made yourself indispensable, my dear."

"Thank you, Mister Boothroyd, one tries one's best."

"I think you should take a break," Boothroyd suggested.

Earnestine realised that she did fancy a cup of tea, but Boothroyd instead suggested the Duelling Machine in the warehouse.

"An excellent way to blow off steam," he said and he left her to it.

Earnestine examined the instructions, squinting at the spidery additions in the margins. The Jacquard cards, hard and made from a material Earnestine didn't know, went in a slot at the back... no, this way round and the handle wound the internal springs. There were three: back, right – quite stiff – and the front, which whirred away until she realised that there was a catch. Finally, the instructions said it was started by dropping a gauntlet on the Activation Plate, see Fig 1. There was a heavy leather glove supplied for the principle, which had been loaded with lead shot and sewn shut. To deactivate it, all one had to do was press the heart in the centre of the main column with whatever weapon one had selected. This seemed remarkably simple, and the obvious nicks and holes attested to how often this had been achieved in the past.

She marked a line two paces away in the dust with the toe of her Oxford Street boot and experimentally swished a foil this way and that. Finally, she pulled the face mask over, finding she could see through the wire mesh, but realising that her coiffure was ruined.

"En garde," she said, bringing the blade upright, the cold steel guard tucked under her chin, and then, ruining the bold stance, she bent forward and tossed the gauntlet down. It landed squarely on the activation plate.

The metal dropped, the central arm jerked up in a parody of the duelling pose and then the first Jacquard card shunted in at the back, clunking and whirring. The right armature swung round, a counter balance, distracting Earnestine as the other arm came up and prodded forward. It caught her in the midriff; her corset transferred the force across her entire torso, so it flung her over backwards crushing both her bustle and her dignity. The thing carried on, whirling, swirling and stabbing, slashing and probing as the entire pack of cards jostled into the mechanism telling the mechanical combatant to fight and struggle on, despite facing an already fallen opponent.

Earnestine rolled over and hustled out from under the flailing threat and turning, she pulled herself up.

Waiting for the right moment, she stepped in: parried the blow. It clanged backwards and she smiled, knowing that she'd got the hang of this–

"Oooph!"

She was on the ground again, her ear stinging from a swipe. The face mask came free and bounced away like a rugby ball. The machine had known where she was, her blow activating cogs and levers as her parry moved the arm in a certain way and this in turn directed the counter move. She struggled backwards, the device thrashing side-to-side above her and walking!

Walking!

Towards her!

It shunted from one short leg to another, the weights inside throwing it one way and then another in a travesty of motion.

It stopped moving as the internal forces wound down and presently the thrashing slowed, stuttered and stopped.

When it finally ceased, Earnestine stood and brushed the dirt off her dress before she–

"Ah!"

It struck again, the last spring giving its final oomph.

"Right!"

A simpler programme was the answer to expedite a gradual improvement of her skill, she thought.

She selected another: turned the handle again – that right one could do with some oil – and set off the combat once more.

This time she was ready, this time she parried and parried again before the thing somehow twisted its foil and disarmed her.

Second attempt – the oil was in the workshop and… there must be something to get this disgusting stuff off her hands without ruining her lace handkerchief.

"Now!"

Gauntlet down, Earnestine down.

Fourth attempt, the oil had done the trick, and she was soon hopping in the centre of the warehouse around the clever hansom cab, holding her hand and biting her lip to stop her yelling the 'b' word at the top of her voice.

When it had finally subsided, Earnestine glared at it for a long time and then, very deliberately, she stabbed the heart of the machine. The image depressed signifying that the machine was 'off'. It was indeed so easy when the opponent wasn't defending itself.

Oh, it was such a foolish un-ladylike activity anyway.

She made herself a cup of tea, but it was no victory celebration and her hand, ear, derriere and pride smarted dreadfully, so she put the very idea out of her mind completely and went back to filing, banging the doors shut and slamming the stacks of paper down with a certain vehemence.

"My dear, what's the matter?"

"Nothing Mister Boothroyd."

"I think we should have a spot of tea."

They had yet another tea and Earnestine began to sort again, separating items into i) clearly obsolete, ii) interesting and iii) utterly perplexing. There were many on the same lines, often with extremely minor adjustments to their diagrams. If this was school, then clearly these pupils had copied each other's homework. She'd also forgotten some of the mnemonics she'd invented in order to understand her system. The pile under the brick, for example, ought to have been Architecture, but clearly wasn't any more.

She found the pile she'd removed from the fireplace, and decided to chance her luck.

"These ones were already in the fire."

Boothroyd didn't even glance up from his crossword: "Oh very well."

Earnestine rammed them back into the fireplace and lit them quickly in case he changed his mind. The fire produced a lot of smoke that wafted into the room, until the heat allowed the chimney to draw. The paper took and whooshed, so Earnestine added some wood that she'd found and then a few coals. She went into the kitchen to wash her hands, prepare a pot of tea and put together a plate of assorted biscuits.

Boothroyd was sitting in the armchair, perplexed again by the empty desk. He'd finished the crossword, although he'd added some squares to the right hand side to do so.

"May I?" Earnestine asked, putting her hand on the copy of the Times.

"Certainly, my dear."

Earnestine realised that it was, in fact, her newspaper.

The headline was about all these arrests, but Earnestine flicked through to see if there were any columns about explorers. There were no reports of any long lost expeditions being found. She was used to that, but even so she missed her mother and father. It was her regular morning tightness in her chest, but it passed.

"My dear?"

"I'm sorry, Mister Boothroyd, what was the question?"

"What do you think of all this talk about temporal travelling?"

"Oh... er..."

Earnestine glanced at the headline again: 'More arrests' and it went on to talk about men from the future.

"I've not been following it, I'm afraid."

"They've been arresting those responsible."

"Responsible for what?"

"And taking them to the future to stand trial."

"Is that likely?"

"Just think it though, my dear," said Boothroyd.

"It seems rather fantastical and far-fetched."

"Really?"

"Of course. Surely such a..." She looked at the front page for the right expression. "...Temporal Engine would be impossible."

Boothroyd dunked his garibaldi in his tea: "Why do you think that?"

"I'm sure I read somewhere that the Patent Office of the Americas suggested that we were reaching the end of all possible inventions."

"My dear?"

"That all inventions that were possible had already been invented. Or, at the very least, nearly so. There must surely be a limit to the possibilities."

"But we have so many inventions surrounding us. Steam power was unheard of only fifty years ago and now people go on day trips at velocities exceeding thirty miles per hour. There are steam powered boats made of metal. Zeppelins fly through the air. Why should it not be possible to construct a vessel to traverse the ether itself?"

"Because..."

"We could show the people of a hundred years ago marvels beyond their belief."

"I grant you."

"So it follows that in a hundred years' time, there will be marvels that we would struggle to understand."

"But surely time is different."

"Certainly," said Boothroyd. "But you already travel in time."

"One does not," Earnestine scoffed.

"If I were to travel to the continent, France or Italy, then I must reset my watch. I have travelled in time."

"Of course not." Earnestine put down her tea and biscuit to point at the floor. "Here is Greenwich Mean Time. I could easily decide that over there by the door it was half past five in the afternoon. I could go there, turn my watch until it said half past five, but I would not have travelled in time."

Boothroyd stared at the corner: "And you would have missed afternoon tea."

"Travelling to now from a distant age is quite another matter."

Her paper appeared to have a lot of columns devoted to these people and, flicking over, on pages two and three. It was all there in black and white, with editorial comment on page seven, and clearly Earnestine had been living in another world for she had simply missed all of this.

"These people say they have," said Boothroyd, pushing his hand through his grey streaked hair, "so it must be possible."

"They say they have?"

"How else do you explain their appearances and disappearances?"

Earnestine, of course, could not.

"Responsible and trustworthy men have seen it with their own eyes," Boothroyd finished. "And they have shown marvels beyond our current understanding."

It was unfair, Earnestine thought, for everyone to strive so hard for a future that was suddenly, and inexplicably, handed to them on a plate. This department, the Patent Pending Office, was redundant. Why invent when one could simply have someone from the future give one the device, ready-made and, indeed, redeveloped and improved many times over?

"Why paint a picture, when one can go to the future to see it already hanging in the gallery," she said.

Boothroyd snorted: "Why indeed?"

"All this..." Earnestine said, waving her hand to encompass the study and, by suggestion, the warehouses beyond.

"I wondered when you'd realise."

"If they give one the plans and say you invented this, then would one?"

"I'd say so."

"But one wouldn't have actually done it."

"Legally it's whoever signed the patent application."

"Only legally."

"What other definition is there, my dear?"

Earnestine tidied away the cups and small plate, and took them to the kitchen. At some point she'd have to see if she could match cup to saucer.

"I suppose one can't argue with them," Earnestine said raising her voice. "After all, they'll know what one is going to do, won't they?"

Boothroyd didn't answer.

"I mean," Earnestine continued. "They have an unfair advantage."

There was a clatter, like something falling.

"Mister Boothroyd?"

There was a palpable silence and then a scuffle.

"Mister Boothroyd?"

Earnestine stepped back into the main room.

Boothroyd was on his knees, his hands together pleading. Beside him were two tall men dressed in long frock coats and wearing high top hats. They had strange glasses, painted white which made them look blind. Another was suddenly standing beside her. He looked like a fighter or a bull, and he had a weapon in his hand, a brass device with prongs and a strange internal illumination.

"Don't fight them," Boothroyd said.

"What's going on?" Earnestine demanded. She realised that she'd picked the flat iron up off the pile of 'Household and Garden'.

"This man is under arrest," said one of the men. He had a curved sword strapped to his belt. Earnestine saw that the others were similarly armed. Not that she could fight them... except that they were six paces apart and, unlike the duelling machine, they wouldn't be expecting an attack.

"For what crime?" she demanded.

"Genocide."

"Genocide?! But Mister Boothroyd is a harmless old man."

79

The man snorted: "This harmless old man created a weapon that decimated Europe in a great war."

Boothroyd didn't look like a man who would hurt a fly, but then who knew what monstrous devices were tucked away here ready to be discovered when they reached a particular letter of the alphabet or deciphered something on yellow paper. Involuntarily, she glanced at the piles of documents fearing that her attention would alight on the very creation.

"Who are you?"

"I am Scrutiniser Jones," said the burly one. He had a bent nose that spoke of long ago fisticuffs. "This is Chief Examiner Lombard."

"You have no jurisdiction here to arrest anyone," Earnestine replied.

"Jurisdiction? All of time is our precinct."

The men hauled Boothroyd to his feet and frog marched him out. Earnestine took a step to follow, but the taller man blocked her way. As he left, Boothroyd looked directly at Earnestine and said, "By George–" but then he was gone.

"Excuse me," Earnestine said. "But he needs... does he get representation?"

"Oh yes, these monsters get a fair trial."

"Will one be allowed to speak in his defence?"

"Maybe... who are you?"

Earnestine didn't want to tell him.

Somehow, she didn't want to get involved despite desperately wanting to save Boothroyd, but was her loyalty misplaced? Should she side with a mass-murderer just because he gave her a biscuit with her tea? Even Napoleon for all his mad warfare and radical ideas, had probably meant well when he imposed the nonsense of the metric system on the continent.

"Your name?" Chief Examiner Lombard repeated.

"Miss Deering-Dolittle."

The man stumbled back surprised: "Miss *Earnestine* Deering-Dolittle?"

"Yes."

Chief Examiner Lombard took a moment to close his open mouth, and then he chuckled, deep and reflexively.

The others had gone with Boothroyd.

There was only Earnestine and the laughing Temporal Peeler.

Surely, if they had removed Boothroyd from history, then he wouldn't be able to discover the weapon or whatever it was, so he would be innocent. But if it wasn't him, then just as surely it would fall to his replacement, which could very well be Earnestine herself.

He handed her a coin: "For your door."

"My door... oh."

She had to put the flat iron down to examine the gold disc. It was a King Edward sovereign, but Edward was only the Prince of Wales, Queen Victoria was the Monarch.

The man, Lombard, was still chuckling. Under his breath he repeated her name to himself and shook his head: "Earnestine Deering-Dolittle, *the* Earnestine Deering-Dolittle – of all people."

"What is it?" Earnestine asked. "Do you know me?"

"Mrs Frasier isn't going to be happy."

Mrs Arthur Merryweather

Georgina felt she didn't sleep at all and then suddenly she was trying to come round in that befuddled manner which betrayed a late rising. She rubbed her eyes, found the bowl of water for washing and splashed her face to shock herself awake. She found Arthur's pocket watch from under her pillow and, as she did every morning, she carefully wound the mechanism. It was – and this was utterly shocking to her – twenty five past eight!

81

She had a proper wash and dressed, wondering how to tighten her corset without a sister or a maid. She managed, but she wasn't pleased with the result. Finally, it was done up. A familiar sensation rose within her, and rushed to find the chamber pot. She threw up, not much because she'd eaten lightly the day before, but surely she must be going down with something for this was getting far too regular.

Luckily, there was enough water in her glass to rinse her mouth and she'd remembered to bring chalk to clean her teeth.

She thought about writing in Arthur's journal to finish yesterday's interrupted entry, but instead she made her way downstairs, ravenous, and at the foot of the stairs realised that she had no idea where to find the dining room.

She coughed: "Ahem."

She checked Arthur's watch again: nearly five to nine.

Another clock was ticking loudly, an ancient looking grandfather clock tucked by one of the doors. Time was important here, clearly, but why this door? Once she'd asked the question, it was obvious. Everyone needed to know when it was exactly right and proper to enter for a particular meal.

Listening at the door, she could only make out the ticking of the mechanism beside her.

There was nothing for it and she was a member of the Derring-Do Club after all.

She grasped the door knob and swung it open in a single gesture.

The room was occupied and everyone turned to face her.

Loudly, the chimes sounded nine times, forcing everyone to wait, counting in their heads to a number which they were all probably well aware.

It gave Georgina a chance to study the one man and three women.

The man was old and fat with a handlebar moustache, red features and a military bearing, with an appalling yellow waistcoat beneath open, double breasted jacket. The women were as different from each other as it seemed possible to be, in the sense that the eldest was staid and cautiously dressed in a tweed outfit that was protected by an apron; the second was flamboyant, dressed in red and wearing a long lace veil that failed to hide her blood red lips and beet juice rouged cheeks; and, finally, trying to hide in a large armchair was a nervous specimen, much younger and dressed in white. Georgina was reminded of three witches: the crone, the mother and the virgin.

The last chime faded away.

"Ah ha! Our guest," said the military man. He waddled over, took his thumbs out of his waistcoat pockets and put out his hand. Georgina took hold and the man simply held her hand in an unctuous manner with a sweaty, cold palm. "I'm Colonel Fitzwilliam, at your service."

"Colonel," Georgina said as she tried to slip out of his grasp.

"Allow me to introduce everyone," he continued. "This is the indispensable Mrs Jago, who keeps everything in order."

"Mrs Jago," said Georgina, smiling to the stern old woman in the apron. This was the woman, who had piled so much reluctance into letting her in last night. This morning Mrs Jago ladled out a stony silence.

The Colonel continued: "And Miss Millicent."

The young woman bobbed, looked embarrassed and mumbled something into her handkerchief.

"And finally, we are honoured to have staying with us, the great Mrs Falcone!"

The Colonel let go of Georgina's hand to open his arms wide to welcome the strange Mrs Falcone. He beamed at the flamboyant woman as Georgina wiped her hand on her dress.

Mrs Falcone accepted the Colonel's attention with mock humility and then turned to Georgina: "And you?"

"Oh, I'm Georgina Deering-Dolittle; I mean, that is to say Mrs Arth–"

"Because we are so very pleased that you are paying us a short visit."

"Thank you."

"When are you leaving, Miss?"

"Well that depends," Georgina replied, "and it's Mrs. You see, I am Mrs Arthur–"

"Really?"

"Merryweather!"

"Quite a claim."

Georgina wasn't sure what to say, so she looked about for breakfast. There were plates, but the food seemed to be absent.

"I wondered..." Georgina said, pointing at the empty sideboard.

"Breakfast finishes at nine promptly," said Mrs Jago, the housekeeper.

"But the dishes must have been cleared away before nine, because I arrived at exactly nine."

"No-one else wanted any more, Miss."

Georgina wasn't used to staff standing firm in quite such an obnoxious manner: "It's Ma'am. I'm Mrs Arth–"

"You have no right to be here, Miss."

"I have every right according to–"

Mrs Falcone butted in: "There are other claims. The Colonel's for example."

The Colonel smiled deprecatingly.

"Every right according to Messrs Tumble, Judd & Babcock."

"Tumble's an idiot," said Mrs Jago, "everyone knows that, and Babcock drinks."

"And, pray, what is your position here, exactly?"

84

"I am Jago, the housekeeper, Miss."

"And I am the mistress of the house, so I would appreciate it, if you would be civil!"

"I am perfectly civil. I am known for my civility. Everyone knows that, Miss."

"The correct form of address is 'Ma'am'."

"Whatever you say, *Miss*."

"Ma'am... 'em', 'ay', '...arm' – 'ma'am', I am Mrs Arthur Merryweather and Magdalene Chase is–"

"You are not!"

"I am!"

Mrs Falcone stepped between then in a conciliatory fashion: "We shall see what Arthur has to say about this."

"Who's Arthur?"

Mrs Jago saw her chance: "He's the man you are claiming to be married to."

"I'm not claiming, I am."

"Allegedly."

"No, not allegedly, legally."

"That remains to be seen. Legality is not everything, Miss."

"Ma'am!" Georgina caught herself before she stamped her foot and therefore wavered on one leg for a moment. "I married Arthur Philip Merryweather."

"When we ask him," Mrs Jago insisted, "maybe he'll say you did and maybe he'll say you didn't."

"How can you ask him?"

Mrs Falcone beamed: "We'll be holding a séance."

"A what?"

"That'll sort you out, Miss," said Mrs Jago. "Breakfast is over."

Mrs Jago swept out and the others followed, leaving Georgina fuming like a pent-up steam engine.

Miss Charlotte

Charlotte hadn't got to bed until the early hours and she had never been an early riser, so it was lunchtime when she emerged, nervously, from the room. She didn't want to run into any of the other occupants: guests, landlady or even the strumpets; however, this couldn't be avoided as they were all clumped together between her and the door. They were asleep or so befuddled that their eyes did not appear to focus on her at all as she picked her way through the gin soaked lounge and found her canvas bag in the cupboard off the hall.

"That's not yours." It was Odette.

"Yes, it is."

"All belongings become the property of Madam Waggstaff."

"Mine doesn't."

"It's for their own safe-keeping."

Charlotte searched for a good expression: "No!"

"It's the rules of the bordello."

"Bordello?"

"Yes, what this is."

"Oh, well, they don't apply to me."

"They do."

"They do not, I'm not a strumpet!"

Charlotte escaped into a bright crisp new day with her bag over her shoulder.

It was back west towards Uncle Jeremiah's then, she thought.

If she kept up a good pace, she might make it in time for a late lunch and perhaps a story, Uncle Jeremiah told such good stories, and then she remembered that he wasn't there.

"Where do you think you're going?"

Charlotte was off the ground, dangling from a strong arm as Mr Waggstaff yanked her off the pavement. She flailed about, but the man was used to how woman fight.

He held her up in such a way that she slipped down inside her dress, her arms constricted.

"Get off me!" she yelled. "Help, help."

At that moment, two policemen came round the corner.

"Police!" And when they didn't react, she remembered Uncle Jeremiah's advice: "Fire! Fire!! FIRE!!!"

The police came running at once as did a few passers-by. Mr Waggstaff was somewhat perturbed by all the attention, but he kept Charlotte aloft.

"Where's the fire?" said the sergeant, the stripes on his arm identifying his rank.

"This man is accosting me," said Charlotte.

The Sergeant and Mr Waggstaff considered each other: "It's not our concern to help dollymops," said the Sergeant.

Charlotte was indignant: "I'm not a dollymop!"

"She's one of mine, Constable Philips, and I'll see she doesn't cause any more trouble."

The police started to move away: "Right you are, Frank."

"Wait," said Charlotte. "He waters his gin, his house has rats and strumpets, none of them have clothes, and last night the Temporal Pee– *eek!*"

Charlotte hit the ground and bounced.

Mr Waggstaff was surrounded by an angry looking crowd: "We didn't. We had none of them. This one, she's got something wrong with her head. She's nothing to do with me."

Mr Waggstaff backed off and, when he felt he had enough of a head start, he scarpered. No-one chased him and the crowd went on their way leaving Charlotte at the feet of the two policemen.

"Were there Peelers?" Sergeant Philips asked.

"Yes."

"And you're not his dollymop?"

"No."

87

"What are you then?"

"I'm... a detective."

"A detective is it? You're a little short for the Metropolitan Police."

"I'm a consulting detective."

"Like Mister Sherlock Holmes in that Strand Magazine?"

"Yes, that's exactly it."

"Where's your deerstalker then?"

"It's at home, I'm in disguise."

"As a mopsey?"

"I'm sure I don't know what you mean!"

"What's the case then?"

"Missing person... possible kidnap," Charlotte tapped the side of her nose knowingly.

"Foreign spies at the bottom of it, no doubt."

Charlotte hadn't even considered this possibility: "No doubt."

"What's your next move then?"

"Clues. It's wrong..." – she racked her brain for the phrase: she'd read it not two weeks ago – "...to form theories without the facts."

"You're a positive Mrs Gladden, aren't you?"

Charlotte nodded, keen to inhabit her new role.

"Be off with you then, Miss."

It seemed obvious now: her task was to find Uncle Jeremiah and the first place to start would be his rooms. If nothing else, she was sure she could find his biscuit tin.

Charlotte was excited by her new life even before she reached Uncle Jeremiah's street. There was a red pillar box on the corner and black iron railings along the front of the long, smart terrace. Her Uncle had rooms on the first floor of number 34.

Confidence, she thought, and with a swing in her step she sauntered up the stone steps just as a posh gentleman in a top hat was leaving. She skipped past him, through the red door and the tiled porch. It was dark in the hallway. With luck, she wouldn't even be seen by the landlady, but she saw a movement down by the kitchen.

"Just seeing Uncle Jeremiah," she sang out. "He's expecting me."

She took the stairs two at a time and reached Uncle Jeremiah's landing.

The door was locked.

She stood on tiptoe, and could barely reach the top of the door frame. She jumped, once... twice – there were footsteps coming up the stairs behind her – and... she'd got it. She put the key in the door and opened it. She took a smart step backwards, so that when the landlady looked up, she saw Charlotte standing in front of a door that was opened.

"Uncle!" she said brightly and loudly. "What's that? Oh yes, Uncle, I'd love some macaroons. What a lovely idea, Uncle."

She went in and closed the door behind her.

Her breathing was like an express train.

She heard a voice mutter outside: "Kids of today... I don't know..." and then all that blah-blah-blah, which adults always indulge in, was taken downstairs.

Where to start?

If she was honest, she hadn't expected to get this far.

In the Strand Magazine, Sherlock Holmes always went on about not disturbing the evidence, so she decided not to touch anything. Instead, she scanned carefully left to right. Oh, there was his biscuit tin. Charlotte helped herself to two macaroons and then took exactly the same strides backwards to end up by the door again.

She'd left a trail of crumbs across the carpet.

The macaroons were jolly nice and she was so hungry.

She began her observations again: little table, then the door to his bedroom, which was ajar, then his writing desk, shelves with books, fireplace with ash but no fire, fireplace set, his big old lumpy chair, the glass cabinet with all the atlases, window with curtains open and nets drawn,

89

round table with unopened post, sideboard with his clocks and finally a coat stand. His coat, stick and hat were missing, but his long grey scarf was there.

She took two steps into the room and reached the central sofa. From here, she could see Tosca the Tiger lying in front of the hearth, his angry glare dulled as there was no roaring fire.

There was no Uncle Jeremiah here, no toasted muffins and no thrilling tales of faraway places. And there was no mess. The room was tidy.

She went into his bedroom, nervous, and saw his bed made up.

His big travelling trunk was still at the foot of the iron bedstead.

In the wardrobe there were clothes missing. Charlotte didn't know whether he had any suitcases. He must have, she thought, as he'd travelled all over the world and she couldn't see any; therefore, my dear Watson, he had packed and left. That also might explain the tidiness.

Back in the drawing room, she went over to his writing desk.

The blotter had mirror writing on it; not real Leonardo Da Vinci mirror writing, but the writing left from upside-down blottings. She found a shaving mirror amongst his things and examined the messages in the reflection, turning the blotter to read them all.

'...sincerely, Dr Jeremiah Deering.'

'...the fifteenth...'

'...chronostatic charge cannot be deployed to adjust actuality...'

'...cancel the Times forthwith...'

'...per's Ghost and trap...'

She pushed it back into place clumsily: there was nothing here at all.

If she stuck her lips out, she could make herself look like a duck, and even open her mouth wide and show her teeth, so she looked like that stuffed gorilla in the Natural History Museum. She put the shaving mirror down.

There was a book missing from the shelf near the end. After the gap, there was *The Wonderful Visit*, *The Island of Doctor Moreau*, *The Wheels of Chance*, *The Invisible Man* and *The War of the Worlds*. There didn't seem to be any authors for 'X', 'Y' and 'Z', they were forgotten letters.

Letters! The post!

She jumped out of his revolving study chair and raced over to the post.

Oh, but they were sealed.

Three letters: penny blacks, yellow envelope, white envelope, white envelope: all with 'Doctor J. Deering, Esq.' and one with 'FRS' after his name. The postmarks were Kensington, Battersea and smudged. Oh, Kensington! That was the card from Georgina that she'd sent to inform him of Captain Merryweather's funeral, which meant that he hadn't opened his post for weeks.

That was very clever, she thought – positively deductive.

If only she could work out what was in the other two envelopes.

Holmes played the violin to think, but Charlotte hadn't brought hers and she was only allowed to practise when there was no-one else at home, so she never did.

Perhaps she should sit and smoke a pipe, she thought. Holmes was always doing so. Young ladies, however, did not smoke pipes, so perhaps she should cultivate that as her eccentricity.

There was a spare clay pipe on the mantelpiece, tufts of tobacco in a wooden box and matches. She rammed the tobacco into the pipe and lit it, blowing down the tube until it flared and started to burn, the smoke spiralling upwards much as it had when Uncle Jeremiah sat down to tell them a story.

She sat in his lumpy arm chair feeling very grown up.

91

Uncle Jeremiah had blown smoke rings from his mouth, so clearly you also had to suck the smoke into–

"Ga'*aarrgh!*"

Charlotte was suffocating, the pressure of the smoke inside her causing her eyes to bulge. She coughed loudly, her throat trying to turn inside out and she dropped onto her hands and knees, almost retching like Georgina every morning, with tears gushing down her face. As the proverbial cart before the horse, her weeping brought on a desperate feeling of loneliness. She missed Uncle Jeremiah and she missed Georgina... and she even missed her all High and Mightiness, Earnestine, now that she was away every day, all day.

Once she'd remembered the catch, the sash window came up easily enough. Charlotte stuck her head out and breathed the invigorating, horse manure whiff of fresh air. Clearly, she thought, pipe smoking was not going to be her eccentricity, it would just have to be chocolates and cake.

Down below, there were three men in top hats at the door arguing with the landlady. She blustered and objected as they forced their way in and moments later a heavy tread sounded on the stairs along with the unmistakable sound of swords clattering.

It was a long time since she had played 'hide-and-seek' here and she realised that she could no longer fit under the sofa nor would the curtains suffice. Indeed, she realised that Uncle Jeremiah must have been particularly blind not to have realised straight away when she'd hid behind them.

The voices reached the landing: high tones objecting to a lower pitched firmness.

Maybe they were going up to the second floor.

The handle rattled.

"This door's unlocked," said a voice that wasn't Uncle Jeremiah's.

Charlotte light footed it across the room and into the bedroom.

She could hide under the bed – no! It would be the first place they'd look.

In the wardrobe?

Footsteps in the study!

"I must object!" the landlady announced.

"In writing, Mrs Jacobs, in writing."

"But where to?"

"The Chronological Constabulary, care of Scotland Yard."

Trunk!

Blankets out, flung onto bed, Charlotte in, top down.

"It's not on the shelf."

"Search everywhere."

"I can smell fresh tobacco."

"Someone's been here."

The bedroom door creaked open.

She wasn't hiding from Uncle – don't giggle! Don't! Just don't!

"Post... an unpaid bill for glass... galvanic lighting... some funeral."

The cheek, Charlotte thought, they've opened his letters.

"This pipe is warm – go and find out if anyone's been here."

"How?"

"Ask the Jacobs woman."

Footsteps went away, but another step sounded in the bedroom. The light in the crack around the trunk lid moved, split and moved again.

"It's not by his bed... nor under it."

"It was here."

"He's taken it then."

"Looks like it."

"Someone else has been looking for it."

"We'd better tell Mrs Frasier."

"Rather you than me."

"Mrs Frasier isn't going to be happy."

"Is Mrs Frasier ever happy?"

The footsteps receded.

The door closed.

Charlotte lifted the lid a smidge and looked out: they'd gone.

They'd been looking for 'it', they'd not found 'it', so 'it' wasn't here, whatever 'it' was, and Mrs Frasier, whoever she was, wasn't going to be happy.

Back in the drawing room, Charlotte looked around.

The books had been disturbed on the shelf, the gap was now larger and a Jules Verne lay fallen on the blotter.

How do you find something, she thought, that you know isn't here?

What had the man said: "Kronologic Constab... u... lorry."

She fetched down Uncle Jeremiah's big dictionary: 'H'... 'J'... 'K'... 'Krona', 'Kronecker'... It wasn't there. Perhaps it was 'Crone' like an old woman, which would be an excellent word for Earnestine. Charlotte sniggered as she passed 'E' and 'D'. It wasn't in 'C' neither. Could you have a silent letter in front of a 'C' or a 'K', she wondered idly flicking the pages. There it was: 'Chronology – pertaining to, and of, time'.

"Temporal Peelers," she whispered aloud.

So it was true. They had been here looking for Uncle Jeremiah and the mysterious 'it'. Uncle had packed, quickly as he'd left his trunk and scarf, and then gone on the run. Logically he'd taken 'it' with him. 'It' would be small, if 'it' had been on the shelf. But where would he go? Perhaps Battersea or smudged?

She checked the letters they'd discarded on the table. It wasn't wrong, surely, to read them now, because they were open and she'd not opened them herself.

Smudged turned out to be a Birmingham glass making factory – how dull.

She could do this.

The clues were here.

94

Holmes always spotted a footprint or a dropped pair of glasses, and deduced a secret room or whatever. No dog had barked, but then Uncle Jeremiah didn't have a dog.

He hadn't opened the letter about Captain Merryweather's funeral, so he'd not been here for an age, and yet there were only three letters. Perhaps he had arranged to have them forwarded somewhere else. This meant he'd been living somewhere else, but he'd not mentioned anything like that at the theatre, when they'd seen the brass band and that funny sketch about the French Foreign Legion that now seemed so silly in comparison to consulting detective work.

She had another macaroon.

Missing book, stupid factories in Battersea and Birmingham, both places that begin with 'B', packed quickly, gone... west. He'd left his scarf, so perhaps Africa or India, rather than Canada or the Outer Hebrides. He hadn't been arrested, because they were looking for him.

There were no more macaroons.

Oh, it was impossible.

Chapter VI

Miss Deering-Dolittle

Earnestine followed them.

The Temporal Peeler, Chief Examiner Lombard, had left the way he had arrived, but Earnestine knew how to get to the 'treasure house' and thence through a yard and into the street, so, after some undignified running, she was close enough to catch sight of them getting into a four wheeler. As it moved away, fortune smiled on her as a hansom cab came round the corner.

"Follow that carriage," she said, climbing up.

Now they approached Battersea or perhaps further north-east into Vauxhall or Lambeth. She wasn't sure about this side of the river.

The driver was holding back as instructed and Earnestine was trying not to bob up to see over the horse's rump every five minutes.

The trap door above her opened, and she looked up and back at the driver.

"They're stopping, Miss," he said.

"Thank you, stop here please."

The horse snorted loudly as the driver pulled back on the reins. Earnestine opened the doors in front and stepped down from the two-wheeler.

"Here," she said, paying. "Wait."

"Right you are, Miss."

As she stepped away, she had a sudden panic that she'd paid with the strange King Edward sovereign, but it was still there in her carpet bag, along with the flat iron and the poker. She inwardly cursed herself for not bringing any of the Duelling Machine's weaponry.

She was at a factory, she thought, although she wasn't that familiar with such premises.

97

She ran to the entrance, a wrought iron gate between two strong brick pillars with an iron arch between them, and peeked round the corner.

The dark suited men in their top hats and white glasses were bundling Boothroyd from the carriage and into a goods yard. A smart woman dressed in burgundy appeared and the men snapped to attention. They were talking, too far away for Earnestine to make out any words, and then one of the men pointed at the gate. Earnestine ducked away.

When she looked back, they were all going inside.

When the way was clear, Earnestine sprinted across the cobbles and hunkered down in front of the door. Although it had been her plan, now she was near the entrance, she didn't fancy following them inside. There'd be nowhere to run if she was discovered, so she went around the side of the building – *gosh,* it went a long way back – keeping low, and craning her neck into each window to check. By the time she'd reached the third, she saw them – just.

She searched round for something to stand on and found a barrel covered in a black powdery substance that left a soot mark on her fingers. She tilted it on its rim to semi-roll it up against the wall. When she clambered on top, she could just see through the dirty window.

At the end of a long room, the Temporal Peelers and that woman in the long evening dress had gathered on a platform with the Peelers holding the forlorn and dejected form of Boothroyd between them.

They stood in formation, holding their sword scabbards flat against them, almost as if they were posing for a daguerreotype.

All of a sudden, and in unison, they checked their pocket watches: it was a bizarre, almost choreographed, action.

A noise, a galvanic fizzing or a bagpipe drone with a rising tone, ululated, and a light pulsed brightly within.

And then... and then...

They vanished: right before her eyes, the figures faded away to nothing.

The light returned to normal.

She blinked – once, twice – but it didn't bring them back. They had definitely disappeared.

The platform was empty.

She'd had a clear view. The light hadn't dazzled her, she'd blinked, but not closed her eyes, and they'd not stepped off or gone out the back way.

They'd just evaporated.

She'd seen stage magicians dematerialise people in the theatre, but that had always been inside a closed box.

These had simply gone, right in front of her eyes.

So it was true.

Men from the future had come and gone.

What would that herald for her time?

And what to do about it?

When Earnestine arrived back at 12b Zebediah Row, she had a plan. She went straight upstairs and dug out her medium kit bag. The stout canvas contained a variety of useful items: penknife, compass, flashlight, spare batteries, matches, tinder, sewing kit, spare button, handkerchief, whistle, map of London, pencil and notebook, water bottle, dark lantern, extra socks, a bandage, two packs of Kendal mint cake and a clothes peg. She'd take her lucky umbrella too, and money.

The door opened downstairs.

For a moment Earnestine feared that it was the Temporal Peelers come to arrest her and she grabbed her umbrella to defend herself, but it was just silly Charlotte. Earnestine could see that the irresponsible child had been out rough and tumbling, but there was no time to chide her properly now.

"Charlotte! Get cleaned up and packed this instant."

"Ness, I–"

"This instant!"

Money would be useful and that was all in the large kit.

She lifted the trunk out, opened it and hefted out all the spare clothing. Under the false bottom was a wad of big white paper notes, a bag of sovereigns and a smaller purse of silver and bronze. She felt disorganised as she really should have predicted this sort of eventuality and prepared a medium-large adventure... no, not adventure... medium-large emergency kit. She divided the money into evenly distributed portions, one for the kit bag, one for her jacket and one for the cunning pocket that she'd sewn onto the inside of her winter skirt.

Charlotte still hadn't packed!

"Charlotte, pack – now!"

"Ness."

"Now!"

Earnestine found the carpet bag and loaded it with the medium kit bag, a knobkerrie from the Zulu lands and a police truncheon. Father's old belts would hold it all together and she could use the strap from the large kit to carry it over a shoulder. Unfortunately, it would give it a bohemian appearance, but that couldn't be helped.

"Lottie, for goodness sake! Pack."

Earnestine, having had to check upon the youngster three times, took matters into her own hands, stuffed Charlotte's leather luggage bag with clothes pulled from her drawers at random and then bundled it all, including Charlotte herself, down to the front door.

"This is five pounds," said Earnestine.

"Oh, goodness, oh, oh..."

"Spend it only in an emergency."

"Ooh, Ness..."

"Now, hail a cab and go to Uncle Jeremiah's," Earnestine instructed. "Stay there until I say it's safe, and don't go anywhere else."

"I can't."

"Of course you can, stop being silly."

"Uncle Jeremiah's not there."

"I beg your pardon?"

"He's on the run from Temporal Peelers."

Earnestine blanched. All her plans fell away to be replaced instantly by others, but she felt one step behind and awfully in the dark.

"How do you know this?" she asked.

"I went round to his rooms and he hasn't been seen for three weeks."

"Why weren't you at school?"

"And I discovered that he's on the run from Temporal Peelers. They turned up – I hid, wasn't that clever? And they couldn't find him, so I looked for clues."

"That wasn't what I asked."

"Oh Ness, it's a horrid place. We've far more important matters to worry about," said Charlotte, dismissing this minor trifle. "The adventure is afoot!"

Earnestine was appalled: "Adventure?"

"You like adventures."

"I do not."

"What's all this then?" Charlotte pointed at Earnestine's open carpet bag complete with the medium kit, knobkerrie and umbrella. She added the flat iron.

"It's for emergencies."

"Where's your flashlight?"

"It's in the medium adv– I mean, emergen–"

"Ah ha!"

"Well, you'll just have to go with Georgina to the..." Earnestine gritted her teeth, "...seaside."

"Oh, Ness, it'll be a holiday."

"No, it won't. I have to... do whatever it is that needs doing and you have to keep out of trouble. My employer, Mister Boothroyd, was arrested, Uncle Jeremiah's disappeared–"

"An MP has been arrested."

"As have many others, so Georgina and..." Earnestine was suddenly conscious of another disappearance: "Where's Georgina?"

101

Mrs Arthur Merryweather

Georgina wished fervently that she was somewhere else, but she was so ravenous that the dining room was the place she needed to be. Unfortunately, Mrs Falcone was holding court and her tale of Red Indian Medicine in the Americas endlessly delayed the serving of the food. Apparently, the savages caught dreams in large nets. It conjured up an image of red men, dressed as running buffalo, leaping around like so many butterfly-collecting clergymen.

During all this, Georgina could see the hot pots steaming on the side, gradually cooling and then, as the prattle turned to peace pipes, going cold. She could taste the flavours in the still air such was her anticipation. It was torture.

"We shall have a séance on Friday," Mrs Falcone announced. "For we cannot possibly do so without the Reverend Gabriel Milton. He is such an open minded individual when it comes to the spirit world."

Mrs Falcone was seated at the head of the table. This place should have been for her Arthur, Georgina was sure, but she wasn't acquainted with the seating arrangements now. The problem was that this irritating woman, who seemed to receive most of her information from great chieftains disguised as eagles, was acting as if she owned the place. Georgina didn't want Magdalene Chase herself, but she didn't want this Mrs Falcone to have it either. What was she doing here? What was her position? What was a polite way to ask?

"Perhaps we could discuss this over dinner?" Georgina suggested.

"We are."

"Over the actual repast."

"I say, what a splendid idea," agreed Colonel Fitzwilliam, leaning odiously towards her. "Capital."

"My Millicent here! She has an opinion on that, don't you, dear?"

"Perhaps food, Mama... or not," said Millicent, her eyes darting about as if she were the rabbit about to be caught and cooked in a pot.

"Mrs Jago, if you would be so kind," Georgina said.

Mrs Jago glared from the dark corner where she stood in attendance.

"The Colonel," Georgina said.

"Ladies first, my dear."

"So kind, Colonel."

Caught in the pincer movement, Mrs Jago had no choice: "Yes, Miss."

Georgina bit her tongue. Once, just this once, she'd let that pass – anything to have something on her plate.

Mrs Jago served Mrs Falcone, then at an even more glacial pace, Miss Millicent, before tapping the spoons on the pots and placing them on the sideboard.

Georgina clattered her cutlery.

"Miss Dee... my dear," the Colonel said.

Mrs Jago found the spoons again and served Georgina and the Colonel. It was stew, or something, apparently lamb, with vegetables.

The wine was next to Mrs Falcone, the jug of water by Georgina. The Colonel had brought in a whiskey.

"The Reverend Gabriel Milton once communed with William Shakespeare's brother, did you know?"

Georgina swallowed a spoonful; bliss: "No, I did not."

"Then you have a lot to learn, Miss."

Georgina could not say 'Ma'am' with her mouth full.

"We will conjure up the spirits and learn much from them. I always do. They have much to tell us."

Georgina could feel her strength returning: "Will we bring forth the ghosts of Christmas past, present and yet to come?" she asked.

She and her sisters had once played the characters from Charles Dickens' story at a fancy dress party: Earnestine had been the past, Georgina the present and Charlotte had been the ghost of the future. Charlotte had

103

disappeared, she remembered, leaving Earnestine and Georgina as two bereft figures.

"The doubters of youth," Mrs Falcone said, condescendingly. "You may mock, but the spirits will have their retribution."

At that moment, the wind – it was the wind – rattled the windows and howled around the building and wailed down the chimney.

Georgina, who relished reading books on the chemical interactions of daguerreotype printing, found the idea of spirits both ludicrous and deeply disturbing. They were all utterly serious and perhaps, in this God forsaken place, the departed really did communicate from the other side, and science and rationality only worked as far as the reach of the railways.

"Seconds, Colonel?" Georgina said. "And, as you insist, Colonel, for myself too."

"What? Oh, yes dear," the Colonel spluttered.

Mrs Jago served and then removed the bowl to avoid any possibility of thirds.

As for dessert, cream did not come north of Cornwall according to Mrs Jago.

When dinner was over, Georgina checked the master bedroom and found that Mrs Jago had removed the sheets, so Georgina found fresh and made the bed up herself. She found Fellowes in the scullery polishing the silver: the old man bent over his task, one eye concentrating and the other closed.

"Fellowes."

"Miss?"

"Ma'am."

"Ma'am?"

"I would like the key."

"There are only four keys to the front door, mine, Mrs Jago's, Mrs Falcone's and Colonel Fitzwilliam's."

"The key to my bedroom."

"The guest room key is–"

"The master bedroom!"

"Miss, that's—"

"Ma'am!"

"I don't wish to cause friction, but Mrs Falcone—"

"Mrs Falcone, Miss Millicent, Colonel Fitzwilliam and Uncle Tom Cobbley and all are not the legal owners of this property according to Messrs Tumble, Judd & Babcock."

"That, if you pardon me, has to be decided."

"And when it is decided, I shall remember who showed me due courtesy and *who did not!*"

"There is a spare key."

"All of them."

She had three keys, and she locked them and herself safely in the master bedroom.

Mrs Falcone and Miss Millicent were not mentioned in Arthur's journal until the page on which Georgina let fly with her careful handwriting. The Colonel was, however; described in terms that suggested he was a family friend, one who had first interested Arthur in military service. Georgina couldn't reconcile Arthur's descriptions of the Colonel with the man himself.

And then there was that other woman in the picture.

Miss Charlotte

"Perhaps she's been arrested?" Charlotte suggested.

Earnestine's expression was one of derision, followed by another of disquiet.

"We can solve this in an elemental way," Charlotte continued. She nodded with her best sage expression on her face.

"What are you talking about?"

"I observe that you have packed for travelling and so have I."

"I packed yours if you remember."

"Perhaps there are other clues..." Charlotte said, casting about for just such.

"We don't have time for this."

"Ah ha!"

Charlotte pointed at the hall table, atop of which were two parcels wrapped in brown paper.

"So?" said Earnestine. "The post came."

"There's no stamp and they are only addressed to..." Charlotte examined the parcel tags. "You and me... oh goody, a present."

"Charlotte, application."

"Indubitably."

"Do you know what these words mean, Charlotte?"

But Charlotte wasn't listening. The clues she needed were indeed on the hall table, two boxes wrapped up in brown paper. There were parcel tags, one to 'Earnestine' and the other to 'Lottie'. Charlotte examined both parcels: they were different, rattled differently and when she'd carelessly ripped with abandon the wrappings of her own, she revealed a paper bag of macaroons, all fresh and delicious.

As she munched, she picked up Earnestine's box and pushed her nose up against it. Sure enough, it was that pong that Uncle Jeremiah always bought for Earnestine. Her deduction–

"Uncle! Uncle!"

She ran through the house, but there was no-one in the drawing room or the study.

"What's all this commotion, Dearie?" It was Cook, rubbing her hands on her apron as she bumbled out of the kitchen. "Miss Deering-Dolittle, you're back too."

"Where's is he?" Charlotte demanded.

"I don't know who you mean?"

"Uncle Jeremiah."

"He called earlier with his arms full of parcels."

"It was Uncle Jeremiah... he's gone out with Georgina."

The Cook shook her head: "Mrs Merryweather's not been in all day. Or yesterday."

That was strange.

"There are only two parcels," Charlotte said, pointing at the solitary parcel and the discarded brown paper.

"He left two and took one with him," said Cook.

Charlotte narrowed her eyes as she contemplated this.

"Did he do anything else?"

"He waited in the drawing room, Miss, and asked for some boiling water and a piece of candy. I gave him a cup and let him help himself to the jar."

"There's candy in the jar!"

"Lottie," Earnestine warned. "Go on Cook."

"That's all," said Cook. "He didn't drink much. Queer sort of request."

"Hmm... thank you, Cook," said Charlotte.

"Don't you be eating all those biscuits, my dear," said Cook. "You'll ruin your appetite."

"Mmm... mmmm... I know," Charlotte said, realising that events were moving apace.

"Thank you, Cook," said Earnestine.

Cook went back to her duties in the kitchen, leaving Earnestine and Charlotte alone in the hall.

"Mister Boothroyd vanished – literally – and Uncle Jeremiah is being hunted, caught for all we know, and perhaps Georgina has gone too," Earnestine said.

Charlotte raced away, and then rattled about upstairs, causing the hall gas light to swing as she stomped about on the floorboards.

"Charlotte!"

Charlotte shouted down: "When they arrested Boothby–"

"Mister Boothroyd."

"Be that as it may," she said, pattering back downstairs, "did they let him pack?"

"Of course not. They threw him into a carriage, took him to Battersea and then they all disappeared into thin

107

air. I saw it, Charlotte, I saw the Temporal Peelers disappear into thin air."

"Georgina packed for a long trip: clothes from the wardrobe and her travelling trunk have gone."

Earnestine checked the hall table: "She can't have done, she hasn't left a note."

"Perhaps she had to leave in a hurry."

"If she had time to pack her travelling trunk, then she had time to leave a note."

"Uncle Jeremiah knows."

"How do you know that?"

Charlotte linked her hands together behind her back to stride across the carpet. "He came with three parcels and left only two of them. One of them was for me, another for you, so I deduce that the third was for Georgina–"

"Have you been reading my copy of the Strand?"

"I've not even been in your bedroom. So, if he took Georgina's present with him, then logistically–"

"Logically."

"Logically, he's gone to meet Georgina."

"That's jolly clever, Charlotte," Earnestine admitted. "Sensibly reasoned and without any flights of fancy."

Charlotte felt important.

"But where have they gone?" said Earnestine.

"Well, Uncle Jeremiah's on the run from the Temporal Peelers. Perhaps... he's been arrested by now and Georgina too, because Cook hasn't seen her all day or yesterday, so perhaps these Chronological Rozzers have taken them back to Roman times or to the Stone Age to eat Dillpod... Diplod... that skeleton thing in the British Museum."

"Unlikely."

"But possible."

"Where did you pick up a word like 'Rozzer'?"

"School. I told you it was a horrid place."

"Only because you don't apply yourself, whereas Georgina is responsible," Earnestine said. "She'd leave a note."

"Are you saying that I'm not responsible?"

"That is not what I said, but now you mention it: yes, you are decidedly irresponsible."

"Ness!"

"Don't whine. So why isn't there a note on the hall table?"

"Perhaps she didn't think it important enough to leave a note."

"It is a matter of a minute or two to write a note and Georgina never forgot."

"Perhaps it fell down the back."

"Charlotte, it couldn't..." but Earnestine must have realised that it could have done, for she peered down the crack between the wall and the table, and then underneath before she heaved the table away from the wall. "The maids don't clean here properly. There are crumbs down here... your crumbs."

"Too important for a note," said Charlotte.

"There's no such thing. If it's trivial like going into the garden or if you are in a rush to catch a particular post and are only going to the pillar box at the end of the Row, then you wouldn't leave a note, but anything else: we have a system, Lottie. You're the only one who doesn't follow it."

"But some things require explanation, so she'd write a letter."

"Are you suggesting that she'd write us a letter, walk down to the pillar box and post it?"

"Possibly."

Earnestine gesticulated towards the road: "If she posted it in the morning, it would have arrived by third delivery, fourth at the latest, and even if it was the last post it would arrive by first delivery in the morning, and the maids put the post on the hall table. Georgina is not

109

profligate, she wouldn't waste a stamp, she'd have simply put it on the table herself."

Earnestine's speech ended with her pointing at the empty table.

"She packed her trunk," said Charlotte, "which is premeditated–"

"It's not a murder mystery."

"So she left a note... or a message."

"I beg your pardon."

"In code!"

"Code or no code, it would be on the hall table!"

"Important letter... write it in the study..." Charlotte continued mumbling, her hands out in front of her with her fingers acting out the commentary. She wrote a tiny squiggle in the air, slipped nothing into the grip of her other hand and then held the imaginary object out to put down.

She looked round.

Earnestine was standing by the hall table pointing obviously. Red and blue patches shimmered on her stern features as the afternoon sun came through the stained glass of the front door. "I can't see the cab arrive," Charlotte added.

"What cab? We've not ordered a cab. Oh, do think, Charlotte."

"Gina packed a trunk, so she had to have left by cab, so she ordered a cab in the morning–"

"Or whenever she left."

"Or whenever, so she'd wait in the drawing room... and Uncle Jeremiah waited in the drawing room with hot water and candy, and he figured it out."

Charlotte waved her non-existent letter at Earnestine and then opened the door into the drawing room.

"Charlotte! You'll get dirt in... Charlotte?"

The drawing room was still and quiet. Charlotte scanned around quickly and saw it at once.

"Charlotte," Earnestine chided behind her. "She would not–"

"Picture's gone."

Charlotte pointed at the gap on the wall.

Earnestine took a few seconds to change trains as it were, and then she checked the framed pictures that were still there.

"You're right... mother... father... expedition..."

"It was the one taken at the theatre, the new one."

"Why? Oh, Lottie–"

"She wanted one of the three of us together standing shoulder-to-shoulder helping one another."

"Charlotte, really–"

"So be quiet and let me think."

"Oh–"

Earnestine was quiet, silenced by Charlotte's raised finger.

Charlotte closed her eyes, but trying to fathom a deduction was like trying to remember a Latin word when the sun was shining.

The clock ticked and tocked telling her that she was achieving nothing at all.

She conjured up the imaginary letter again trying to feel its texture and weight.

Tick... tock.

Charlotte smiled; she knew and opened her eyes. She gesticulated like a magician and waved towards the mantelpiece clock without looking towards it at all.

Earnestine followed the gesture: saw, jumped forward and snatched down the envelope. The clock tottered on the edge and fell, its glass smashed on the tiled hearth and the delicate mechanism twanged, rattled and ceased.

The silence was as complete as if time had stopped.

Chapter VII

Miss Deering-Dolittle

A quiet shattered by the doorbell.

A tall silhouette complete with top hat stood behind the red and blue stained glass in the porch. It bent down to peer through, a gaunt face bulging in the window with eyes white and covered.

Earnestine and Charlotte simply faced each other in the drawing room, each a mirror of the other's fear.

"They know my name," Earnestine whispered.

"Do they?"

"Yes."

"I saw them arrest someone," Charlotte hissed back.

"Then they've come to arrest one of us."

"Oh lummy."

"You or me?"

"Or maybe neither."

"I doubt they've popped round because they heard we have candy in the jar."

"We have to find Georgina."

"I agree."

"Once the Derring-Do Club is back together," said Charlotte, "it'll be like old times."

"I sincerely hope not."

The doorbell rang again, followed by a loud hammering knock.

"Garden!"

Charlotte hadn't needed the instruction as she and Earnestine scurried through the kitchen. Earnestine managed to grab the kit bag.

"Careful!" Cook cried as they hastened past. "And be back for dinner."

They ran across the lawn and circled the rose garden. At the far end, hidden by trees, was a wall. This wall had

113

been the defences of many fortresses and castles in their youth.

"Give me a leg up!" Earnestine ordered.

"Can't you make it on your own?"

"Just–"

"Getting too old?"

"Don't be impertinent. I'm carrying the Adventuring Kit."

"Adventuring?"

"You know what I mean."

Charlotte linked her hands to take the dig of Earnestine's Baker Street boots and launch her sister upwards. Earnestine scrambled at the top and then offered a helping hand, but Charlotte had already jumped up further along. Over they went into the alley beyond. Without any discussion, they started making along in the direction of Kensington Station, but two figures appeared at the far end. They were tall, dressed in black frock coats and wearing top hats. Their eyes looked huge and sinister with the glasses.

The sisters came to the same conclusion.

"Perhaps..."

"Yes..."

They scuttled away.

"Don't look back," Earnestine said. "Don't look back."

Charlotte glanced over her shoulder: "Run!"

They ran.

They came out the other side and into the busy street. Earnestine craned her neck up and looked right and left. There were no hansoms visible in either direction. There was never one when one needed one.

They worked their way along the pavement.

Earnestine was trying to think ahead: "Make for Addison Road or try and find a cab?"

"Split up!?"

"Absolutely not."

"Derring-Do Club forever."

They pelted along ignoring the 'Oi' of workmen.

At the corner were two men in top hats.

"Shortcut," said Charlotte, grabbing Earnestine's arm and yanking her round. She disappeared into a narrow alley between a butcher's and a tobacconist. They had to go single file, the clatter of their heels echoing off the brick walls. There was a tiny yard with two exits created by the gap between outside privies. Children playing barefoot there scattered when they arrived, and then gathered to point and joke.

The first exit led to a street full of pawnbrokers and across the road two men in top hats turned to look at them.

Back at the yard, the children were bolder and prepared, and plucked at their clothing practising their pick-pocketing skills. Both Earnestine and Charlotte had to swat their thieving hands away and snatch their bag back.

The second exit led to a side road with two banks facing each other on the corner. They turned left and went with the flow of people, ladies out for a stroll and labourers carrying coal from a parked cart.

"Top hats!" said Charlotte and she took off, running towards the banks. Earnestine followed, caught up and tapped Charlotte on her shoulder.

"Stop!"

"We must keep moving."

Earnestine paused, bent over slightly to ease the line of her corset across her ribs and panted for breath: "Wait... wait!"

"But–"

"We're running from top hats."

"Yes–"

"All top hats. That man... he's talking to another gent in a bowler."

"We must run."

115

"They're probably bankers or... independent means... and not Temporal Peelers. They don't have... swords."

Charlotte turned her attention to the distant top hat. Sure enough, he was talking amiably to another two men, who were both wearing bowler hats. Earnestine wondered just how many upper class gentlemen they'd run from in the course of their desperate flight.

"Where now?"

"We'll get off the streets," Earnestine said, and she pointed across the road: "Tea shop! Read letter... come up with... plan."

Hunkered down to hide their faces, Earnestine and Charlotte waited for a gap in the traffic and then sprinted across to the tea shop. As they went in, a bell jangled to startle a waitress.

"Ladies?"

"Table for two, please," said Earnestine, trying to avoid panting.

The waitress picked up two menus and directed them towards the window.

"Can we have one at the back?" Charlotte asked.

The waitress looked at them quizzically.

"My friend gets the chills very easily."

"It is warm."

"Please. She's old."

The waitress frowned, but nonetheless took them to a different table towards the back. They settled and ordered tea with scones.

"I'm younger than the waitress," Earnestine said.

"It worked."

Earnestine lips narrowed.

"Letter?"

Earnestine got out the letter and opened–

The tea shop bell rang and a man entered. He took off his top hat and placed it on the coat stand before taking a seat by the window. He gazed out into the street watching the traffic and only looked into the shop when the waitress went over to take his order.

Earnestine relaxed and opened the envelope. She had her finger on the letter when the waitress returned with a steaming pot, cups and saucers.

When the waitress had gone, she took out the letter and began reading. It started thus: '*To My Dearest Sis-*'

The waitress brought an elegant jug of milk. Earnestine smiled at her forcefully, returning to the letter when she'd gone.

'*Sisters, Ness-*'.

Their scones arrived, and looked very tasty and came with butter on a small dish, whipped cream in a bowl and strawberry jam in a jar.

'*Dearest Sisters, Ness and Lot-*'

"Will that be all, Miss?"

"Yes," said Earnestine through clenched teeth. "That will be all, thank you."

Earnestine waited until the waitress has returned to her counter. '*Dearest Sisters, Ness and Lottie.*'

"Shall I be Mother?" Charlotte asked.

"Please."

Earnestine read.

Charlotte had poured both teas, added milk and scoffed half a scone with lashings of jam and cream by the time Earnestine had read and re-read the letter three times.

"Ness?" said Charlotte, entirely failing to keep the impatience out of her voice.

"She's gone to Magdalene Chase."

"Where?"

"It's... near Tenning Halt."

"I've never heard of it."

"Neither have I."

"Let's see," Charlotte demanded. She scanned down the letter. "Why is it spelt funny?"

"It's how you spell 'Magdalene'."

117

"But it would be 'em', 'ay', 'you', 'dee...' 'el', 'eye', 'en'."

"Why ever would it be spelt like that?"

"It's more logical."

"No, it isn't."

"Why?"

"Because... if you'd pay more attention to your lessons, you'd know."

"But why has she gone to *Magdalene* Chase?"

"It's her ancestral home."

"Her ancestral home is 12b Zebediah Row."

"Her ancestral home on the Merryweather side."

"Merry... oh!"

"I think we should visit our sister," Earnestine announced. "Apparently it's in the middle of nowhere, so it would be a perfect place to hide."

"Uncle Jeremiah will be there and might be able to explain."

"Absolutely."

"Are you suggesting we wander down to the station with all the Temporal Peelers after us?" Charlotte asked.

Earnestine thought for a moment: "We'll lie low for a while."

Outside the street was still full of men in top hats, but there were bowlers, flat caps and many, many ladies' bonnets.

"Which nowhere is it in the middle of?" Charlotte asked.

Earnestine lips tightened: "Gina didn't say."

They made their way back to the banks on the crossroads and checked the street names, and it was easy to walk along keeping pace with the traffic as they looked for a hansom. Luck was not with them and in the end Earnestine and Charlotte had to walk all the way to Queensbury Road.

Mrs Arthur Merryweather

The view from the bedroom was bleak and when the clouds blotted out the weak sun, Georgina could see her reflection in the window. She would have stood here with Arthur and he would have put his arm around her. She'd have been able to glance – just there – and see him, just as now she saw a ghostly figure standing at her shoulder made from the clouds beyond

A shaft of sunlight escaped and played about the moors much like the galvanic spotlight had at the theatre. She could walk there in the place that she'd been warned against (but then she'd been warned against this house too) and the moors would claim her. The others wouldn't miss her, although no doubt Mrs Falcone would contact her to ask about eagles and wigwams.

Downstairs in the drawing room, Mrs Falcone was in full swing with Miss Millicent alternating between fluttering and downtrodden.

"My grandmother was an actress," she announced. "Can you believe it? No better than she ought to have been, I declare. She duped the great Maestro Falcone, didn't she Millicent – don't hunch – and – you take after her, you know – and bore him nine children and only five of those died, but luckily we take after the Falcone side... with exceptions."

"Mama, I..."

"Quite."

"Sorry, Mama."

"I have the acting blood in me, you see. Proper acting, not that cheap stuff of women who should know better, but perhaps a Shakespeare or a Marlowe or a recitation of poetry. I was known for my recitation. Perhaps this is why I am such a sensitive."

Georgina almost sniggered aloud: "Sensitive?"

"Indeed," Mrs Falcone's tongue was sharp. "I feel things beyond the reach of ordinary people and that is

119

why I can commune with the departed. They reach out, you know, looking for a suitable vessel."

Georgina didn't know how to answer this. It seemed tantamount to black magic, but the idea of communicating with her late husband drew her in. If only...

"You are an unbeliever," Mrs Falcone announced. "I sense these things."

"We live in a rational world," Georgina replied calmly. "Everything works according to God's laws, the immutable workings of the Universe as discovered by Sir Isaac Newton. The natural world functions like a clockwork mechanism or an engine."

"That may be true in London, I dare say," Mrs Falcone replied, "but there are more things in heaven and hell than in that new-fangled philosophy."

"Science holds that the same laws apply everywhere and–"

"Hmm, there are daguerreotype pictures of spirits and ghosts, and that isn't explained by your Newman, Sir or otherwise."

"Newton."

"I have communicated, regularly, with the spirit world and the spirit of this Newton hasn't come to argue his case that spirits don't exist."

"That makes no sense."

"Well, that's because you are closed-minded."

Georgina felt her mouth open, but no words came out. She simply couldn't argue with this woman, who flatly ignored rational discourse and instead relied on pure statement. Also, Georgina still wasn't sure what this woman was doing here. She'd assumed that the house would be occupied by Merryweathers, relations of her husband, but there didn't seem to be any at all. Fellowes, Mrs Jago and the rest of the staff made sense, but Mrs Falcone, Colonel Fitzwilliam and Miss Millicent did not. Unless, she supposed, Miss Millicent was a Merryweather.

120

She resolved to visit every room and did so, disturbing the cook and Fellowes, who was polishing the silver again, and discovered that the guests were in the East Wing, whereas the master bedroom was in the West Wing.

Outside, there was a small formal garden at the back, blasted by the seemingly endless gale, and then the land rose into undulating hills from which burst outcrops of sharp granite. The elements had carved these into blocks as if the landscape was littered with fallen megaliths.

"Tors."

Georgina jumped.

It was Colonel Fitzwilliam, who had appeared from nowhere, it seemed, and now stood far too close. He tucked his thumbs into his garish yellow waistcoat.

"I beg your pardon," Georgina said, taking a few steps away for propriety's sake.

The Colonel took a step even closer.

"You were thinking about the hills. The rocks, like cairns, are called 'tors'. Some say the devil made them."

They did look like satanic markers. Now she looked, Georgina could see that some of the stones formed the outlines of buildings long ago destroyed.

"Witches' houses," the Colonel added.

"There are perfectly natural explanations for these geological features," she said.

"I'm sure there are, my dear, but all rather complicated for an old duffer like myself."

"Well, thank you for the information. I think I shall take a stroll up to one and examine it more closely."

"Mac was here," said the Colonel.

"Mac?"

"Lieutenant McKendry, last year. He stayed for a few months, walked all round. He had such awful trouble pronouncing Magdalene, he kept saying 'Mag-da-lene'. He was probably investigating the lights."

"Lights?"

"In the sky. At night."

121

"Shooting stars?"

"Rum shooting stars that hover and change direction."

"Oh."

"Be careful," the Colonel added. "Peat bogs can easily suck the unwary into the ground."

"I shall be careful."

The walk was bracing and the wind howled stronger still once she was away from the shelter of the Chase. She thought about going back for a shawl, but she knew she was being watched and she didn't want to give anyone the satisfaction of seeing a weakness. The slope uphill was mostly gentle, the ground sprung underfoot and, where it was steep, it was like a giant green staircase. Once she reached the rocks of the Tor, she had to use her hands to pull herself up the tricky sections, but soon enough she was standing atop the summit.

The view was spectacular in a bleak fashion.

Magdalene Chase was below, the driveway leading out to the main road, a narrow affair between stunted hedges that wound along a contour. There was a village, its church tower dominating a small clutch of cottages and beyond... nothing.

Behind her, in the near distance, were other Tors, each higher than the last and very like cairns marking a route, tempting her to go ever further from civilisation.

The derelict houses came from another era, an ancient one. She had read, and seen exhibits in museums, of prehistoric times when barely human cavemen had eked out a savage existence. Mankind progressed, inventing all the time, so logically earlier times were more primitive and any Golden Ages, like that of Atlantis or Troy, were entirely mythical. Further back still would be Darwin's hypothesized (oh, very well, she knew that *On the Origin of Species* only implied it) ape-like ancestors of mankind. These pre-humans must have lived here despite the lack of trees.

There had been Dark Ages when knowledge had been lost, dips between the hills of enlightenment, but the direction was always upwards. The people who lived here, who built these rude houses, must have been as barbarous as those modern day natives in the jungles of the far flung colonies of the Empire.

If one stopped looking back, she wondered, and turned one's mental gaze in the opposite direction, what marvels would the future offer?

Or would the likes of Mrs Falcone and her fellow spiritualists suck mankind down into the bog of another Dark Age of Superstition?

She shuddered and made her way back down, conscious that there were eyes behind the dark windows of the Chase watching her, both the living and perhaps a multitude of dead ancestors, by marriage, going all the way back to the primitive.

Miss Charlotte

Charlotte had not liked the Patent Pending Office as it looked stuffy, full of papers, documents and other tedious matters of uninterest.

Earnestine took a flat iron out of her bag and put it on a stack of papers. There were other items on other piles: a brick, a statue of a knight–

"Don't touch that!"

"I was only looking."

"Look, but don't touch."

"Can I ahoy-hoy someone up?"

"I beg your pardon."

"On the thingamajig?"

"No, and you don't know anyone who has a telephonic apparatus anyway."

"Can I–"

"No."

"What about–"

123

"No. Nor that... Here, I know what you need."

Charlotte's heart sank when she saw Earnestine reach for a book. She was going to force her to read some stuffy text, but instead it was a disguised switch and the book shelf swung open.

"A secret door... an actual secret door. Oh, Ness."

"If you'd close it behind you, please," said Earnestine.

Charlotte, still failing to contain her excitement, did so. The whole shelf rotated back into position on carefully balanced brass hinges, and stopped with a satisfying click.

"This way."

Charlotte followed into a huge store house full of delights.

"Ness, is this–"

"Don't touch anything."

"But Ness."

"For any reason."

"Ness."

"Ever. And don't whine."

Earnestine was like some evil witch, who showed children sweets and then chopped off their hands.

"Look at this!"

Charlotte saw a wooden scarecrow arrangement with metal rods and an odd heart in the middle of the wooden central column. Earnestine handed Charlotte a sword, a foil with a red protective end.

"This is Ridley's Automatic Fencing Exerciser," said Earnestine.

"It's a fighting machine!" Charlotte said, her eyes gleaming with excitement.

"You wind it here."

Earnestine indicated the holes where a crank could be fitted. Charlotte set to work, and it was work, jolly hard work, particularly the one at the front. When she paused, Earnestine tutted.

"You must learn application," Earnestine commanded.

Charlotte looked at the previously exciting sword with its silly red bobble. It was only a short Pariser.

"Do I have to wind the machine every time?" she asked.

Earnestine was now some way down the corridor going back to the office: "Yes!"

"Do I–"

"Yes!"

"And–"

"Yes."

Fine, Charlotte thought.

The stupid machine required three stupid mechanisms to be wound up, the front and the side and the back and the stupid card things and the stupid gauntlet and finally she could fight the stupid thing.

It slashed right and left. Charlotte parried, tried to get past to stab at the heart, but it countered. Slash, slash, parry, slash... she backed off, got her breath back and went in again... finally stabbing the heart when the front and side springs were spent.

It stopped.

It was only five past two... a whole two hours was simply impossible. Earnestine was mad. No-one, absolutely no-one, except Earnestine, who had a black heart, could concentrate on one thing for *two hours!*

It took forever to rewind the springs, utterly stupid, round and crankingly round again and it was still only seven minutes past, but at least the fighting was fun.

She hadn't changed the pack of cards, so she was able to anticipate the machine's movements somewhat, but they changed when she struck the sword. It was clever and disarmed her. She was holding the hilt too tightly, she realised. She should be using... what was it? The French grip. Grip, grip, grips, gripped, gripping, grippamus... yuk.

Her third attempt met with no success either.

"Stupid."

She tried again.

125

Slashing with great abandon, while screaming at the top of her voice, didn't work either.

If only there was some way to pause the machine, rather than having to start again from the beginning, and a display to show if she was gaining points.

She flung her foil down and stomped off.

However, there was nothing else to do in this boring place.

In the end, she found the pamphlets and read them, which was like doing homework. One of them covered the machine itself and outlined the winding, the maintenance and then listed the four techniques: direct thrust, indirect thrust, cut over and counter disengage. These were all explained in another pamphlet in great detail, but in French. With disgust, Charlotte recognised the present tense.

The packs of cards had French words on them too, which were duelling schools of thought, she guessed. There were daggers on them, one, two or three crosses, referring to a level of difficulty. She didn't want to be someone who fought against the beginner's 'one dagger' level, but no-one was looking.

Direct thrust was simply stabbing the heart. Indirect was probably knocking the machine's sword aside and then going for the heart. Cut over was... ah, a little wiggle. It was skill rather than brute force that won every time, when she did win. And she began to win more often.

Her shoulder muscles ached from the winding. It was a torture device, because it alternated the heavy work with the delicate twizzling of the foil. These actions had as much in common with each other as chopping wood had with embroidery.

Now another trick, she realised, was to bounce in and out using the back foot as the guide. And counter disengage was what you did when it did an indirect thrust. So, now, she thought–

"Time's up!"

Earnestine had just re-entered the room.

"But Ness, I'm just—"

"You'll have to complete your practise tomorrow."

"But Ness—"

"Tomorrow."

"But—"

"No buts."

"I never get any fun."

It was so utterly unfair, Charlotte knew, that she was only allowed two hours. How was she going to learn anything that way? Charlotte made a face. Earnestine was such a spoil sport.

Chapter VIII

Miss Deering-Dolittle

Earnestine had been outside. She knew it was a risk, and every passer-by filled her with a dread and every pair of eyes seemed to be staring at her. Charlotte seemed to have taken to the duelling machine and if only she could transfer that dedication to more useful activities like French, Greek and Latin. They couldn't stay hiding in the office forever and the logic that Temporal Peelers had been there, so they wouldn't search there again, seemed flawed, even when she was feeling optimistic.

It was Friday, three days later, and the hue-and-cry might have settled, so it was time to make a move.

She knew that her nervousness was making her suspicious and therefore made matters worse, but she couldn't stay in the Patent Pending Office indefinitely and she had to find out what was going on. She'd bought a few newspapers, the Times and Telegraph, and a Bradshaw for the train times. Georgina had gone to this Magdalene Chase near Tenning Halt with her trunk, so it had to be some distance, and then Earnestine realised that this logic didn't work. Even if she was only moving next door in Zebediah Row, she'd have packed her trunk. Even so, a travelling trunk suggested a distance, so either a long coach journey or a train. Georgina had modern ideas, so it was the train. Also, Tenning Halt was very suggestive of a station.

She found the place, eventually, in the Bradshaw: Tenning Halt was on Dartmoor!

The actual Magdalene Chase could be some distance from the station too. Georgina's use of the word 'near' showed an imprecision that was unlike her, so it seemed advisable – flicking through the pages, she saw that the London terminus in question was Paddington Station – to

129

set off early, so that they could cover the unknown number of miles at the far end during daylight.

She cooked a light meal of bacon and eggs with kippers for breakfast.

"We have to find Uncle Jeremiah," Earnestine announced as she poured a second cup of tea from the pot.

"He's gone to see Georgina," Charlotte said.

"That does seem sound and one doesn't speak when one is chewing."

Charlotte made a face, which Earnestine chose to ignore.

"He can tell us what this is all about and then we can work out how to stop these Temporal Peelers."

"Why?" said Charlotte. "So we can allow the destruction of the world?"

"Oh... I hadn't thought of that."

Charlotte swallowed: "Uncle Jeremiah has something they want."

"Does he?"

"He's disappeared with it."

"He's gone to the future?"

"No, he packed and went out, weeks ago," said Charlotte and she recounted her experience at Uncle Jeremiah's rooms.

"So the notification of Captain Merryweather's funeral was unopened?"

"Yes."

"But he came to the funeral," said Earnestine, "so he must have moved to somewhere in London and read it in the paper, otherwise he wouldn't have been there."

Charlotte pointed at her mouth and exaggerated her chewing motions.

Earnestine summed up: "So he has an 'it' that they want. Any idea what it could be? Size? Shape?"

"I don't know," Charlotte admitted: "But whatever 'it' is, Mrs Frasier won't be happy that they haven't got it."

"Mrs Frasier!"

"Yes, I overheard them."

"Mrs Frasier won't be happy that I'm Earnestine Deering-Dolittle."

"That's the spirit, Ness."

"No, it's something the Peeler, Chief Examiner Lombard, said when he wasn't laughing at me," Earnestine frowned. "And Uncle Jeremiah's mixed up in this."

"You'd have thought he'd have left us a note."

"He probably realised that he couldn't."

"He could have done. In code. He always liked codes. I didn't find it."

"And then you saw this Member of Parliament arrested at Uncle Jeremiah's rooms."

"No, that was in the bordello," said Charlotte, taking another mouthful of bacon and egg.

Earnestine suffered a strange bee-like buzzing noise and the other side of the kitchen table seemed very far away. She felt a strangling in her throat and a difficulty swallowing. She took a sip of tea, her hand shaking and then she managed a single word in reply: "Bordello!"

"It's a sort of hotel, but you don't get breakfast."

"Breakfast!"

"I only stayed one night. I was going to join the French Foreign Legion, but I changed my mind."

"French!"

Earnestine's hands gesticulated in jerks and she mouthed the word 'soap' to herself.

"You're not going to clean my mouth out," said Charlotte, "because I don't know what the words mean. There were loads of other words too: strumpet–"

"Charlotte Deering-Dolittle!"

"I don't know what they mean."

"Mean? If you'd... paid attention at school!"

"Reverend Long doesn't teach those words."

"Of course, the Reverend *Mister* Long doesn't!"

"What do they mean then?"

131

"I... absolutely do not know and would not know and couldn't repeat the definitions even if I did and neither will you."

The horror of it chilled Earnestine's flesh: selfishly she thought of herself, the middle sister married before her, the younger becoming a woman falling... it beggared belief.

"Have you..." Earnestine phrased it very carefully, "kept your honour?"

But Charlotte had stuffed her filthy mouth with her bread and Earnestine had to wait while she masticated, all the time drooling butter that clearly did melt in her mouth.

Finally, Earnestine could stand it no longer: "Did you keep your honour?"

"I don't know what you mean."

"Did a man... touch you?"

"Yes... it was horrible. He wanted me to take my clothes off."

Earnestine managed a squeak: "Did you?"

"I hit him with the chamber pot."

The strange distant buzzing sensation evaporated and Earnestine smirked, imagining the moment. Charlotte smiled too, then grinned and before long the two were chuckling, laughing, and finally shrieking until tears rolled down their cheeks. Thank goodness no-one had been around to witness such the unseemly display.

"The... contents went all over him," Charlotte howled.

"No!"

"Not mine."

Earnestine banged the table with her fist.

"And then he was arrested," Charlotte said, when they had finally calmed down.

"But they couldn't find Uncle Jeremiah."

"No."

"These people must read the history books, their history books which are our future books, so any message, any written note, would be accessible to them, so they ought to know exactly where he is."

"They'd need to know when he was there too."

"You're right, well done Lottie. They need to know time and place."

"Well, we know the time."

"Do we?"

"Well, yes. We can't travel in time, so for us it has to be now."

"So where is Uncle Jeremiah now?"

"Somewhere warm," said Charlotte.

"Why do you say that?"

"He left his scarf behind."

"Dartmoor is hardly warm."

"Dartmoor?"

"Magdalene Chase, Georgina's new home, is on Dartmoor."

After the breakfast dishes were tidied away and washed, the two sisters sorted themselves out and collected what they thought they might need for the journey. Without discussing it, they both packed lightly being well aware that they might have to hotfoot it from pursuing Temporal Peelers.

Earnestine re-checked the Bradshaw for the time of the next locomotive to Plymouth and they caught a hansom at the corner to Paddington Station. Earnestine kept glancing backwards along the way, but there didn't appear to be anyone following them.

The station brimmed over with the capital's bustle. A multitude of businessmen from Bristol were just disembarking and a disturbing number wore top hats. Earnestine and Charlotte were on edge as every stove pipe and chimney pot approached.

"Everyone wears black," Earnestine said. "You'd have thought these Peelers would have a different uniform: blue or yellow or something that stands out."

"Silver in the future," said Charlotte. "I would guess."

133

"Why silver?"

"Everything will be made of metal."

"Not all metals are silver."

"Steel is."

"What's wrong with brass?"

At the ticket office, Earnestine had to contend with the interminable queue for two or three minutes before she was bombarded with all the diverse ticket options: first, second or third, single or return. She bought two return tickets in second.

"We're not really dressed for first," she explained. Their dresses were certainly in need of cleaning and ironing after their mad dash across West London and the days of hiding in an office.

"Where do we go?"

"The Great Western departs from Platform One."

"Oh, oh, Great Western, London to Plymouth... will we catch the Flying Dutchman?" Charlotte asked, excited.

"The Flying Dutchman went out of service nearly ten years ago when they changed the gauge."

They waited in the clock room and later, when the train was getting ready, they stood impatiently under Isambard Kingdom Brunel's wrought iron arches as the rain pattered on the glazed roof. The big clock ticked towards their departure time and the train was awfully late boarding, so they only had twenty minutes to find their carriage and settle.

Finally, the platform guard checked his pocket watch, nodding to himself while the second hand ticked round to the prescribed moment, and then he blew his whistle and waved his flag, and the steam locomotive powered the train out into the drizzle towards the countryside.

Earnestine asked for cushions when the conductor came round and they slept.

Mrs Arthur Merryweather

"The dead are but sleeping."

Mrs Falcone snuffed out the candles on the sideboard, so that the only light came from the nearly spent flames flickering on the hexagonal card table. The rest of the room was in complete darkness. When the woman sat down, she appeared frightening and otherworldly.

"Hold hands in a circle," she commanded.

Georgina gripped the icy claws of Miss Millicent and the clammy palm of Colonel Fitzwilliam. The fifth member of this strange cabal smiled benevolently, his white dog collar shining in the satanic light, one corner of the five pointed star angled towards him. The Reverend Mr. Milton seemed at ease with a display, which frankly worried Georgina alarmingly.

"Shall I say grace?" the Reverend asked.

"That would not be appropriate, Vicar," said Mrs Falcone. Suddenly, the woman's eyes fluttered and then showed the whites only, causing Georgina to shy away.

"I feel that the spirits are close tonight... yes, we will have contact. Here the curtain between our material world and the beyond is thin."

She moaned, pushed her hands forward, the catalyst of a fearful ripple transmitted around the table from hand to hand.

A low moan wavered distantly.

A sudden chill came over Georgina, her exposed neck feeling a cold breath. It was close, so close, and she wanted to turn around, but she couldn't.

A shriek rent the air.

Mrs Falcone looked utterly different as if her skull beneath her flesh had been replaced by another's.

"No, no," she cried. "I am plagued by the tainted, by those heathens who died here so long ago. They plead for release, but that cannot be."

135

"Steady on," said the Colonel, but even his bluster was shrivelled by the grating sound of Mrs Falcone's unearthly voice.

She began shuddering.

The table lifted, shook and dropped.

An object flew across the room to shatter by the fireplace.

"Keep to the circle!" Mrs Falcone demanded. "Do not falter, it is dangerous to break the circle."

Even Colonel Fitzwilliam's clammy hand felt comforting and Miss Millicent's bony fingers dug deeper.

"I feel a presence... is it? Yes, I can hear you. There is one here, ooooh my, an imposter... the name begins with a 'G'... Yes, Arthur. I hear you, Arthur."

An icy wind prickled across Georgina's bare neck, a terrible cold, freezing. Georgina gasped, her breath forming a ghostly mist to spread across the table. The air that flowed back nearly froze her lungs. As she spoke, Mrs Falcone's words condescended like phantoms themselves.

"We should cast her out. We should—"

"It's not Arthur."

Georgina was as shocked as anyone that she had spoken.

"It is Arthur, oh harlot, oh Jezebel."

"Then ask him what he bought for me at the seaside."

"The spirits do not like to be tested in this manner."

"Ask him!"

"Arthur? What did you buy? It is difficult to make out what he is saying... rock... cand— a sweetmeat of some kind."

"No, it was not."

"A dress... a bonnet... a ribbon..."

"No."

"He does not remember."

"It was when he proposed."

"He did not propose, you are a harlot, a wanton fallen women, an imposter, sent by the Devil himself to test us... oh, Arthur, tell me Arthur, tell me and we can cast her aside."

The table shook with rage.

The cold freezing intensified.

Georgina yanked her hands back: Miss Millicent held on tight, but her hand slipped out from Colonel Fitzwilliam's sweaty grasp. Her chair clattered backwards causing a cry from the person standing just behind her. Georgina caught the hair of... the maid. Ice cubes ricocheted off the furniture and the bellows fell to the floor.

The maid fought and screamed, but Georgina held firm and pulled down.

The light came up.

Colonel Fitzwilliam was standing by the gas taps.

Mrs Jago stood to one side with a collection of theatrical contraptions, tubes and metal sheets for making noises.

Mrs Falcone was incensed: "Miss, you have done something terrible–"

"Ma'am – it's 'Ma'am' to you."

"Miss, I think–"

"Fellowes! Take this fake and her bunkum and throw her *out of my house!*"

"Miss–" Fellowes said, but Georgina gave him a glare that Earnestine herself would have been proud of. He didn't need further prompting: "Ma'am," he said, correcting himself.

"Perhaps we have been improper..." Mrs Falcone began, but Georgina spoke over her in a deep booming voice that she'd once used to frighten Charlotte.

"You have tried to defile Arthur's memory, which is unforgiveable."

"...but we meant well and..."

"Out!"

137

"Miss," said Mrs Jago. "I have served the Merryweather family for three generations."

"You did not serve them tonight!"

"Miss–"

"Ma'am!"

Mrs Falcone held her hands out pleading: "Perhaps in the morning we could have Mister Tumble of Tumble–"

"Out!"

"Gabriel, do say something."

"Fellowes!" Georgina ordered: "Set the dogs on them!"

Mrs Falcone, Miss Millicent, the Reverend Mr. Milton, who was still smiling, Mrs Jago and the maid scuttled out.

Presently the front door slammed and Georgina's heavy breathing relented and settled to a more ladylike depth and rhythm.

"Remarkable," said Colonel Fitzwilliam. Georgina hadn't realised he was still there. "You don't actually possess any dogs."

"Colonel."

"I will leave if you wish, but I assure you I was as hoodwinked by those bounders as anyone," he replied, smiling to show his missing tooth. "Ma'am."

Georgina havered between outrage and shock, and found herself laughing. The Colonel chuckled and then Georgina couldn't stop herself, she threw her head back and convulsed even when her corset dug deep into her splitting sides.

It was a generous brandy that appeared under her nose. The Colonel fixed himself one, taking his time to let Georgina regain control of her faculties. She practically snorted the brandy as another spasm timed itself to coincide with a swift gulp of the burning liquid.

"Quite a show, quite a show, you were forceful."

"I'm nothing compared to my elder sister. You should meet her."

"I fear to do so as she must be quite something, for you, my dear, are a remarkable young lady, if I may say so."

"I have such a lot to write in Arthur's journal."

"What did Arthur buy you?"

"An umbrella. I gave it to my sister."

The Colonel nodded: "Arthur was a lucky man."

"He died."

"Men die. Men like him die all the time. It is a risk that those in the service gladly accept. But he had you during his time on Earth."

"You haven't died."

The Colonel looked heavyhearted: "No, I was unlucky enough to be assigned to a desk and merely sent men to their deaths."

"I'm sorry."

"And I never met someone like you. Captain Merryweather was more fortunate than I in many ways."

Georgina saw beneath the bluster and bravado a very different man.

"Thank you," she said.

"You are most welcome."

They sat and swilled their brandies in their glasses to warm them.

"You knew Arthur?"

"See this," said the Colonel. He opened his shirt – shockingly! – and showed her a savage scar, a spider's web of lines around a central divot. "I got this in India from one of those Kali cultists, and Merry said I took it for him."

"You saved him?"

"Probably."

"Probably?"

"They all claimed the bullet was meant for them: Caruthers, Merry, McKendry, Williams, even the coolie. It might have been Merry. I was at the front. I've no idea who was behind me, except that they all were."

139

Georgina blinked away her tears before they arrived. It sounded exciting and wonderful. They had a real brotherhood, which was far more than a mere Derring-Do Club with all its pretend camaraderie. The Colonel referred to a proper regiment. The Deering-Dolittle sisters only played at adventure and that was firmly in her past now.

"We all took turns in saving the others," the Colonel continued. "It was a competition, each of us going out to bat as it were. Marvellous days. They make a man of you. Whereas now you don't know who to trust and the cold seeps into your bones. I'm sorry, my dear, old soldiers make the worst company."

Georgina put her hand on his arm: "I don't think so."

Distantly a bell rang.

"You must let him go," the Colonel said.

"I can't, it's—"

The bell rang again.

"Arthur would not want you to pine."

The bell rang a third time.

"Fellowes!" Georgina shouted.

"Ma'am."

Georgina couldn't help smiling as the butler – her butler – made his way to the door.

Colonel Fitzwilliam grinned too: "Well done, my dear, well done."

Miss Charlotte

For a journey that started in Second Class, it ended somewhere below Third, when Earnestine and Charlotte persuaded a farmer to deliver them in a cart full of damp hay to Magdalene Chase with the help of a full shilling. There was money still hidden in the baggage, but all Earnestine had left in her purse was a shiny gold sovereign that Earnestine let Charlotte hold. It wouldn't become legal tender for another twelve years. The glittering coin held such promise, but it was also a portent of death for it meant that Queen Victoria's days were numbered, or so Earnestine said.

But they made it.

An old butler opened the door and looked at them with one eye as if he were taking aim.

"We're here to see the mistress of the house," Earnestine announced.

"Who shall I say?"

"Miss Deering-Dolittle and Miss Charlotte."

"Very well, Miss and Miss."

The man let them in, noted the state of them and then showed them into a huge room filled with books.

"Please wait in the library," he said, rather obviously.

"Lots of books," said Charlotte.

"You could study," Earnestine suggested.

"What?"

"Latin or Greek."

"Latin is so useless, and Greek–"

A flurry of quick footsteps on the marble outside announced the arrival of Georgina.

"Ness! Lottie! It is you!"

"Gina!"

"Gina."

141

CHAPTER IX

<u>Miss Deering-Dolittle</u>

"Where's Uncle Jeremiah?" Earnestine asked, getting straight to the point.

"He's not here," Georgina said. "What made you think he was here?"

"He's on the run from the Temporal Peelers."

"The... pardon?"

"Temporal Peelers," Earnestine said. "Surely you've heard the news?"

"This is the country."

"So it is."

The old butler took their coats and bags, and Georgina led them into a fine drawing room complete with a welcome roaring fire. An old man with military bearing stood as they entered. Seeing their dishevelled appearance, he went over to a sideboard and poured two brandies. Earnestine was grateful for the medicinal warmth.

Georgina examined her sisters carefully: "Is this some sort of adven–"

"It most certainly is not," said Earnestine.

Charlotte nodded to Georgina.

"This would be your elder sister?" said the man.

"I'm sorry," Georgina said. "Colonel Fitzwilliam, may I present my sisters, Miss Deering-Dolittle and Miss Charlotte."

"Charmed, charmed, three peas in a pod," said the Colonel.

Earnestine thought this a most bizarre choice of expression as she and her sisters weren't alike at all.

"I beg your pardon for interrupting introductions," Earnestine said. "But it really is important that we locate Uncle Jeremiah."

143

"What made you think he was here?" Georgina asked.

"We deduced that he followed you after he'd read your letter to us," Earnestine explained.

"He used boiled water to open your letter and candy as glue to reseal it," Charlotte said.

"Thank you, Charlotte, and he set off with a present for you."

Georgina was surprised: "For me?"

"I got macaroons and Ness got perfume," Charlotte said.

"Oh, but I've too many ribbons as it is," said Georgina.

Earnestine ignored the interruption: "We assumed that he came here to hide from the Temporal Peelers. He has something they want."

"Perhaps, my dear," the Colonel said, "the man lost his way coming here."

"Uncle Jeremiah is an explorer," Charlotte said, "he wouldn't get lost."

"Ah, of course," said the Colonel beaming. "Deering-Dolittle... explorers. Such a famous family."

Earnestine smiled: "Yes, we are." What a nice man, she thought.

"The Zambezi and Karnak in '85, wasn't it?"

"That's the Surrey branch of the family, we're from Kent."

"But that's the family that... oh. I'm most dreadfully sorry."

"That's all right," said Earnestine sharply. "We've more important matters that require our attention. Where is Uncle Jeremiah Deering?"

Charlotte stood and paced the room: "He left ours for Paddington. If he caught the train then he'd have arrived at Tenning Halt. Then there's the carriage trip along the lanes and finally here. He must have been intercepted somewhere along the way."

"But you took the same route, surely?" Georgina said.

"Yes," said Charlotte. "Indubitably."

144

"Ness?"

"She's read The Strand," Earnestine said.

Georgina's face fell: "Oh no."

"The point is that if he came here, then you'd know about it," Charlotte concluded.

"Not necessarily," Georgina said. "You see, I had some issues with guests and the staff."

"Then if he reached here and failed to find you, where would he go?" said Charlotte. "Late at night... lost on the moors, sucked beneath the mire and eaten by a terrible hound or–"

Earnestine felt cross: "Charlotte, please."

"The Dragon," said the Colonel.

"A dragon!?" This was the very limit, Earnestine thought, it was as if they'd stepped back to the Middle Ages. Honestly, the superstition of the countryside.

"The George and Dragon," the Colonel insisted. "It's the pub. It's the only possible accommodation for miles around."

"We'll go in the morning," Georgina said.

"We'll go directly," said Earnestine.

Georgina marched into the hallway: "Fellowes, have the trap made ready at once."

"This is such an adventure," said Charlotte.

"No, it's not," Earnestine said, swiping her brandy off her. "No brandy, you're too young."

"But–"

"Don't whine."

The trap, when it arrived outside, sat four, so Colonel Fitzwilliam would drive accompanied by Earnestine and Georgina, with the fourth place reserved for Uncle Jeremiah in the hope that he'd be with them on the return journey.

"But–"

"Don't whine."

"Gid'up," said the Colonel and the trap skittered off to plunge down the driveway.

145

The sun was setting, the sky a Shepherd's Delight, as they wended their way along the narrow lane to the village. They passed a small, forlorn group trekking through the gathering dusk. Georgina explained that they were Mrs Falcone, Miss Millicent, the Reverend Mr. Milton, Mrs Jago and the maid.

"My recent guests and staff," she said.

The village itself consisted of a few cottages made of local stone and arranged loosely around a green with a church, St Jude's, some way off on higher ground. The large clock tower loomed against the blood red background of light and clouds. It had been a race to reach this destination, and it was as if there was a huge stopwatch looming over them to count off the final minutes.

The public hostelry was at the furthest corner from the church.

As they entered, Colonel Fitzwilliam ducked under the beams, revealing that he was a regular patron. Earnestine stumbled on the uneven floor confused for a moment by the tilt of the walls.

"Frank, my good man," Colonel Fitzwilliam said to the landlord.

"Colonel?"

"Is there a gentleman staying here by the name of Jeremiah Deering?"

"No-one of that name here."

"He'll be using a false name," Earnestine whispered.

"May we check," said the Colonel, leaning on the counter and putting his foot up on the brass rail.

The landlord's eyes flickered to the right. There was a visitors' book with a fountain pen on top at the end of the bar.

"These matters are confidential," said the landlord.

"Of course, of course, maybe a... bottle of India Pale Ale, then, my good man."

"Those bottles are kept in the cellar."

"Are they?" said the Colonel, oozing unctuousness.

The landlord knew, but had little choice: "I won't be a moment."

"Take your time, Frank."

Earnestine was at the visitors' book in an instant, flicking to the current page. The last entry jumped to her attention.

"Uncle's handwriting, unmistakable... Let's see, Wells, Room Three."

She shut the book and the small party was all smiles when the landlord returned with a bottle of IPA. He pulled the cork and poured the liquid.

"And the ladies?"

The Colonel turned.

"Perhaps a sherry," Earnestine said.

Georgina nodded.

"Two sherries."

The landlord looked at his visitors' book and the pen now clearly to one side: "You won't be needing that from the cellar I notice."

"Not at all."

The landlord poured two sherries.

"And, perhaps, whatever Mr Wells in Room Three would like," the Colonel added.

"Stout," Georgina said, helpfully, but the Landlord had already put his hand on that pump. Once the pint had settled, the landlord very deliberately moved to the far end and placed the pint there.

"From the Gentleman at the end," the Landlord said.

Earnestine saw him first: "Uncle!"

She led the rush towards their elderly Uncle who was sitting at a table in the window alcove, his hair sticking out and his eyes sparkling above his half-moon glasses.

"Earnestine and, oh my, Gina," Uncle Jeremiah said, flustered. "I went to the house and this woman turned me away."

147

Georgina was incensed: "That would be Mrs Jago or Mrs Falcone. They had no right."

Earnestine sat opposite him: "Uncle, we know that you are on the run from the Temporal Peelers."

"You know!" Uncle Jeremiah clutched his chest. "Whatever they said about me, it's a lie."

"We know, Uncle, you'd never destroy the world."

"So she's issued the arrest warrant. I knew she would. It was only a matter of time. I had thought here, and with a false name, I would not be discovered..."

Uncle Jeremiah froze in position, staring out of the window.

A carriage clattered across the road, its lanterns spreading an eerie glow across the green. Men disembarked, adjusted their sword belts and put top hats upon their heads. Their eyes looked white and ghostly in the darkness.

"She's found me..." Uncle Jeremiah's voice was full of dread. "Earnestine, I'm so sorry, this is all my fault."

"To the carriage," said the Colonel, suddenly sprightly despite his age and size, "tactical withdrawal."

"Come on," said Earnestine to her Uncle. He protested, but he was no match for the tugging of his two nieces. They made it out of the door, and crossed to their trap as three top hats marched across the green.

The Colonel plucked the reins as Earnestine and Georgina helped their Uncle up, and then they were off.

The Temporal Peelers saw them, turned and sprinted back to their carriage, one of them losing his hat in the process.

The Colonel's driving was more erratic and swift than it had been on the outward leg. Branches lashed out at them from the darkness threatening to pluck them away. They nearly mowed down Mrs Falcone, Miss Millicent, the Reverend Mr. Milton, Mrs Jago and the maid. This time Mrs Falcone was ready for them.

"A curse upon you, upon you all," the woman cried out, shouting above the noise of the horses and shaking her fist. "I'll have my revenge."

As they turned into the driveway, they saw another carriage coming up towards them.

Uncle Jeremiah gasped: "She's here."

"Who's here?" Earnestine asked.

"You," Uncle Jeremiah's intense gaze mesmerised Earnestine. "You led her here."

"Who?"

"She's not going to be happy."

Mrs Arthur Merryweather

When they pulled up outside Magdalene Chase's main door, Georgina struggled out of the trap. The other carriage turned towards them, its lights shining down the driveway.

Charlotte appeared: "Uncle!"

"They're here," said Earnestine.

"Man the battlements," the Colonel shouted.

They rushed inside, knowing that the Peelers were due any second, and everyone set about defending the Chase. It seemed that each person knew their role: Georgina rallied the remaining staff – a butler, a cook and the boy – the Colonel postured and huffed, Earnestine locked the front door and Charlotte ran off to close the windows and check the other exits.

"It's all my fault," Uncle Jeremiah fretted.

"What's your fault?" Earnestine asked.

"The chronological mechanisms."

"You invented their time apparatus?"

"Yes, yes, that's it, but I never thought for a moment that it would all come back to haunt me. It was theoretical, all theoretical, but that woman... that dreadful woman."

149

There were shouts, and the clatter of horses and carriages on the driveway.

"A better world, we all want that, surely?" Uncle Jeremiah was pleading, almost going cap in hand to each of them in turn. "A new age: an enlightened age, where reason and merit and common sense hold sway, a best of times. The Law of Time was to free the masses from poverty and overcrowding, gift women with suffrage and education, protect the countryside from the blot of dark, satanic mills and grant the colonies a say in their administration. England would become a Utopia, where a man could walk down the street and be appreciated for his ideas and not for his background."

"He's rambling," said the Colonel.

"It's the means that I don't agree with: the means, not the end. It's the end I want."

A loud percussive hammering signalled that the intruders had reached the main door.

"So I ran away... oh dear, she's so cruel when she's not happy."

Miss Charlotte

Charlotte had finished checking the windows and doors downstairs. Everyone had gathered in the hallway, stepping back involuntarily with each heavy crunch on the oak.

"All secure," she said and she saluted the Colonel.

He blinked in surprise and saluted in return.

"We led them here," Earnestine said, berating herself. "I'm to blame."

Charlotte realised that at every place they'd stopped, the tea shop, the station – oh, the station, where they'd done nothing to disguise themselves and it was such an obvious place to watch – and the streets in-between had been full of men in top hats. All they had to do was remove their white glasses and they look like any upper

150

class Gentleman. Swap the hat for a bowler and they could mix with anyone of the middle ranks too. Their uniform was the same uniform that everyone in the Empire wore: black. Only their strange glasses made them look alien and those would fit in a pocket.

But this was no time for recriminations.

"Fellowes," said Georgina, but she meant the butler and not all of them as soldiers. "Are there any weapons?"

"We have a gun room, Ma'am."

"Excellent," said Charlotte, positively rubbing her hands together with glee.

"But no guns, Miss."

"A shotgun, surely?"

"In the outhouse."

Fellowes pointed out of the window: it was pitch black outside and the outhouse was unlit, but the steep angle of his arm betrayed its distance. It was the other side of the courtyard at least and the Top Hats were at the walls already. It was bare hands. Charlotte realised that she had adopted a fencing position despite having nothing at the end of her sword arm.

"Escape tunnel," Georgina cried suddenly. "Fellowes?"

"Ma'am?"

"The escape tunnel that takes the hiding priest from the priest hole to the outside. The building's of the right age, early Elizabethan at least."

"The Merryweathers, and the Fitzwilliams before them, were good staunch Protestants."

"I finally belong to a reputable family and it's just at the wrong time."

"The Captain had some golf clubs, Ma'am."

Georgina led the party up the stairs and along the landing to the master bedroom. Sure enough, tucked at the back of the wardrobe was a filthy set of clubs. When she'd pulled it out and bumped it down on the floor, a ring of dried dirt cascaded down onto the carpet.

151

Georgina handed out clubs. Earnestine armed herself with the knobkerrie from her Adventure Kit. Charlotte swapped hers, a wood for a five iron, but it was still an axe or club rather than a sword.

The banging on the front door stopped.

"They've given up, Ma'am," said Fellowes.

"I doubt it. Calm before and all that," said the Colonel. He raised his putter. "One for all?"

"The Derring–Do Club against the world," said Charlotte.

"The Derring–Do Club?"

"It's an adventuring club," said Charlotte. "And you've just joined what might be our last stand."

"It is not an adventuring club," Earnestine insisted.

"You might as well face facts, Ness," Georgina said. "It's always an adventure."

"Gina, we have to at least make an effort."

They made their way back to the top of the stairs and peered down. Lights moved, apparently haphazardly, behind the frosted panes to either side of the solid oak door. The iron fittings arranged to reinforce and strengthen made the entrance look impenetrable.

There was a cry outside, something fizzed loudly and then the edges of the door were highlighted by a bright white light. It focused on the lock, shining in a beam through the keyhole, until sparks burst through the door. The piercing brightness that was so intense everyone had to look away. On the far wall of the landing, their shadows jerked and pranced as if they were trying to run away.

"If we can keep our heads," Earnestine shouted.

The metal of the lock melted away, the liquid shrapnel scouring the stone flooring as it splashed and flared.

The door opened, its heavy lock falling away.

A man in a frock coat and a welder's mask stood up from his kneeling position and backed away.

Now, looking at the empty doorway, it did feel like the calm before the storm.

"Earnestine," said Uncle Jeremiah. "Saint George."

"For England, yes," Earnestine replied, gripping her golf club.

"No, Saint George."

Two lines of Temporal Peelers entered holding weapons that even Charlotte herself didn't recognize, although she spotted a few of those galvanic pistols she'd seen earlier. The troops went left and right, but instead of storming the staircase they formed an honour guard.

"St George!" Uncle Jeremiah insisted.

"And the Dragon," Charlotte said, not understanding.

"Booth–"

A woman entered, her heels clicking on the floor as she sidestepped the glowing debris from the door lock.

"I am here," she announced.

She tilted her head, haughty and superior, upwards to spy them all clustered at the top of the stairs. She wore a burgundy dress, tight fitting at the waist and splayed out in a fashionable manner, and she carried a matching velvet bag over her arm. Perched upon her head was a pillbox hat with a tiny, black veil pushed up to reveal her chiselled features.

She smiled – a thin, tight smile of satisfaction.

"I am Mrs Frasier."

153

Chapter X

Miss Deering‑Dolittle

Whereas the idea of a desperate last stand against a squad of Temporal Peelers armed with strange weapons had seemed viable, a heroic Rorke's Drift, no‑one wanted to fight this woman. Their defiance simply wilted away. The Temporal Peelers confiscated their weapons and the Colonel even handed them the golf bag in which to store them. Earnestine relinquished her knobkerrie without even realising it was being taken. They had handcuffs for Uncle Jeremiah.

"There's no need for those," Georgina said.

They ignored her and pulled the poor old man down the staircase to face Mrs Frasier.

"Jeremiah Deering?"

"I told them nothing, Mrs Frasier, nothing."

"But they must have asked."

"I told them nothing."

"Do you have it?"

Uncle Jeremiah looked furtive: "Yes."

"Give it to me – now!"

The defeated man fished into the inside pocket of his jacket, but he couldn't extract anything due to the handcuffs. Mrs Frasier herself reached into his coat, a strangely intimate gesture, and plucked it out. It was a book, yellow with an Egyptian sphinx on the cover and–

Earnestine just couldn't make out any letters before Mrs Frasier tucked it away in her velvet bag.

"We wouldn't want this falling into the wrong hands, would we?"

Uncle Jeremiah looked away.

"I have a warrant for your arrest, signed, stamped and... post‑dated."

"I haven't done anything."

155

"You haven't done anything *yet!*" she corrected. "Nor will you, now. Take him away!"

The Peelers removed their prisoner, frog marching him out into the night. Carriage doors slammed, a horse whinnied, and then their vehicle clattered away. They all listened well beyond the final crunch of gravel.

Mrs Frasier clapped her hands: "Let's have dinner, I'm famished."

The Derring-Do Club sidled down the stairs with its tail between its legs. Mrs Fraser examined them from a distance and then made a closer review as if inspecting the decidedly motley, military unit.

"In view of the circumstances, let's all be rebels and not dress for dinner."

They trooped past the ticking clock to the dining room.

Mrs Frasier called out: "Earnestine."

Earnestine paused and then turned back.

"That's close enough," said Mrs Frasier.

Earnestine halted, feeling much like a little girl called before a headmistress. There were only the two of them in the hall, the cold Dartmoor atmosphere drifting in through the broken door. Earnestine knew she could flee, run out into the darkness, but what would have been the point? She knew she could not escape this woman. Indeed, such was the power of the woman's gaze that it held Earnestine's attention completely.

As far as Earnestine could tell, Mrs Frasier wasn't just *not unhappy*, she was taking a positive delight in everything she said. A gold tooth flashed when she smiled.

"You are the honest one."

Earnestine answered back: "We're all honest."

"Did – *ha* – Uncle Jeremiah tell you anything?"

"No."

"Come now, the truth will out."

"He said he was responsible, that he created the Temporal Apparatus and the plan for a new world order."

"And the details, the theory?"

"We were interrupted."

Mrs Frasier glanced at the damage to the hallway: "Ah, yes."

"How long has Uncle Jeremiah been mixed up in all this?"

"Not until a few years yet."

"Then how?"

"He created it all and then popped back to let himself in on it, as it were."

"But surely one can't meet oneself... can one?"

"Most assuredly one can."

Mrs Frasier picked her way across the hallway, kicking the damaged lock with the toe of her Oxford boot. Earnestine did not like her overbearing attitude and standoffish manner.

"Have we met?"

"Yes... a long time ago and just now."

"You come from the future?"

"Yes, your future, my past."

"Your present."

"Yes, but here and now it's my past."

Earnestine said nothing and waited for Mrs Frasier to continue.

"The present is your personal here and now; your personal past is what you remember, so, Ness, your future is my past."

"Please don't call me 'Ness'."

"You think you don't like me, you think of me as your enemy, but you will come to think of me as... your elder sister."

"I don't have an elder sister."

"Always the responsible one, Ness. The weight always rests on the shoulders of people like you... and me. One must accept it, embrace it."

"Miss Deering-Dolittle, if you please."

"So keen to be taken seriously."

"What's wrong with wanting to be taken seriously?"

157

"Do you trust yourself?"

"Of course."

"But make allowance for their doubting too."

"I beg your pardon?"

"This way," said Mrs Frasier, showing the way to the dining room.

But make allowance for their doubting... *oh!* The lines came unbidden: ...*doubting too: If you can wait and not be tired of waiting.* 'If–', Kipling.

"It's all part of growing up," said Mrs Frasier, "you'll learn that, when the time comes."

The clock chimed.

Mrs Arthur Merryweather

For her first evening meal since coming to power in Magdalene Chase, Georgina felt deeply ashamed of the fare on offer. There was practically nothing on the table: simply a cold ham, some beef, pheasant that hadn't been hung long enough, only quickly steamed vegetables of carrots, parsnips, runner beans, peas and new potatoes, some pickles and preserves in ill-matching condiment sets, a truly pathetic fish course, and all with only the cooking wine from the kitchen rather than any choice vintage from the cellar. There wasn't even icing on the cake.

The Cook had conscripted the Boy to help, but clearly that had been a desperate measure. Mrs Jago would take some replacing, Georgina admitted to herself.

Mrs Frasier had chosen the seating plan: she sat at the head of the table, Earnestine at the foot and then the Colonel to her right with Georgina herself relegated down one with Charlotte opposite. The place to Mrs Frasier's left hand was set, but vacant throughout.

When they'd entered, Mrs Frasier and Earnestine had been discussing poetry of all things; something privately circulated, but not published yet. The conversation, thankfully, settled down to other matters.

"More pickle, I see, Gina," the woman said, tucking into her meat.

Georgina looked down: there was far too much pickle on her plate. She ate it anyway – she didn't want to give the woman the satisfaction – and had some more afterwards as well.

"Music I adore," Mrs Frasier said. "In the future, it's all automatic by recording. I want to listen to the Berlin Philharmonic, I just ring for it to come out of the cupboard."

"Wax cylinders?" Georgina asked.

"Vinyl Chloride."

"It sounds thrilling," Charlotte said.

"Thank you, Lottie – no wine though – and what else? Automatic carriages, which your driver operates, but it has no horse."

"Automobile," Georgina said.

"Ah, you have them already. Despite being able to dip in and out as it were, my knowledge of history is appalling, quite appalling."

"Does everyone travel by Zeppelin?" Charlotte asked eagerly. "We've been in a Zeppelin."

"The sky is full of them and we have personal Zeppelins too."

"Amazing."

The main course was finished. Fellowes, flanked by two Temporal Peelers, cleared away the dishes.

"Fellowes," Georgina asked as he passed her. "Can we do cheese and biscuits?"

Fellowes looked panicked: "Yes, Ma'am."

Mrs Frasier chortled: "Ma'am! Capital, capital."

Georgina seethed inside, but tried to remain the good hostess. On her right, Earnestine was staring straight ahead, her lips disappearing such was her silence. Charlotte – silly girl – was entranced by all the talk of the future, which seemed to be full of toys and trinkets, gadgets and gearing, contrivances and contraptions.

159

While Fellowes brought in brandy with the cheese and biscuits, Mrs Frasier lit a thin cigar, inhaling deeply.

"Would you like one, Colonel?" Mrs Frasier said offering them to the Colonel, who shook his head. She then indicated Earnestine.

"I don't smoke," said Earnestine.

Mrs Frasier corrected her: "You don't smoke yet."

As she took another long drag on her cigar, the tip glowed brighter than the candles.

"Should the ladies retire?" the Colonel asked, confused.

"We won't leave you on your own," Mrs Frasier said. She poured herself a generous glass of Armagnac. She swirled it around expertly.

"And then came the Great War," she continued.

Charlotte was confused: "Do you mean the Napoleonic War?"

"The Greater War then."

Knives scraped across cream crackers. The hall clock chimed the half-hour. No-one dared speak. The chill in the air had nothing to do with ice and bellows this time.

"You've had wars in which thousands died. In this war, millions died. It almost never ended. We were in blood stepped in so far that should we wade no more, returning were as tedious as go o'er. Whole landscapes became indistinguishable from the mires of Dartmoor. The dead envied the living. And it all began here!"

Mrs Fraser struck the table with her fist. Ash fell from her cigar leaving black marks on the tablecloth.

"These people must be held accountable. They will be held accountable."

She pointed now, stabbing forward.

"We arrest them. We give them a fair trial and then... we change history."

She took up her brandy again, swirled it and caused the light from the candle to flicker around her haughty features.

160

"We mould it, shape it, make it our own."

She knocked her glass back, draining it.

"But Uncle Jeremiah?" Georgina said.

"And Mister Boothroyd?" said Earnestine. The first words she'd spoken since they'd started.

"And the man in the bordello?" Charlotte added.

Georgina was aghast: "Bordello!?"

Mrs Frasier laughed: "Oh yes, the bordello..."

"They've not done anything," said Earnestine.

Mrs Frasier corrected her once again: "Not done anything *yet!*"

The woman stood suddenly.

Colonel Fitzwilliam was taken completely by surprise and struggled to get out of his chair.

"We should get some sleep," said Mrs Frasier. She stubbed out her cigar on her plate. "We've a long journey tomorrow. I'll take the guest room."

"I'll show you the way," Georgina said, dropping her napkin on the tablecloth.

"I know the way," Mrs Frasier replied sharply. "I have an advantage, you see."

"You have these thugs to do your bidding," said Earnestine.

"More than that... I know what happens next."

"How?"

"Gina wrote it down," said Mrs Frasier, "but just not yet."

Mrs Frasier chuckled as she climbed the stairs and unerringly turned towards the East Wing. In her wake, everyone fussed and prepared until accommodation was found for everyone. Fellowes found bedding for the Peelers, who slept on the floor in the library and guarded the hallway. Georgina found another bedroom for Earnestine and Charlotte to share.

And then – "good night" – and Georgina was suddenly alone in her own room.

161

She changed for bed and then, as was her new habit, she picked up Arthur's journal and took out the fountain pen. So much to write, she thought, and she needed to do so now, while it was fresh in her memory, but when she tried to make sense of it all, she realised it was all a jumble, events falling over each other in the wrong order in her mind. Arrests before the crimes? It was as if she were reading a story with all the pages in the wrong order.

Moreover, as the pen touched the page, she remembered what Mrs Frasier had said: 'Gina wrote it down, but just not yet.'

With a numbing shock, she realised that the woman had meant after dinner. Now! This was the very moment that had been predicted.

These blank pages would be where she'd write about the séance, her sisters' sudden appearance, the flight through the night to the George and Dragon, Uncle Jeremiah's arrest and Mrs Frasier claiming the guest room.

But what if she didn't write it down, and instead left it blank? What if, this instant, she dashed the book into the fire? What if? If?

But had events already gone too far: in the blood so deep it's best go on wading through the mire? Mrs Frasier had said that, hadn't she? Something like that anyway.

And she'd said that history could be moulded, changed and shaped. Did Georgina herself have that power in this moment? She could write anything, make something up, phrase it such that Mrs Frasier spent the night in the library. Would Mrs Frasier then read the journal years hence, and therefore know, without a shadow of a doubt, that she'd slept in the library, and therefore choose that room instead?

What else could Georgina change?

Could she cross out Arthur going to see Major Dan? Would they then never meet? Have met? But that had happened: cause followed by effect.

Except now, it didn't.

162

This wasn't the fakery of séance and mysticism, easily swept aside by turning up a gas light: this was science and engineering with its chronological mechanisms and time apparatuses. Even so, one of the basic tenets of science, cause followed by effect, had been overturned. They'd not stepped back to a Dark Age, but forward... into what?

Such was the pressure of her hand on the pen that the ink blotched on the page making a mark and recording for all time her indecision.

Miss Charlotte

Charlotte had not slept well: Earnestine snored.

The London they returned to, after a long carriage trip and an uneventful train journey, seemed on edge and very different from the one they had left. People went about their business much the same, the bustle at Paddington was as busy as ever, but it was subdued. Soldiers from another train fell into neat columns to march along the platform, but they were all in khaki rather than their proper dress uniforms. The newspaper hawkers no longer shouted their headlines, but merely held up a sign saying 'more arrests' or 'Lord Farthing to address the House'.

The sisters arrived back at 12b Zebediah Row exhausted and defeated. They had failed to protect one of their own and the fate of Uncle Jeremiah was a mystery.

"We could break into their secret base," Charlotte suggested, "steal a time machine and voyage to whenever and rescue Uncle."

Neither Earnestine nor Georgina had the energy to object. Cook made them tea and brought cake, but by the time they'd finished it, they couldn't remember what sort of cake it had been.

Their unpacking was lacklustre too. Luggage was simply put down rather than everyone's belongings being returned to their rightful place. The picture of them all by the theatre, which Georgina had removed, remained in her bag and so the blank space on the drawing room wall remained.

Outside, a fog descended.

"Will you be going to work?" Georgina asked.

"I suppose I must," Earnestine said. "Mister Boothroyd was arrested, but the work still needs to be done."

"Booth?" Charlotte said.

"Boothroyd," Earnestine corrected. "And to you, it's Mister Boothroyd."

"It was the last thing Uncle Jeremiah said to us: 'booth' and before that 'Saint George'. It's a clue."

"Not now, Charlotte."

"It's inventions, isn't it?" Georgina asked Earnestine.

"That's right, although perhaps it'll just become a museum for tourists from the future."

That got Charlotte's attention: "Will there be ice cream?"

"Charlotte!"

They had a simple meal of bread and cheese with ham from a tin, and then Charlotte was sent to bed.

"This is all jolly unfair!" she shouted from the stairs before she 'climbed the wooden hill' completely. They were both being so moody. No-one had even mentioned when she was going to get her personal Zeppelin.

Tomorrow, she thought, would be another day.

CHAPTER XI

Miss Deering-Dolittle

When Earnestine rose and came downstairs early the morning after next, a Monday, there was a card and a gentleman waiting in the drawing room: it was Captain Caruthers, DSO & bar, MC.

She knocked and entered.

He was standing in uniform looking out of the window, clearly ready for action.

"Captain Caruthers?"

"Ah, Miss Deering-Dolittle, we're wanted."

"Jolly good."

Earnestine let Cook know she was going to be out, grabbed her bag and then joined the impatient Captain on the path to the road. There was a hansom waiting.

As they jostled out into the traffic, Earnestine had to ask: "Can you tell me what this is about?"

"Ah, thing is... I don't know."

"I see."

"Major Dan sent a telegram. Urgent. Hush-hush. All that."

"I see."

Earnestine decided to wait patiently. She could do that, she knew: keep her head while all about her were losing theirs. They turned onto the main road and picked up speed, before–

"Where are we going?" she asked.

Caruthers gave her a smile and patted her hand.

This seemed rather familiar and Earnestine remembered a similar journey with this man when they'd been to the theatre.

When they arrived at their destination, Earnestine didn't recognize the area. It was somewhere near Whitehall, she guessed, and the buildings were tall, stone

165

and Romanesque, like temples, and the one they entered was austere, august and reeked of power and money.

Caruthers took her through the main hall and up a flight of wide, well carpeted stairs. As they passed through, various Gentlemen saw her and harrumphed, flapped their papers and made a point of turning their heads away. This was a realm of men: women were clearly not welcome, so the person they had come to see surprised her.

"Mrs Frasier!"

Earnestine felt her lips tighten: this was the woman who had so rudely invaded her sister's house and who had, without a moment's thought, taken their Uncle from them. Here she was, almost larger than life, in the very heart of London.

"Ah, Earnestine, come in," Mrs Frasier smiled warmly, her gold tooth evident, a replaced canine.

It was a smoking room and, like the rest of the building, it was grand, high ceilinged with enormous oil paintings of serious looking and important historical figures hanging everywhere, each looking down on the meeting with disapproval. The expectations of the past loomed over them. The smoke from Mrs Frasier's cigar spiralled up to the ornate fresco ceiling.

There were others here, important looking men in well-made black frock coats. Earnestine glanced at the tables and sideboard, but she couldn't see any top hats or white glasses. Perhaps they had been given to the Porter and stored in a cloakroom.

She stood prim and proper.

"I should introduce these people," said Mrs Frasier. "But I have forgotten your names... again."

The gathering smiled at her admission.

"Suffice to say this is a Judge, a Bishop, a Peer of the Realm, General, Admiral, rich man... poor man.... the others are all Lords."

There was a cough.

"Oh, I beg your pardon... or Members of the Commons."

The Peer, a young man, came forward: "Miss Deering-Dolittle, we are very pleased you are here. I am Lord Farthing; here is General Saunders, Sir Neptune Atkinson, Admiral Tempington, the Right Reverend Samuel Lilliworth..."

He went on.

Earnestine tried to take them in, but there were too many and they were introduced too quickly.

"Anything to be of service," said Earnestine, "although I do not understand why I am here."

"Of service," said Lord Farthing, his jovial repetition directed to the others. "Now where were we?"

"It's a question of trust," said the Judge.

"We cannot trust you," said Mrs Frasier, "that is the point. This era, as every schoolboy in my time knows, was full of conspiracy: German spies, Russian agents and those followers of Marx and Engels. But there are conspirators in the Entente Cordiale and the Triple Alliance, American industrialists, expansionists on all sides and warmongers, those who want this terrible conflict to engulf the entire globe, for the purposes of profit. They must be stopped."

"Then I see an impasse," said the Judge.

"There is a way."

Everyone was all ears.

"We have decided," continued Mrs Frasier, magnanimously, "to allow a representative of this time to visit the future, so they can see for themselves the extraordinary progress and the vital nature of our work here in the past. Once they are reassured, we will return them safely. Their word would be your guarantee."

"That seems to have potential."

"But it must be someone we can all trust, someone above suspicion, and, as a compromise, someone whom you know is not a temporal agent."

167

There were many opinions from the assembled company:-

A Judge: "Perhaps someone from the judiciary."

The Cabinet Minister: "A Member of Parliament."

The General: "The military, wot?"

Earnestine put her hands together as she tried to follow the conversation. Opinions had clearly gone round and round in circles for some time.

"I'm afraid we have had to arrest a Member of Parliament. The Chronological Committee will never accept someone from such a historically tainted organisation."

"Then who?" Caruthers asked.

"A member of a club," Mrs Frasier suggested

Again, there were many opinions.

"The Reform."

"I think not. The Cuckoo?"

"The Diogenes, surely?"

Mrs Frasier steepled her hands, imitating Earnestine's thoughtful posture. She waited until an expectant hush had settled onto everyone assembled.

"I thought the Derring-Do Club," Mrs Frasier said.

Earnestine's hands fluttered as she became the focus of attention.

"A young lady!?" General Saunders exclaimed.

"And what is wrong with the fairer sex?" said Mrs Frasier. "She is eminently qualified: born of your time and not of the Committee's, too young and innocent to have been swayed by the Conspiracy and yet someone who has proved herself a staunch supporter and able warrior for the Empire."

There were shakes of the head and nods, glances for support and persuasion, until finally the 'aye's had it.

"A capital choice," said Lord Farthing.

Captain Caruthers caught Earnestine's eye, but when she took a step towards him, he signalled her away and slipped out of a side door.

168

The various dignitaries came to shake her hand: Lord Farthing, General Saunders, Sir Neptune Atkinson, the Judge, a man smelling of formaldehyde, and finally, with an embrace, Mrs Frasier.

"We have a saying in the future," said Mrs Frasier, playing to the throng. "No time like the present."

They all agreed with that polite chortle given to a clever phrase.

Mrs Frasier indicated Earnestine, and then the door and together they left the room.

Earnestine wasn't aware she'd said 'yes'. Perhaps, she thought, she could rescue Uncle Jeremiah and Mister Boothroyd.

Captain Caruthers caught up with them in the corridor.

"May I just have a quick word," he said.

"By all means," said Mrs Frasier. She moved on, pretending to examine the paintings and the elegant chairs that lined the panelled walls. The one she chose showed St George, the English flag behind him fluttering in the breeze and a wounded dragon sprawled at his feet.

"I just want to wish you the best of British," Caruthers said. He shuffled in order to put Earnestine between Mrs Frasier and himself. He fiddled with his jacket and then plonked a heavy object into Earnestine's bag. It was about the size and shape of a house brick and made of metal.

"What is it?" she whispered.

"Latest thing," Caruthers replied quietly. "It's a miniature camera."

"I beg your pardon."

"Just click the button on the top and wind the dial anti-clockwise."

"Anti-clockwise."

"Against the clock, yes."

"I know what it means," Earnestine said, so sharply that Captain Caruthers felt it necessary to look to Mrs Frasier to exchange a smile. "I was just startled that it was so small, but what's it for?"

169

"Evidence. For Queen and Country."

"Saint George."

"That's the spirit."

"No, tell Georgina... no, tell Charlotte, she was right: find Saint George."

"I have to see Major Dan."

"Then please send a telegram: Charlotte was right, find Saint George."

"Will do. Good luck."

He stepped away and Earnestine, feeling somewhat further put upon, joined Mrs Frasier.

Outside there was a carriage waiting. Mrs Frasier held the door open.

"Where are we going?" Earnestine asked.

"Not where... when," Mrs Frasier announced. "The future, Earnestine, the future."

The carriage took them to the place south of the river, under the wrought iron archway and into the yard.

This time, Earnestine went up the steps and in via the front door, rather than sneaking around the side of the building. She noticed the substantial but discreet security: hired heavies outside and Temporal Peelers within.

They went along a bright and shiny corridor that reeked of new paint. At the end was a raised platform with a strange mat consisting of lines of copper wire woven into the material. The platform was edged with thick brass rails.

Earnestine stepped up nervously.

One of the Temporal Peelers grabbed her arm and pulled her across so that she was properly positioned in the formation. There was a window along the corridor (she half-expected to see someone staring in as she had done) and she could see the sky. She wondered if this was the last time she'd see her era.

They moved a protective glass screen across, partly obscuring the technician, who stood at a lectern covered in dials and controls. He pulled a lever and made adjustments before he took a rod or baton from his pocket and screwed it into the centre. The light caught a jewel fitted in the end as it turned.

"Fourteen fifty nine," he said.

That was the continental system, Earnestine realised, and she managed to glance at her fob watch as she subtracted twelve: nearly three, post meridiem. Everyone else, including Mrs Frasier, checked their watches with a flourish of clicking covers.

The technician slammed a lever home: "Fifteen hundred."

The lights began to flicker and the smell of galvanic charge filled the air. She felt the hairs on her head start to stand on end and her skin prickled.

"Close your eyes," said the Peeler, tapping his white glasses.

She saw the corridor begin to fade and distort, disappearing from sight as it changed. Even if she hadn't been instructed to do so, the bright light forced her to close her eyes

A note rose in tone ringing in her ears and then–

And then–

The world fell away.

Mrs Arthur Merryweather

Georgina made herself another pickle sandwich. Cook wasn't around, presumably shopping, and the maids were busy with the laundry. Earnestine was away with Captain Caruthers, and without a chaperone – shocking really – but then good old Earnestine: it really was about time. She hoped Colonel Fitzwilliam was fixing her front door back at Magdalene Chase.

All this business with the Chronological – she checked the paper – Committee was quite perplexing, but it was good to have something to worry over. She was concerned about Uncle Jeremiah – arrested. Surely it

171

would turn out to be a mistake. Hopefully, the Surrey branch of the Deering-Dolittle family had a Jeremiah or Jeremy or a Jemima even, and the resulting scandal would go some way to redressing the balance between the Surreys and the Kents. It all took her mind off her grief over Arthur and–

She shouldn't have thought that.

She choked on the pickle, tears streaming down her face.

This was terrible, just awful – and she coughed a bit of bread across the kitchen table. She swallowed, drank some water and cleaned up, wiping mess away. Thank goodness Earnestine hadn't seen her carrying on like that.

Distraction, that's what she needed.

There was a telegram on the table in the hall.

Georgina found Charlotte reading the Strand magazine in her bedroom.

"Where did you get that?" she asked.

"Earnestine let me."

"You have a telegram."

"For me?"

Charlotte swivelled off her bed and took the proffered message.

"It's from Captain Caruthers," Charlotte said.

"Why is he sending you a message?"

"Maybe he wants to propose."

"Charlotte!"

"Oh, it's from Earnestine: CHARLOTTE STOP... isn't it funny the way they write these."

"Charlotte!!"

"CHARLOTTE STOP NESS SAYS... Ness, it's to save money on letters."

"Charlotte!!!"

"CHARLOTTE STOP NESS SAYS YOU... Why didn't he shorten Charlotte?"

"Lottie!"

"Sorry... CHARLOTTE STOP NESS SAYS YOU WERE RIGHT STOP FIND ST GEORGE STOP CARUTHERS STOP."

"Saint George?"

Charlotte flourished the telegram: "Ness says I was right."

"Oh, do concentrate."

"I was right."

"You were right, jolly good," Georgina conceded. "Now, what were you right about?"

"Uncle Jeremiah said 'Saint George' and 'Booth'."

"Saint George and the Dragon, where he was staying, yes... and?"

"No, I said 'and the Dragon', he just said 'Saint George'. Find Saint George, Earnestine says, and if 'Booth' is 'Boothroyd', it'll be at the Patent Pending Office."

"Well that's the end of that, because it's secret and we're not allowed."

"I've been there and I know where the key is hidden. Ness doesn't think I saw, but I did. Come on, it'll be an adventure."

"No."

"But—"

"Don't whine."

"But—"

"Oh very well," said Georgina. "We'll go directly, but we don't tell Earnestine that we thought it was an adventure. Agreed?"

The hansom took Georgina and Charlotte to Queensbury Road. They found the actual door with some difficulty even though Charlotte had been there before. Charlotte insisted that Georgina turn around while she found the key.

Inside, it was a dark passageway and then the... storage warehouse for paperwork. It certainly wasn't the study or library that Earnestine had described. Atop the piles of

173

papers were large weights: vases, pieces of rock, a brick, iron objects and tat.

"There's no Saint George here," Georgina said.

"Don't whine."

"Don't be cheeky."

But Charlotte ignored her and rushed about bent double looking at the floor: "Waste paper basket... no, fireplace... here..."

"We've no time to play consulting detectives."

"Ah ha!" Charlotte had found a slip of paper. "Telegram: B STOP AT G AND D NEAR TENNING HALT STOP WELLS."

"That could be anything."

"Boothroyd, I'm at the George and Dragon near Tenning Halt signed 'Wells'. Who's Wells?"

"Uncle Jeremiah used that name to check-in."

"That settles it then."

"I'll admit it is suggestive."

"It must be."

"So?"

"It means that Uncle Jeremiah told Mister Boothroyd where he was, and Mister Boothroyd told him about Saint George."

"Really?"

"Most likely, so indubitably one of the papers refers to some invention that's codenamed Saint George."

"Oh, Charlotte, there are thousands of pieces of paper here."

"We look, but don't touch anything."

"How can I look at the paper if I can't touch it?"

They looked and didn't touch.

There was a line across the room, diagonally, that divided a region of chaos from an area of organisation. In the latter, the documents were piled neatly with paperweights to keep them from floating away. It struck Georgina suddenly that this was like a chessboard; the paperweights were pieces being moved from square to square as each pile gave up some of its confusion to other stacks.

The important one was a knight.

Georgina found it: "Saint George."

It was a pewter statue, about six inches high, depicting a knight on a horse with his lance stabbing into a dragon that writhed along the base. Underneath was a thankfully small stack of paper.

Charlotte helped her move it to the empty desk.

In here, then, was something from Uncle Jeremiah, a patent that had been transferred to this office when its importance to the Empire had been realised.

They sat opposite each other and began sifting through.

"Let's have tea?" said Charlotte sometime later.

Georgina checked Arthur's watch: "We've only been at this for fifteen minutes."

They carried on.

There was so much of it and– "ow!"

Charlotte's fidgeting had grown to the point where her swinging feet had caught Georgina on the shin.

"Sorry."

"Just... concentrate."

But Charlotte couldn't and the girl was distracting. Eventually, and against her better judgement, Georgina realised that she'd make better progress on her own, which she supposed was Charlotte's strategy all along.

"Charlotte, is there something else you could be doing?"

"There's this machine in the other room."

"All right, you may."

Charlotte bounced out of her chair and rushed across to the shelves on one wall. Something happened and Charlotte disappeared into a dark opening. Georgina just caught sight of the secret door closing.

Wonders never cease, she thought.

175

All of this material – gosh, there was a lot – was about camouflage and espionage. None of it was about clocks or temporal mechanisms.

She found it: Jeremiah Deering.

It was old, dated a decade or so back.

Oh, and it was in Uncle Jeremiah's excuse for handwriting. His esses looked like effs.

Georgina did make herself a cup of tea, although she used lemon as the milk was lumpy and smelt.

She found an armchair with better light and settled down, her cup and saucer on the nearest stack nestled against a flat iron. Georgina wondered what Earnestine's system was regarding the choice of paperweight or whether it was random. There must be a notebook, she realised, with the explanation: object to subject.

Uncle Jeremiah's treatise wasn't in order. His conclusions, according to the header at the top of the page, were first.

'*These mechanics might work in civilised countries with a proper accountable governing system, a judiciary and a civil service. In other nations, they would require adaptation.*'

It didn't seem to Georgina much of an introduction and the following pages were just diagrams, boxes connected to other boxes with letters in them. They probably stood for something, but there was no key. Ah, she saw the squiggle at the top and realised that these pages were the appendix. She had the last page of the document and some notes, so the rest...

After a long sigh, and a final sip of her tea, she set about working through the rest of the stack for the other pages. At least she knew that it was on white foolscap with blue ink handwriting.

But there wasn't anything else.

Perhaps they were hidden in another stack of papers?

The room was overwhelming, as if she were being asked to do an Easter egg hunt in a garden that was the Amazon rainforest.

She'd never be able to sort out what Earnestine meant without the other pages.

She glanced at Arthur's pocket watch.

She had to try.

One half of the room was organised, clearly the area that Earnestine had worked on, so it wouldn't be there. She'd have seen it.

The other half was topsy-turvydom... and Boothroyd had told Uncle Jeremiah that it was under St George, therefore Boothroyd had found it, so it couldn't be in the chaotic area either.

It was a dead end.

Maybe... she turned the heavy pewter over in her hands, but, try as she might, the St George and the Dragon sculpture did not reveal any hidden compartments or secret codes other than a maker's stamp. Perhaps it was symbolic, the dragon representing Mrs Frasier and St George standing for Captain Caruthers or someone?

They had established a link.

Mister Boothroyd was involved with paperwork, invention and the like; whereas Uncle Jeremiah studied books about stories, fables and myths from other lands. This made sense: researchers undergoing temporal relocation to times without a proper history would have to rely on myths as their guide.

Perhaps Uncle Jeremiah's thesis on Atlantis had finally became useful?

They were connected in as much as Mister Boothroyd had had Uncle Jeremiah's patent application, they'd been sending each other telegrams and they had both been arrested. How could a harmless man like Uncle Jeremiah be involved in a conspiracy to destroy the world? That made no sense. Perhaps he'd been led astray by this Mister Boothroyd character, who might come across as affable, but was instead somehow devious and cunning. Georgina hadn't met him, so she had no way of telling.

177

And how did an MP and all the others – she must start a proper list – fit into it? If it was a conglomerate of arms dealers, then it would... but even they wouldn't destroy the world. You can't sell bullets to dead people. Even the most insane megalomaniac wouldn't invent a weapon that could destroy the world.

There were too many questions.

Maybe someone could bring back a history book from the future and then she could just consult that for answers.

Miss Charlotte

When the day was nearly over and she wouldn't be forced to do paperwork, Charlotte came back to see how Georgina was getting along. Charlotte felt flushed and alive, glowing from her activities, but, in contrast, Georgina looked like her blood had been leeched from her face by this dusty place.

Charlotte was bursting to tell her news: "I got Edgar up to the–"

"Edgar?"

"I've called the Duelling Machine 'Edgar' – come and see."

Georgina allowed herself to be dragged through the secret door and beyond into a warehouse. Charlotte ignored all the machines and took Georgina to the Duelling Machine.

"Don't you think it looks like an 'Edgar'?"

Georgina considered the wooden and metal contraption, armatures sticking out at odd angles and a sword stuck in one.

"Not really."

"Well, Edgar's on the highest level."

"Wonderful."

"Yes, and I beat it."

"It's time to go," said Georgina, clearly a spoilsport.

"How did you get on?" Charlotte asked when they'd returned to the office.

"I found Uncle's patent application, but most of it is missing. There's only this page and some notes."

Charlotte glanced at it: "Ripped off."

"I beg your pardon?"

"Here, see the ripped edge. It was attached with a little string thing."

"Treasury tag."

"Yes, and someone pulled the pages away quickly and these sheets were left."

"Yes, but how..." Georgina waved her arm about the masses of paper, a haystack of needles within which they were searching for a particular needle.

"It's not here," Charlotte said.

"How can you say that?"

"It's elementary. Ness has sorted all these piles into type or whatever, they've got a weight on them, so she put all of Uncle's pages into one pile. Ergo and Quod Erat Demonstrated."

"Demonstrandum."

"Yes, that."

"I had worked that out for myself." Georgina got her coat and bonnet: "We'd better lock up."

"Why are you looking so dejected?"

"By not finding the complete application, we've failed Ness."

"Ness knew the pages were missing."

"Then why did she send us on this fool's errand?"

"Because she wanted us to find something else."

"But what? And where?" said Georgina, indicating the room. "What's the right move?"

"The right move?"

"Well, it does look like a giant chessboard, doesn't it?"

Charlotte considered this and saw what her sister meant: St George from Uncle Jeremiah's pile, the flat iron to the armchair stack, the book to the secret room. They were all moves – a game. But what did it mean? A book, a secret book, like Uncle Jeremiah's.

"The dog didn't bark," Charlotte said.

"I beg your pardon?"

"Can I buy a deer stalker?"

"Pardon?"

"A hat, a deer stalker hat."

"Charlotte, you'd look ridiculous."

"But Gina—"

"Don't whine."

Charlotte was hurt, but then she remembered something about Uncle Jeremiah's rooms.

"Uncle Jeremiah had a missing book as well."

"Charlotte, what was the missing book?"

"I don't know."

"Well, think, Lottie, think. This could be very important."

"I don't know because it was missing."

"We saw Mrs Frasier take a book off him, didn't we? 'Do you have it', she said."

"It was between Verne and Wells."

"I beg your pardon."

"On Uncle Jeremiah's shelf."

"How do you know that?"

"When I went round that was where the gap was, between Verne and Wells."

"So an author between 'vee ee' and 'double you ee'."

"Or Verne or Wells themselves."

"Yes, that's right, but it's gone."

The Patent Pending Office was in such a state that whole sections could disappear and no-one would be the wiser. However, Charlotte realised there was a link, a gap in Uncle Jeremiah's shelf, the book that Mrs Frasier wanted, and the missing patent. The invention sounded like it would be like a textbook, but the missing book might be an adventure. It was in Fiction in Uncle Jeremiah's study after all. Or maybe he just hid it in fiction? A reference book disguised as a work of fiction, just the sort of wheeze that Uncle Jeremiah liked. She'd loved listening to Uncle Jeremiah tell her stories about far off lands.

"I like Jules Verne's *A Journey to the Centre of the Earth* and *Eight Hundred Leagues on the Amazon* and—"

"Yes, thank you Lottie."

Charlotte made a face.

Chapter XII

Miss Deering-Dolittle

Earnestine stumbled to her knees, her hands falling onto the strange mat with its copper wires, as her stomach heaved. She kept her breakfast and was thankful for that. When she blinked away the glare, she saw that she was exactly where she had been, the same position on the mat, the same men standing around her and the same view down the corridor, except that it was lit with the strange yellow glow of galvanic lighting. The gas taps had been replaced.

Through the window it was night-time. The same window she'd stared through when she saw Mrs Frasier and the Temporal Peelers disappear, but, of course, this meant that she was now one of the 'disappeared'.

"Time?" Mrs Frasier asked.

A different technician stood at the control lectern: "Zero zero ten."

The operator – a different person, of course! – started unscrewing a lever from the controls.

Those around her adjusted their pocket watches, but Earnestine felt too disorientated to follow suit.

"Come!"

Mrs Frasier led them all back the way they had taken when they'd arrived, but the interior was subtly different. The new paint was old and peeled now, and other areas had clearly been renovated. Strange posters adorned the walls of brave men in heroic poses wearing top hats and white glasses: 'Policing Yesterday for a Better Tomorrow', 'Correcting Mistakes' and 'History in the Re-making'.

Instead of leaving, they turned a corner and went deeper into the building. Further along was a rotunda, a large, open circular room that served as an atrium with four main corridors leading off. The signs pronounced

183

Judiciary, Prison and Accommodation. Earnestine glanced back: they had come from the 'Temporal Engineering'.

Mrs Frasier took them left and they went past rooms labelled variously: dormitory, canteen, billiards and smoking room. Finally, they reached a solid door and Mrs Frasier showed Earnestine the interior. It was a bedroom, more of a box room, with a simple bed, small table and chair.

"I thought I was going on a tour," Earnestine said.

"Impossible now. Everything is closed up for the night."

"But it was day."

"It was day, seventy odd years ago."

"I suppose, I just assumed."

Mrs Frasier had a tight smile: "I'm used to it, I forget how disconcerting it can be."

"I'll be all right."

"I know. I'll wake you in the morning."

"But it's only... three in the afternoon."

Mrs Frasier took two watches from her bag, a gold and a silver one: "More like a quarter after midnight."

Earnestine nodded.

"Get some sleep," Mrs Frasier said. "Early start."

Mrs Frasier shut the door behind her and Earnestine heard the lock turn.

She was a prisoner, as much as if she had been arrested. Uncle Jeremiah was here somewhere, she realised, although maybe he had been tried years ago or possibly there were still years to wait. She prepared herself for bed, but her heart wasn't in it. How could she sleep? It was the middle of the afternoon for her, but the next day would start in six or seven hours, which would be nine or ten in the evening for her.

She lay down, and then had to get up to switch off the galvanic light. She was used to blowing out a candle, so she was thrown by the severe disadvantage of this future technology. It was all familiar and yet unfamiliar, English words but with twisted meanings, strange noises that could be plumbing or machinery in this cross between a factory and who knew what.

She wasn't going to sleep.

There was a glass of water, but it had an acrid taste.

She checked her fob watch, but couldn't see it in the dark, so, in the end, she risked the cold to turn the light on. It was still only twenty five to four. She turned the light out, stubbed her toe and hid in the warm covers.

She stared into the dark.

How was she going to fulfil her duties as an Ambassador for the Yesteryears? It was such a weight for her young shoulders, she hadn't the experience – it was too much to ask. She was only twenty and felt so alone, and she wanted Uncle Jeremiah to tell her a story, an adventure that she'd heard before and knew, because she'd read the book, one that had a happily ever after and, at the end... the adventurers returned to England with tales to tell and riches to distribute, and they hadn't left their daughter to look after her two sisters all on her own, before she was whisked off into this hereafter.

She snored.

"Rise and shine," said a jolly lady standing in the doorway, the light shining around her.

"What time–"

But she was suddenly dazzled when the room's galvanic light came on.

"It's eight o'clock, sleepy."

"Is it?"

Earnestine felt panicked, not really knowing where she was and then it dawned on her that she didn't know *when* she was. She fumbled for her pocket watch: it was quarter to eleven... eleven, ante meridiem or post meridiem, she wasn't sure, but she did the arithmetic in her head and realised that it was very late. She was something like nine

185

and one quarter hours ahead... or rather many years and nine and one quarter hours ahead.

She washed; the woman had bought in a bowl of tepid water and waited patiently as Earnestine dressed.

Outside it was daylight, back in her time it would be – *would have been* – night time.

The woman showed her down a corridor and into a canteen. There were men seated at the benches eating porridge. Once it was pointed out to her, she found the serving bowls and helped herself.

"We don't have much, my dear," said her guide, "what with the war and everything."

"Thank you, it's delicious."

It was.

She ate in silence, blowing on the surface to cool each spoonful.

Some of the Temporal Peelers left, their swords clattering as they went, and other men arrived. They wore white, slatted glasses and sullen expressions. Obviously, having been brought up properly, Earnestine would not have introduced herself, but their bearing forbade any conversation, even if someone could have acted as a chaperone.

"I'm Miss Androlucia," said the jolly woman.

"Pleased to meet you, I'm Miss Deering-Dolittle."

"Oh yes, we've heard such a lot about you. You're famous, although I know I shouldn't be telling you that now, should I?"

"Famous? But I was only appointed yesterday."

"Oh, that was just the start, just the start. I've read the history books. It's such an honour. To think, me, cleaning out your bedpan."

She laughed and made her way out.

Another man intercepted Miss Androlucia and they conversed. The pointing convinced Earnestine that she was the topic on everyone's lips. She felt her face burning, so she concentrated on finishing her breakfast.

Afterwards, she was taken to Mrs Frasier's office which was straight over the Rotunda and off to one side of Judiciary.

Whereas the rest of the building had been plain walls, with only a few high windows like a fortress, this was plush, wood panelled with an old fireplace, bookcases and swords over the mantelpiece. Mrs Frasier was seated behind an oak desk, its green leather surface sparsely occupied by various objects.

"...yes, yes... but it's important..." Mrs Frasier waved Earnestine towards a chair. "...get it done. The Chronological Transfer Points must be maintained otherwise the conveyor is likely to send the subject to who knows when. Thank you."

She took a small device off her head and saw Earnestine's quizzical expression.

"It's a telephone," Mrs Frasier explained. "The sound first travels – how shall I put this – through the ether as radio waves. You've heard of a telephone?"

"Yes."

"And radio waves?"

"Tesla, isn't it?"

"That's right; and the bulky devices of your day have been distilled down to this contraption that you wear like a headband."

"How wonderful."

"You are concerned about your Uncle Jeremiah," Mrs Frasier said. "Don't worry. There are mitigating circumstances. He and I... He helped design all this and, well, he was led astray."

"Can I see him?"

"Sadly no, but I assure you that he is alive and well. I would not see any harm come to him."

"And–"

"Boothroyd is also safe and sound."

"I would still–"

"It is not the purpose of your visit. You have a duty here that you must perform."

"Yes. Certainly."

"Are you ready to start?"

"I am, directly."

Mrs Frasier came out from behind the desk and she was wearing trousers!

Mrs Frasier saw Earnestine's shocked expression and laughed: "Women wear trousers. Not all, but most. What was the word that we used to use... rampant... what was it?"

"Rampant bloomerism."

"Bloomerism, yes, as if we needed to control our flowering." Mrs Frasier chuckled as she opened the door for Earnestine. "Indeed, we have flowered. Women have complete suffrage. Look at me, the woman in charge."

They went down a long corridor and reached a doorway. The place was something of a maze.

"This is the future," Mrs Frasier announced. "We can't stay long on account of the poison from the war."

They went through and *outside*.

There was a square, open to the sky, and guarded by men in breathing masks that looked at odds with their black frock coats. Down the long alleyway, Earnestine could see the blue sky and, distantly, extraordinary glass towers soared above the skyline dwarfing the distant Houses of Parliament. High up, a strange Zeppelin hovered.

It was utterly fantastical.

"Use these," said Mrs Frasier and she handed Earnestine a pair of opera glasses.

Earnestine put them to her eyes, adjusted them ever so slightly and was able to look along the Thames to the Palace of Westminster. The optics were so good that she could read the time on the distant clock of Big Ben accurately showing this future hour, so different from her own fob watch.

"May we go and walk the streets?" Earnestine asked, taking down the opera glasses. "I would like to see what Zebediah Row looks like now."

"Perhaps, when we've finished our duties, but it is forbidden to interact."

"How can people live out here, if one has to use a mask?"

"The people of this time are used to it, adapted so to speak, whereas those from other times, yourself for example, would have illnesses when exposed to too much of the aerial poison."

"You are from another time?"

"Another time from this one, yes."

"That's–"

"Camera please."

Earnestine jerked like a school girl caught with her hand in the candy jar. Mrs Frasier took it off her. Earnestine had taken one picture and had been struggling with the anti-clockwise mechanism.

"I've not seen one of these in years," said Mrs Frasier, turning it over in her hands. She wound it on, expertly, and then waved Earnestine over towards the quad.

"Smile!"

Earnestine didn't feel like smiling: she tried, but she was sure she was grimacing. And one didn't smile for a daguerreotype as it was unseemly. Mrs Frasier took a picture, moved around and took another. She motioned again and took a third, and a fourth – the profligate expense was astounding.

"Let me get the Zeppelin in," she ordered and clicked again. "Perhaps one with both of us."

One of the guards came over to Mrs Frasier's beckoning.

"There," she instructed. "Mask off to see through there."

She stood next to Earnestine, both of them with their hands crossed neatly in front.

189

The man clicked.

"Take another!"

He did, then he looked confused.

Mrs Frasier took the device off him and checked it: "Ah, only twelve plates on the strip – never mind. We've been out long enough as it is."

She gave the camera back to Earnestine, who dropped it in her bag feeling guilty.

"There's no need to be the spy, we've nothing to hide," said Mrs Frasier. "Quite the contrary."

Back inside the building, Mrs Fraser took her to a study or small library constructed of wood panelling, high book shelves and a large central table.

"I have some books," said Mrs Frasier. She went to a particular shelf and brought down a variety of leather bound volumes of different weights and sizes. "Read these... this one would be the best to begin with."

Earnestine sat at the table and opened the first volume that Mrs Frasier had selected. There was a daguerreotype image of three ranks of soldiers, the officers at the front were seated and those behind stood to attention. They all had the same stern expression. No smiling for this picture. The caption read 'Sandhurst Passing Out Parade, Year of 1912'. She was looking at the future a dozen years from her own time and it was history, preserved and strangely sacred.

Earnestine felt a hand on her shoulder. It was Mrs Frasier.

"I am sorry that you have to grow up so quickly," Mrs Frasier said before leaving.

Earnestine was alone.

She began reading, first looking at the pictures, then the captions, the newspaper clippings and finally the articles and journal entries. At first she couldn't make sense of it. There were daguerreotypes of young men in military uniforms, strange mechanisms and machines,

190

mud, explosions, and it was all such a mess of information.

However, slowly, the pieces fell into a sequence in her mind. It was the same story, repeated over and over, relentlessly, until Earnestine felt that she had lived in these trenches and flown these aerial machines and dived beneath the cold waves, and still the terrible events went on and on and on.

Part of her wanted to push the books away, shut their heavy covers to deny the dreadful horrors within. She wanted to return to the picture books of her youth, the innocent adventure stories that Uncle Jeremiah had made up, but she knew her duty was to learn.

But there was just so much of it and there was no peace.

Just endless war.
Bombs.
Shelling.
Bullets.
Armoured land ironclads.
Poison gas.
Massacres.
Starvation.
Disease.
Execution camps.
Death, always death.

The flower of youth, all those brave young men who had stood so proudly in ranks were plucked from their pictures to be ruined on the battlefields of Europe and the rest of the world.

She felt sick, drained utterly.

"Here," said Mrs Frasier, giving her a glass of water. Earnestine had not been aware that she had returned, she'd slipped in behind her and she must have been watching for some time.

Earnestine blinked: "It tastes..."

"It has chemicals to replenish the blood."

191

"Thank you."

"I have someone who would like to see you."

"See me?"

Mrs Frasier showed an old man in. He doddered, his hair white and he looked to Earnestine like someone's Uncle. Not hers, not Uncle Jeremiah, but someone familiar and–

"Mister Boothroyd!"

"Ha, ha," he said, "yes, yes, such a long time ago, you haven't aged a day, not a day I say, it feels – oh my dear, like yesterday and yet... and yet."

"They say... no, please sit," Earnestine showed him to a seat and he gently settled. Grey streaks had now conquered the man's pate completely, and when she saw him close up, she was shocked by the ragged appearance of his skin.

"You..." Earnestine looked to Mrs Frasier. "Is it the poisons?"

"No Ness," Mrs Frasier replied, "not the poisons."

"The years," said Mister Boothroyd. "So many."

"Were you... guilty of..."

"Genocide. Yes. The evidence was incontestable."

Earnestine stepped back: "Oh my!"

"I have been lucky," Boothroyd said. "The Chronological Committee commuted my sentence and I've been able to serve. My ideas have been used to rebuild the world, do you see, and make amends. It's been how long? A decade? Ten years, imagine... and to see you, bright and new like a polished coin, after all this time."

"That's good," said Earnestine.

"If I had my time again... Miss Deering-Dolittle, make them see, make them understand," he said, his eyes alight with fiery energy. "You can go back. Change it. Save the world."

"Yes, Mister Boothroyd, I will."

Mister Boothroyd looked to Mrs Frasier: "Have I done the right thing?"

Mrs Frasier nodded.

"I've made up for it then, done my penance?"

"Yes, Boothroyd, you have. The new future will thank you for it. I'm proud of you."

He clasped his hands, stared ahead in an ecstatic, religious fervour: "Oh!"

"You should both rest now," said Mrs Frasier.

"Yes... no, wait," Earnestine said. "I should get back – warn everyone! As soon as possible!"

Mrs Frasier laughed: "We travel in time. We could drop you five minutes after you left, or a year, or three months earlier."

"Yes, of course," said Earnestine, trying to get her head around the idea.

Mrs Frasier opened the door: "Come."

"Good night, Mister Boothroyd," Earnestine said. "I'll do the right thing."

Mister Boothroyd nodded: "I know you have. Thank you, my dear, thank you."

Mrs Frasier led Earnestine back to her room with a kindly arm around her shoulder to guide her.

"I'll say good night, then," said Mrs Frasier. "I'd say sweet dreams, but I know what you've read. It is worse for us, we have experienced some of it at first hand."

Earnestine nodded, aware of the images jostling for attention in her memory as they queued to become nightmares.

Mrs Fraser got out her key.

"Do I have to be locked in?"

"It's for your own safety."

"My safety?"

"You are too important to me to allow anyone to hurt you. You and I have enemies, even here and now. We must be cautious."

193

Earnestine prepared for bed, her mind buzzing with everything she'd seen. It was eight o'clock when she'd finished reading in the small library, a meal had been brought in, and on her watch it was eleven o'clock by the time she was undressed and washed. Eleven o'clock in the morning, she thought, but it was night. Night here, but morning back in her own time. Her mind felt befuddled. She was exhausted, her mind was like an over-stuffed travelling trunk, and she was almost asleep before her head hit the pillow.

Mrs Arthur Merryweather

The first that Georgina knew was the sound of shattering glass and the shrieks of the maid. She found her robe and ran barefoot downstairs to see what all the commotion was about. As she turned on the stair, she saw something flicker through the hallway, a crashing of glass, and she heard a deep crump of a noise as a heavy object hit the hallway table. Earnestine's umbrella danced in its stand. A brick lay on the floor amidst the shards of debris.

She hesitated – the tiles were covered in glass, red and blue from the porch, glinting with a fiery light.

The maid redoubled her screeching.

What was she called?

It was night and Georgina hadn't woken yet.

"Mary, Mary…"

The screeching stopped abruptly: "It's Jane."

"Jane, what's–"

Another object bounced off the door.

Georgina could hear shouts outside, deep and indistinct, but numerous and angry. Georgina risked going down to the first step, felt a shard of glass beneath her foot depress in the stair carpet, and hunkered down to look.

There was a crowd in the street, shaking raised lanterns and brandishing sticks. The tiny garden gate that squeaked and was in need of paint, kept them at bay by force of demarcating the property line, but it was clearly little real protection.

A cheer went up – another object hurled at the house arced through the air.

The mob was stirring itself like a wild animal building its courage towards a tipping point.

"We're done for," said the maid, "all because you've sided with them Chronies."

"Chronies?"

"Chronologics, them Peelers wot take innocent folk."

"Mar– Jane, don't be ridiculous."

The noise outside hushed. Somehow this was more frightening than the shouting. The central cohort parted, gathering around a gap, and into it stepped a woman.

Her voice was strident, livid with rage: "This is the house of those who plot against you!"

The mob 'aye'd and 'yea'd.

"Should we stand idly by, while our loved ones are taken from us?"

"Nay, nay."

"We should act, act and protect ourselves!"

"Here, here."

The woman turned, screamed something incoherent as she pointed at the house.

Georgina recognized the ring-leader, and she wasn't going to take any more of this nonsense.

Quickly, she stepped across the hallway, ignoring the sharp stabbing pain on her icy feet, and went out. As the door opened, the crowd divided between those jeering and those quietened into guilty silence. Georgina was half-way down the path when the woman, who had her hand on the unlocked gate, turned to look.

On the hockey pitch, Georgina used to shout louder than everyone else: "Mrs Fal*CONE!*"

The crowd shushed itself into an audience.

"What is the meaning of this?"

195

Mrs Falcone smiled, her opportunity had come: "You sell people out to the Temporal Peelers."

"Nonsense!"

"It's true."

"Evidence!"

"We know all about it."

Georgina realised that she was never going to convince this woman. In an instant she knew that they were mortal enemies even before they'd met. Georgina represented something to this woman and, whatever it was, there was no changing it. So Georgina changed tack.

"You would damn people on the word of this woman, without evidence, without trial, without a jury."

"We're a jury," came a reply from the back.

"Then be a jury! Be twelve good men and true."

"Aye."

"Don't listen to her," Mrs Falcone yelled.

"So, this woman does not allow a defence, she does not allow a fair trial, she does not allow you, good men and true, to reach your own verdict before she, and she is no judge, pronounces sentence."

"She's trying to trick you," Mrs Falcone said. "Smash the house, take your revenge."

The gate opened.

"Are you English?"

"Yes," came a shout from another direction, and then another. "And we won't stand for this."

Mrs Falcone stepped back; of course, she wasn't going to do the dirty work, and three men barged forward. They crossed the property line and took a stride along the garden path.

Georgina had one last throw of the dice: "Is this cricket!?"

The men stopped.

"No," said the leader.

"There are rules!" Georgina said, using her most outraged tone.

196

"Yes, there are," the man admitted, and he stepped back, almost as if the beefy workman had been woken from sleepwalking.

"These rules are here for everyone's protection, yours and mine," Georgina said, using her best schoolmarm impression. "We're in England, not some foreign clime where the foreigners don't understand justice and fair play. We don't throw things at people's houses, we bowl. We don't shout and scream, but we accept the word of the Umpire and walk calmly to the pavilion. We don't brawl, we box. We don't hit someone else, unless for a roquet. There are rules: Marylebone Cricket Club's or the Marquis of Queensbury's or John Jaques'."

The men nodded as did those around him.

Georgina waggled her finger like a vexed, but loving mother: "Let that be a lesson to you."

The man nodded, forlorn and apologetic. He took his cloth cap off and rung it in his hands.

"Most sorry and apologise, Miss."

"Ma'am."

"Sorry, Ma'am, of course, Ma'am. And apologies to Mister Deering-Dolittle too."

"Well, be off with you then."

The man left, stumbling and the crowd dispersed.

"Come back, come back," Mrs Falcone pleaded.

When they were all gone, Georgina went to the garden gate, closed it with a click and then, when she was confident no-one could see, she punched Mrs Falcone.

Miss Charlotte

Charlotte was absolutely flabbergasted: Georgina, of all people.

"That was fantastic," she said to her sister. The crazed woman had gone down like a felled tree – one punch. "Marvellous."

Georgina pushed straight past her.

197

Charlotte waved Earnestine's umbrella at the empty street: "Ha ha!"

She caught up with Georgina in the kitchen throwing up into a bucket.

"Every morning," Georgina said.

"Brilliant," Charlotte said.

"I've broken my hand."

"You've probably broken her jaw."

Georgina looked like she was praying, kneeling on the tiles with her hands holding her dark hair away from the bucket and her feet sticking out from under her robe and nightdress.

"You've cut your feet," Charlotte said.

"Oh... have I? Oh, I have too... ow! Ow!"

Charlotte bent down: "Here, let me."

She eased a piece of glass out, and another. Little dribbles of red gathered, threatened to flow and then did, trickling as a stream along the arch and then welling up in a lake between her toes.

"Mary– Jane get the iodine!" Georgina shouted.

"But Miss, it's–"

"Ma'am!!!"

"Yes, Ma'am."

Jane bobbed and rushed away, her feet cracking glass in the hallway: "And sweep the hallway."

"You were amazing," Charlotte said.

"Were you really going to take them on with an umbrella?"

Charlotte smiled: "I was going to make a last stand. I've been practising."

"Better with a point three oh three."

Charlotte laughed: "Yes, absolutely."

"Lottie, you're wearing trousers."

"They're practical."

"It's rampant bloomerism."

"No one can see."

"Everyone saw," said Georgina. "Change at once."

The maid came back with the medicine box and then dithered.

Charlotte took the iodine off the flapping Jane: "This'll sting," she said to her sister.

Georgina gritted her teeth as Charlotte dabbed here and there.

"Brush, pan... hallway," said Georgina. "And get Jane."

"I am Jane."

"Then... get the other one."

"Yes, Ma'am," said Jane with another bob.

"You should raise your legs to stop the bleeding," said Charlotte.

Georgina did so, looking quite ridiculous lying on the kitchen floor with her legs stuck up in the air.

"Matters are becoming serious with the Chronological business," Georgina said.

Charlotte nodded.

"It's not just Uncle Jeremiah, Mister Boothroyd and now Earnestine disappearing, but the whole world seems to be going mad."

"What can we do?"

There was a clatter from the hallway.

"Fix the windows," said Georgina, "and carry on."

Chapter XIII

Miss Deering-Dolittle

Earnestine awoke to the bustle of Mrs Androlucia. She felt awful, groggy, as if this future did not agree with her. Mrs Androlucia's friendly smile did not help at all.

"You feeling a little rough, my dear?"

"Yes."

"Temporal Ague, it'll pass, don't you worry."

"I feel..."

"Headache? Tired?"

"That's it."

"It's something to do with the process."

Once Earnestine had washed and dressed, she was taken along a group of passages she'd not seen before, up and down stairs, until she arrived at a nurse's station. A woman filled in forms, checked her heartbeat and looked into her ears.

"Nurse, what's this for?" Earnestine asked.

"Doctor," the woman replied without looking up. "I'm a Doctor."

"Oh, a woman Doctor."

"Yes, why, what's wrong with that?"

"Nothing, just..."

"You olden days people... honestly."

"I beg your pardon," Earnestine said, "but what is this all for?"

"Temporal ague and poisoning check."

"Oh!"

"Hmm..."

The Doctor, her starched uniform as stern as her expression, stuck a wooden spatula in Earnestine's mouth and peered down.

"What's your date of birth?"

"Ah... uh. *Eh*... ah."

201

"How old?"

Why did Doctors and Dentists always ask questions, when they knew full well that one couldn't answer them: "Twe – nee... *ah*... nee."

"Biologically twenty, good, and what's your Chronostatic Displacement?"

"Ma... wah?"

"Never mind, you'll live."

With that over, Earnestine was taken back, up and down stairs, and finally returned to the Conveyor Chamber where she'd first arrived. She was positioned on the mat between two Peelers. Mrs Frasier arrived and stood by the technician.

"Are you coming?" Earnestine asked Mrs Frasier.

"Back to that misogynistic smog ridden era? Not likely."

The technician glanced at the controls and gripped the jewelled lever: "Eight fifty nine..."

Again, everyone checked their pocket watches. Earnestine, ready for this, did the same: it was 11:45 for her. She still hadn't adjusted it and there was no point now.

"Scrutiniser Jones," Mrs Frasier said.

"Ma'am," said the big man to Earnestine's right. With their black frock coats, top hats and strange white glasses, they all looked the same, except for this shaven bear of a man.

"Take good care of her," Mrs Frasier said. "Earnestine. When you get back there to those days seventy five years ago, tell them what it's like here, tell them of good work we're doing here, but, above all, tell them the truth."

"I will," Earnestine replied.

"If you can talk with crowds and keep your virtue," Mrs Frasier said, quoting Kipling. "And risk it all on one turn of pitch-and-toss."

The light built, that strange noise grew in volume, and Mrs Frasier, and her gold toothed smile, began fading from view.

Earnestine steeled herself, closed her eyes tightly and that awful sensation built in her stomach and legs, but this time somehow in reverse. She felt dizzy, flailed out with her arms as if she were losing balance and she was caught by the two Peelers travelling with her.

Finally, the sensation stopped with a jerk and she was back in her own time: still daylight. The galvanic lights had become gas taps and the paintwork was no longer peeling and old, but fresh and new.

"When is it?" she asked.

"Oh nine hundred," said the new technician, but not in reply. He was still carrying out his checks before unscrewing the control lever.

"Good conveyance," said Scrutiniser Jones. "Always nice to arrive at the same time of day."

Earnestine's own watch said 11:46. She ought to change it and realised that this awkwardness must exist for those travelling east or west on, say, the Orient Express or by Zeppelin.

Scrutiniser Jones stepped off the platform: "Did we arrive on the right day?"

"Depends when you were aiming for?" the technician said. "It's the morning of Friday the seventeenth."

"Excellent, spot on."

Earnestine fumbled for her watch: she was nine and one quarter hours... behind, because for her it was Wednesday–

"What did you say!?"

"Friday the seventee–"

"But I've lost two days!"

"That's Chronological Conveyance for you," the technician replied. He waved the lever he'd removed and the light shone through it, casting speckles across the ceiling.

203

She was closer to her birthday, she realised. Did that count or would she have to wait two more days for her cake and candles?

The Peelers escorted Earnestine outside to a waiting carriage. Caruthers was smoking a cigarette and his impatient strides had taken him some way down the street, so he had to trot back.

"Everything all right?" he asked the Peelers.

"She's been, she's back," said Scrutiniser Jones. "Straight on with her."

Caruthers nodded.

They clambered into the carriage and it clattered away. Caruthers drew the blinds and handed Earnestine a hip flask. She unscrewed the top and took a swig, feeling the metal thread with her lips and then the stinging liquid hit her palette. She snorted, swallowed and took another, much slower draught. The warmth spread down her insides burning her stomach.

"It's an acquired taste, sorry," he said, smoothing his chevron moustache in thought.

Earnestine had another experiment at acquiring it, and a fourth.

"Steady on," said Caruthers.

The carriage went through Lambeth heading for Westminster Bridge.

"Did you manage, you know?" said Caruthers.

Earnestine hefted the miniature camera out of her bag and gave it to him.

"Excellent."

"Mrs Frasier knew."

"She has a tendency of knowing."

"She let me... or rather she took the pictures."

"I'll get them developed," said Caruthers.

The carriage turned and took them across the river and then pulled up outside the Houses of Parliament.

As she disembarked from the cab, Earnestine noticed the number of soldiers dressed in military khaki and armed with rifles. They stood at ease in pairs here at the set down point, by the door, further along towards Westminster Bridge and around the corner towards Whitehall.

"There are a lot of soldiers," she said.

"Things are changing."

"So quickly?"

"You've been away a long time," said Caruthers. "Five days."

"Seventy five years," Earnestine said.

Caruthers, tight lipped, brought her straight through the security details and along the plush corridors of power. They stopped by an entrance to the second chamber.

"The House of Lords," said Caruthers, putting his finger to his lips, although Earnestine could not imagine actually speaking in such an august building.

He opened the door and they slipped inside.

The chamber was like a high church or cathedral, but with wooden panelling around the lower part of the walls and gothic stained glass windows stretching up towards the elaborate ceiling. The rows of benches on either side were upholstered in red leather and the far end was a statement of gold decoration, dominated by a magnificent throne. Every space, even the balcony that went around the walls, was crowded with men. They all wore fine clothes, some in wigs and gowns and others in religious regalia, and they generated such brouhaha as they all tried to shout at once.

A clerk stepped in to stop them: one eye looked at Earnestine, the other at Caruthers, and then disconcertingly it swivelled of its own accord to gaze over Earnestine's shoulder.

Captain Caruthers gave his card to the man and pointed. They had a whispered conversation, mouth to cupped ear, and then the man with the lazy eye threaded his way through the gathering.

205

The speaker called for order – "Order, order!" and eventually a quiet settled: "Lord Farthing!"

Earnestine recognized the surprisingly young man when he stood, dressed smartly in white tie and tails, and waved his order sheet in front of him like a baton.

"Gentlemen, my Lords, a little more time please."

There was a general bellowing of disapproval.

Some wag's sharp voice carried: "You have plenty of time with time travel."

The clerk reached Lord Farthing and handed him the card. Lord Farthing checked it and then noticed the clerk's pointing finger. He looked across, his gaze locked with Earnestine's. For a moment the noise faded.

Lord Farthing threw his arms wide: "You have asked – rightly – for proof."

"Aye, aye," came a chorus of responses.

"And here she is."

He gestured like a compère introducing an act at the theatre and, like the parting of the Red Sea, people stood aside to create a clear passage between the Peer and Earnestine. Even Captain Caruthers stepped to one side leaving her standing alone.

A dreadful hush.

Earnestine's mouth went dry.

Lord Farthing flexed his finger – come, come.

Earnestine walked into the centre of the high-ceilinged chamber until the ranks of seats on either side, and the general press of standing room only, surrounded her.

"This is Miss Deering-Dolittle," said Lord Farthing, his voice seemed to float far away. "She was selected as a trustworthy person, an innocent, someone untouched by Conspiracy or Committee. Come, Child, tell us!"

"My Lords–"

Her voice was an awful squeak like Charlotte's violin practise. A glass of water was thrust into her hand and she took a grateful drink, washing away the taste of Caruthers' brandy.

"What day is it?"

After some confusion, a Bishop answered: "Friday."

"My watch..." she weighed it in her hand, "On Monday I went away for a day and a half, and I find I have been deposited here on Friday – five days later."

There was a wave of murmured comments.

The Speaker of the House intervened: "Order!"

"I have been to the future, transported from a room to the same room, but seventy five years hence. I saw this very building in which I now stand from a distance and the sky was full of flying machines. I saw wonders I could not comprehend, devices and mechanisms beyond our understanding as a steam engine is worshipped by natives in our own far flung colonies and people... and misery and hardship in a world devastated by war."

She paused; it was all too much as if the enormity of it was only now beginning to manifest itself.

She was prompted: "Go on", "Tell us", "Quiet", "Let her speak."

"There was a Great War, a World War that touched every land in the Empire with armies on every continent, navies on every sea, air machines in every sky and it involved every nation. It nearly destroyed everything. Millions – that's *millions* – killed on the battlefields, bombs from the air, civilians – women and children – massacred. There were unstoppable land behemoths churning the mud across Europe, men tunnelling like animals to kill each other underground, metal tubes like undersea dreadnoughts plying the very oceans hunting merchant shipping like monstrous sharks. A whole generation of young men cut down like... like... a crop."

No-one spoke now, not a whisper, as expressions betrayed every man's inner struggle to comprehend this horror. Earnestine wanted to say more, to explain over and over until they understood, but she held her tongue.

The question was finally asked: "But, Miss, do you believe it?"

"How could I not when I saw it with my own eyes."

Captain Caruthers came up and took her elbow, guiding her away.

"Lord Farthing," said a voice behind her, "you ask us to surrender our hard won powers to this... committee."

"My Lords, My Lords, please," Lord Farthing commanded, his clear voice cutting through the hubbub. "We are not discussing the demise of this House, far from it. Just as we defer to the lower house upon occasion, we now defer to a higher chamber. This Chronological Committee was formed by the Crown and Government of the Empire for a particular task. We are simply following our own orders, though before we have made them."

Another Lord jumped to his feet: "Lord Farthing, my Lord."

"I give ground," said Lord Farthing.

"My Lord, what you say is all very well, but there is a long standing legal precedent. Laws cannot be applied retroactively."

"But the... excuse me." Lord Farthing consulted his notes. "The Law of Retroactive Application as pertaining to Chronological Police Act of 1962 does make it so."

"But it does not apply."

"It does not apply *yet!*"

Lord Farthing's turn of phrase struck Earnestine as belonging to Mrs Frasier.

"Gentlemen, Gentlemen," Lord Farthing continued, "their desperate times – such desperate times – led them to desperate measures. They want to save the world. Our world. And who would not want that? Who stands here for destruction? Who stands for Death? Who stands for War? I most certainly do not. Do you? Or you? You Sir, do you?"

The man picked out, and his neighbours, shook and then bowed their heads.

"Of course not. And their desperate times will be our desperate times unless we act *now* in our own time. We are simply endorsing a decision that will be made. I ask you to vote for the motion, stand up for law and order and save our very future!"

A shout rang from the back: "This is a fait accompli!"

"No, Sir, it is not: it will be a *fate avoided*."

As the Members of the House of Lords filed out to 'vote with their feet' through one door for 'aye' and another for 'nay', a small group gathered in a committee room: Captain Caruthers, Earnestine and a few others.

The room, although gloriously decorated, seemed Spartan in comparison to the great chamber of the Lords. Earnestine felt desperately tired as she waited. How could it take so long to count... but there had been hundreds of men packed into the cathedral-like space.

A clerk arrived with a note for Caruthers. He seemed shifty, his eyes looking in different directions as if he were permanently suspicious of everything and everybody.

"Major Dan," the Captain said by way of explanation. He didn't show it to Earnestine, but instead scrunched it up into his pocket.

"It's on a knife edge, it could go either way," said Lord Farthing as he entered. "Miss Deering-Dolittle, you performed splendidly."

"Thank you, my Lord."

"Ah, yes... yes, Mrs Frasier was right, you are a fine young lady. Weren't you something to do with defeating that Austro-Hungarian business?"

"She was, my Lord," said Caruthers.

"Nasty, nasty, that was a terrible business, but it wasn't the end of the world, was it?"

"No, sir."

"Whereas this is."

The clerk with the lazy eye came in, bowed and handed Lord Farthing a slip of paper.

"Our future," said Lord Farthing. "One wonders whether it is right to know, but nonetheless we must look.

209

We have been shown the future in the hope of avoiding it and with this we might."

He opened the folded page.

His face revealed nothing, his eyes merely showing that he read it, read it again and finally checked a third time, then he whooped and jumped off the ground.

"We have it, by Jove, we have it! The Laws of the Future take precedence over the laws of the past from this moment on. I did not believe we could pull it off, but we did. You did, my dear. You tipped the balance of the scales. We would have got there, don't you doubt it, but this makes things so much easier, all above board and by the book."

"Good news, my Lord," said Earnestine.

"Yes, now we can begin the arrests in earnest."

Mrs Arthur Merryweather

"Ness, we were so worried," said Georgina as she led Earnestine to a seat. Her elder sister looked shattered and groggy. "You've been gone nearly a week."

"A week, but I was only gone a day and a half."

Finally, they guided Earnestine into the hallway of 12b Zebediah Row. Earnestine raised her head as if she didn't recognize her own home. She seemed to shy away from the light, darker now that so few panes of red and blue stained glass remained. Just as the porch was boarded up, so Earnestine's countenance seemed shuttered.

"Shall I get you a glass of water?" Charlotte asked.

"Brandy," said Georgina. It did look like Earnestine was ill.

"I've Temporal Ague," Earnestine answered, clearly reading Georgina's expression.

"Temporal Ague?"

Charlotte backed away: "Is it catching?"

"Don't be silly, Charlotte – brandy!"

"I was going."

Charlotte went to the drinks cabinet and brought back the bottle of brandy.

"Glass, Lottie," Georgina said, and then softly. "Is it catching?"

"No, it's... because I've travelled in time," said Earnestine.

Once Earnestine had taken a sip, and coughed, the colour seemed to come back to her cheeks. Thank heavens for medicinal alcohol, Georgina thought.

"What happened to the porch?" Earnestine asked.

Charlotte piped up: "It was–"

"Nothing to worry about," Georgina said.

"It was an angry mob with pitchforks and everything, chanting, and out for blood–"

"Charlotte!"

"They shouted, woke up the whole neighbourhood."

"Charlotte!"

"They said we were in league with the Chronological Committee. Gina was amazing."

"Charlotte!!!"

Charlotte was quiet.

"Did that really happen?" Earnestine asked.

"I was amazing, yes," said Georgina. "A lot has changed while you've been away."

"They say a week is a long time in politics?"

"Yes."

"A day in the future seems like an eternity," Earnestine said. "A lot changes in the next seventy five years. Millions. They died in their millions... will die. In a Great War, the whole world was laid to waste. Every nation: the British Empire, Germany, France, the United States, Japan, every nation, and they just killed each other, and then there was starvation, disease, tuberculosis and the real killers like influenza. Whole communities just swept away."

"Oh Ness."

211

"This is what we have to look forward to if we don't stop the conspiracy."

"Then we're joining forces with the Chronological Committee?"

"I don't know."

"With Mrs Frasier?"

"If you can trust yourself when all men doubt you."

"Keep your head when all about you are losing theirs. Yes?"

"But I doubt myself when all men believe me."

"Why are you quoting 'If–'?"

"Mrs Frasier quoted it in the future."

"It just means that, like you, she knows her Kipling."

Earnestine hesitated: "She's not telling us everything."

Miss Charlotte

The doorbell rang.

"I'll get it," Charlotte shouted. She ran to the door and then came back looking shamefaced. There were Temporal Peelers behind her, tall and imposing, and when they parted, there was Mrs Frasier.

"Earnestine," she said, "I've not seen you in such a long time."

"It's only been..." Earnestine looked at her fob watch. She still hadn't changed it, so it made no sense. Half past nine: was that a late breakfast or a supper?

Mrs Frasier consulted her two fob watches: "Nearly a month for me, but less than a day for yourself, I believe. I thought I'd pop back and visit you for afternoon tea."

"Afternoon tea?"

Mrs Frasier smiled: "Because of you, things have moved forward. We can begin the next phase."

"I see," said Earnestine, her lips tightening.

"Tea then," said Mrs Frasier, and then she raised her voice: "Jane, Jane... tea, chop-chop."

"Can we have cake?" Charlotte asked.

"Of course, Lottie," said Mrs Frasier. "It'll be a proper little feast, all of the Derring-Do Club together again. In the drawing room I think."

Mrs Frasier swept past, her burgundy dress trailing the floor. The others had no choice but to follow.

"Still got that picture in your bag I see," said Mrs Frasier.

"I beg your pardon?" Earnestine said.

Mrs Frasier pointed to the gap in the wall: "Gina?"

"Oh, yes, I forgot," said Georgina. "It's in my... how did you know?"

Mrs Frasier made a little writing gesture in the air.

Jane bought the tea, a pot and the best china on a metal tray.

Mrs Frasier took charge: "Thank you, Jane."

She sat; they all sat, except for Earnestine.

"I'll be Mother," said Mrs Frasier. She poured: lemon for Earnestine, milk for Georgina and Charlotte, and two lumps deposited into Georgina's with the silver tongs. "And lemon for me."

They took their tea, blew gently on the surface to create ripples that spread outwards.

"Such a good picture too," said Mrs Frasier. "All of us together at the theatre: the Captain and the Lieutenant, Uncle, and then *Earnestine*, Georgina and Charlotte. Did we count the men then? I think we did, even then. The Derring-Do Club."

"You're not a member of the Derring-Do Club," said Earnestine.

"Of course I am," said Mrs Frasier. "You really are such a silly little girl, Earnestine."

"I am not a little girl."

"And petulant too."

"Who are you?"

"I am Mrs Frasier, of course."

"We'll find out what you're up to and put a stop to it."

"You didn't."

213

"We will."

"So much fire, so little wisdom," said Mrs Frasier, not unkindly. "You'll join us."

"I will not!" said Earnestine.

"Yes, you will, because I did," said Mrs Frasier with a smile. "We have so much in common, you and I. You see, I'm Mrs Marcus Frasier now, but my name is Earnestine too–"

"That's my name?"

"Yes, I'm Earnestine Frasier, née Deering-Dolittle."

CHAPTER XIV

Mrs Frasier

She smiled at the three sisters and their shocked faces. Earnestine – the younger Earnestine – looked utterly aghast, amusingly so; while the other two, Georgina and Charlotte, looked from their elder sister to their... more elder sister and back again.

Mrs Frasier relished Earnestine's startled reaction. She knew she shouldn't. She should feel sympathy for this young lady. Mrs Frasier did, after all, know what was in store for her.

She took a calm sip of her tea, tasting the sharp tang of lemon.

"Yes, Earnestine," she said, "I was you, Earnestine Deering-Dolittle, and you will be me, Mrs Marcus Frasier."

"No, it can't be," cried Earnestine.

Mrs Frasier stood, took two decisive strides right up to Earnestine. Nose to nose, they had the same angle and shape making an even 'V' between them. She put her hand upon her head and shifted it across. They were the same height. She pulled her earlobes to signify that they were identical apart from the slight elongation caused by the older version's heavy earrings, but their ears each had the same shell-like appearance.

Mrs Frasier stepped back and smiled.

"You have a gold tooth," Earnestine said. "I don't."

"You don't... *yet*."

Earnestine put out her arm behind her, feeling for a chair, but it wasn't positioned straight on. Georgina leaned in and guided her down.

"No, no..." said Earnestine.

"You see, we are on the same side... in fact, we are the same side."

215

Georgina glanced back and forth, comparing eye colour, hair, shape of chin, everything. Mrs Frasier let her examine fully, knowing that Georgina was finding it suddenly obvious – of course it was. If one sees two people who look similar, perhaps one thinks of a family relationship, but one never for a moment thinks they are the same person.

Still, she had a part to play.

"Now, if I remember rightly, we have some foolish questions and then I went... I *will go* and attend to certain matters."

"What foolish questions?" Charlotte asked.

"Quite."

Earnestine found her voice: "You can't be me?"

"Really? Why not?"

"Because... you're nothing like me."

"I'm older, lost some of my puppy fat, and clearly I've grown up, but we're the same."

"Ness," Georgina put her hand on her sister's arm, "she does look like you, the same sharp nose and red hair."

Earnestine snatched her arm away: "I don't have a sharp nose."

"I prefer regal," said Mrs Frasier, touching the sharp edge with her index finger.

She considered the three young ladies in front of her and she felt happy. It was such a pleasant experience to see them again, all together, and the need for pretence gone.

"Well, I'll leave you three alone as I have duties. Thank you for the tea," Mrs Frasier said. "I remember... so long ago. It's like one of those fairground exhibits – the Hall of Mirrors. Do you remember them? Of course you do. They make you thin or fat or like an hour glass or... young again."

"Or old," Earnestine managed to say.

"I'd forgotten that part of the conversation until now."

Mrs Frasier nodded and then walked away closing the drawing room door behind her.

"We'll be going then, Ma'am?" Scrutiniser Jones asked.

"Yes, indeed," Mrs Frasier said. She put her finger to her lips and then shooed the big man away. He cottoned on. Bright man, she thought, despite his ogre-like frame.

Once the Peelers had gone out through the ruined porch, Mrs Frasier tip-toed back to the drawing room door to listen.

Earnestine was whining: "She can't be me, oh Gina!"

"She's as bossy as you," said Charlotte, brightly. Silly girl, Mrs Frasier thought, she'd have to have words with her as it wasn't 'bossy', just 'forceful'... but later, when the ramifications of her identity had had time to settle in.

"Lottie! Can't you see Ness has had a shock?"

Ah, yes, Gina, always the caring diplomat. She remembered... but that was a long time ago, a long, long time ago when she was young.

"Shall I get the brandy?"

"Lottie."

She heard Earnestine wail loudly.

Young and silly, she thought: a little girl of a mere twenty years, but destined – she smiled to herself at this thought – for greatness.

Was that pride?

Mrs Frasier decided to leave them to it and slipped away.

Scrutiniser Jones held the carriage door open and then Checker Rogers whipped the horses into a canter. They sped through London, not openly yet, but that would come. Soon, very soon.

Their posters were up, bold and decisive, with striking images of noble men looking to the distance and towards a brave new future. Boys and men had been employed to travel round with buckets of glue and brushes pasting their message over adverts and exhortations to visit the theatre

217

or the music hall. True, some had been defaced, but the inexorable tide of words would win through.

Mrs Frasier's 'certain matters' were waiting for her when she reached her new office. There was something refined about the Houses of Parliament, a wood panelled room had been set aside for her with an oak desk complete with green leather surface. There was something positively British about oak. It reeked with the centuries of polishing, a perfume of power.

Her lists were ready on her desk. All these troublesome individuals with their dissenting opinions enumerated in fine ink, a beautiful hand, in neat columns and arranged in alphabetical order: title, name, letters and occupation. A few had a note appended: these were always the first to consider. The ink well on the desk was stocked with fine red vermilion and Mrs Frasier would dip her pen, flick, and then write a single letter.

'A' meaning 'Arrest'.

When she'd finished, she used a wooden rocking blotter dry the ink. She always pondered the little 'A's imprinted on the underside of the absorbent paper like so many squashed insects. It was satisfying to do something properly: everything in its place and a place for everything.

The book was shut, the Chief Examiner came and took it away and then, somewhere, all the Peelers went to work, scurrying hither and thither, and thus the names turned into cowering men each pleading ignorance as a defence as they were taken to the Battersea Conveyor Terminal and whisked away.

'A' was for 'Apple', a bad apple, and soon the insidious cancer would be cut away for good.

Once that was done, there was the rebuilding: suffrage, voting rights, an end to poverty, health improvements, education and so on and so forth. She knew that she would never finish the task she had set herself. Saving the world was not something one did, collected the medal and then had tea: it was a vocation.

It would be never ending, but they had made a good start: out with the old.

She leant back and the leather of her chair squeaked. She allowed herself a thin cigar, letting the swirling smoke rise to its limits and spread across the ceiling. Outside a ship sounded its horn with a bellowing cry like a bull walrus claiming its territory – commerce. This was the centre, the very axle around which the British Empire turned. Ships sailed and steamed from here all over the world, a world where the sun never set. From this very room messages were influencing Whitehall, soon London, England, the Empire... and the World, why not?

But Rome was not built in a day.

This New World would take decades to construct and she would not live to see it flower. Like those great men of old, who planted trees so that later generations could enjoy an elm lined avenue they themselves would never walk along, or men who designed great cathedrals that they knew they would not live to worship within; so she, a mere woman, would not live to see this bold future, except through the eyes of some bronze statue cast to keep her memory alive.

However, she knew that she could hand the baton on, so to speak, into safe hands.

She smiled, letting the tobacco calm her raging blood. It was delicious. All this effort and finally – and worth savouring – here was this moment of triumph to enjoy with a deep satisfaction.

In the oil paintings around the room, crusty old men stared down at her from the past – disapproving, she thought – and, although they were great statesmen, generals and thinkers, they were all men. She had a picture of a woman on her wall in the future: Boudicca. She would replace these pictures here with those of Cleopatra, Marie Curie, Queen Elizabeth, Queen Victoria and...

She laughed aloud.

219

"Earnestine Deering-Dolittle," she announced to the empty room.

When she was older, much older, and the years had taken their inevitable toll, she would hand the reins of power to someone younger, but as equally deserving as herself.

Herself.

<u>Miss Deering-Dolittle</u>

Even though Earnestine was alone in her room, Mrs Frasier was staring right at her with an expression of disbelief.

Earnestine washed her face, cupped her hands in the bowl and washed it again and wanted to wash even more, but every time she looked up at the mirror she saw that woman. As her disquiet increased, despair clutched at her heart, so her features became more haggard, older, and then, even more so, Mrs Frasier glared back at her through the mist of moistened eyes.

I am a monster, Earnestine thought, the very person I mistrust – all my life I have been impatient to grow up, to be taken seriously, but all the time I have been striving to become Mrs Frasier.

One must pull oneself together.

Stiff upper lip.

Calm in a crisis.

When all about are losing their heads and blaming it on you... but it was her fault, she was Mrs Frasier. She was the one who arrested... would arrest Mister Boothroyd and Uncle Jeremiah.

No, she must trust herself when all men doubt... she'd be a man about it.

But she felt relegated to a lower form. All her hopes, her dreams of adventure – yes, that word – and expedition. They belonged to someone else. Her life was no longer her own, it had been usurped. Trumped.

She went back to the drawing room to face her sisters again. If you can keep your head when all about you are losing theirs and blaming it on you... she would be brave, she decided, and not let it show.

"Can I just ask," said Charlotte. "Who's Mister Frasier?"

Earnestine felt not just her lip, but her entire face tremble.

Mrs Arthur Merryweather

"Ness, sit down," said Georgina taking hold of her sister. "That was a stupid thing to say, Charlotte."

"Me?"

Earnestine made a strange sound, grief stricken: "No... some man is..."

"Marcus," said Charlotte, brightly. "Some man called Marcus Frasier."

Georgina struggled to hold her sister upright: "Ness, I think..."

But Earnestine knees gave way and she sat rather unceremoniously on the floor.

"There's an obvious question," Georgina said.

"Yes," Charlotte said. "Who's Marcus Frasier?"

"Oh no," Earnestine wailed in a very un-Earnestine manner.

"Lottie, you're not helping," Georgina chided.

"I feel sick," said Earnestine.

"You're not in the bun club, are you?" Charlotte asked.

Georgina jerked back from her elder sister: "Charlotte, you are seriously out of order. Of course, she's not in the 'bun club' as you so crudely put it. Clearly she can't be as she isn't married."

"She is now," Charlotte said, pointing at the door to indicate Mrs Frasier. "She's married to Mister Frasier."

"Lottie! She's not said 'yes'."

"But Mrs Frasier has and aren't laws retroactive now?"

221

"Lottie!"

"What's the obvious question?" Earnestine asked.

Georgina couldn't think. She felt utterly flustered.

"Will I be a bridesmaid?" Charlotte asked.

Georgina ignored her: "We have to find Uncle Jeremiah."

"Isn't he in the future?" Charlotte said. "We could go there. Use the Temporal Engine."

"We could," said Georgina. Earnestine looked pale; perhaps something to occupy her mind was just what was needed. "Couldn't we? Ness? You're in charge of the Derring-Do Club."

Earnestine's retort was without expression: "Mrs Frasier is now the ranking officer."

"Ness?"

"If I was supposed to, then Mrs Frasier... I'd have told myself."

"You might meet Marcus Frasier?" Charlotte suggested.

Earnestine glared at Charlotte.

"Perhaps we're meant to," Georgina said quickly.

"We have to do something," Earnestine agreed.

"That's the spirit."

"We could talk to Captain Caruthers."

"Yes, that would be sensible," Georgina agreed. "The men will know what to do."

"That wasn't quite what I meant."

Charlotte had an idea: "Perhaps Captain Caruthers knows Marcus Frasier."

"Oh do be quiet, Lottie!" Georgina shouted.

"I was only trying to help."

"Perhaps, Lottie, you should stay here," said Georgina.

"No," Earnestine said, "otherwise she might run away and join the French Foreign Legion or a bordello. Or we might discover that she's our great grandmother."

"That's settled then," said Georgina, "we'll ask the men."

They collected their bags and Earnestine's umbrella, and set off.

Their assumption was that Captain Caruthers would be at his Club, or at least they'd have information as to his whereabouts, and a Hansom dropped them off outside.

The front of the building was like a Greek temple and inside the lobby was the most austere of libraries, lit by shafts of sunlight from a skylight and with a silence that stunned the motes of dust floating in the air into immobility. The Porter behind his desk considered them as both unwelcome and unbelievable.

"Good day," Earnestine began, but a 'shhh' of a finger raise made her quiet. He pointed to the exit.

Earnestine stood and folded her arms.

He pointed again.

"We are here–"

This was too much and he quickly shuffled them across the marble floor to a room marked 'Ladies Drawing Room'. It was a waiting room with chairs with backs designed to make sitting with a bustle difficult and persuasively suggesting that a 'message left' would be more beneficial than a 'female waiting'.

"Captain Caruthers, please," Earnestine said.

"He may be in."

"He is in."

"I will check."

"If you check and come back to say he isn't here, *then we will check*."

The man's expression of utter horror was a brief picture before he fled.

A clock ticked with an interval that seemed far too long for a mere second.

Captain Caruthers came in smartly, followed by Lieutenant McKendry.

"Miss Deering-Dolittle, Mrs Merryweather, Miss Charlotte, how can I be of service?"

"You know about matters," Earnestine said.

"I beg your pardon."

"I was away for five days and you were... consorting with Temporal Peelers, so we have questions."

"Yes," said Charlotte. "For instance, do you know Marc– *Ow!*"

Georgina smiled sweetly at the Captain as if she had done absolutely nothing untoward.

"Is there somewhere we can go to discuss matters?" Earnestine asked.

Captain Caruthers hesitated: "This is the Ladies Drawing Room."

Earnestine simply waited.

"There's the Wellington Room," McKendry said. "Ted's the porter."

"Mac, they are young ladies... oh, very well."

They went back into the hallway. Ted the Porter had their gloves and umbrella ready in a jiffy, so he was wrong-footed when they went up the wide flight of stairs.

"Just taking them to the Wellington," said Caruthers breezily, "don't worry, it'll all become legal in 1920 or so, I expect."

"Captain," said Ted, "Lord Farthing–"

"Yes, we'll be out before his cronies arrive."

The Wellington Room had a number of red leather arm chairs clumped around small tables under the watchful eye of the Iron Duke himself, who stared down from a tall portrait over the mantelpiece. Caruthers directed them away from the door and across the open space of the marble floor to an area behind a display cabinet. Charlotte gazed up in wonder at all the weapons and military exhibits.

"Waterloo," McKendry explained. "The Club famously won more medals than the Diogenes. They have a Nelson Room. We're not so good on water."

They settled: Earnestine sat with her hands neatly in her lap, Georgina was concerned about her sister, and Charlotte fidgeted.

"I have some news," said Earnestine.

Caruthers nodded.

"It appears... that is to say... I am... I will become: Mrs Frasier."

Caruthers let out a breath and fell back in his chair.

"Well, I'll be..." said McKendry as he tugged on his chin puff beard.

"I suspected as much," Caruthers said, recovering. "Mrs Frasier herself let something slip, you could see she feared she had, and she knows too much about us all. There's been a rumour circulating. I don't know where it started."

Earnestine was shocked: "A rumour!"

"It was in the Standard," McKendry added.

"Not the Times?"

"Perhaps the evening edition."

"Then we are inextricably linked with all this," Earnestine said. "I find myself at odds with the situation."

"Mrs Frasier said you'd come round eventually."

The silence that followed was palpable. No-one really knew what they were supposed to do, as if the other side in the game, if it was the other side, was allowed to dictate their moves and change the rules.

Charlotte broke the silence: "Do you know—"

Georgina hit her sharply across the arm, then said, "We're worried about Uncle Jeremiah, Doctor Deering."

Caruthers looked to McKendry.

"He was arrested last week," McKendry added.

"In front of us," Georgina added. "In Magdalene Chase by Mrs Frasier herself."

"By..." Caruthers glanced at Earnestine and then nodded. "Who else has been arrested?"

McKendry took a sheet of paper from his jacket pocket and unfolded it.

"Colonel Jefferies, Lord Stockton, the Right Honourable James Foxley—"

Charlotte sniggered.

"...Doctor Deering, Chief Constable Rodman, Mister Mellers, our own Mister Boothroyd–"

"Poor Mister Boothroyd," Earnestine said. "I met him in the future."

"How was he?" Caruthers asked.

"Much older, repentant, and pleased to see me."

"Older?"

"He'd been there for ten years at least."

Caruthers brushed down his moustache as he reflected on this: "Not the same time in the future every journey then?"

"No."

"Mac?"

"There are a few others," McKendry finished.

"And the pattern?" Caruthers asked.

"They are all important, not high ranking exactly, and they are all supposedly involved in this conspiracy. We can't see how."

"Because there isn't a how," Earnestine said. "They aren't involved yet."

"You sound like Mrs Frasier," said Caruthers, and then when he saw Earnestine's expression, he added: "No offence."

"And this conspiracy will destroy the world?" Georgina said.

"That's the one," McKendry confirmed.

"I've had those pictures developed," said Caruthers. He reached into his inside jacket pocket and produced some daguerreotype prints. He handed them around, and Georgina had to wait patiently until Earnestine had seen them.

Charlotte reached out, desperate to see for herself, but Earnestine gave them to Georgina next.

There were images of a street quite unlike anything she had seen before, and then one of Earnestine standing in the foreground which gave the scene a sense of scale. She could see the Houses of Parliament in the far distance.

The next one had Earnestine standing next to Mrs Frasier. They did look alike, so very alike, and yet Georgina could not reconcile their characters.

"So we're right to support this Chronological Committee," said Georgina. "Don't snatch."

"My turn," said Charlotte.

"That's the kit and caboodle of it," said McKendry. "Our hands are tied by destiny."

"Particularly as Miss Deering-Dolittle will end up in charge of it," Caruthers said.

There was another longer pause.

"There's nothing to be done then," Earnestine said.

"We can find Uncle Jeremiah and defend him," Georgina said. "At least mitigating circumstances."

Caruthers nodded.

A cry sounded from the doorway: "There she is!"

A man dressed in formal evening attire with his bow tie awry and his white silk scarf in disarray, strode forward. He was flanked by another man in a frock coat,

Caruthers stood and faced the newcomer: "Foxley... Schofield, I know Club rules and all that, but I couldn't leave them in the Ladies Drawing Room, it's not decent. And anyway, Mrs Frasier says that suffrage and all that, and it's retroactive, so we should perhaps move with the times and allow Ladies into some of the other rooms."

"My brother was arrested by that creature."

"I don't know anything about it," Earnestine replied.

Foxley's face twisted and his tone was sarcastic: "Ignorance is no excuse."

"Your brother?"

"Yes, the Right Honourable James Foxley, MP."

"Oh, the man I saw at the brothel," said Charlotte.

"That's a damn slander!" the man spat, dribbling. "My brother is a paragon of virtue. He always supported bills in the house that promote family values."

Caruthers tried to step between them: "Foxley, perhaps when you've sobered—"

227

"Go to hell!"

The man, Foxley, lurched over to the other, Schofield, grabbed something off him, and then Foxley came to Earnestine. She stood her ground as the man threw a glove into her face. It rebounded and flopped onto the floor.

"You are a monster!" Foxley shouted. "I challenge you!"

"I say," said Captain Caruthers, "steady on. You can't challenge a lady, it's simply not cricket."

"Ha! That's where you are wrong. Mrs Frasier made it legal," said Foxley. He changed his voice, twisting it to imitate Caruthers' clipped accent. "Suffrage and all that, and it's retroactive, so we should perhaps move with the times."

He went to the wall and extricated two cutlasses from the display. He handed them to Schofield, who weighed them and then brought them over.

"Doesn't the challenged party choose the type of weapon?" Charlotte said, helpfully.

"What would you like?" Schofield asked.

"Hockey sticks," Earnestine suggested.

"Oh, be serious," Foxley said.

"They can be jolly vicious," Charlotte said.

"We can't do this with the child here," said McKendry.

"Quite right," said Caruthers.

"Then get her out!" Foxley screamed.

"Charlotte," said Earnestine, "I think–"

"Oh, but–"

"Don't whine."

"I could be your second."

Earnestine picked a sword, experimenting with the grip. Schofield returned the other to Foxley, who lashed out, slicing the air angrily.

"Miss?" said Caruthers to Charlotte indicating the door.

228

"Oh, this is so unfair," said Charlotte. She stamped her foot.

"Lottie," said Earnestine, firmly.

"Edgar," said Charlotte.

"I beg your pardon," said Earnestine, "but who?"

"The..." Charlotte lowered her voice to a whisper. "Duelling machine."

"Oh, that. Why is it called Edgar?"

"After Uncle... never mind," Charlotte glanced at McKendry as he gently took hold of her arm and moved her towards the exit. "It's not cricket."

"I beg your pardon?"

"Men: they play cricket," said Charlotte, "it's all sportsmanship and gentlemanly behaviour. Duelling is like that."

"I suppose."

"Girls play hockey," said Charlotte, and she winked at Earnestine in an overly obvious manner.

Finally, McKendry moved Charlotte out of the Wellington Room and into the corridor beyond: "Just stay there, please," he said.

Foxley pointed at Georgina: "And the other one!"

"She's my second," said Earnestine.

"I'd rather... may I have your handkerchiefs please," said Georgina, and she went to Caruthers and McKendry for their clean spares. "For the... blood."

For Georgina, this was suddenly real, and the act of gathering materials to staunch blood brought it home to her. Earnestine was going to let her pride get her chopped up by this inebriated blackguard.

It shouldn't be allowed: fighting women was clearly suffrage gone mad.

She went over to Earnestine and whispered: "Ness, don't do this!"

"I must."

"What did Charlotte mean about cricket and hockey?"

"She's been practising on the Duelling Machine."

229

"Duelling Machine?" said Georgina. "Oh, at the Patent Pending Office. She called it Edgar after Uncle Edgar, because it wobbled."

Foxley, Georgina decided, didn't look like Uncle Edgar or a Duelling Machine. Any contraption would be a cuddly child's doll in comparison to this obvious bounder. Although he looked drunk and smelt of brandy, he was agile on his feet, unlike the real Uncle Edgar. It was obvious from his movements that Foxley was practised in the art of fencing.

"Oh, cricket! Playing by the rules, of course."

"What?" Georgina asked urgently.

"I did learn one trick from the Duelling Machine."

"Which is?"

"Ready?" Schofield asked.

"I need a second," Earnestine replied.

The man shrugged: "Take as long as you like, a minute, two even – let's just get on with it."

"No, I meant a person to assist me. Captain Caruthers," Earnestine said. "Would you mind awfully?"

"Not at all, Miss Deering-Dolittle," Caruthers said. "I could get the Duty Porter."

"Oh shut up, Caruthers," Foxley said, spitting, as he brought his cutlass up to the ready position. "En garde!"

"En garde," Earnestine replied, gingerly bringing the blade closer to her nose.

She bowed and, when the man followed suit, she stabbed forward, straight, like one does when one is skewering beef steak and the man jerked back, wrenching the sword from her grip. It vibrated side to side, stuck as it was in his chest.

He stared down, surprised, at the growing red stain that seeped angrily across his starched white shirt front, before his eyes turned as if he were trying to see the inside of his skull and then he toppled backwards like a felled tree. His cutlass clattered from his grasp to skitter across the marble floor.

"I say," said Caruthers, "you can see why we're not allowed to fight the weaker sex."

"Yes," McKendry agreed. "We wouldn't stand a chance."

"Excuse me!" said Schofield: "That wasn't a legal move."

"Oh," said Earnestine, her voice soft, her eyes wide with innocence and her demeanour positively exuding the sense that butter wouldn't melt in her mouth. "Is there something you forgot to explain to me?"

Schofield's face muscles tensed: "Yes, there is."

"Oh?"

"You are supposed to raise your sword thus!" Schofield brought his pointed finger in front of him like an angry teacher. "Swipe it to one side, and then fight."

"Oh, silly me."

"Silly–"

"Thank you for letting me know," said Earnestine. "It won't happen again."

"It won't– but... he's dead now."

"Yes, and a good job he's not on any carpet. Blood is awfully tricky to scrub out."

Caruthers coughed: "I think honour has been satisfied."

Earnestine could see the Captain's eyes twinkling with the effort of trying to keep a straight face.

Georgina was horrified: a man was dead and they, including her sister, were practically joking about it. She saw a side of Earnestine she didn't like, a side that would become manifest when she turned into Mrs Frasier.

"Honour has not been satisfied," Schofield insisted. "The Earl will want to... well, that is to say..."

"Perhaps next time he'll pick on someone his own size, or at least over six foot, rather than on some slip of a young lady who's only five foot eight," Caruthers pointed out.

"Next time!? But he's dead."

231

"He was an Earl?" Earnestine asked.

"Was? Yes. I suppose his brother is the Earl now."

"He'll be pleased," said Caruthers.

"Except that he's been arrested and taken to the future," said Schofield. "By her!"

McKendry coughed and shuffled forward to Schofield, taking him to one side in a conspiratorial way.

"I think we ought not to mention this," he said.

"Why ever not?" Schofield demanded.

"There are plenty of witnesses to the late Earl's rather unsporting behaviour. Fighting young ladies, not exactly on, is it?"

"She proved herself quite capable."

"I'm sure the Earl wouldn't want it known that he fought a young lady *and lost*."

Schofield considered the dead body and Earnestine, and then he nodded.

"Best inform the Duty Porter," McKendry said.

"Who's the Duty Porter?" Schofield asked.

"Ted. There will be something in the rule book to cover this."

Schofield nodded and left.

Georgina returned the handkerchiefs to Caruthers and McKendry, glaring at them to express her disapproval.

"We're going to have to keep you all away from the public," said Caruthers, folding his handkerchief back into his pocket. "What with tempers already inflamed, when this gets out..."

"If?" said McKendry.

"If, yes. We must keep our heads about us," said Caruthers. "But things are getting out all the time."

"Almost as if it's orchestrated," said McKendry.

"Where shall we take you?" said Captain Caruthers. "Will Kensington still be safe?"

232

Miss Charlotte

It was jolly tedious and unfair of Earnestine and Georgina – why should they have all the fun? She'd been sent out like a naughty schoolgirl. And she hadn't done anything wrong this time. It would be lines next. She waited in the corridor as she'd been told for an absolute age and then she went to have a little look around.

The first room she came across was full of old men sitting around in comfortable armchairs reading boring papers and drinking port. When one of them, and then all of them, realised she was there, their faces became jolly comical as they tried to reconcile their outrage at the feminine incursion and the rule of absolute silence.

She went up to the bar.

"Excuse me," she said. Her voice carried like a tornado, wrenching items from gentlemen's hands and dashing them to the floor. "Could I have a lemonade, please?"

The barman opened his mouth, paused and then closed it again.

"Please."

He pointed at a sign: 'All Men Must Maintain Absolute Silence At All Times'.

Charlotte smiled sweetly: "But I'm a girl."

"I can see..." The barman closed his eyes and swallowed, before, like a condemned man, he mixed a lemonade. It arrived with a clink of ice, wonderfully cool and enticing. Charlotte picked it up.

"Do you have any of those sherbet–"

In a flurry of taffeta, skirts, bustles and clicking heels, Earnestine and Georgina swept in, picked her up and she flew between them out into the corridor. Her feet touched the ground briefly and then she was floating down the staircase.

"Weee*eee...*"

"Hush," said Georgina.

"Quiet!" said Earnestine. "We're in enough trouble with... an unfortunate incident as it is."

On the pavement outside, Charlotte sipped her lemonade. She hadn't wanted to be in the stuffy place anyway.

Captain Caruthers joined them, waving a hand aloft to attract the attention of a cab driver.

"Perhaps, they won't believe what just happened," said Caruthers.

"Perhaps," said Earnestine.

"Did you win?" Charlotte asked.

"Yes."

"On points?"

"No, on... never you mind."

A hansom cab arrived and a young toff descended: Lord Farthing.

"Caruthers," he said, touching the brim of his top hat with his cane.

"My Lord."

"Miss Deering-Dolittle," said Lord Farthing.

"My Lord," said Earnestine.

He paused: "The python and the egg."

"I beg your pardon."

"Mrs Frasier, like the pythoness, the Sibyl of Greek legend, foretelling the future and you are her in the egg, as it were."

"I see."

"Caruthers," said Lord Farthing, and they moved to one side: "We've a meeting here tonight."

"Sir."

"Very good," Lord Farthing said, and he doffed his hat slightly and then strode up the steps to the Club.

"Captain," said Georgina, once his Lordship had disappeared inside. "We would like to find out what happened to our Uncle Jeremiah."

"Doctor Deering?"

"The very same."

"I think it would be best if you all didn't get into any more trouble."

"We can help," said Earnestine.

"We won't be any trouble," said Georgina.

"I've finished my lemonade," said Charlotte, handing Caruthers the empty glass.

Caruthers smiled, genuinely amused: "I shall be fined by the Club."

"That death was not my fault," Earnestine insisted.

"Ooh, well done Ness!" Charlotte squealed.

"Lottie!"

Caruthers looked confused for a moment: "Not that... clearly self-defence. However, I let women in and they'll say that was the cause. I can probably argue a reduction on account of your being children."

Earnestine's lips narrowed and she glared at him: "I am not a—"

"We should find out what's going on!" Georgina implored.

"Absolutely not, it's no task for young ladies," said Captain Caruthers. "I'll contact Major Dan to make a more permanent arrangement for your protection."

Earnestine found her voice: "I think—"

"Leave it to the grown-ups."

"I'm twenty," Earnestine said. "Nearly twen—"

"Driver, Driver, take them to Kensington, Zebediah Row."

The driver lifted his cap slightly: "Right ho, Squire."

The sisters all squeezed in.

The reins flicked and the horse set off. It took a route out of Whitehall and along Pall Mall towards Buckingham Palace. The Royal Standard fluttered from the flagpole, so they knew Queen Victoria was in residence.

"The men aren't going to do anything," said Georgina.

"It's unlikely," said Earnestine.

"But what could we do?"

"Precisely."

235

"But we're the Derring-Do Club," Charlotte said.

"Exactly."

Earnestine rapped on the trap door above with her umbrella and redirected them to Battersea.

"This is it," said Earnestine, when they arrived.

There were guards, but they were clustered by the door of the large factory, so Earnestine was able to sneak them around the cobbled courtyard. At the side, the barrel was still conveniently placed against the wall, and Earnestine clambered up to look through the dirty window.

"Can I see, can I see," said Charlotte.

Earnestine came down and Charlotte jumped up.

"There's a Technician on duty," Earnestine said.

Charlotte could see a man standing by a lectern covered in galvanic switches and levers. There was a stage area cordoned off with brass railings further on. Whereas the outside looked dilapidated, the interior appeared brand new.

"Just two matters," Georgina said. "How are we going to get past the Technician and how are we going to operate this temporal conveyor?"

"We don't need the Technician for one and we do for the other," Charlotte added, wanting to be a part of the planning.

Earnestine took a deep breath: "We'll brazen it out."

"I beg–" Georgina began, but Earnestine was already marching around to the front of the building. The others rushed to fall into step, as they dropped all attempt at subterfuge and instead strode up the stairs, nodding to the guards as they past, and went along to the Technician.

"We'll be sent to the future now, if you please," Earnestine announced.

Georgina and Charlotte came to a halt behind her.

The Technician appeared flummoxed: "I have no orders." He reached into his pocket, his hand gathering about an object within.

236

"I'm giving you your orders now in person!" said Earnestine.

The man blinked in confusion, consulted his paperwork and then looked back.

"I am Mrs Frasier," said Earnestine.

"Ah... yes... I know... that is... I take orders from *Mrs* Frasier, not *Miss* Deering-Dolittle."

"If you don't do as I say, then Mrs Frasier – when I am Mrs Frasier – won't be happy."

Another man appeared from further inside the complex: "What's happening here?"

It was Scrutiniser Jones, his top hat and white glasses in his hand, his black frock coat stretched across his broad chest. He was completely bald.

The Technician explained: "This is... Mrs Frasier and she wants... to go to the future."

Scrutiniser Jones smiled: "Then we had best do as she says."

The nervous Technician busied himself at the controls. Only now did he remove his hand from his pocket and screw a jewelled control rod into the device.

"Unscheduled Chronological Conveyance, time... fifteen thirty eight and nineteen... twenty."

"You stand on the dais," said the Scrutiniser, holding out his hand.

Earnestine led the way around the protective glass screen. The others joined her as did the Scrutiniser. Georgina held onto the brass rail, but the Scrutiniser shook his head and repositioned everyone into a formation in the centre.

A hum grew in pitch and intensity.

"Forty seconds... forty five... stand by."

"Close your eyes," said Scrutiniser Jones.

"Do we make a wish?" Charlotte asked.

"This is the part that's unpleasant," Earnestine said.

"Unpleasant? How?" Georgina asked, worried.

237

The hairs on the back of Charlotte's neck prickled and she was scared. This wasn't an heroic charge, the Light Brigade hurtling towards glory, but a trap.

The Scrutiniser put on his white glasses as the Technician in front of them began to fade to nothing. The gas lights, flicking in the taps on the walls, started to become fixed and galvanic.

The growing radiance suddenly dazzled and the pit of Charlotte's stomach lurched as if she were on a fairground ride.

The past disappeared.

Chapter XV

Mrs Frasier

Earnestine, Georgina and Charlotte appeared in front of her, simply materialising out of thin air. It always took her breath away.

Georgina crumpled to her knees. The others kept their feet. Charlotte leaned down to help her sister up. Earnestine stood as regally as she could, blinking desperately against the effect.

"There I am," said Mrs Frasier. She stood calmly with her velvet bag over her arm and her hands held together in front of her just like Earnestine did herself. She wore a burgundy pill box hat, a fine, simple jacket and trousers flared at the thighs and tucked into her calf length boots.

"Oh Ness!" Charlotte cried. She jumped forward down from the dais, came around the brass rails and then threw her arms around Mrs Frasier. "I've missed you so."

"And I've missed you too, Lottie," said Mrs Frasier, disentangling herself from Charlotte's embrace. "There now."

"It's an amazing trick."

"It's not a trick, it's engineering."

"And you just stand on that stage thing and appear in the future."

"All the world's a stage."

"Can I have cake?"

"Later perhaps."

"How did you know?" Earnestine asked.

"How did I know?" Mrs Frasier answered. "Rather obvious isn't it."

"This was an unscheduled conveyance."

Mrs Frasier smiled: "Yes, I remember."

"Why didn't you stop us then?"

"I thought it best to teach you a lesson of sorts."

"Did you?"

"I remember it as a lesson," said Mrs Frasier and she took Earnestine's umbrella off her: "Oh... this! Zeppelins." She laughed.

"Do you remember what I'm going to say next?"

"No," Mrs Frasier admitted, "I don't remember that."

"Why not?"

"Because... I came to realise that I had been very childish, so I tried to put these events in my past and go forward with my life."

"But–"

"Scrutiniser Jones!"

The big man stood to attention: "Ma'am."

"Please find appropriate quarters for my sisters and take them there."

"What about Uncle Jeremiah?" Georgina demanded.

"He's a prisoner. He'll be tried soon enough."

"And Mister Boothroyd?" Earnestine asked.

"He has been returned to the past."

"But Uncle Jeremiah is your Uncle too," Georgina insisted.

"He would destroy our world."

"This is wrong," Georgina insisted.

"I am bound by the rules," said Mrs Frasier. "We have our duty. I understand that, Mister Boothroyd understands that and I'm sure that Uncle Jeremiah will too, soon enough."

"But he would never–"

Mrs Frasier interrupted: "Scrutiniser Jones."

"Ma'am."

"Make sure they are settled safely."

"Yes, Ma'am."

Mrs Frasier held up a finger to silence anything the newly arrived young ladies might have to say, took her silver fob watch from her trouser pocked and checked the time.

"I have an appointment seventy five years ago," she said, and then with a smile added: "And I don't want to be late."

"Mrs Frasier, what about Uncle–"

"Gina! That is enough."

Georgina looked her right in the eye: "Ness, please!"

Mrs Frasier softened: "Gina, once you see what we are building here, you'll understand, I'm sure. Jones, if you would be so kind."

Scrutiniser Jones and Checker Rogers, who had been with her, escorted the sisters away. She watched them go and stand further down the dingy corridor.

This unscheduled conveyance had changed her plans. By this stage, it should all be going like clockwork, but as the Committee moved, so too did the Conspiracy. Wheels within wheels, gears moving gears, it all interlocked like a mechanism, but unfortunately with the occasional lurch when a particular cog proved awkward.

She gave Earnestine back her umbrella.

"Technician," she said.

"Ma'am," said the operator. "Fourteen sixteen... now!"

These changes rippled outwards, but then that was the whole commission of the Chronological Committee and the Temporal Peelers.

The Derring-Do Club, for example, was one such belligerent component, but then what did she expect them to do, sit down and quietly crochet? She smiled at the spirit, such vitality, such tempestuousness: *oh wonder! How many godly creatures are there here! How beauteous mankind is! Oh brave new world that has such people in't.* The fire would inherit the Earth.

The technician moved the controls, adjusting a number of sliders one way or the other. The lights flashed and the machine howled, and Mrs Frasier's view of the Deering-Dolittle sisters vanished to be replaced by images of another time.

241

Miss Deering-Dolittle

Earnestine saw her future self stand on the Chronological Conveyor's dais and fade from view: gone.

She felt herself fading too: going.

Scrutiniser Jones took them down a corridor that Earnestine recognized well.

It was months until she was twenty-one... or years ago. She'd been a child and treated like a child, but held out knowing that she would be an adult eventually. Now, that future had been stolen by that woman.

"Can I wear trousers?" Charlotte asked, brightly.

"No," said Earnestine. "It's rampant bloomerism."

"But you wear trousers."

"I do not... Oh!"

"Don't be unkind, Lottie," said Georgina.

They reached the Rotunda and came suddenly upon a small gathering. The crowd burst into applause.

Earnestine heard cries of "The Derring-Do Club" and "Look! It's Mrs Frasier, doesn't she look young".

Mrs Arthur Merryweather

Georgina found their reception strange. It was heartwarming to be appreciated, of course, but utterly peculiar. Scrutiniser Jones took them further into the building along a corridor marked for Accommodation.

There were posters on the wall: 'History in the Remaking', 'Correcting Mistakes' and 'Bringing the Past to Book'. They depicted heroic men like Captain Caruthers, Lieutenant McKendry, Major Dan and even her own dear departed Captain Merryweather. Each was a stylised rendering showing their square jaws, determined expressions and smart uniforms.

They passed a canteen and a smoking room before reaching their destination.

Scrutiniser Jones opened the first of a long line of plain doors.

Earnestine went in, saying nothing. As Earnestine propped her umbrella against the wall, the big man closed the door and locked it just as if he were a gaoler.

The next door revealed a room for Georgina. It was small, positively Spartan and more like a cell than anything else.

"Your room, Miss," said Scrutiniser Jones.

"Ma'am," said Georgina. It looked worse than the Eden College for Young Ladies.

She stepped in, turned and the door was closed in her face.

"Why are we locked in?" she asked through the door.

"Safety."

"Yours or mine?"

"Both."

A key turned.

She heard Scrutiniser Jones and Charlotte's footsteps move along, presumably to the next door.

She was a prisoner now.

They had been waiting for them.

Why had they rushed headlong into the future? It had been so stupid. Going up the river was the family curse: charging in where those angels of the Surrey Deering-Dolittles feared to tread.

There was a washbowl, a small table, a chair and a bed. No cupboard or wardrobe or press, and underneath the iron bedstead, there was only a chamber pot.

Dreading they'd be searched, Georgina pushed her bag under the mattress and sat down on it, leaning slightly due to the resulting bulge. She was in the future, she knew, and it was hard to fathom. Seventy five years. It meant that everyone she knew, everyone, was long dead and buried. Captain Caruthers, so handsome and virile, dead; McKendry, dead; Major Dan... Cook, their two maids,

243

even Mrs Jago and Mrs Falcone, and her daughter Miss Millicent, all dead.

In sudden desperation, Georgina scrabbled under the mattress and fished out the picture from her bag. There was Caruthers, Earnestine the younger, McKendry, herself, Uncle Jeremiah and, of course, Charlotte.

If they ever managed to return to their own time, then they too would pass away from old age.

Mrs Falcone had conversed with the dead, so she claimed.

In this time, Georgina herself was no more.

If God allowed her the three score years and ten, then she would have died... twelve years ago. Was she already with her sweet Arthur now? Could she find a Ouija board and communicate with her own ghost? Join hands and say:

"Am I there?"

Georgina gasped, held her hand to her face.

It was ridiculous.

Saying it out loud made it more so: you can't meet your own ghost.

She returned the daguerreotype to its hiding place.

Except, she thought, Earnestine had met herself.

Miss Charlotte

Charlotte decided to escape.

She'd started out on this adventure – and she didn't care what Earnestine thought – searching for Uncle Jeremiah and she intended – *ow, wretched brooch pin* – to finish what she'd started. She'd played hide-and-seek with Uncle Jeremiah many times, always winning, but, with its rush to Dartmoor and the added interference of Earnestine the Even Elder, this round was proving the most challenging.

Charlotte smiled to herself: she'd outwitted that Earnestine. Older and wiser indeed. *'I missed you so'*, ha!

Gulled good and proper, and the woman hadn't even realised.

But still, an older Earnestine!

What could be worse?

Now Charlotte had not two, but three older sisters. They'd all gang up on her, she knew it. Three against one was not odds she fancied.

It wasn't fair.

It would be 'Lottie, do this', 'Lottie, sit up straight', 'Lottie, elbows', 'Lottie, homework', 'Lottie, French tenses are important', 'be quiet, Lottie', 'careful, you'll break it', 'oh, look what you've done now', 'that brooch was expensive and *you've just bent it*', 'you'll never amount to anything if you have that attitude', 'language', 'do as you are told', 'don't whine' and 'Oh, Charlotte, honestly!'

Ah ha, locked door opens, mystery investigation begins.

Chapter XVI

Mrs Frasier

"Lord Farthing."

The young Peer looked away to stare out of the window at the far horizon, and Mrs Frasier smiled. It always amused her to have a man under her spell. The dominant sex indeed, when they were often putty in her hands. It amazed her that in all the centuries since the creation of Eve, the sons of Adam had not been overthrown. *Yet*, she reminded herself.

"Everything proceeds, Mrs Frasier. The laws are phrased ready to go before the House."

"Good."

Lord Farthing tidied some papers on his desk.

"No clerk?" Mrs Frasier asked.

"Not today," he said quickly. "You are prepared if things go badly?"

"I am," said Mrs Frasier, and she lit another thin cigar. "Are you prepared if they go well?"

Lord Farthing coughed and nodded.

"We shall treat those two imposters just the same," Mrs Frasier said.

"I beg your pardon."

"Triumph and Disaster; it's from a poem I had on my bedroom wall back in Zebediah Row."

"Oh," he said, with studied casualness. "I hear that you are hiring workmen."

"A few, yes."

"I would have thought that the working class of your time had far more skills than our backward types."

"We lack certain abilities in the future," said Mrs Frasier. "The war left us bereft of a whole generation of men."

"Men that we will now save."

"Yes."

"But won't that change the future and render your existence impossible?"

"Time is mutable," said Mrs Frasier. "To change things is the Chronological Committee's intention."

"But to destroy yourself?"

"The Ultimate Sanction will remove all trace, wipe us from the face of history as it were."

"Is it really necessary?"

"So that you have a fresh start, a clean slate as it were," said Mrs Frasier and she waved her cigar at him playfully like a schoolmarm telling off a pupil, "so be careful not to waste it and repeat the mistakes of the future."

"But to throw away that power? For whoever controls the Temporal Peelers, controls everything."

"A power I would hand over gladly to make a better world."

"You are a remarkable woman."

Mrs Frasier inhaled and let the smoke flow from her lungs to drift through the office: "Thank you, but I shall live on in my younger self."

"Isn't she your Achilles heel?"

"She is safely tucked away in the future."

"Safe? Surely the changes we make tomorrow will render that future null and void?"

"I returned... pardon me. She *will* return in plenty of time and grow up in the Utopian future we strive to deliver."

"She is like your child."

Mrs Frasier chuckled: "Although I am not her mother, she is my child."

"Women have such a wondrous gift, the gift of bringing life into the world. Why would you want the vote?"

"It's the future."

"So you say."

"You've seen the evidence with your own eyes."

"Her Majesty will sign it into law, of course," Lord Farthing said.

"The woman will do as you men command," Mrs Frasier said and, when she saw his expression, she added: "I'm teasing you, forgive me."

"I never know with your sort."

"My sort?"

"Strong women," said Lord Farthing. "Remember Doctor Mordant."

"Elizabeth, yes. I met her at the Fabians."

"She was the same. What happened to her?"

"She went to do some research in Austro-Hungary, I believe. Dead now."

Mrs Frasier steadied herself with a draw on her cigar, and moved to the window to stare out across the Thames. They were high up in the Palace of Westminster and Big Ben chimed loudly. Reflected in the window, she saw the burning ember of her cigar. It reminded her of something – ah yes, remember, remember...

"Guido Fawkes," she said, "once put barrels of gunpowder beneath this very building in an attempt to change politics."

"And now we overthrow the established order with a proper legal framework," said Lord Farthing. "Who is on trial next?"

"The Right Honourable James Foxley."

"Earl Foxley."

"Earl?"

"Yes, his brother was killed in an unfortunate duelling accident."

"Really?"

"You killed him."

"Ah yes, I remember," said Mrs Frasier. "I was teasing. I still have the pertinent skill, you understand."

Mrs Frasier flicked her arm up and pretended to parry and thrust.

"Of course you do," Lord Farthing agreed. "And I have the cut and thrust of debate to win, and we will."

"I know."

"Tomorrow, it will all be decided, one way or another."

"It will be our way," Mrs Frasier stated.

"Yes, it'll be a day to remember, but our opponents will regroup and form an opposition. They may prove difficult."

"First they will have a meeting to scheme and contrive. Men like meetings." Mrs Frasier returned to the view of Parliament: "Remember... remember..."

Lord Farthing poured himself a brandy and offered a second glass to Mrs Frasier. She nodded, so he poured a generous measure, and brought it over.

"Mrs Frasier," he said.

"Please, call me Earnestine... Ness."

"A toast, Ness."

Mrs Frasier raised her glass: "To tomorrow."

"And tomorrow's tomorrow."

"Yes, I know of no reason why the day after tomorrow should ever be forgot."

Miss Deering-Dolittle

The lock in the door rattled.

Earnestine stood: she hadn't been asleep and had no idea what time it was or what time it was supposed to be. Did it matter?

The same thoughts circled within her mind: she was merely a prototype, just a–

A man came in suddenly, his hands up and he lurched towards her as he went for her throat. Earnestine threw her arms up instinctively, blocking his grip, but his momentum caused them both to stumble back. She caught the edge of the bed as she went down, crashed against the chair, and heard the water basin bounce and clatter over the hard floor and her water jug shatter.

"You bitch!"

His right eye stared into her face with an angry hatred, but his left eye looked sideways.

Earnestine couldn't cry out, such was the man's stranglehold. Her own hands were fully occupied in fighting his inexorable grip and her legs trapped by her chemise. Her vision blurred, the galvanic light burnt her sight, but it was the only direction she could look.

He banged her head back on the floor: "We will."

Again: "Not have."

She was blacking out, her struggling fingers felt like they belonged to someone else.

"A dynasty of Frasiers."

The man jerked, a spasm running through his entire body, then he wrestled around in twitches.

Earnestine gagged as the air came back into her lungs.

Despite her arms being partially pinned, she hit back with small, savage blows, striking again and again, nails gouging, but the man ignored her.

Instead, he twisted, then bucked, yelped and then toppled awkwardly.

Above, standing heroically, was Charlotte: her left hand raised high above her head and her right directed forward and down in a classic fencing posture. Her sword was black, evil, with a curved handle.

"Lott – *ah...*"

Charlotte beamed: "I killed him just like in a duel. Just like you."

"It's not..." Earnestine coughed, clearing her bruised throat, "...a competition."

"Still, that's one each and–"

"Be quiet, Lottie."

Charlotte pulled her sword out of the man and brought it up to the En Garde position.

Earnestine pushed the dead man off her, wriggling out awkwardly: "And it wasn't a duel, because you stabbed him in the back *with my umbrella.*"

251

"He was trying to kill you."

"He was succeeding."

There was a scuffle at the door and the frame was filled with the bulk of Scrutiniser Jones.

"What's this?" he demanded.

"I was attacked," Earnestine announced.

"By?"

"I don't know," she shouted, straining her voice. She pointed. "Him."

"I killed him," said Charlotte with a big grin.

Earnestine finally pulled herself up and clambered onto the bed.

Scrutiniser Jones surveyed the scene, his thick head rotating about, then he bent down to check the dead man's pulse before glancing up at Earnestine, concerned.

"A glass of water, if you'd be so kind," she said.

"Your jug is broken."

"Can you... kind Sir."

The big man hesitated, but then stood, pushed past Charlotte and went out.

Charlotte started to give advice: "Ness, just lean back and–"

But quick as a flash, Earnestine was going through the man's belongings. He wore a thick workman's coat with pockets on either side, but, as Earnestine discovered, only one inside. The total contents were an oily rag, some shillings with Queen Victoria on them, a small penknife, a bottle opener... hardly the stuff of a proper kit.

"From the past," Earnestine said.

"Not a workman," Charlotte replied. "His hands."

"I am aware of his hands."

"They're clean and uncalloused."

Earnestine checked. Sure enough, his big, murderous hands were quite soft and fine. His face was familiar.

"I've seen him before," said Earnestine.

"Where?"

"Not where, when?" Earnestine tapped her forehead, it vexed her.

"Can you remember anything?"

"He doesn't look right with his eyes looking upwards." Earnestine reached out to close his eyelids and saw that his eyes didn't match. "I was with Captain Caruthers."

Scrutiniser Jones returned with a metal mug, spritely enough to take Earnestine by surprise.

She pulled back, guiltily.

The big man knew: "What did you find, Miss?"

"I'm afraid he has no identification."

"Your water, Miss."

Earnestine took the proffered mug and sipped, her first taste turning into a gulp as the cool water soothed the inside of her neck.

Scrutiniser Jones turned to Charlotte.

"What are you doing out of your room?" he asked.

"Oh, am I supposed to be in there?" Charlotte replied in her sweetest voice. Earnestine winced when she remembered all those times she'd heard that particular tone of innocence.

Scrutiniser Jones fished out his keys, loud and clattering.

"I'd rather not be locked in," Charlotte said.

"It's for your own protection."

"Protection," said Earnestine, rubbing her neck obviously, "that's jolly thoughtful of you. What would I have done just now, if it hadn't been for the locked door?"

Scrutiniser Jones didn't reply. What could he have said?

"Could I have another room please?" Earnestine asked.

"This is the one allocated."

"It has a corpse in it."

"That is... unfortunate."

"Excellent, that's settled then," said Earnestine. "Something with a view perhaps."

253

The three of them moved into the corridor, went past one closed door.

"Charlotte," said Earnestine. "You've broken your brooch."

"I used it–"

"You must take more care of your belongings. That brooch was expensive," Earnestine chided, and she snatched back her umbrella. "And don't take things that don't belong to you."

"But–"

"Don't whine."

Scrutiniser Jones let Charlotte back to her room and locked it. He checked the handle twice.

Earnestine was given the next room along.

She went in, propped her umbrella up in the corner and then thought better of that. She took it up, intending to put it by the bed just in case, but she saw a mark of blood left on the floor by the point.

She was frightened by this.

The evidence, far more than her sore neck, made it suddenly real and frightening, but she couldn't admit that to herself, so she felt angry instead.

"Oh, Charlotte, honestly."

<u>Mrs Arthur Merryweather</u>

The next day, Georgina was surprised by all the extra security. There were six Temporal Peelers in their long frock coats, top hats and sinister white glasses. She recognised the bulk of Scrutiniser Jones and the lofty stature of Chief Examiner Lombard.

"You're going to court," said Chief Examiner Lombard.

"I've not done anything," Georgina protested.

"Public Gallery, Miss," he replied. "Justice must be seen to be done."

Charlotte appeared from the next door along.

"Yes, of course, and it's 'Ma'am'. I'm widowed."

"As you wish, Ma'am."

"Where are we going?" Charlotte asked.

"Public Gallery of the court, Miss."

"That sounds exciting," said Charlotte.

"Mrs Frasier wanted you to know what we do here," the Chief Examiner replied. "This visit is to be part of your education."

"Oh no," Charlotte whined.

"Why all the guards?" Georgina asked.

Chief Examiner answered her: "Mrs Frasier... sorry, Miss Deering-Dolittle was attacked."

Georgina jerked her head round to look at the first door on the corridor. It was closed; there was no sign of Earnestine.

"Oh, please no."

"It's fine, Gina," said Charlotte.

"Don't be silly, Charlotte. Earnestine's been attacked."

"I know."

"You know?"

"Yes, I saved her."

The Chief Examiner had reached the fourth door and unlocked it to reveal Earnestine.

"Ness!"

"Gina?"

"Are you all right?"

"I'm fine."

"But–"

"Stiff upper lip, Gina."

Georgina saw the bruising around Earnestine's neck and the tightness with which she held her umbrella. Georgina felt a flutter in her chest, a cross between worry and panic.

"Why do you fight people?" she demanded.

"He attacked me," Earnestine replied.

"Yes, but why do they keep attacking you?"

The two sisters glared at each other.

"Shall we go?" said Chief Examiner Lombard.

Earnestine nodded sharply.

They fell into an easier formation, Charlotte skipping to fall into step with the surrounding Peelers. Their swords clattered and their boots stamped in time.

When they reached the Rotunda, an excited man in overalls stepped in front of them, causing Earnestine to flinch noticeably.

"Hello, hello," he said.

"Please make way," said Chief Examiner Lombard.

"I just want to... that is..."

"Oh, Albert, yes, of course."

The Peelers stepped away, leaving the Deering-Dolittle sisters exposed.

"Mrs Frasier," said this Albert as he stuck out his hand towards Earnestine eagerly. "We are so grateful for what you are doing. My family, my family... the recent arrests, I learn that because of the great endeavour, they are back, returned to us. We are so grateful. The world is grateful."

"I'm not Mrs Frasier."

"Not yet," he smiled. "I know, I know, of course, still Miss Deering-Dolittle. Marcus is going to be a lucky man. And these must be your sisters – the Derring-Do Club. I've read about you in the History Books, of course, so brave, so sad, so mysterious, and to meet you in person. I'm honoured, honoured."

He shook Georgina's hand and then Charlotte's.

"So brave, so sad," he said. "We're so grateful."

"Move along now," said Scrutiniser Jones, but good-heartedly.

The man went on his way, smiling, talking to passers-by and pointing back.

"We're famous," Charlotte beamed.

Earnestine tightened her lips.

Miss Charlotte

The Rotunda had four corridors, each labelled: Judiciary, Temporal Engineering, Accommodation and Prison. They moved straight on, entering a wood panelled corridor. Charlotte craned her neck round to look into the Prison area as they went past, but she didn't see much with the tall Peelers in the way.

It had been jolly bad luck that she happened to be passing Earnestine's door during her escape and so seen that man attack Earnestine. Well, maybe not bad luck, but her rescue of Uncle Jeremiah had had to be put aside.

Uncle Jeremiah was down there somewhere in the Prison section, she thought, and if she could just–

"Charlotte, stand up straight," Earnestine snapped.

"I am."

It was foolish to have all these extra guards, when they could just as easily have given her a sword and then she could protect them all.

Hadn't she proved herself saving their precious, and ungrateful, Mrs Frasier the Younger?

Or a revolver, that would be better.

They arrived in a waiting area with long wooden seats like pews. They sat. Charlotte fidgeted.

"Can I go for a walk?" she asked Earnestine.

"No."

"Just to stretch my legs."

"No."

"I won't be long."

"Charlotte, honestly."

"Lottie," said Georgina, "be a good girl now."

Charlotte made a face.

They never took her seriously, even though – she sniggered – she had discovered what all this was about. But she wasn't going to tell them, the bossy older sisters; at least not until she'd figured out what it meant.

257

Chapter XVII

Mrs Frasier

A new day, Mrs Frasier thought, a great day. Now she had returned to the future, she decided she'd see the next trial in person. It would be a distraction, something to take her mind off Lord Farthing and the debate.

She checked her watches, touched the lettering within the golden cover: '*For Our Future, J. J. D.*' in a fine italic script. She felt confident. A penny for your thoughts: a shilling perhaps, but this mighty one was a gold sovereign of an idea.

There was a knock at the door.

"Come in."

Chief Examiner Lombard came in, stiffly, and closed the door behind him. He took a pace inside and stopped well short of Mrs Frasier's desk.

"Ma'am."

"Lombard, why are you standing to attention?"

"I've some news."

"News?"

"Bad news, Ma'am."

"Divvy it out."

"You won't be happy."

Mrs Frasier waved her hand to prompt him to continue.

"Last night, one of the new workmen attacked one of the Deering-Dolittle–"

"What!?"

"She's fine."

"Which one?"

"Miss Deering-Dolittle, Earnestine."

Mrs Frasier felt a cold chill: "Me?"

"Yes."

"Who did this?"

259

"We don't know."

"Don't know? How is that possible?"

"He was one of the latest batch brought in, but I asked and none of the other workmen knew him. He was counterfeit, didn't know one end of a pipe from the other."

"Then beat him until he tells you."

"He's dead, Ma'am."

Mrs Frasier practically screeched into Chief Examiner Lombard's face: "What the hell was he doing here?"

"He was a workman, Ma'am."

"Why couldn't one of ours do it?"

"It's the old pumps, Ma'am; we brought a team here to fix them. None of us know how those old things work. And the water is seeping in."

"Could we not have left it until after... oh hell."

It was petrifying.

A man from the past here, without so much as a scribbled note anywhere, wandering about with murderous intent. He could have gone anywhere. He could have done anything.

And why?

"Where?" she demanded.

"In her room."

The man had found Miss Deering-Dolittle's room and attacked her.

"It's just one of those things, Ma'am."

"Lombard, what sort of gulpy do you take me for? He was some bloody bludger, no less than a political assassin."

"He only attacked one of the girls and she's fine, there was no harm done."

Mrs Frasier saw the picture of Boudicca on her wall. That woman had waged war against men, Ro*men*, because her daughters were attacked, and now her successor had been assaulted. The painting showed the Iceni Warrior

Queen going into battle and that was how Mrs Frasier felt too.

"He went for me!"

"Ma'am."

"Find out who he was – everything."

"He was one of the plumbers who–"

"No he wasn't. He was an assassin, a spy, a bloody nose. Lombard, don't be such a glocky cove. This goes deep. Find the trail, follow it to its source and report back."

Lombard stiffened.

"Get on with it!"

Chief Examiner Lombard was a tall man, cadaverous and frightening in his appearance, but he saluted and turned to the door.

"Elijah!"

"Ma'am."

"I'm sorry."

"Ma'am?"

"It's just... we're so close."

"Yes, ma'am."

"Please forgive me."

"There's nothing to forgive, Ma'am."

"You are too kind, but I was wrong."

"We'll find out who he was, directly," said Lombard, his gaunt face set and determined. "We'll get to the bottom of it."

Mrs Frasier nodded with a tight lipped smile.

"I know you'll do your best."

"We're your Peelers, Ma'am, we wouldn't do anything less."

"Thank you."

After he'd gone, Mrs Frasier gripped her desk with both hands and breathed, trying to force herself to be calm. Anger never did her any favours, she knew. She dropped her cigar case twice before she managed to retrieve one. She couldn't get the damn thing into the

261

cutter and nearly took the end of her finger off. Finally, she had it lit and the first inhalation calmed her, even before the smoke reached her lungs. Thank goodness for Double Claro.

When she felt in control again, she checked her watch. Always and always checking her watch, *'For the Future'*, willing the seconds to pass, the long dreamed for day to be over: *if you can keep your head.*

Her hand was still shaking.

No good panicking about it: *if you can force your heart and nerve and sinew to serve.* Work, that's what she needed: *'Hold on!'*

She clipped her gold fob watch shut and stubbed out her cigar, leaving half the greenish length in the ash tray.

Down the corridor towards the court rooms, she found Judge Smythe in his rooms.

"Oh! Mrs Frasier, you gave me such a turn."

The man, his head bald and his whiskers busy and ginger, looked guilty before he went back to hanging up his formal robes in a wardrobe.

"Judge, who is in the dock next? Foxley, isn't it?"

"Foxley... I say, yes: guilty. Do you think hard labour will be too harsh?"

"For that man?"

"I suppose, I suppose, sherry?"

His trembling hand poured two glasses to the rim without spilling a drop.

"Although he is technically innocent at the moment," said Mrs Frasier.

"Of course, of course, Mrs Frasier, justice must be seen."

The man dithered, hesitating as to which way around his oak desk he ought to walk to his chair. There were papers on the desk tucked away in fine covers and tied shut with thin ribbons of various colours.

Mrs Frasier sat and sipped her sherry. It was a fine vintage. She smiled, wondering what was on the bottle:

1897, which made it a few years old or nearly eighty. It depended on how it arrived, she supposed.

"It's Earl Foxley," said Mrs Frasier, correcting the Judge. "His brother died, so naturally the title falls to him."

"When did his brother die?"

"Seventy five years ago."

"Oh yes, of course, of course."

"I mean he did. I just found out when I was there. In a duel."

The Judge was surprised and amused: "A duel?"

Mrs Frasier made a stabbing motion as if she were skewering an invisible man: "It was very quick."

"Swords? Was it over some woman?"

Mrs Frasier gave him a tight smile: "By a woman."

There was a tap at the door.

"Come!"

An assistant came in: "Bert, it's– Mrs Frasier! I beg your pardon, Ma'am."

Mrs Frasier signalled him to continue.

"Mrs Frasier... Your Honour, the court has gathered."

"Oh, very well," the Judge put down his sherry glass. "I say, help me with this, won't you?"

The assistant stepped forward to help him take his robes down again and fuss with them.

"Put on a good show," said Mrs Frasier. "The Derring-Do Club is in."

Miss Deering-Dolittle

Scrutiniser Jones and five other Peelers, their hands on the hilts of their swords, led the sisters through the complex and into the Judiciary section. Earnestine had not been there before.

The new eldest sister, Mrs Frasier, had been there before, of course. Probably many times, but she would remember this time, if this sightseeing meant anything, as

263

it had been her first visit. Now! When she had been Miss Deering-Dolittle.

Earnestine felt she was set on rails: do this, do that, it's fate, because she had already done this and done that. All she was doing was storing up memories for her older self. And, if Mrs Frasier had forgotten, then what was the point of doing it in the first place?

They reached the entrance to the Public Gallery and Scrutiniser Jones held the door open.

With nothing else she could do, Earnestine, as if she were controlled by a train timetable, followed the signal and went along the track indicated.

<u>Mrs Arthur Merryweather</u>

There were about twenty people in the Public Gallery overlooking the main court room. Earnestine asked a woman if she would make room to let the three of them sit together. The lady was only too delighted to move along once she realised who had made the request.

It was like a theatre and they were high up in the circle. Down below, the room was divided into distinct sections. To one side was a kind of box filled in two rows by a motley collection of individuals: the jury, both men and surprisingly women, while in the main area there were a variety of stages: one for the Judge, another for the accused, and a long bench facing the judge for the Prosecution and Defence council. The two opposing lawyers, bewigged, were already in position busy with their papers.

"That's the 'Gentleman Caller'," said Charlotte pointing.

The man in the dock was seated between two Temporal Peelers. He looked haggard, head down and his arms flopped in front, even his wide whiskers drooped.

The Clerk came in and a hush descended.

After a few moments, the Clerk stood: "All stand."

Everyone was on their feet, although the accused needed to be helped up.

The Judge, resplendent in formal red and black robes, entered. He took his seat under a coat of arms that resembled a giant clock set to eleven. He sat, and then stood again as Mrs Frasier, dressed in a fine burgundy dress and matching bonnet, came in from the Judge's rooms. She took a place to the right of the Judge, who then sat, and then everyone else sat too.

The Clerk got back on his feet.

"Your Honour, my Lords... Mrs Frasier, I beg your pardon. Mrs Frasier, Your Honour, my Lords, Members of the Jury, Ladies and Gentlemen, we continue the trial of the Right Honourable James Foxley, Earl and Member of Parliament."

The accused brought his head up: "Earl?"

The Clerk looked to Mrs Frasier, who smiled sweetly.

"If I may continue? The *Earl*, because in his Temporal Thread his older brother has recently become deceased, although for us he died seventy five years ago–"

"John? Dead?"

The Judge intervened: "Silence! He died in a duel, but that is not the matter at hand and we will not be sidetracked. Clerk, pray continue."

Even though Earnestine had her head down, Georgina noticed that her elder sister's face had blushed. Good, because she should feel guilty killing a man, whatever mitigating reasons she may have in her defence.

"James Albert Foxley is accused of diverse crimes of mass murder, conspiracy to war and so forth. He was arrested on... let me see, Temporal Edict, 301, issued by the Chronological Committee, July Twelfth, in the Year of our Lord, nineteen forty five and subsequently arrested in the year nineteen hundred. Confirmation of Historical Adjustment, pleaded 'not guilty', etcetera, etcetera. Adjourned yesterday. We now move to the Summing Up."

The Clerk sat.

The Prosecution lawyer stood.

It was like some strange variation of musical chairs.

The man put his thumbs into the lapels of his robes, turned to address the jury and glanced to the Public Gallery.

"Mrs Frasier – an honour that you could join us – and Your Honour, Members of the Jury, we have all lived through such terrible times, an age of destruction created by the Conspiracy. If it wasn't for the sterling work of Mrs Frasier and the Chronological Committee, we would still be... well, I dread to think. Mrs Frasier's work – our work – is concerned with rectifying these awful crimes, one crime at a time, and one of those criminals is this Earl Foxley. Look at him, guilt written all over his face, and his defence has been nothing but whining complaints and insults. Do we know who he is? Do we? Of course we do, but he's no Member of Parliament here. Here, and now, he's a murderer, a warmonger, a Conspirator!"

Angry shouts erupted from all around Earnestine, Georgina and Charlotte.

"There is but one verdict: guilty, guilty, GUILTY!"

The Prosecutor looked to the Public Gallery, bowed slightly and then sat down. There was a ripple of applause.

The Judge looked to the other bench and the Defence lawyer stood. He adjusted his wig before addressing the main bench.

"Mrs Frasier, Your Honour, Members of the Jury – what can we offer, but our sincere apologies, my client is full of remorse for his actions–"

Foxley jumped to his feet: "NO!"

The Judge banged his gavel: "Silence!"

"My Lord, Your Honour," Foxley said, "I wish to sum up myself."

"You wish to dismiss your council?"

"Yes, Your Honour."

"Oh... very well. Clerk, make a note, I say."

Foxley straightened his jacket, his hands up at his lapels like a lawyer: "My Lord, no evidence has been produced against me."

"Your Honour," the Prosecution interrupted. "We've been through this time and time again. Of course, there is no evidence. History has been changed, that is the point of the Chronological Corrections. This man was arrested to wipe that slate clean, and so the marks of his guilt have gone. However, if he had been allowed to continue, then he would have committed these atrocities. For this, the accused is on trial."

"Outrageous!" Foxley shouted.

The Prosecutor leaned forward, his hands gripping the desk in front of him and all the invective he could muster was directed at the accused: "Were you, or would you have become, a member of the Conspiracy?"

"I don't know anything about–"

"Were you, or would you have become, a member of the Conspiracy?"

"I don't know–"

"Were you, or would you have become, a member of the Conspiracy?"

"I don't–"

"Silence!" The Judge turned: "It has already been well established by legal precedent that an arrest by the Temporal Peelers is authorised by the Chronological Committee and is thus legally admissible in court. No other evidence is needed, and indeed the very lack of evidence proves that the Temporal Peelers arrested the right man. Has this not been explained to you?"

"But that means that I have no defence."

The Prosecutor was ecstatic: "Finally, he admits his guilt!"

Foxley shouted over him: "I refuse to recognize this court."

"Silence!" the Judge banged his gavel. "Mister Foxley, it matters little whether you recognize this court or not. The court recognizes you."

"This is a travesty. Mrs Frasier is a dictator."

The court was in immediate uproar. Objects were hurled at the accused from the Public Gallery. Those by the sisters waved their fists and shouted, jostling them as the fury welled up.

"Silence! Silence!" the Judge commanded. "Mrs Frasier is above your slander! She indulges mass murderers and monsters like yourself out of the kindness of her heart and her fine sense of fair play, in order to restore justice and the liberties that your Conspiracy so wantonly sought to destroy. Silence! We will have silence!"

The Clerk of the Court quietened matters, fluttering his hands up and down to direct people to settle, but the damage had been done.

"Look at all this," said the Judge, referring to the litter and mess thrown from the Public Gallery. "Your kind brings nothing but chaos and destruction. You are finished. Scrutiniser Jones, keep him quiet, I say, keep him quiet."

Scrutiniser Jones, sturdy in his uniform and impassive behind his white glasses stepped forward. Foxley was subdued.

"Now, members of the Jury," the Judge said. "You have heard the evidence, you have heard the accused himself attempt to overturn law and order, please consider your verdicts... no, I insist, please retire and discuss your verdict even if you feel you have made up your minds already. Give to this man that courtesy and consideration that he and his kind so malevolently denied millions of others."

The Foreman stood, nodded, and the jury, the twelve good men (and women) and true, filed out.

"I'm not guilty," Foxley shouted. "Not guilty."

A man next to Georgina shouted abuse.

Charlotte sniggered: "He used the 'B' word,"

"Charlotte, language!" Earnestine warned.

The Clerk busied himself with his papers and the lawyers, both Prosecution and the redundant Defence, put their documents away. The Judge simply stayed in his position impassively. No-one had to wait long; Georgina was just looking at Arthur's watch when the Foreman led the Jury back to their places.

Once they were settled, the Judge addressed them: "Members of the Jury, have you reached a verdict?"

"We have, Your Honour."

"Is this verdict unanimous?"

"It is, Your Honour."

"And what is that verdict?"

There was no pause between the Judge's question and the Foreman's answer. It was immediate and certain, but the heightened tension in the court room was such that it seemed to take an age to arrive.

"Guilty."

The Public Gallery erupted with shouts: "Yes", "send him on his way", "the rope", "hang him", but this hushed when the Judge placed a small square of black cloth upon his head. Foxley seemed to fold in upon himself like a figure in a pop-up book when its part was finished and the covers were closed shut.

"There can be only one punishment for your crime: death! You will be taken..."

The Judge paused.

Mrs Frasier had attracted his attention with a slight raise of her index finger. She leant over to whisper to him.

"Ma'am," said the Judge, "you are too... wonderful."

The Judge coughed and addressed the court again.

"Mrs Frasier of the Chronological Committee – the very person you accused of being a Dictator – has kindly consented to give you the chance to redeem yourself. It

269

recognizes that you are like a serpent in an egg, unformed in your evil. So, even though you are legally guilty, the Committee will generously allow you to seek redemption and make amends."

"Anything," said Foxley, a man clutching at straws.

"So, will you diligently work for the Committee to make reparation?"

"Yes, yes."

"Very well, you accept any labours given to you?"

"Yes."

"No matter what may come to light in the fullness of time?"

"Yes."

"Done... make him sign, I say, make him sign and take him away."

Scrutiniser Jones took Foxley by his collar and led him away. There were jeers, but already people were collecting their belongings and making for the door.

"I'm glad he was found guilty," said Charlotte. "Horrible man."

"Uncle Jeremiah can't go through this," Georgina said in a low voice.

"He might have done already," Earnestine replied.

"Excuse me?" Georgina said to the woman next to her.

The woman appeared very nervous: "Miss?"

"Ma'am. Has Unc– Doctor Deering been tried yet?"

"Doctor Deering?"

"Yes, his case. Has it happened?"

"No."

"And Mister Boothroyd?" Earnestine asked.

"Oh, yes..." said the woman. "Guilty I'm afraid, but given reparations."

"Thank you."

The woman darted away and Earnestine, Georgina and Charlotte joined the exodus, conscious of the glances in their direction. They were known by everyone.

Once they were clear of the crowd, Earnestine pulled Georgina to one side. Charlotte followed. The eldest sister tilted her head to one side, a tiny jerk, and they followed her. She led them to a small room full of book shelves.

"This is the library where I saw all the histories. I thought it might be a good place to prepare a proper legal case," Earnestine explained. She went over the Law section full of bright new volumes. "We need books."

"Will this be those presidents?" asked Charlotte, already swinging her arms about in boredom.

"Precedents," Earnestine said.

"We need case law from this age too," said Georgina.

Earnestine had already put three heavy volumes down on the table.

"This is impossible," said Charlotte.

"No, it isn't, Charlotte," said Earnestine. "We can't compete on case law; we aren't lawyers, so we will have to base our argument on legal principles: Habeas Corpus and so forth."

"Do they still apply?" Georgina asked.

"No civilised nation would discard Habeas Corpus."

"What's Habeas Corpus?" Charlotte asked.

"It's a writ that brings a prisoner before the judge."

Charlotte made a face: "Paperwork, yuk."

"Important paperwork: if a legal process is not followed, then it is invalid."

"There's Magnus Carter," Charlotte suggested.

"Magna Charta."

"And Deus Ex Machina."

"That's Aristotle."

"And—"

"Charlotte, be quiet! You don't know your French tenses, so how are you going to know your Latin legal terms? All that time you complained that Latin was useless; well, now you see how vital it is. It's not possible to run a proper law-abiding country without it."

271

The books were piled high on the table in irregular groups. They were leather bound volumes, red, black and blue, and looked like piles of bricks ready for an ornate wall to be built.

"The answer is in here," Earnestine said, leaning forward and putting her fists down on the table.

Georgina picked up the book nearest and skimmed the words, and then flicked through others, but, if she was completely honest, none of the actual words made that much sense and the volumes were old, dreadfully old.

She picked another at random. It had been first published in 1882 and updated in 1895, this edition 1897, which may only be a handful of years ago for her, but this was the future. It was as if this book was written in 1800 before the Married Women's Property Act of 1884, the Great Reform Act of 1832 and all the other great advances of her own century. It was useless against this Chronological Judiciary. If the last hundred years for her meant that married women gained the right to own property, and the whole electoral system was overhauled, then what would the next hundred years have brought? Perhaps even women's suffrage was possible. It was as if she were trying to play chess, but knowing only the rules of draughts. It just wasn't... cricket.

Something chimed in her head, something just on the edge of her mind like a half-remembered dream.

Charlotte snuffled and shuffled.

It was gone.

Georgina tried to recover it, thought about cricket, chess, cricket... but it wasn't there anymore. It had vanished as if to another time.

"It's impossible," said Charlotte. "Do you really want to spend all day going through some dusty old books?"

"Knowledge is king," said Earnestine.

"Bleurgghh."

Charlotte picked up Earnestine's umbrella and swizzled it experimentally like a sword.

272

"LOTTIE!" Earnestine yelled. "Oh, Gina, take her somewhere please."

Georgina ushered Charlotte out and back to their rooms. There were Peelers on duty, but they didn't escort them.

Once they were back in Georgina's room, unlocked during the day, and Georgina had taken the umbrella off Charlotte to stop her playing with it, they sat down. Charlotte perched on the bed, fiddling with a yellow book, and Georgina chose the chair.

Georgina checked Arthur's watch. She really ought to help Earnestine, return her umbrella, but... oh, that fidgety girl was so distracting. She never did anything useful.

"Charlotte, did you take that from the library?"

"No."

"Well, either read that or put it down!"

"I've read it. Ages ago."

"Well, read it again."

"It's Uncle Jeremiah's."

"Really... I beg your pardon?"

Charlotte handed it over.

"Where did you get this?" Georgina asked.

"It was in Mrs Frasier's bag when we arrived."

"You stole it!?"

"She took it off Uncle Jeremiah."

"Charlotte Deering-Dolittle," said Georgina, utterly beyond exasperation, "how could you steal such an item *and then keep it a secret!*"

Charlotte made a face, but Georgina ignored her and examined the book. If this was Uncle Jeremiah's book and if she could find his patent application, then...

It was '*The Time Machine*' by H. G. Wells – a novel of all things and disturbingly ironic considering what was going on. That was probably why he had chosen it for whatever it was he'd chosen it for. She flicked through it. She'd read this when it came out and remembered the yellow cover with the simple sphinx motif in the centre.

273

Ah ha!

She had it: this title was an aide memoire and inside he had hidden the answer.

Holding it upside down and flicking through the pages did not produce the hoped for secret letter. She then riffled through the pages from the back, even pages first and then looking at the odd pages. There was no hand-written marginalia.

"I've done all that," said Charlotte.

Georgina carefully opened the first few pages.

"And that."

On the flyleaf was written '*To J. J. D. Love C. M.*', but there were no other apparent annotations. The book didn't fall open at any particular page when she dropped it slightly on its spine. The binding hadn't been interfered with. It appeared to be an ordinary copy of... who was 'C.M.'? And 'Love'? 'J. J. D.' was Jeremiah James Deering, Uncle Jeremiah.

"Gina, why is your bed lumpy?"

"I hid my bag under the mattress."

"Who's C. M.?"

"You're the detective."

"Oh, yes, can I get a deer stalker hat?"

"If you solve this, I'll buy you one."

"Oh yes, please."

They dropped the book on the simple bed between them, squaring it so they could consider it as an object.

"Perhaps it's a cipher key," Charlotte said.

"A what?"

"A book used to encode secret messages. If so, it'll have little marks on some pages where the decoder counted words."

Charlotte set about examining it.

Maybe, thought Georgina, the clue wasn't in the book, so maybe it *was* the book.

Uncle Jeremiah read the novel, he was inspired by it and therefore he invented a time machine. That made a kind of sense. After that, logically, he'd have filled in a patent application and this in turn must have ended up at the Patent Pending Office, thus involving Mister Boothroyd, and then it had been side-tracked to the more nefarious divisions of the civil service and so on... until at some point in the future someone had actually built it and used it to come back in time.

Although the Chronological Conveyor wasn't so much a carriage as a... well, there wasn't a word for it as there wasn't anything like it. Any form of transport required one to be in, or on, something, which was usually connected to a horse or a steam engine, and one needed to physically journey through the intervening space.

With this device, one simply stayed put – literally.

It was hard to see what physical property could gather one up and convey one to another place, let alone another year. However, many marvels were fathomed, created and reported all the time. She herself often read a number of scientific journals during her visits to the library and was suitably amazed by various propositions.

However, Uncle Jeremiah wasn't an engineer or an inventor, he didn't know one end of a steam engine from the other and he used to say 'yes dear' a lot when Georgina explained the daguerreotype process.

So someone else, not Uncle Jeremiah, invented the temporal process and came back in time, etcetera, etcetera – perhaps pretending that Uncle Jeremiah had invented it – and if so, what was the point of this book!?

Would being unable to invent a time machine prove Uncle Jeremiah's innocence?

Had some devious future engineer framed him?

Charlotte was still going through it page by page. She could be quite studious when she wanted to be and–

"Hopeless!"

Charlotte pushed it away, the sphinx tilted at an angle.

Sphinx – the riddle of the sphinx.

275

Georgina felt an icy chill. She couldn't remember the story.

"What's the riddle of the sphinx?" she asked.

"I don't know."

"Oh think, Charlotte, think."

"It's... oh, what has three legs for breakfast... no, it's what has four legs in the morning, two legs in the afternoon and three legs in the evening?"

"What?"

"A man!"

"How can it be a man?"

"When he's a baby, he crawls on four legs; when he's grown up, he walks on two legs, and old men use a walking stick, which is three legs."

"What does that mean?"

"That's the answer: a man. A baby crawls on four legs, a man walks on—"

"I know what a baby does!" Georgina snapped, rather more sharply than she intended. Why, why, why did Uncle Jeremiah want them to know about the Sphinx? Perhaps it... "Charlotte, what's the story of the riddle, not the riddle itself, but the story?"

"It's Greek."

"Yes."

"I don't do Greek. Only Latin and French – *yuk* – but I've read about their battles, Alexander the Great, the three hundred Spartans and—"

"Yes, thank you Charlotte."

"There's another riddle."

"Yes?"

"Two sisters: one gives birth to the other, who then gives birth to the first."

"And?"

"It's the second riddle in some versions of.... Oedipus!"

Oedipus, of course, Georgina remembered: a man who killed his father, married his mother and put his own eyes out. Uncle Jeremiah's brother was their father and married their mother. There were three Derring-Do sisters... or four now, not two. The riddle had nothing to do with them that she could understand.

"What's the answer to the second riddle?"

"You have to guess."

"Charlotte!"

"Night and day, each gives birth to the other. The words are feminine in Greek – why do languages have genders for words, it's stupid?"

"It's so that we can have lessons in school."

Charlotte made a face.

Three sisters in the Derring-Do Club: a baby, an adult and... but Earnestine didn't use a stick, but she did have an umbrella. The child, the virgin and the crone, but Georgina had been married. The crone, the mother and the child, like Mrs Jago, Mrs Falcone and Miss Millicent, but Georgina herself couldn't be a mother without storks and gooseberry bushes. They were all sisters and there were four sisters now: Earnestine, like the day, begetting the night that was Mrs Frasier.

Georgina threw her arms wide: "This is impossible!"

"I did say."

Miss Charlotte

But, thought Charlotte, when you've eliminated the impossible, then only the possible is left. That didn't sound right.

"Allow me," Charlotte said.

"Be my guest."

"I get a deer stalker hat, a magnifying glass and a pipe."

"This isn't the time to make demands."

Charlotte folded her arms.

"Very well, but no pipe."

Charlotte drew herself up to her full five foot two: "Facts!"

"You know the facts."

277

"Why don't we ask him?"

"Ask who? Sherlock Holmes? Conan Doyle?"

"Uncle Jeremiah." Charlotte raised a silencing finger to Georgina's gathering objection. "There may be visiting hours."

"What if we're stopped?"

"We say we're going to visit our Uncle in prison."

"What if they don't allow visits?"

"We say 'oh, that's a shame'."

"This is your trick, isn't it? To have your excuses worked out beforehand."

"No."

"What if he doesn't want to talk to us?"

"Gina, we could always wrangle another story out of him. He can't say 'no' to us."

"You have a point."

"He might have macaroons."

"In prison!?"

"They have to eat something other than gruel."

Georgina opened the door and peeked out: "No-one about."

Charlotte picked up the umbrella and opened the door properly.

"What are you doing with that?"

"Protection."

"Give it to me, Lottie," Georgina chided. "You could take someone's eye out with that."

They set off, down the corridor and into the canteen. They knew that this wasn't the way to the prison; the walls had very clearly marked labels directing people to the Judiciary, the Prison and Temporal Engineering. However, the canteen made a useful psychological base camp. It had biscuits too, hard oatcakes that were dry and again fit the bill for an expedition. Once they'd sat at the rude tables long enough to see a few people enter and leave, they decided, without a word, that it was now or never.

At the Rotunda, they turned left towards the Prison section.

Charlotte leant again the wall to peer along the various corridors.

When she was sure, Charlotte said, "It's clear."

"Thank goodness."

"This is cold."

"What's cold?"

"The wall."

"Well, of course it is."

"It's slightly damp."

"I dare say this glorious new world has a few building problems same as any era."

They went straight ahead, fighting both the impulse to stride purposefully and to shuffle furtively. At the end, there was a stone staircase, wide and open, leading both up and down. Charlotte followed the stair up to the landing, where it backed around to go up to the next level. There was a barrier across the landing, heavy wood with iron reinforcing. Looking down, there was a similar obstruction below, but this was just wooden.

"Why is their security heavier to leave than to keep people in the prison?" she asked quietly.

"I was wondering that. There must be something upstairs. The cells are down."

They went down.

Although the barrier was all the way across the half-landing, there was a normal sized door cut into the middle and this was open. They went through, crossing the line between simply pretending to be lost and genuinely trespassing. On the wall facing them, there was a curved mirror designed to allow the Desk Sergeant to see up the staircase. It also allowed them to see that the man was reading a penny-dreadful.

Georgina started to ask the obvious: "How are we going... Charlotte?"

Charlotte sauntered over to desk.

"Hello," she said.

The Sergeant started, his feet jerking off the desk and his chair nearly capsizing.

"Miss... I..."

"That's *Half-penny Marvel*, isn't it?"

The man glanced at the cover of his lurid magazine: "Yes."

"Is there a Sexton Blake story?"

"Yes."

"Is it good?"

"I've not read it yet."

"Oh, but it's the best bit."

"I think so too, so I leave it until last."

"Georgina and I shouldn't be long."

"Right you are, Miss."

As she went past, Charlotte saw Georgina smiling at the Sergeant with a crookedness to her mouth as if her face didn't agree with the deception.

"Excuse me, Miss, but–"

"Ma'am," said Georgina. "I'm married."

"Sorry Ma'am."

They rounded the corner.

It was all they could do to stop themselves giggling with excitement and relief.

Further on, they found a Warder.

"Excuse me," Georgina asked. "We're here to visit Unc– Jeremiah Deering, a prisoner."

The man considered them suspiciously, but he went to a ledger and checked.

"Deering... Deering... Let me see. Carstairs, Conway, Danton, Deering – Doctor Deering, here we are. No, I'm afraid no visits are allowed."

"Why not?"

"Says here, 'NK', that's 'Non-contemporaneous Knowledge' – means he can tell people things that could lead to the end of the world."

280

"Oh – what if we promised not to ask him about that?"

He snorted, his moustache flaring with the exhalation.

"We'll be going then," said Georgina. "Sorry to have bothered you."

"Miss."

"It's Ma'am."

Georgina led Charlotte back around the corner.

"But–" Charlotte began, but Georgina raised her finger and moved closer to whisper.

"I saw the ledger, number nineteen, along there. If I keep him occupied, then you can slip along the corridor and see Uncle."

Charlotte nodded.

"Find out about the... find out everything."

Charlotte saluted: "Yes Ma'am."

Georgina strode back and rapped the desk top with the umbrella handle to gain the man's complete attention: "Excuse me, but I wondered who I might ask for permission to see Doctor Deering?"

"That would be Mrs Frasier. I can ring through."

"That would be most satisfactory."

The man turned to the contraption on the wall, lifted the earpiece off and wound a small handle. Georgina's hand waved desperately around her bustle and Charlotte, keeping low, snuck past and down the corridor.

The passage ahead was dark and narrow with doors on either side. They were numbered in big white letters like the houses on streets with the odd numbers on the left and the even numbers on the right. Each door was cast iron, spotted with rivets around the edge with a slot for parcels in the centre and a spy hole. Charlotte tiptoed along, ducking in case the prisoner inside might be looking out. After three doors, there was a gap created by a buttress and arch, then another three doors. That was one to six, seven to twelve and another supporting arch and, finally, thirteen to eighteen before a blank wall.

281

There wasn't a nineteen!

Wait, as her eyes had become accustomed to the gloom, she saw that the end wall, contained an iron door, black on dark brick, with no number.

When she reached it, her eyes were level with the slot because she was bent so low. It was designed to put things in, and then shunt them into the cell, without ever having to open the door.

She stood.

The eyehole was higher than her forehead and designed for tall Warders and Peelers, rather than little girls who were out-of-bounds.

She raised herself on tiptoe and could just see through.

The view was strange, distorted like a Hall of Mirrors at the fairground, as the image was stretched out, so she could observe the whole room, everything except the door itself. There was little to see: a simple bed and a desk. Uncle Jeremiah, his wild sideburns as unruly as his thinning hair, sat on the bed peering over his half-moon glasses at a book.

Charlotte knocked.

The iron door was too big to carry the noise.

"Uncle Jeremiah... Uncle Jeremiah..."

She tapped the service hatch. It sounded like a cymbal and Charlotte jumped, afraid that the noise would attract the Warder. The corridor behind her was dark and empty, but still full of menace.

"Who's there?"

"It's me, Charlotte... Charlotte Deer–"

"Lottie! Little Lottie!"

"Shhh..."

"Lottie – whatever are you doing here? How? You can't be here. You'll get into trouble. Why are you always getting into trouble, Lottie?"

"Uncle, we need to know what's going on."

"But if you are here, then you already know."

"We know about the Temporal Peelers and the Chronological Court, but there's more."

"More?"

"You had a patent under St. George's statue in Earnestine's office, the Patent Pending Office, and—"

"So that's what Boothroyd meant."

"Yes, and there was a book missing from your rooms, the one you gave..." Charlotte lowered her voice. "Mrs Frasier."

"Mrs Frasier?"

"Yes, and we know that she's... well, Ness."

"You know that she's Earnestine!?"

"Yes."

"Oh dear Lord."

"But there's more isn't there?"

Charlotte became aware of her breathing, a faraway moan and distant footsteps.

"Uncle?"

"I can't... this is terrible. What have I done?"

"Uncle, the book, I got it off Mrs Frasier."

"You did," said Uncle Jeremiah. "She won't be happy about that."

She heard him stumble around inside the cell and other noises, a striding thump-thump and a sharper clack-clack: many boots and one set of narrower heels.

"Uncle?"

She jumped at the clattering noise. The service hatch shifted, pulled into the cell and something landing in it making it resound like a drum.

"Who's C. M.?" Charlotte asked.

"The hatch."

Charlotte pulled the metal handle back and the hatch clunked towards her. Inside was a rod or sceptre with a jewel at the end. She reached for it like a little girl pushing her hand into the jar for some humbugs.

The footsteps increased in volume and pace, closing in.

"Charlotte," Uncle Jeremiah whispered urgently. "I must tell you everything."

Charlotte put her ear to the door: "Go on."

She listened, clutching the book to herself, the book called... and her Uncle tried to explain. He'd told her so many stories of adventure when she was young as she'd sat by the roaring fire on Tosca the Tiger, tales that began 'once upon a time...' and ended 'happily ever after'. This one too was about 'once' and 'time' and 'ever after'.

"Well, well, well."

Charlotte turned to see the familiar face of Earnestine looming over her, full of tight lipped disapproval and anger, but it wasn't her sister: it was Mrs Frasier flanked by two Scrutinisers.

"Lottie, dear Lottie," said Mrs Frasier and she snatched the book off her. "The Time Machine – mine I think."

"What you're doing, it's–"

"What has he told you?"

"Everything! I know–"

But she never got to finish her sentence.

Chapter XVIII

Mrs Frasier

Mrs Frasier examined the scrawl inside the flyleaf and then snapped the book shut. H. G. Wells, she thought, had a lot to answer for.

She put it down on her desk, her finger resting on the cover as if she were holding the sphinx down. It was... unfortunate that Jeremiah had talked to Charlotte.

If only she could go back and change it, if only she could undo those five minutes – and they couldn't have talked for longer than that – and make everything right again.

But then she did have a time machine and agents at her beck and call, so it was moderately straight forward.

Yes, she could save Georgina and, mostly importantly, Earnestine. Save Earnestine, that was essential. To save herself, she'd have to do that. And there had been an attempt on the young girl here in the future: it beggared belief. Posterity – that was all that mattered, and as for the others: well, the Derring-Do Club would have to make sacrifices.

She picked up the telephone and spun the handle.

A voice sounded, distant and distorted.

"Get me Scrutiniser Jones – at once."

There was a kerfuffle at the other end of the line, a shouted instruction across the Peelers' guardroom, but before the long the officer came on.

"I have a mission for you," Mrs Frasier said. "A little searching and a little rubbing out."

"Expunction, Ma'am?" said the distant Scrutiniser.

"Yes."

She busied herself with papers until Scrutiniser Jones and Chief Examiner Lombard arrived in her office. The details needed going through, the time and place, but her

285

sisters had been together in the court room. Georgina would have talked to Earnestine back in the small library, of course, but that couldn't be helped. Ripples always spread outwards with unforeseen consequences. The two of them were out of the way, which was the main thing, and so Lombard and his team had plenty of time.

Time – ha! It felt like it was running out.

Lombard knew what to do, the tall man nodding as she gave him his instructions.

"Have you found out anything about that assassin?"

"No, Ma'am," said the Chief Examiner. "We're working on it. Checker Rogers had a hunch and he's... well, checking."

Mrs Frasier smiled at the gaunt, tall Chief Examiner, so unsuited in appearance for making a joke.

And what about Uncle Jeremiah, Mrs Frasier thought.

He really could no longer be trusted. He had been there at the start telling her stories by the roaring fire, planting ideas of adventure and exploration in her head, and suggesting, oh so casually, the thoughts that had changed her life.

He'd have to be tried next. Incommunicado, so that he didn't say anything inopportune at the wrong moment, even though that went against her policy. Due process was important. She'd put it off for as long as she could, but now he was simply too dangerous. If only... but he had objected to their use of the technology. It was time.

Time... she huffed: that book, that bloody book.

Try as she might to ignore the impulse, the bonds were too strong. She had to see him. She set off along the corridor with Scrutiniser Jones in tow before she actively considered the decision, but she was walking there, so somehow she had already made the choice.

The room did not have a roaring fire and there was no glass of port to have on the sly. Doctor Deering sat on the edge of the bed with his books clutched to his chest and his half-moon glasses perched on his nose. She was conscious for the first time of how old he was. It had never mattered before, but now he seemed shrunk, diminished, as if somehow he was being reduced by some Temporal Ague as he readied himself to be rubbed away.

The man had always been so vital and alive, needing the merest of nudges to send him back in time from 'happily ever after' to 'once upon a time'.

"Uncle," she said, "I would like a story, a simple tale of Derring-Do, an adventure with heroes and heroines, where the villains all talk in funny foreign accents."

"You don't have to do this, my dear."

Mrs Frasier towered above him.

"I am in blood stepped so far that, should I wade no more, returning were so tedious as go o'er."

"Earnestine–"

"Yes," she said, kneeling down in front of him and taking his hand. "And I do have to do this. But the young Earnestine will take over and be me, but with my slate wiped clean, my innocence and my honour will be restored."

"But–"

"I trust her when all men doubt me, but make allowance for their doubting."

"Charity, have pity."

"We're nearly there, so close..."

"Mrs Frasier... please?"

"Call me Ness."

Doctor Deering looked at her, pleading in his eyes.

"We have our parts to play, Jeremiah," she prompted.

"Only her friends call her 'Ness'."

Scrutiniser Jones appeared at the door: "It's time, Ma'am."

"Jeremiah?"

Mrs Frasier waited. She knew that time was running out, that the act must be completed, but she knew that she couldn't rush the dear old man.

Doctor Deering for his part considered for a long time, his unruly brows furrowed and animated by the turmoil within until, finally, he spoke.

"I will... Earnestine."

Miss Deering-Dolittle

Earnestine went through the legal process again: reading the charges, pleas, prosecution, defence, summing up, jury deliberation, verdict and finally the sentencing. Her tapping count added another pencil mark to the list and each step had a few, tiny smudges of graphite attention already. She had copies of the paperwork, even blank forms that could be filled in, but none of it seemed like an answer.

"She was caught," said Georgina summing up. She had paced about the room, distractingly. The oak tables, floor and shelves were used to silence and study for a 100 years... 200 years now, and not the agitation of an angry and distraught young lady.

"She'll be told off, detention, lines," said Earnestine. "The usual."

"The usual?!"

Earnestine sighed: Charlotte was a handful. Georgina and Earnestine had always had to endure those lectures in the Principal's study about their errant sibling. She seemed to get away with murder. Perhaps not killing exactly, but crimes that the schools sometimes claimed were worse, and they'd had to endure Charlotte's telling-off second-hand.

"Yes, Georgina, it was foolish of you to try and see Uncle Jeremiah."

Privately Earnestine thought it would have been a jolly good idea, if it had worked. She was sure a long talk with their Uncle would clear up a lot of things, as it always had. She'd much rather be sitting by his roaring fire listening to his stories, they filled her head with such ideas.

"Ness?"

"Did she talk to him?"

"I think so," said Georgina. "We found out he was in cell nineteen and Charlotte made it down the corridor."

"Then when you find her, she'll tell you what she's learnt."

"When will that be?"

"Look," Earnestine snapped, her hand hovering over her books. "I have a lot to do here and you aren't helping."

"What's the point of all this?"

"Mrs Frasier–"

"You."

"Me, then, is using the legal system to cement power," Earnestine said and she held her hands wide to encompass all the books: "This is the playing field–"

"It's not hockey."

"*And* if we can prove Uncle Jeremiah is innocent, then we can have as many conversations with him as we want."

Georgina pointed her finger and flushed even more with anger, but she said nothing: it made sense, Earnestine thought, it did make sense.

"Thank you."

Georgina bowed her head: "What can I do to help?"

"Read these and find something we can use."

"Where do I start?"

"Anywhere is as good as anywhere else."

Georgina pulled a chair out, but as she did so there was a sharp knock at the door. Two Peelers came in. One of them was the bulky Scrutiniser Jones.

"We're here to escort Mrs Merryweather to her room."

"I'm not a prisoner."

"Of course not," he replied. "We're here to escort you to your room."

"It's not time," said Georgina. Earnestine noticed that she was fiddling with that man's watch, yet again.

"Your room, Ma'am."

289

Georgina pushed the chair back making Earnestine smirk because of the scraping noise she managed to generate.

"And you, Miss?" said Scrutiniser Jones to Earnestine.

"I need some more time to consult the books," Earnestine said.

The big man nodded.

"I'll find Charlotte," Georgina said.

"Yes," said Earnestine, distracted. "Sort the silly girl out."

Left alone, Earnestine turned her attention back to the books, but the case studies blurred in front of her tired eyes. Her neck hurt, the recent bruising kept rubbing against her collar.

There must be a loophole.

There were probably dozens of them, but she'd need to study law, and Universities frowned upon women reading male subjects.

And she wasn't a woman yet; she was only a girl.

Reading the charges, pleas, prosecution, defence, summing up, jury deliberation, verdict and finally the sentencing. The point of her pencil broke with a certain finality.

They were like stations on a railway line and the timetable was quite clear and rigid. She needed to adjust the points somewhere, get the court onto a branch line or...

"Oh!"

She scrabbled through the heap of all her notes and found the list of charges.

"Ah!"

There it was – a branch line into the unknown.

And risk it on one turn of pitch-and-toss...

She'd confront the woman first, of course: play by the rules.

Mrs Arthur Merryweather

Georgina was practically frog-marched from Judiciary to the Accommodation wing and, she realised, she still had Earnestine's umbrella with her, such was her annoyance. When they reached the Rotunda, Mrs Frasier happened to be coming out of Temporal Engineering with Chief Examiner Lombard.

"Gina," Mrs Frasier said.

"Mrs Frasier."

"Please, Gina, you've always called me Ness."

Georgina moved on, biting her lip and then, best foot forward she thought. She broke away from the two Peelers and ran back.

"What have you done with Charlotte?" she demanded.

Mrs Frasier turned to her in surprise: "Gina, what is it?"

"Charlotte! Don't deny it, I was there, I saw you and those thugs go to the cell."

"Me?"

"Yes, you, when the Warder tele-voiced you."

"I simply do not know who you are referring to. I've been to the past," Mrs Frasier said. "I've not been here."

"Don't lie!"

Mrs Frasier turned to Chief Examiner Lombard: "Do you know what this is about?"

Georgina was infuriated: "Where is Charlotte?"

Mrs Frasier turned a kindly eye towards Georgina and smiled: "Charlotte? I'm afraid I don't recall anyone named Charlotte."

The Chief Examiner coughed: "You were in the past, Ma'am, outside the aethereal field."

"Oh, you changed something?"

"Yes, Ma'am, on your orders."

"I see."

"You changed..." Georgina tried to understand. All these euphemisms and strange words: aethereal fields,

fields of aether, the fundamental substance of time and space, and 'changed'...

"You've killed her!"

"We have not," the Chief Examiner replied, "we have removed her from history."

"That's.... murder!"

"No, no, you don't understand. She was never born. You can't kill someone who was never born."

"Never..."

The Chief Examiner grinned, showing his bad teeth.

Mrs Frasier spoke in soft, understanding tones: "Georgina, whatever it was, it was for the best. You must understand that."

"I'll never understand."

"Please Gina, there's no need to create a scene."

"Create a scene!?"

"Jones, I think my sister needs to lie down."

"Ma'am," said the big man. He put his big hand on Georgina's shoulder and guided her, she had no choice, to her room. Mrs Frasier came too, keeping an eye on her until they'd locked the door.

For a few moments Georgina heard Mrs Frasier talking: "What was that about? She mentioned a sister... Charlotte, I think she said."

"Nothing to worry about, Ma'am," Chief Examiner Lombard answered. "All gone now."

"Will there be plaque to this 'Charlotte' on the memorial wall?"

"Already seen to, Ma'am."

"Jolly good," said Mrs Frasier as their voices and footsteps receded. "We need to increase security..."

A cold grip spread across Georgina's chest as if the fire had long died in a room.

Charlotte removed from history.

Mrs Frasier, Charlotte's own sister, didn't even remember her.

It was unthinkable.

292

Charlotte gone.

How many others?

Had they had a fourth sister? A fifth? Or a brother? Was she next? Or Earnestine?

Georgina's hands twisted into claws in front of her as if she were trying to grasp Charlotte's ghost from the air and hold on. There was nothing there, of course, not even phantoms, but if Charlotte had never been born, never lived, then she was even denied the afterlife.

'The usual' and 'sort the silly girl out' – that's what Mrs Frasier had... what Earnestine had said, mere minutes ago. She didn't care about Charlotte, didn't care now and didn't care then... won't care *whenever*.

There was a strange noise, a gasping and when it happened again, Georgina realised that it was her own fractured breathing.

She sat on the bed, abruptly and with force, and the springs heaved and shifted beneath her weight, but awkwardly.

Her bag was still hidden beneath the mattress. She took it out, mechanically and with no real feeling. Her emotions were draining away, leeching from her body and leaving her like a cold, broken mechanism.

There was something sharp in the bag, a corner of a hard rectangle. It was the framed daguerreotype. She took it out, turned it over and saw the image of a happier time, when the six of them had been outside the theatre – except that there were only five figures: Caruthers and Earnestine standing to the back and in the front row, McKendry, Uncle Jeremiah and herself. To Georgina's left, the right edge of the frame, there was... nothing. The building was there, the poster, the smeared figure of a man walking behind them, who was now less obscured by the party in the picture, and the empty steps.

She stared at it for a long time, uncomprehendingly, before she cried out, a formless, pitiful syllable that meant nothing and everything. Crying would be a release, an

293

*un*English display in this private cell, but the bottleneck of her tear ducts was too narrow for the floodgates of her despair. She wanted to scream and shout, she wanted to destroy them, to bring down upon them the terrible war because they deserved it. If they had a form for the Conspiracy, then she'd sign it now in a futile gesture of defiance.

Maybe they'd blot her out, rub her away from diaries and letters and pictures, and it would be a blessed relief.

And then there'd be one – the winner.

She remembered hearing that the winners wrote the history books, and these people could *rewrite* the history books.

How could that woman, Earnestine, lose?

Miss Charlotte

Charlotte Rosemary Deering-Dolittle

1885-1975
R. I. P.
Died Aged 15

Victis Honor

Chapter XIX

Mrs Frasier

Aethereal field or no aethereal field, all this jumping about in time was playing havoc with her sleeping pattern. Perhaps she should leave her office and catch up on some rest, but she knew, on today of all days, the hopelessness of that idea. Mrs Frasier checked her watches and did that oft-repeated mathematical calculation in her head. If it was half past ten here... morning, then it was–

The rap at the door was sharp: tap, tap, tap.

"Come in."

Checker Rogers came in smartly: "Ma'am."

"You have a report."

"Yes, Ma'am."

He didn't say anything further. Mrs Frasier understood why ancient rulers executed messengers bearing bad news: they wasted so much time putting off the inevitable.

"Rogers?"

"I found out who our corpse was."

"Corpse?"

"The man who tried to kill Miss Deering-Dolittle."

"And?"

"I had a hunch."

"Please Rogers, just tell me."

"He worked for a parliamentary group, a sort of clerk or fixer."

Rogers stopped talking.

Mrs Frasier sat back in her fine chair, heard the leather squeak and felt her back stretch over her bustle. This day was never going to end and she'd thought the months and months leading up to it were purgatory.

"He was a Fadge Man," said Rogers.

"Fadge Man?"

"You know what 'fadge' means?"

"It's a quarter penny... oh, farthing."

"Yes, Ma'am."

"I thought he'd come into line rather too smartly."

"You're not angry, Ma'am."

"No, Rogers – I'm not happy, not happy at all – but any ill feelings are directed against Lord Farthing," she nodded and smiled, tight-lipped, but containing some warmth. "You've done well, Rogers."

"Do you want me to..."

"No... not yet."

Rogers shuffled uncomfortably.

"I realise the danger," she said, "but we can't remove him from history before he's made history."

Mrs Frasier mulled over the news and found she wasn't surprised. Somewhere there was a piece of paper with all the possible groupings: helper, hinderer, hanger-on. Lord Farthing had been in one division, now she knew he was in another. Well, it was merely a matter of a few seconds to add his name to the list, but vexing to have to wait until his usefulness was over.

"Bloody Farthing," said Mrs Frasier, aloud. A penny for her thoughts? She should not have trusted a man whose title only came up to a quarter of a penny: a fadge by any other name. "Does Chief Examiner Lombard know?"

"No, Ma'am. I came straight here."

"We'd better brief everyone, double the guard and everyone carries swords."

"Yes, Ma'am."

Mrs Frasier stood and Checker Rogers opened the door for her. She strode out along the corridor towards the Rotunda, conscious that she'd left her own sword in her office. She should go back for it.

"Mrs Frasier, Mrs Frasier?" It was a female voice.

She rounded: "What now?"

It was Earnestine.

"Yes?"

"Mrs Frasier, I need to talk to you."
"I don't have time right now."
"But Mrs Frasier–"
"Don't whine."
Earnestine's lips went tight and she flushed, angrily.
"Earnestine," Mrs Frasier said, "don't be such a child!"

Miss Deering-Dolittle

Earnestine's face burned with shame.

To be told off *by herself.*

Like a child.

Mrs Frasier, having cut her to the quick, had departed towards Temporal Engineering, striding without a care or a backward glance. She was happy to see others put on trial, but she'd clearly never been brought to book herself.

Well, I'll show her, Earnestine thought, so she hurried too, taking tiny steps, with her dress clutched and held above the ground as if she were running for a train. The Clerk of the Court was hastening along too. Earnestine picked a spot, tucked into a doorway and chose her moment perfectly.

She stepped out.

They crashed in a flurry of apologies and papers.

"Oh, oh, I'm so sorry," she said automatically, as she bent down to retrieve his fallen documents, her own falling into the mix. Quickly, she gathered them back up.

"It's fine, fine," said the Clerk, flustered.

They were both standing upright soon enough, each with a disordered collection. The clerk sorted his, trying to straighten them to bring order back to the world.

"Is everything satisfactory?" Earnestine asked.

The man glanced at his paperwork.

"So sorry," said Earnestine, handing him his wig.

He'd checked, a quick glance, she'd seen his eyes scan the page.

"Everything is in order," the Clerk said. The man's face furrowed showing confusion and suspicion, his eyes narrowed. It was obvious that he knew he'd been gulled and – yes – he checked that his watch and chain were in order with a pat of his stomach.

"Good day, Miss," he said, and he went on his way.

Earnestine skipped to catch up.

"Mrs Frasier said I could attend the court," she said. "I have a note."

She gave it to him.

Now he was suspicious.

"It's in her handwriting," Earnestine said sweetly, hoping her handwriting wasn't due to change in the years to come.

"Oh, very well," he said.

They went on, through the side entrance and into the court proper.

"Just sit... there," said the Clerk.

She sat, meekly, and folded her hands together in her lap once she'd placed her own papers on the table. She waited patiently, fighting her agitation down, and eventually the court was called to stand.

The judge came in, blinked in surprise at Earnestine's presence. He sat on his throne on the higher bench and looked down at the Clerk.

The Clerk stood.

He read from the charge sheet: "For conspiracy to thwart the course of justice, the accused one Miss Earn–"

The man baulked.

"Go on, I say, go on."

"There is some mistake, Your Honour."

"Nonsense, read the sheet, I say, read the sheet."

"Your Honour, I must decline."

"Who signed it?"

The Clerk checked the foot of the page: "Mrs Frasier."

The functionary glanced at Earnestine, realising.

"If it's written down, then it must be true," said Earnestine softly, but audibly.

"Quite so," the Judge agreed.

The Clerk straightened: "For conspiracy to–"

"We've heard all that," said the Judge.

"Your Honour, the Chronological Committee arraigns one, Miss Earnestine Deering-Dolittle."

There was a sharp intake of breath. This hadn't been in anyone's script.

Earnestine walked calmly, but quickly to avoid Checker Rogers' move to intercept her, and she climbed the wooden steps to the dock. High above the lawyers, and on show in this box, she could see the whole panorama of the legal process spread out before her. She stood erect and took hold of the brass railing around the raised wooden stage to steady herself.

The Public Gallery was writhing with punching fist gestures and angry faces.

The Clerk pounded his gavel: "Silence, silence!"

The Judge adjusted his wig.

"Please state your name for the records," the Clerk demanded.

"I am Miss Earnestine Deering-Dolittle."

"This woman is known to us," said the Judge. "She is our own Mrs Frasier. Take her down from the dock. Take her down, I say."

"Your Honour, I wish to plead."

"But you are innocent. This is known. This is a matter for the history books only."

"Nonetheless, I am here and proper process demands that I enter a plea. It is important that justice is seen to be done. In my time terrible events were planned and so, in effect, everyone from my time must stand partially accountable."

"But there is no crime against your name."

"There is a crime listed upon the arraignment," Earnestine replied.

"Clerk?" the Judge prompted.

The Clerk fussed with his papers: "Your Honour, it was conspiracy to thwart the course of justice."

How apt, Earnestine thought: "Then I will plead against that."

"Oh, very well," said the Judge. "Clerk, do note this down. Note it down, I say."

The Clerk returned to his desk and dipped his pen in his inkwell.

"And you, Prosecutor," the Judge demanded with a stabbing finger motion, "will present no evidence."

"I have no evidence to present, Your Honour," said the lawyer in question, jerked to his feet when his title was mentioned.

The Judge turned to Earnestine: "How do you plead... not guilty? Note it down, Clerk, note it down, I say."

The Clerk started to write in his records with a bold 'N' and then Earnestine spoke, clearly and loudly:

"Guilty."

Mrs Arthur Merryweather

Georgina wore black, of course: she was still in mourning for her late husband. Scrutiniser Jones stood to one side, quiet as a mouse despite his rhino-like build. He had knocked on her door, apologised, and wondered if it would help her to pay her respects.

The wall was tucked away down a side corridor from Judiciary and it looked like the bricks were made of brass. They were plaques, row upon row, column by column, filling the space from the left until they stopped, abruptly, a third of the way along. They contained names, unsorted, hopelessly out of sequence with names, dates and sometimes an epitaph.

She found Charlotte complete with dates that made no sense and '*Victis Honor*' as if she needed encouragement.

"Honour to the vanq... vanquished."

Scrutiniser Jones had a clean handkerchief for her.

"She wouldn't have felt anything, if that's what you are wondering."

"Gone, but not forgotten."

"That's it, Mrs Merryweather."

But it wasn't that at all. It was 'never been and... made up' or some such expression. How long was one supposed to mourn a sister who never was, who never came into being 15 years earlier... or, adding another 75 for the temporal motion, a hundred. It was a century and Georgina was reminded of cricket again.

This was surely against the rules.

A bellow cut through her thoughts. Checker Rogers ran up to them, breathless.

"Jackson..." he stopped short when he saw Georgina. "I beg your pardon Mrs Merryweather. Scrutiniser Jones, we're to arm ourselves and, worse, Miss Deering-Dolittle is for the rope."

"Rope!?"

"Begging you pardon again, Mrs Merryweather, but there's been a court case. Miss Deering-Dolittle stood on trial."

"She's not on the lists," Scrutiniser Jones said.

"That may be as may be, but she was tried nonetheless and guilty it is."

"Guilty! I must see her at once," Georgina demanded.

"She's in the library," said Checker Rogers.

"Take me there, directly."

"Ma'am?"

"Best to do so," said Scrutiniser Jones. "I'll find Lombard and see what's what."

"If you are sure, Jackson."

"You jump along, Gideon."

"Yes, Gov."

Checker Rogers led the way to the small library, eagerly and somewhat forgetful about opening the doors, and

303

Georgina saw Earnestine sitting calmly sitting at the large oak table and dwarfed by the tome laden shelves.

"Ness?"

Earnestine explained what she'd done, enumerating the steps on her fingers and reaching 'guilty' long before her thumb.

"I beg your pardon?"

Earnestine went through it again.

"I..." Georgina began, but words did fail her.

"It was an idea."

"Ness, of all the stupid things, honestly."

Georgina paced up and down in the small library, back and forth as she repeated "of all", "stupid" and "honestly" in various combinations.

"If I am guilty, then Mrs Frasier is guilty and..."

"You are Mrs Frasier. She won't be happy."

"I dare say."

"What's your plan?" Georgina demanded as she stopped pacing for the first time. "Break out of prison, run down the corridor, steal a time vessel and run off to Elizabethan times or the Jurassic or... whatever they call the Year of our Lord, nineteen thousand."

"I will present my case."

Georgina was aghast: "You've pleaded guilty. That's an end to it. All that's left is for the Judge to put on his black cap, pronounce the verdict, you eat a hearty breakfast and then there's the scaffold and the rope."

"I get to make a statement."

"How can you be so calm?"

"I'm–"

"What about me? I've lost Arthur, then Charlotte and now you."

"Charlotte's just in detention."

"She's been erased from history!"

"History detention?"

"No, they went back in time and changed... something and now she was never born. Being erased is worse than being killed. At least with being killed there's a funeral, tea and cucumber sandwiches."

Georgina broke off, fumbled desperately in her bag for Arthur's pocket watch to feel its comforting cold brass in her hand. She touched the frame of the daguerreotype.

"Not me," said Earnestine.

"Not you... yet."

Georgina grabbed the picture and thrust it under Earnestine's face.

"This was taken on that evening after the theatre," Earnestine said, "but–"

Georgina pointed: "Charlotte!!"

"She's... gone."

"She's been erased from history," Georgina said and then, deliberately and slowly, "they went back and changed events so that she was never born."

"But–"

"That's what they do."

"We'll see about that."

Earnestine touched the image lightly, thinking, and then gave the frame back to Georgina.

"We could use the machine ourselves," Earnestine said. "It's just down the corridor. And anyone who has control of time can control anything. Think: we could change history so that Napoleon was never born. Or persuade people not to take part in the Boston Tea Party. The British Empire wouldn't just be a quarter of the globe, but half of it. Pax Britannica would bring peace to so many more people."

"It's too much power."

"Think of the good we could do."

"It's evil."

"Only because of the way it's been used."

"It's meddling in history."

"We could change everything back, restore Charlotte," said Earnestine. "We could teach the Surrey Deering-Dolittles a lesson."

"We could stop Graf Zala before he started and..." Georgina swallowed, her mouth dry and her palms sweating, the watch slippery in her hand, "...save Arthur."

"Would it be right?" Earnestine said. "Perhaps there is a natural course to events that shouldn't be interfered with: God's plan."

"God's plan! To have those monsters kill Arthur!?" Georgina grabbed her sister's arms, her face pleading: "To save Arthur, my husband... we must, we have no choice."

If Earnestine had a reply, she didn't get the chance; there was a sharp rattle of the door as the handle was turned.

"Come in," said Earnestine, her voice faltering.

The door opened and Scrutiniser Jones filled the opening.

"Yes?" Earnestine asked.

Scrutiniser Jones coughed: "The adjournment is over. You are to come with me."

"I'm ready," said Earnestine.

"Honestly, of all... words fail me," Georgina said to Earnestine.

The Scrutiniser led the way and Earnestine followed.

Georgina stayed where she was, wondering when the picture would lose another figure. She shivered: in the morning the Derring-Do Club would consist of one member and then it wouldn't be a club at all.

Georgina picked up Earnestine's umbrella.

But maybe, just maybe, it was her turn to disappear.

Chapter XX

Mrs Frasier

What was the silly child doing?

There was so much to do and now this.

Mrs Frasier heard that familiar voice in the courtroom through the air vent into the Judge's chamber. She'd pleaded guilty – stupidly – and she'd refused counsel, which made things tricky, and now she wanted to make a statement.

What did she know?

What could she say?

She said: "I call to the stand, myself."

The Judge ruled: "You may make your statement from there, Miss."

"I call myself, Your Honour, from my future: Mrs Frasier."

There was a commotion in the Public Gallery. The Judge banged his gavel until there was silence.

"This is most irregular, I say, irregular."

"The accused, upon pleading guilty, is entitled to make a statement," said Earnestine, "and so I call the accused to the stand."

"Mrs Frasier is not accused."

"I am accused, therefore Mrs Earnestine Frasier, née Deering-Dolittle, is accused."

Clever, clever girl, Mrs Frasier thought looking at the air vent, and most unexpected.

The Judge spoke: "You are separate entities."

"Marriage does not wipe the slate clean."

The Judge fumbled with his papers and then looked at the Clerk of the Court: "This is most irregular. Do we have a ruling on this?"

"No, Your Honour," said the Clerk.

"This is most unusual, I say. Most unusual."

307

"Yes, Your Honour."

"Mrs Frasier isn't going to be happy."

"No, Your Honour."

"Very well. Call Mrs Frasier."

The cry went up, repeated along the corridors as a polite hue and cry. Mrs Frasier picked up her skirts and quickly ran to the corridor. It would not do for her to enter from the Judge's chambers: the executive and the judiciary must be seen to be separate, and she'd been most lax about that lately.

She let a Peeler find her.

"Mrs Frasier, Ma'am," he said. "You are wanted in court."

"I know," she said.

She let him lead her around the room to the main door and, when she came in, the tumultuous kerfuffle in the court quietened. Observers didn't know why and so craned their necks around and over their neighbours, until all eyes were focused on her entrance.

Mrs Frasier had arrived.

She moved regally to the centre of the room almost chilling the air as she passed. Finally, her footsteps rang out in the eerie silence as she ascended the witness box.

The Clerk of the Court suddenly realised he was on, so he shuffled forward.

"If it please your... Mrs Frasier – the oath."

His hands shook as he handed up the card and Bible.

"I shall use the Dictionary," she said.

"Ah... I don't think, that is–"

"It's on your desk, red leather."

The Clerk turned to his desk and was shocked to discover the object nestled amongst his reference books. When he pulled it out, he dropped the Bible onto the floor, bent to collect it and then clearly thought better of delaying Mrs Frasier any further.

She swiped the book off him.

"I promise to tell the truth."

"Er... the whole truth and nothing but the truth?"

"That is the truth."

"The whole truth."

"The truth is everything, all things, the whole, and nothing other: the truth."

"Yes, of course, thank you for the lesson," said the Clerk, and he looked to the Judge for support and clarification.

"That is quite acceptable, Mrs Frasier; indeed more than acceptable, I'd say," said the Judge. "And may I add the court's sincere apologies for disturbing you from your important and vital work."

"Thank you."

"It is just..." The Judge held his arms wide in apology. "Due process and all that."

"Of course," Mrs Frasier agreed. "Justice must be seen to be done."

She smiled now at Earnestine, and the girl's face betrayed that she had thought this far in the game, but no further. The young lady shuffled her papers. There was nothing on them, Mrs Frasier knew, and clearly the girl had no idea what she was going to say. Mrs Frasier decided to use her most beneficent of smiles, while she waited for her cue.

"Mrs Frasier," Earnestine began.

"Miss Deering-Dolittle."

"You are guilty of conspiracy to thwart the course of justice."

"I am not."

"You have already pleaded guilty."

"I am not guilty," said Mrs Frasier, "therefore, *you* cannot possible be guilty."

"But now laws are applied retroactively."

"Only if one breaks them."

"Who are we to believe?" Earnestine asked the court sweeping her attention to the Jury.

309

"You are not of age, child, and thus you are too young to plead, one way or the other," said Mrs Frasier, "whereas I am an adult. You are a child."

"I am not!" Earnestine shouted.

The Judge leant forward: "Mrs Frasier's word is such that it cannot be called into question."

Earnestine leaned slightly, having raised her foot, but she didn't stamp it down. "But I'm... 95."

There was a guffaw from the Public Gallery at the ludicrousness of Earnestine's assertion. The young lady went red, which made her appear far more youthful than her twenty biological years.

"Please, Your Honour, forgive her," said Mrs Frasier. "I was impetuous in my youth."

"If Mrs Frasier's word cannot be questioned, then my word cannot be questioned," Earnestine said.

"My dear," said the Judge, "we take Mrs Frasier's word, the elder of our Earnestines as it were."

"It is foolish of us to argue," said Mrs Frasier. "Again."

"Obviously we did. Are. We can't both win this argument."

Mrs Frasier considered Earnestine carefully, weighing up the options: "You are saying that one of us is Triumph and the other Disaster."

"Yes," said Earnestine. "If you can bear to hear the truth you've spoken."

Ah, she's got it, Mrs Frasier realised: "Twisted by knaves to make a trap for fools."

The Judge interrupted: "I beg your pardon, Mrs Frasier."

"We're quoting Kipling, Your Honour."

"Our sister, Charlotte," Earnestine said, "has been removed from history."

"I know," said Mrs Frasier.

Earnestine pounced on this: "How can you suddenly know?"

"When our sister Georgina mentioned it, I decided to read the report."

"Oh, but it was by you? This is murder, Your Honour."

"Habeas Corpus!" said Mrs Frasier. "Show me the body!"

"But my sister... our sister! Do you have no pity?"

"Sacrifices have to be made," said Mrs Frasier. Why wouldn't the silly girl *understand*?

"You–"

"I could do nothing, and even if I could, weighed against the survival of the human species, what is the life of one man? Or child? Not just this generation or yours, but for all generations to come from now until time eternal."

Mrs Frasier pinched the bridge of her imperial nose. She was getting a headache, strong, powerful and full of those flashing lights that somehow whirled inside her cranium. She smoothed down her dress, pulled herself together and faced the young Earnestine for another round, but the child had no more fight in her. She was like a drowning kitten, helpless and forlorn.

"We must stand together," Mrs Frasier said, "now more than ever. The point of changing events is to bring about a better outcome."

"Here, here," came a shout from the Public Gallery.

Mrs Frasier smiled: "Earnestine, it's for your own good."

"That would be your own good."

"Yes! And for the good of all."

"God Bless Mrs Frasier," came another shout from above. "God Bless Mrs Frasier."

The saying was taken up, repeated, and culminated in applause.

Mrs Frasier held up her hand and a hush descended.

"I was charged with perverting the course of justice," she looked around the assembly and it was as if she were

311

addressing each person individually. "I pleaded 'guilty', when I was not of age to do so, but now, today, when perverse justice is being swept aside by true justice, I can at last honestly change my plea to 'not guilty'."

"Very good, very good," said the Judge. "Clerk, upon appeal, I say, upon appeal."

"As I give myself a second chance, so we give the world a second chance."

<u>Miss Deering-Dolittle</u>

Earnestine jumped up, shouting to make herself heard above the clapping: "But, but—"

"No, my dear," said the Judge, and he pointed towards Mrs Frasier. "You have spoken."

The Jury huddled together.

Earnestine felt like a told-off child. All her arguments were nothing, and generated nothing more than a 'there, there' and a pat on the head. She thought that Mrs Frasier, remembering exactly how this had made her feel, would have been more sympathetic. It was so unfair.

"Members of the Jury," said the Judge, "have you reached a verdict?"

"We have, Your Honour."

"Is it unanimous?"

"It is, Your Honour."

"And what is that verdict?"

"Not guilty."

There was applause again from the Public Gallery.

"Mrs Frasier is not guilty," said the Judge. "Clerk, note it down, I say, note it down."

The Clerk picked up his pen and then noticed that he'd already inscribed the letter 'N' by Earnestine Deering-Dolittle's name.

Mrs Frasier smiled: she was happy.

312

Mrs Arthur Merryweather

Whatever Earnestine was doing in the courtroom, Georgina thought, she was generating an excellent distraction. Everyone had left the prison area sometime back, either to cram into the Public Gallery or to hover nearby. This might be her chance.

She gripped the umbrella. If she met anyone, she'd just say she was returning Earnestine's property. She replayed a phrase or two over in her mind like a voice on a wax cylinder, and it sounded just as unconvincing.

When she reached the Rotunda, Mrs Frasier appeared from the courtroom, flanked by Peelers with a downtrodden Earnestine in her wake. They marched through, turning left into the Prison area.

"Move along now," Chief Examiner Lombard announced.

With mumbles and complaints, the crowd moved away, filtering along to the accommodation area with its canteen and smoking room.

Georgina let the crowd push her to one side, closer and closer to the entrance to the Temporal Engineering section.

Chief Lombard checked the area, his height enabling his gaunt face to loom over people's heads. He checked right and left, saw Georgina, looked back to the court room.

Georgina seized the moment, hunched low and sidled behind a loitering workman and slipped down the corridor towards the engineering area.

Did he see her?

She mustn't look back.

He would see her, surely.

She glanced.

Saw his face.

Even so, she nipped around a corner, pressed herself against the wall, and waited, panting with dread.

He'd seen her, definitely seen her.

313

Any moment.

He couldn't have missed her.

She heard something: a foot fall, the clink of sword against buckle, breathing?

And then she'd be hauled off to the court, tried, found guilty and then she'd meet the same fate as poor Charlotte. She wondered what the Latin inscription on her brass plaque would be.

She heard a ruckus behind her.

Don't look.

She twisted her hands around the umbrella handle.

Don't look.

She looked – the Rotunda was empty.

She wasted no more time and moved further along. Soon she reached the Chronological Conveyor itself. There was the dais, surrounded by a brass railing, and there was the technician's post. It was deserted. Her luck was holding out.

She went over to the control lectern.

The surface was covered in a bewildering array of brass dials that could be turned for a date and time. The main slider wouldn't budge, it needed unlocking somehow. In the centre was a hole with a screw thread cut into it. She remembered that something had caught the light when the technician had operated it. Something like... but she didn't know.

However, she was at the machine, so surely she had command of time.

She looked beside the control lectern and found a sword hanging there, but no extra temporal devices. She added Earnestine's umbrella to a spare hook, so that her hands were free.

One person, at the right moment, could alter history. She could erase the Chronological Committee, rescue Charlotte, save Arthur... anything. All she needed to know was the moment in time when the smallest of actions would tip the balance.

Arthur first, she decided, and then he'd know what was for the best.

There were dials to turn, so she did so, slowly at first and then with greater rapidity. They were linked together so that the 18th March 1975 was a Tuesday... Wednesday for the 19th and...

"Bother!"

She was going the wrong way.

She turned them in the other direction moving the dates back from the future... no, from the current present, and then into this era's past.

She must go back to the moment before Arthur was killed.

But when?

Exactly.

If she changed history, stopped him from leaving Magdalene Chase, then they'd never meet. He'd think her some mad woman if she just turned up: 'Oh, Arthur dear, we're going to fall in love, but you mustn't go to Austro-Hungary.' All those moments abutted perfectly, one event following the other, and to change one link would surely cause everything to fall apart.

They could burst in at the last, critical moment – she was sure she would be able to find her way – and then she could save him. She would save the brave Captain Merryweather, but then that would mean that she would see herself.

No, that wouldn't do at all.

Major Dan!

No-one had known where he had been on that fateful day. She could go back the day before and find him, explain and then they could be waiting to save Arthur.

But then what would she do as Arthur saved his bride, her earlier self, while being blissfully unaware of his ex-widow. Perhaps she could go and live on an island knowing he was safe and that would be enough. Would

315

she be jealous of her younger self? If she never saw him again, how would she know he was safe?

Perhaps Charlotte first?

She'd been removed from history, so it must be easier to change those events back again. The proper moment would be just before whenever it was that the Temporal Peelers removed her.

Or was it the instant before they set off back from their time to the past?

She had access to the machine, she could control the destinies of men and nations, but she lacked the knowledge to use it properly.

She stopped turning and let the whirring dials come to rest: Friday 25th August 1922. It was as useless a date as any other she could think of.

Perhaps she could escape? Jump to the 1920s, change her name and stay there. But she would not be able to reset the machine once she was in the Chrononauts' past, so they'd know exactly when, and presumably where, she materialised. They could simply go back to Thursday 24th August 1922 and wait for her to appear.

Or just an hour beforehand with this other panel and its clocks and wotnot.

A critical minute would be all that was needed.

She could go back to when this infernal contraption was invented and smash it up before it was ever used. Everything would then return to normal. All the erased people would be restored to life and daguerreotype.

And how would she operate the controls when she didn't know how and she had to stand on the dais *at the same time*?

Should her first action be to come back to this very moment and operate the controls for herself?

But she wasn't here to save herself.

She glanced at the dais: she didn't appear.

And what would happen to this version of herself afterwards?

But the Chronological Conveyor wasn't invented in the past, it was invented in the future. A railway line only works if it has two stations, so how did the future create a destination conveyor in the past?

"Tricky deciding, isn't it?"

Georgina turned, recognizing Earnestine's voice.

"All of time, every age, every moment, every historic event... but how to choose," said Mrs Frasier.

Georgina fumbled around the control lectern, grabbed Earnestine's umbrella hanging and then saw a sword. She dropped the umbrella and snatched down the weapon, drew it and faced the woman.

"That's not a very polite way to greet your sister."

"I'll use this if I must."

Mrs Frasier's lips tightened in that familiar 'oh-so' superior way: "Really?"

"Yes," Georgina said firmly, "so you just come and operate this while I stand on the dais."

Mrs Frasier folded her arms.

"I'm warning you," Georgina said, and she took a step forward, the sharp tip pointing waveringly at Mrs Frasier's throat. "I don't have all day."

Quick as lightning, Mrs Frasier swiped the sword to one side and then, stepping close, she struck Georgina's wrist hard.

The sword clattered away.

Mrs Frasier used the back of her other hand to slap Georgina across the face. The young lady fell, more out of shock than the actual impact.

"Oh, dear," said Mrs Frasier, "another interfering Derring-Do."

Georgina put her hand to her mouth, tasting blood.

"Jones! Get the sword."

Scrutiniser Jones appeared: Georgina hadn't even realised he was there. With a scraping noise, the man, agile for his bulk, picked up the fallen weapon. It looked like a hat pin in his huge hands.

317

"What were you thinking?" Mrs Frasier said.

"I was going to undo whatever you did to Charlotte."

"This Charlotte again!"

"Yes, so... please."

"Just Charlotte?"

Georgina knew what she meant. This older Earnestine could see straight through her just as the younger Earnestine knew when she was bluffing in Bridge.

"I wanted to save my husband."

Scrutiniser Jones gave the sword to Mrs Frasier. She slashed it back and forth testing its weight. Clearly she knew what she was doing, whereas Georgina hadn't had a clue. Sword fighting looked easy when she'd seen it in the theatre, Shakespeare and so forth, but the reality was so much harder. Mrs Frasier slipped the blade back into its scabbard, but Georgina was under no illusions that this made her any safer.

"Are you going to kill me?" she asked.

"What do you think?"

"I'm not afraid."

"It's not the lack of fear that counts; it's the controlling of one's fear."

"Charlotte, me... you can't remove everyone."

"Oh, I think I can," said Mrs Frasier, "there are only thirty million people in the country, a hundred million in the Empire and, say, four times that in the whole world."

"You're mad," said Georgina. "Your own sisters! You've already erased Charlotte, if you *un*make me that would leave only Ness."

"And then there were two," said Mrs Frasier.

"One!"

"Ness and myself."

"That's one."

"Counted twice."

"She doesn't agree with you."

"She doesn't agree with me *yet*."

"What if she never does?"

"Oh, I have a plan," Mrs Frasier said, pointing the sheathed sword straight towards her, "I think, Georgina, it's time you met Arthur Merryweather."

Chapter XXI

Mrs Frasier

It was as if nothing had happened. Indeed nothing had happened, and it was all proceeding splendidly again.

Earnestine was in a cell like a naughty child to learn her lesson, Jones was taking Georgina to wait in the library and little Lottie, according to her report, wouldn't be bothering anyone. The pieces were in position at last, she thought.

Mrs Frasier drew her sword. It felt familiar in her hand, the ridges of the handle and the central bulge meaning that her grip was firm. She touched the edge with her finger, felt the sharp point, and tested the balance – far, far better than she was used to – and an excellent weapon. All she had to ensure was that she followed through.

The blade fitted the scabbard well and the baldric went over her shoulder easily. The blade didn't hang properly at first as the hilt couldn't decide whether to lean over or behind the hard edge of her corset, but eventually, sliding the strap backwards and moving it outside her bosom, it found a natural lay. She made her way through the future to her office comforted by the slap and flick that the weapon made as she marched.

She had an appointment.

She checked her gold pocket watch just as a double knock resounded loudly on the door.

Mrs Frasier tidied her papers before calling out: "Come in."

The door opened and Chief Examiner Lombard came in with another young Temporal Peeler, a young man with the start of a fine horseshoe moustache.

"Ma'am, this is Checker–"

321

"Ah! Come in, come in," said Mrs Frasier, standing and coming around her desk with her hand extended. "It has been such a long time."

The man shuffled, embarrassed, and shook his leader's hand.

"You've been briefed?"

"Yes, Ma'am."

Mrs Frasier smiled like a proud aunt: "If you are sure you can face her."

"I can, I want to."

"That's my brave boy."

"Ma'am," said Lombard. "It'll be time soon for Miss Deering-Dolittle."

"Oh, yes, of course, I remember. She's in her cell, isn't she?"

"Yes, Ma'am... only a matter of time."

"You wait for years and then it all happens at once."

"Yes, Ma'am. The little bird will fly soon."

"There's a special providence in the fall of a sparrow. If it be now, 'tis not to come; if it be not to come, it will be now; if it be not now, yet it will come: the readiness is all."

"Hamlet," said the young Checker.

"Act five," the Chief Examiner said. "Well chosen, Ma'am, a date with destiny for all of us."

"Are we ready?" said Mrs Frasier as she looked from one man to the other: they both nodded. "Then we should put our best foot forward."

Miss Deering-Dolittle

The cell door and the jam weren't aligned properly.

A fringe of light cast around one edge of the doorway, not enough to penetrate the cell, but a hint that the Scrutiniser hadn't closed the door properly. Chief Lombard had arrived suddenly. Earnestine hadn't caught the hurried conversation as they'd bundled her into the cell quickly and then trooped off. It was an appalling lapse.

On her toes, Earnestine stepped over and listened.

There was silence.

A cry, distant... maybe.

There was no handle on the inside of the door and she couldn't get her fingers around the edge. It was heavy, cast iron. She tried high up and low down, even trying to find a gap under the door. It was no use. In frustration she thumped it and the tiny gap vanished with a heart rending clang. Call herself an Adventuress: she couldn't even escape from an unlocked cell.

NO, it wasn't an adventure!

She thumped the door again, punishing her hand because of her own foolishness. She was such a baby sometimes and–

The gap was back.

She put her fingers to the solid iron and pushed. When she let go, the door sprang back – just not enough.

She tried with both hands, and then again pushing opposite the massive hinges.

Oh, so close now, just... she broke a nail, but, by sixteenths of an inch, she eased the door open until she could squeeze the ends of her fingers into the gap and pull.

Outside, the corridor was empty.

Georgina had said that she and Charlotte had found out that Uncle Jeremiah was in Cell 19. Earnestine glanced at the doors to get her bearings and then she scooted down to the far end.

"Uncle! Uncle!" she hissed.

She peered through the tiny hole in the door and saw the magnified and distorted cell interior.

It was empty.

Just as she was about to leave, she saw the hatch and nestling at the bottom was a sparkling object. She picked

323

it out and saw a thing of beauty, a rod with a jewel attached to the end. She tucked it into her belt.

Back she went, carefully, slipping into the shadows of the cell doorways, until she could peek around the corner.

The desk was empty.

The Warder was nowhere to be seen.

Despite her best attempts, she had been found 'not guilty' and yet they'd locked her up. Or rather not. She been taken to a cell and Mrs Frasier had been called away by Chief Examiner Lombard. This odd kerfuffle was why the cell door had not been locked. It had seemed to Earnestine strangely choreographed, moves on a chessboard being played out to some unknown end.

It felt like a trap.

Or was that destiny breathing down her neck?

But she'd been locked up, or could have been, so how could it be a trap?

They were all acting out some pre-arranged sequence, but then that was history. Wasn't it?

She made it to the stone stairs and went up, step by step, craning her neck to see if anyone was above her. She couldn't go any higher as the stairwell was blocked off. So, she had to get out on this level, where the Rotunda was effectively a crossroads linking the prison cells, the dormitories, the court rooms and ahead was Temporal Engineering with the Chronological Conveyor.

She heard some people approaching, so she slipped through a door held it open a crack, so it wouldn't slam and so she could see who was passing.

It was Mrs Frasier striding along with Chief Examiner Lombard and a much younger Temporal Peeler.

"It is the essence of time travel," Mrs Frasier said loudly, "that means one is always a step ahead."

They'd gone.

She'd give it a couple of minutes just to be on the safe side.

Earnestine was in a cloakroom full of Temporal Peeler equipment and uniforms. She considered a disguise, but she'd not seen a female Peeler. Even so, she strapped on a sword and stole a pair of the peculiar white glasses. Amazingly she could see through them and the sword felt comforting, reminding her of the Duelling Machine back at the Patent Pending Office. She checked the blade, Sheffield steel, and it slipped easily back into its scabbard.

Peering through the gap again, she satisfied herself that the coast was clear and stepped out.

Mrs Arthur Merryweather

"You wanted your Arthur back... here he is."

Georgina stood, pushing the chair back with her legs, and placed her hands in front of her. She was in the small library with all its heavy books, taken there by Mrs Frasier and Scrutiniser Jones, and told to wait. Scrutiniser Jones had stayed to keep an eye on her and his big bulk had blocked any chance of another escape attempt.

The man with Mrs Frasier was a youngster, barely a man, and yet she saw, vaguely, a hint in his features of the man she had fallen in love with.

"Who is this?" she asked.

"Arthur Merryweather."

Georgina shook her head: "He isn't my Arthur."

"Oh, but he is," Mrs Frasier said, and she turned to the young man, who stared at Georgina open mouthed. "Arthur, this is Georgina, Mrs Arthur Merryweather, your mother."

"My... mother," he said, shocked. He seemed to go pale in front of Georgina's eyes.

"He was named after his father."

He shook his head adamantly: "You aren't my mother: my mother abandoned me, left me."

Georgina swallowed, trying to think of something to say. Her legs felt hollow.

325

"You abandoned me!" said Arthur.

"I—"

"I was all alone at Magdalene Chase, left in that windswept desolation. If mother... if Mrs Fitzwilliam had not been there for me? She was more of a mother to me than you ever were."

"Mrs Fitzwilliam? Who is Mrs Fitzwilliam?"

Mrs Frasier chuckled: "You knew her... know her as Mrs Falcone. She married the Colonel and brought up young Arthur as if he were her own."

"Falcone – no!"

"Yes, *mother*," said the young man. "You left me. All those years in that dark, dark place... a Bleak House. You left me there and Mrs Fitzwilliam was the only one who really cared for me."

Mrs Frasier coughed.

"And Auntie Ness, of course," he added.

"But why would I do such a thing?" Georgina asked.

"It was the great curse of the Deering-Dolittles, you went up the river," said Mrs Frasier.

"No! I would not!"

"You are not my mother," Arthur said. "I want nothing to do with you."

The lad turned on his heel and with long strides left the room. He didn't look back, he didn't even close the door behind him and the dark rectangle in the wall emphasised the empty space.

"I would never take a child on an expedition," Georgina wailed.

"Ever the Greek scholar, young Arthur, such a fine nephew," said Mrs Frasier, not unkindly. "He doesn't mean the family river, he means the Styx."

Georgina gaped at the woman uncomprehendingly.

"What?"

"You died in childbirth."

"I'm not pregnant... I would not... Arthur was the only one for me."

"He is Merry's, he is your son, you are with child now."
Georgina was emphatic: "No."

But she knew it was true, she knew the morning sickness for what it was and she had run from it, run to Dartmoor and Magdalene Chase, and all the time she'd been running towards this other Arthur. This apparition of her future hadn't been a ghost come to haunt her, but a living man made of flesh and blood, her flesh and blood, her Arthur's flesh and blood.

The moment he'd said 'you are not my Mother', she had felt something move inside her, something alive and real, not a kick as such, but a feeling, and with it came a solid and certain knowledge.

Mrs Frasier confirmed it: "You died bringing young Arthur Merryweather into the world."

CHAPTER XXII

Mrs Frasier

Juggling: keeping three balls in the air, but she'd dropped one. Scrutiniser Jones was taking Georgina back to her room and by now Earnestine would be...

Mrs Frasier checked her gold pocket watch.

Time – that was the key.

She checked her silver watch.

Lord Farthing was taking the laws from the House of Lords to the House of Commons, a short walk down two corridors in the Palace of Westminster, with its many fancily dressed errand boys rushing back and forth. It was going through. He'd rung on the contraption and Mrs Frasier knew it was working. They'd baulked at some of it, of course, but the heavy, inexorable logic of history had forced it along. One law, one vote and a whole raft of changes would become legally binding. The future would be assured as the Sovereign's pen moved across the vellum.

Mrs Frasier checked the sword slid from its scabbard easily. There were still dangers, it wasn't in the bag.

Yet.

Earnestine was – she checked her pocket watch again – why didn't Farthing send a message? There were enough of their agents now for someone to come via the Chronological Conveyor. Or was Lord Farthing making his move early? No, she thought. The bill had to pass a first and second reading, that was why. These things took time.

The man had tried to assassinate her: he'd thought of Earnestine as the serpent's egg and so had sought to kill her in the shell. Calpurnia, wife of Caesar, so afeared of portents of the future.

She felt a rage: much like Boudicca of the Iceni in her painting as that Queen charged down on the Romans, a woman defeating men with scythes on her wheels. If only things could be that simple.

Did Farthing know she suspected him?

He understood that she didn't have to rely on thunderstorms and omens: she could simply read a history book to know all and that should make him cautious. Or was he betting on time's mutability? He couldn't move until this day was over, could he? This date in history, when the law was passed.

Some dates were fixed: one always remembered where one was. The 22nd June a few years ago, when the Queen celebrated her Diamond Jubilee, or the 17th May, when one heard the news of the relief of the Siege of Mafeking, for instance.

Beware the Ides of March and remember, remember the Fifth of November.

She should prepare the Ultimate Sanction just to be safe. Safe! All these people were her responsibility... but so was the future.

Time.

She must be patient.

The young Earnestine was a concern.

Mrs Frasier checked her watch and decided she'd left it long enough. She checked the straps of her baldric and then walked as calmly as she could.

As she went down a corridor, through the Rotunda and along another corridor, she realised that her journey mirrored that of the law passing along the Peers Corridor, the Central Lobby and then along the Commons Corridor.

She entered the Temporal Engineering section, where she'd caught one sister: time to catch another.

Miss Deering-Dolittle

Earnestine reached the Chronological Conveyor with its raised dais, brass railings and control lectern. Lying on the floor next to the device was her old umbrella. She picked it up, wondered what to do with it and how on Earth it came to be lying there. She placed it on one of the hooks fitted into the wall.

The controls were complicated and she fiddled with the dials, altering the date display, and then found the place where the technician operated the mechanism. There was no handle, just a hole with a screw thread as if something needed to be attached.

Something like... the rod tucked in her belt!

She took it out: its multi-faceted stone caught the light, sometimes green, sometimes violet. At the end of the brass rod was the spiral of a thread.

It fit.

Earnestine turned it clockwise, round and round, faster and faster and then slowing as it reached the end. Finally, the brass stopped turning all together.

Now what?

She set the dials; the application seemed straight forward, to her own present. The Chronological Committee was manipulating events in that time, so, logically, hers was the critical era. That seemed certain to her.

"Tricky deciding, isn't it?"

Earnestine turned, recognizing her own voice.

The woman stepped forward and Earnestine backed away until the older version stood between the machine and the younger. Mrs Frasier took hold of the jewelled control lever, her painted nails obvious as her hand enveloped it. She shunted the rod sideways and carelessly reset the date to her present, before she unscrewed it.

"I never understood why I let myself run around so," she said. "But now... I do. It's a lesson, don't you see? A lesson in the futility of fighting inexorable forces."

331

"Charlotte..." Earnestine could feel her eyes watering, but there was no grit being blown around in this airless fortress and so no excuse for showing weakness.

"One learns too that there are responsibilities to the Empire and to civilisation that outweigh all other concerns. One is... you and I have an extra weight upon our shoulders."

"What gives one the right?"

"Nothing gives one the right – nothing!"

"Then why?"

"Because one can." Mrs Frasier grabbed Earnestine by the shoulders, the brass rod in her hand digging into the young lady's collar bone. The older woman shook the younger: "We can and so we must, because – you must understand – if we don't, then we are responsible. Standing by is as bad as if we had been the ones who turned the wheels and pulled the levers that blew up the world. That is our remit."

"It's wrong."

"It's necessary."

Mrs Frasier let go and smoothed down the creases she'd made.

"There now," she said. "You would risk your life for others?"

"Yes."

"As would Charlotte?"

"Yes. But–"

"She did, didn't she? In the sewers that time when the Austro-Hungarian faction raised that untoten army."

"Yes."

"So, she gave her life for the Empire."

"No-one knows about her."

"We know, and we can keep a tomb for this unknown soldier in our hearts."

"But it's so cold."

"Yes, safe in our cold hearts."

Mrs Fraser put her hand on Earnestine's shoulder in a gesture that ought to have been comforting.

"We are not the same person," Mrs Frasier said. "I am older, experiences change one, moments like this mould one's character and after a few more, you will think as I do."

"I'm not the same person," said Earnestine. "And I don't agree with you."

"You don't agree with me *yet*."

Earnestine pulled away savagely and drew her sword, pointing it at Mrs Frasier to keep her distance.

"The impetuosity of youth," said Mrs Frasier. She put the jewelled rod down on the control panel and drew her own weapon. "There is nothing that you can know about fencing that I do not."

"I've been secretly practising on a machine."

"I know, but I've learnt a few tricks since I was you and, most importantly, I learnt the limitations of fighting mechanical devices."

"When did you learn that?"

"In about five minutes' time when Mrs Frasier beat me," said Mrs Frasier. "En garde!"

Earnestine was taken by surprise by the ferocity of the attack. Mrs Frasier's left hand went upwards with her fingers splayed, and she kicked forward lightly on her feet in a skip that covered the ground so quickly. Her sword was a blur of motion.

Earnestine stumbled backwards.

Mrs Frasier hopped sideways in a manner utterly unlike a large bulky duelling machine.

Earnestine lashed out, but her moves were blocked. The older version knew before she did, and her steel was there clashing back any attack. Mrs Frasier reclaimed the offence; any initiative Earnestine might have stolen was whipped away by Mrs Frasier's jab and stab. She wasn't keeping to one school of fencing, but mixing cards from many decks.

333

Mrs Frasier circled, stabbing, testing, playing and always keeping Earnestine off-balance.

Earnestine twisted round, parried – just – and the heels of her Oxford boots slipped across the polished floor. It was all she could do to keep her feet under her and she swept her arms wide like a bird taking flight in an attempt to keep her balance. Her sword was pointing away, she was utterly defenceless.

Mrs Frasier thrust forward.

The blow struck true.

Earnestine yelped and gripped her hand, the flat of the blade had struck her hard and her own sword skittered away.

Even so, the glare she gave Mrs Frasier was defiant.

"You can't kill me," said Earnestine. "If you do, then you'd cease to exist."

"Don't be ridiculous," said Mrs Frasier.

"Kill me then."

"No, no, you'll come round."

"I will not."

"If you can talk with crowds and keep your virtue."

"...or walk with Kings – nor lose the common touch."

"Yours is the Earth, Earnestine, the whole wide world."

"To defeat you, all I need to do is change something," Earnestine said. "Choose Earl Grey instead of Assam, or... refuse Marcus Frasier's proposal and then there will never be a Mrs Frasier."

Mrs Frasier laughed to herself: "Marcus... we had such a wonderful two weeks in Brighton. He was such a wonderful lover."

"I don't care."

Mrs Frasier's eyes narrowed: "And then, behind the Theatre Royal, he proposed and we married."

"I don't care, so you can... what!" Earnestine yelped, the pain of her hand forgotten in an instant. "Before we were married?! Do you mean I'm some sort of common strumpet?"

"Hardly common."

"I would never... ever..."

"It's a new world, Ness, with suffrage and rights and an equal share of the wealth. Such old fashioned ideas have no place in our Utopia."

"No!"

"It's strange how all these obsessions fade away and one sees them for what they are: pointless and trivial when compared to the bigger picture."

"The bigger picture?"

"They will be planning to meet now, all the Conspirators, all those opposed to a fair society and all in one obvious place."

"Then they are going to move against you."

"Against us? Us! You and me," Mrs Frasier insisted. "But we're going to blow the whole thing up and blame it on the Conspiracy. Guido Fawkes would be so proud. People will flock to our cause: the women, full suffrage – will you vote for that? The poor, proper state organised benefits. An end to the workhouse and all the vile prostitution of women. Men will have to be as good as their word. There'll be proper funding for the arts."

"You're mad. And people like Charlotte? The people you've murdered."

"I didn't want to do it, but she left me no choice."

"She was my... *your sister*. You were responsible for her!"

"Yes, our little girl, the baby of the family, our Lottie. And because it was me who gave the order–"

"You!"

"Yes, as the eldest, Earnestine, you are responsible for her, and then again when you become me, and then you give the order – thrice damned."

Mrs Frasier went over to the control lectern and picked up the jewelled control rod. She held it in her hand, weighing it.

Earnestine swallowed: "Can it not be... *un*corrected?"

As if in answer, Mrs Frasier went over to the galvanic connector set in the wall.

"Once our Utopia is established, we'll bring them back: Charlotte, Boothroyd, Jerry, even Foxley."

"How?"

"We have a time machine!" said Mrs Frasier as she gripped the lever and pulled it down. It sparked with life, the control lectern lit up and hummed, almost demanding to be used.

"We can turn the clocks back," said Mrs Frasier, and she flicked a switch. "You and I can shape the future. We'll be able to do anything!"

From nowhere, Charlotte appeared on the dais.

Mrs Arthur Merryweather

Georgina had no more tears.

She would be with Arthur, her Arthur, soon enough, and that ungrateful son would... but wasn't he Arthur's legacy, his way of carrying on in the world? Kidnapped by Mrs Falcone.

Arthur, her husband, had wanted a son, and he had wanted him to be named after his father, Major Philip Merryweather, but as Georgina was destined to die in childbirth, then that wish would die with her. She had promised to love, honour and obey: *obey,* and she would fail to carry out the single order he had given her.

She took out the photograph: breathed a sigh of relief that Earnestine's stern appearance was still evident. Caruthers, McKendry, Uncle Jeremiah and herself were arranged around her. Then there was that disturbing and dreadful gap – poor Charlotte.

Georgina didn't want Earnestine to go the same way.

Perhaps if she stared at it, the very act of observation would fix it in position. George Berkley had suggested something similar when he'd asked if a tree falls in a forest, and no one was around to hear it, does it make a sound? But that was ridiculous. Things were, or weren't, whether anyone was looking at them or not.

She remembered the moment the picture was taken, but the figures without Charlotte looked so strange. They were proud, as any Englishman and Englishwoman should be. There was the same dazzle of the flash reflected in the windows, the same smeared figure walking behind them... except that Charlotte was absent.

It was too awful: staring at Earnestine to fix her in place meant that she also saw where Charlotte had been erased, removed from this picture, and from all of history to become an *un*person. How could they oppose people who merely had to go back and snub out someone before they were grown, or born, or even conceived? It was like playing chess against an opponent who was allowed to change any of their previous moves. There were no rules to this.

Would staring really fix Earnestine in place or would she see her sister fading from the picture?

How did it happen?

What was the natural process that caused it?

"How?" she said aloud.

There were reports pictures of ghosts and fairies.

She considered the actual daguerreotype again.

The silver iodide caused a chemical reaction, light activated, and this fixed the pigment on the special paper. History then, changed, must mean that the light that entered the camera was different from the light that she herself had seen. She remembered seeing Charlotte standing there, before and after the glare and dazzle of the

337

flash subsided. That light, the light that entered her eyes, was unchanged. Perhaps the way in which her mind stored memories was so fundamentally different from the physics of photography that the historical alteration could not affect it. Charlotte was closer to her heart, perhaps, than her impression was to the 2d-a-box Kodak paper.

Or was it some aethereal field that held their memory dyed in their mind?

But the daguerreotype had been with her the whole time, so whatever affected it, must also have influenced her thoughts.

And if history was changed and Charlotte had never existed, then she had never accompanied them to the theatre. When they all posed outside: McKendry, Uncle Jeremiah, Caruthers, Earnestine and Georgina – Charlotte had not been there. If that was the case, then they would never have needed to all huddle closer to fit on the steps. She remembered the apparently headless photographer signalling them to move together. However, here they were crowded to one side, the taller Caruthers and Earnestine standing slightly to the back *and the photographer would surely have turned the camera to move the group into the centre of the frame!*

No-one took a group arrangement like this and left a wide gap on one side, a gap big enough for a sixth person.

Georgina could imagine the crystals upon the paper changing, a process dictated by chemical laws, but what possible process could reach to the photograph, once it was exposed, printed and framed safe under glass, to modify it.

Whether history had been rewritten or not, an invisible presence was pushing everyone to the picture's left.

But who?

It could only be Charlotte's ghost.

Miss Charlotte

Charlotte had been in the netherworld between one world and the next.

She'd gone up, towards the light and towards heaven, but she did not find Saint Peter waiting for her. This purgatory was cramped, full of pipes and brick dust, and by the time she'd crawled through the opening, she was filthy. Her skirts were ripped, her bustle snagged, so she got rid of it, and she'd taken the skin off the knuckles of her right hand. She smashed through, the breaking of plywood gave the lie to its appearance of metal and rivets, and then she'd wriggled out through the hole.

After the lights of the Chronological Conveyor had subsided, Charlotte found herself standing on the dais.

She thought that, perhaps, she could hear a voice: Earnestine arguing with herself, but there was no-one there.

The place by the control lectern was empty.

Everywhere the paint was fresh and the windows bright as it had been in the past, so long ago in her own personal chronology. She must have crawled through a time tunnel or something.

In front of her a corridor that led to the outside world. Nothing could stop her leaving and going into that world: the past, the future or whenever it was.

Unless it was locked?

She took a bold step forward and smashed straight into an invisible barrier.

She fell back and, because she'd discarded her bustle to get through the hole, she hurt her pelvis when she landed on her backside. She sat there with her feet sticking out at a comical angle from her under her rucked up dress.

There was nothing there, except... the protective glass wall.

She went round it and over to the control console and tried a switch. Nothing happened, and then she remembered the heavy galvanic connector on the wall.

She flicked it, jumped as it sparked, but nonetheless she pushed it home.

If you slid the slider, she thought, but it needed the jewelled rod to be screwed in place. Uncle Jeremiah had tried to give it to her and she'd seen it in the movable hatch tantalisingly close, but Mrs Frasier had arrived too soon.

However, when she tried sticking her finger into the hole and moving it, it slid easily enough. Everything hummed and flashed with light, blinding, and then the damage she'd done to the Chronological Conveyor disappeared. Perhaps she had transported it to the past or future, she thought, but when she moving the slider back again, the action recreated the hole she'd made in the dais wall. She tried it again with different settings and found the switch for the humming and another for the flashing light. Soon, she had all the effects turned off and the slider merely changed the view – damage there, damage gone, damage there, damage gone.

When one conveyor was lit, it could be seen; slide the control and the other became visible. The glass wall either let you see through or see a reflection: yes, it *faded from view*.

This was how you saw people literally disappear.

She could stop the slider just so and see the damage as a ghostly apparition.

It was that trick they'd seen in the theatre!

The hairs on the back of her neck and her bare arms stood on end, a rippling of her skin just like she felt when a fancy dessert was served.

She checked: now the light was shining that way, she could see the alternative Chronological Conveyor down a side corridor. There was another passage opposite with a copy of the control lectern. Each had been hidden in the darkness. When you stood on the dais, then the same lighting effect would fade the view from one corridor to the other.

But that didn't explain the stomach churning feeling of Temporal Transference.

But if this was a trick, then there must be an explanation. The 'chimney' she'd crawled into, and then up, had contained huge metal post, gears and cogs and mechanisms and all sorts of things that Georgina would find fascinating. It would – she moved the mechanism in her mind – cause the floor to rise and fall.

It was a lift.

Like in the Savoy.

With a sliding ceiling.

So, anyone watching would see the person standing on the dais fade from existence.

For the temporal voyager, they'd see the view fade, be blinded by the bright light, and then, with their eyes persuaded closed, they'd feel a falling sensation and then the corridor would have changed.

There must be another version of this mechanism in the basement.

It was a conjuring trick, nothing more.

She left the control lectern as she'd found it.

If they really wanted to keep her a prisoner, she thought, they ought to have locked her in one of the cells instead of a store cupboard with a weak ceiling. The cells had been full. Charlotte had vowed never to let herself be locked in a small room again, ever since she was shut into the pantry when she was seven – and that had been Earnestine too!

She must escape.

The door to the outside world was locked with both a key and padlocks across the iron bolts. Charlotte glanced around looking for something that might be of service, but there was nothing. She'd have to try another route.

Going back towards the court and prison didn't appeal, but that was downstairs. On this level, amongst the mirrors and glass maze of the Chronological Conveyor, she found a side exit. It took her outside and into a small courtyard.

"Oh!"

On all sides were the brick walls of the old factory, but ahead, down an alley, was a truly remarkable sight. It was the future, there for all to see, with giant buildings of glass and crystal. High up a Zeppelin of extraordinary design was moored to a rooftop.

This was the future, it really was.

And there, in the distance along the Thames, was the clock tower of Big Ben. The real Big Ben. You couldn't fake that.

She went forward, her head craned back so she could see the marvels, but, as she moved along the alleyway, her perspective changed. The marvels became flat and distorted, changing in front of her eyes until the illusion became obvious. They were painted walls of wood and models of plaster, the giant Zeppelin was made of canvas, small and hollow, the towers of glass were fake. Only the distant Houses of Parliament were the real MacKay giving the imitation a depth and believability. When she reached the far end and looked back, the view was tawdry and ersatz.

It was a lie.

It was like... the theatre.

All the world's a stage, Mrs Frasier had said.

Everyone had been gulled, good and proper.

Chapter XXIII

Mrs Frasier

"Anything?" Earnestine asked.

"Yes, anything, you can do anything!"

"In that case, tell me what's really going on."

This was the moment that Mrs Frasier had been dreading: "I keep six honest serving men," she said.

"I beg your pardon."

"Kipling."

"Really?"

"He's not published it in your time, but there is an elephant in the class room."

"I'm afraid you're not making sense."

"I'm not making sense yet."

Mrs Frasier took two narrow cigars from her pocket and handed one to Earnestine. The child took it, wrinkling her sharp nose. Mrs Frasier leaned against the brass rail of the Chronological Conveyor, struck a match, lit the end and took a long inhalation.

"Their names are – let me get them in the right order: What and Why and When and How and Where and Who. They taught me all I knew."

Earnestine didn't answer, so Mrs Frasier continued.

"If you ask What, Why, When, How... Where and Who, then you learn everything about a situation."

"Oh, I see: Chronological Committee, to save the world... what was the third?"

"When."

"My time and this future; how, with this machine; here and by you and your... Temporal Peelers."

"My six and more honest men."

"Your thugs."

"I beg your pardon," Mrs Frasier retorted. "Scrutiniser Jones may look like a thug, but he has a softer side and a mind if you look beyond the brawn. They are all good, trustworthy men."

"I'm sure. Why don't we all have tea and cake?"

"Why not?"

"You're happy to sacrifice others, but not–"

"I am fully prepared to sacrifice myself, the Ultimate Sanction," Mrs Frasier declared. "I have gunpowder enough to blow everything to kingdom come."

"Other people: the past isn't your playground to do as you please."

"The past? Indeed. *When* is the interesting question?"

Earnestine checked the dials on the lectern: "The Year of our Lord, one thousand, nine hundred and ninety nine... two years before the millennium, according to this."

"I bet they celebrate it early."

"That wouldn't be proper," said Earnestine. "You said it was seventy five years in the future."

Mrs Frasier flicked a little ash away, picked something from her tongue and then took another drag. The smoke curled upwards in a spiral. It seemed that there was more than one trail.

Mrs Frasier made the decision: she knew it was necessary. She'd have preferred to wait until Queen Victoria's signature on the bottom of the page had dried, but time waits for no man.

"Do you see that control on the lectern," she said.

Earnestine looked: "Which one?"

"Ah! 'Which' isn't one of the honest serving men."

"Look, just tell me which one?"

"The white one with the round top."

Earnestine fussed over the lectern and finally put her hand on the slider.

"You should smoke," said Mrs Frasier. "It calms the nerves and thins the blood."

"I'm quite calm!" Earnestine snapped.

"Slide the control and... *catch!*"

Mrs Frasier threw the matches to Earnestine.

344

Miss Deering-Dolittle

Earnestine caught them.

Her hand operated the control at the same time.

Mrs Frasier had gone.

It was true.

And it meant that it was possible to make a better world, to nudge everything forward towards a Utopia. Earnestine felt oddly proud that she was the one who would make it happen.

Her voice came from nowhere: "Move the slider back."

Earnestine did so and Mrs Frasier materialised on the dais from nowhere.

"So it's true," said Earnestine. She'd seen it again with her own eyes and this time hers had been the hand upon the control.

"Come here."

Nervously, Earnestine did so, a step and another, and then strangely her own face materialised within Mrs Frasier's until she could see both herself and her own future.

"You see," Mrs Frasier began, "it's–" but she was interrupted by a distant scream.

Earnestine grabbed her umbrella.

Mrs Arthur Merryweather

Georgina saw a ghost: she ran straight into it, and then she screamed and screamed.

Charlotte threw herself over Georgina and clamped her hand over her mouth: "Shhh, shhh..."

"Don't – *ow* – mmmm me!"

"It's all fake."

"I know," Georgina replied.

"Oh."

"And it also means that I'm not expecting."

345

"Not expecting what?"

"Never you mind," Georgina said, quickly. "We have to warn Captain Caruthers. He can get a message to Major Dan."

"Can't we just fight them off like last time?"

"Charlotte, don't be so foolish."

They both got up – Charlotte picking up a small wooden barrel – and they set off in opposite directions.

"That's the dormitory!" Georgina said.

"And over there is the future," Charlotte replied, "and the gate is too high to climb."

"We'll have to try."

"You won't be able to, Gina, you're getting pudgy."

"I am not."

But she knew she was. Her corset had no cord left to tie a knot these days. It was all the pickle she'd been eating.

"So I thought the main door," said Charlotte.

"It'll be locked."

Charlotte hefted the barrel higher: "I've got a key."

Georgina followed Charlotte and they made their way up some stairs and then along to the Chronological Conveyor.

"The floor falls away," Charlotte explained. "And this glass wall here–"

"Pepper's Ghost," said Georgina realising. "We saw it in the theatre."

"That's it."

Charlotte kicked the barrel until the wood split and then started to leave a trail of powder.

"Do you know what you're doing?" Georgina asked nervously.

"It's only a priming barrel."

"That's not what I asked... *quiet.*"

Georgina heard voices: female voices from below. She moved over to stand upon the dais. There was a hole at the side that led downwards. Moving closer, she began to make them out: Earnestine and Earnestine; no, Earnestine and Mrs Frasier. She leaned closer, trying to understand the words.

"It's ready!" Charlotte shouted. She sprinted from where she'd left the barrel against the door.

Georgina jumped: "Shhh..."

Mrs Frasier's voice came up loud and clear: "What was that?"

"Oh lummy," said Charlotte. "Match?"

Georgina had a box of Bryant and May in her bag.

There were only three left, rattling around, so Charlotte took out all of them at once, rubbed them across the sandpaper and they flared brightly. She held them expertly, letting the initial conflagration die down and waiting for the wood to burn properly. She touched the end of her powder trail and that flared just like the match only ten times brighter. The ignition spat and jerked as it took and then the fire began to rush along the line turning the dark powder into ash.

"That's jolly quick," Georgina said.

"Take cover!" Charlotte yelled.

They dodged round the corner into the other version of the Conveyor, the one that would appear when the control slider had been moved to change the lighting.

Mrs Frasier and Earnestine appeared in the first interpretation of the Conveyor. The haphazard flaring of the gunpowder trail flicked them on and off as if they were trying to materialise there.

The fire reached the barrel, leapt upwards to the damaged area and–

Miss Charlotte

Exploded!
It was fantastically exciting.
Wow!

347

The heavy door split, its planks separated, but held in places by the iron reinforcements, and the ceiling divested itself of a whole heap of plaster.

Bits everywhere.

And Charlotte had done it all by herself.

"Stop! Stop! You don't understand," shouted Mrs Frasier.

"What are you going to do?" Georgina demanded. "Wipe us out? Break into our house and remove us from all our daguerreotypes? We've found you out!"

"Come on!" Charlotte shouted.

Georgina needed no other prompting and they ran for the door.

Mrs Frasier tried chasing their reflections.

"Peelers! Peelers!" she shouted.

Male voices replied: "Oi!" and "What was that?"

Charlotte kicked away the last of the debris and jumped through into the daylight.

Georgina reached it seconds later and stopped. She looked back.

Earnestine was standing there half way along between her and Mrs Frasier.

"Earnestine!" Mrs Frasier shouted, "Stop them! Before they ruin everything. The greater good!"

Earnestine turned back, clearly torn as she gripped her umbrella in both hands.

"Ness!"

Georgina held her hand out beckoning.

Chapter XXIV

Mrs Frasier

Earnestine was hesitating: she was in the way!

Mrs Frasier started to chase them, pushing past Earnestine to do so, but then she realised the foolishness of that.

"Guards! Guards!" she shouted.

The squad of Temporal Peelers, panicked by the explosion, were hurriedly fastening on their sword belts as they stumbled into the corridor.

"Where were you?" Mrs Frasier demanded.

"Ma'am, we–"

"Never mind, get after them!"

"Who?"

"The Derring-Do Club."

Scrutiniser Jones glanced at Earnestine.

"Not her, the other two."

"Other two? But one's been erased."

"She unerased herself – now move!"

Scrutiniser Jones led the pursuit, rushing into the mist of plaster dust that still hovered over the remains of the door. The others stumbled after him becoming organised as they went.

When they'd left, the Chronological Conveyor became quiet, peaceful. Mrs Frasier saw that Earnestine was standing with her arm half extended.

"I want to understand," Earnestine said.

"You are coming around to my side," Mrs Frasier replied.

"But I'm not on your side."

"You're not on my side *yet.*"

Chief Examiner Lombard appeared: "What happened?"

"The Derring-Do Club escaped."

349

"No!"

"Jones is after them, but... best if we prepare the Ultimate Sanction."

"Are you sure?"

"Yes, without evidence who's going to believe two children?" said Mrs Frasier. She pointed to Earnestine. "Bring her to my office."

Chief Examiner Lombard was tall and forceful, his gaunt face brooked no argument, and Earnestine had no choice but to follow Mrs Frasier.

"Mrs Frasier!" Earnestine shouted.

Mrs Frasier didn't look round. Her mind was awhirl. From working along one plan, she was now forced to consider one of the other contingencies.

"That will be all," she said, when they reached her office, but the tall Temporal Peeler stayed at attention.

"Ma'am," he said.

"Lombard, I've beaten this girl once, I can do it again."

"Ma'am," he nodded and left. "I'll see to the Sanction."

"Good man."

Mrs Frasier collected a few papers from her desk and put them in a case. Earnestine tried to stand up straight to regain some dignity. An awful, gory picture of a mad woman in a chariot going into battle stared down at her. There was a dreadful whine in her voice when she finally spoke.

"This isn't the future."

"No."

"This isn't real."

"No."

"And you aren't me."

"No."

Earnestine let out a breath, a single exhalation: the audacity must have struck home, Mrs Frasier realised: all those people gulled by this fantastic fairy tale.

"You may applaud," said Mrs Frasier.

"Who are you?"

She twirled her hand theatrically and bowed: "Miss Charity Mulligan at your service."

"Never heard of you."

"Oh! That cuts to the quick."

"Why did you do all this?"

"To make a better world for all."

"How?"

"Are we going to get all six of Rudyard Kipling's questions?"

"Yes."

"It is a simple idea," said Mrs Frasier. "We present our credentials with a trick, a vanishing act. Audiences love it when things appear and disappear. That's what stage magicians do: pledge, turn and prestige. And people lap it up."

"But it's a trick."

"People want to believe the trick, just as people want to believe in a better future, a war to end all wars between good and evil. Revelations, séances, fortune telling... it's all the same promise. We appeared as if by magic and so, with no evidence to the contrary, they had to believe our scientific explanation. Queen Victoria's reign has marked an age of wonders, so why not temporal engines. And once they'd swallowed the big lie, then others, the forged books for example, followed easily. This Imperial world with its factories and fogs and endless drudgery isn't the world people want, they want hope and betterment."

"But someone must have suspected."

"Many," Mrs Frasier admitted with a shrug. "We presented proofs as we did with you. Some were convinced, some came over to our side and some we arrested and locked downstairs. But most doubters just sat still. It was too big, you see, too gigantic – easier to accept it all than point out the Emperor's new clothes. It's truly amazing how the masses will go along with the herd."

351

"But it's a lie!"

"Don't you occasionally lie to make things better?"

"No."

"Ah well, that's why I'm grown up and you're not."

"The world is good as it is."

"Oh really, that is too much. Please, don't even bother to defend it. Most women in this fine city are prostitutes, forced into it by financial necessity and the lack of opportunity. These stalwart gentlemen may have banned slavery in the Empire, but they revel in it here in the capital. They keep their wives, their Angels of the Home, locked away in their airless houses and go off to fornicate every night with gin-riddled opium addicts desperate for a few pennies. And ever so grateful for the attention. I wanted more. I wanted a better world. Not just for me, and not just for men, but for everyone. Is that wrong? Is that not the ultimate act of doing good?"

Mrs Frasier waved her hand as if she were trying to conjure this new world from the air. She could see in Earnestine's eyes that the girl was wavering, entranced by the spell.

"We will do it, why not – you and me, side by side, making a better tomorrow," Mrs Frasier said. "The plan can still work."

"You're a strumpet."

"I am not! I'm an actress."

"They'll stop you."

"Who?"

"Men like Major Dan and Captain Caruthers."

"Men!" Mrs Frasier laughed. "With all their brass buttons and smart uniforms, their wars and death and destruction. This is a modern age, an age of reason and law. If you want to conquer, there are armies and battles, but better yet to come up with a good, solid legitimate reason and fight it–"

"What sort of–"

"And then you fight it through the courts. That's where laws are made, not over in the Houses of Parliament, not by Kings and Queens, but by the judges and the lawyers. They interpret the law, they create precedent. In a civilised country, that's what establishes the laws. And he who makes the rules, wins the game."

"What sort of legitimate reason?"

"One was descended from King Harold or one took a sword from a stone or a burning bush talked to one. It doesn't matter, and if one doesn't have a legitimate reason, then one makes one up. Then one fights it through the courts and we have the best lawyers."

"You have the best lawyers?"

"Of course, we locked all the others up."

Earnestine screamed in frustration: "But it's a lie!"

"Not a lie, a story. One of Jerry's finest."

"Jerry?"

"Uncle Jere–"

"I'd never call him 'Jerry'."

"Why not?"

"Uncle's stories are make-believe," Earnestine protested. "This I thought was real... and I wanted to believe it all, suffrage and a fair deal for everyone, a Utopia, but you've let everyone down because it's not true."

"Why not still believe and then make it happen," said Mrs Frasier, leaning forward and down. "Stories can change the world. It's not true *yet*."

"But you are blackened by your actions," Earnestine said. "You're tainted. How can you rule fairly if you've done these unspeakable acts?"

"By handing the reins to someone who is good enough to rule."

"Who?"

"You, of course."

"Me!?"

"Yes. The ends never justify the means, I know that, but I am the means that can be discarded and you can make the ends work."

Earnestine tightened her lips and shook her head.

Mrs Frasier's expression softened: "If you don't wish to be part of this, then go. I won't stop you."

Mrs Frasier stepped back, one foot neatly tucked behind the other and her hand unfurled in a theatrical gesture to present a side door.

Miss Deering-Dolittle

Earnestine hesitated.

She knew when she was going to be gulled.

"It's a trick."

Mrs Frasier smiled: "Of course."

What choice did she have? She didn't want to be included in this insane plan. Instead, she wanted to sit in her room, look at her maps and read her adventure books, so she went to the door, slowly, carefully and–

It was locked.

Mrs Frasier had a clutch of keys.

"There's always an answer," she said as she picked out a particular fob.

Earnestine took it, placed the big, black key in the lock and turned. She offered it back to Mrs Frasier. A fob dangled and Earnestine saw the legend '*The Future*'.

"I have mine here," Mrs Frasier said, holding up a copy. "Keep yours, in case you change your mind."

"I won't."

"Indulge me."

Earnestine pushed the key up her sleeve, opened the door and then, fearful that she was going to be plucked back inside at any moment, she sprang through.

The outside!

The time: her present.

No-one stopped her.

She walked away, carefully, and when she heard the door close and lock behind her, she scarpered as fast as she could. She was soon down the side street by the factory wall and then out into the safety of the crowds.

A newspaper vendor shouted and waved an example of his wares aloft.

"Brave New World! Law passed today!"

She reached an open space, hardly a park, and there were children using sticks to knock makeshift hoops along, and others poking their fingers into a patch of dirty water. Ladies, dressed in outrageous outfits, staggered about due to the effects of gin, only to be propositioned by the occasional man making lewd gestures. Everything was dilapidated, grey and unpleasant.

The more Earnestine looked, the more she saw the streets for what they really were. These children had no real future, these women were used and beaten, and these men were no gentlemen.

The present was exposed to her in all the waifs and strays, filthy, barefooted and marked with bruises, cuts and smallpox scars.

There!

A man threatened his women, forcing them to be whores; even the Nannies with their prams and charges were slaves to necessity, like the servants running errands for those imprisoned by polite convention in their plush houses. Servants like their own cook and their maids... whose names she could not even recall, and whom she treated like instruments to fetch and carry and cook and clean. They should be free and she should be more caring and responsible.

The flowering Empire had brought prosperity, but not to everyone. The rich industrialists were fat from the proceeds created by those chained by poverty to work in the factories. The rich became richer, investors paid themselves dividends and bankers hoarded the wealth, while those too destitute to pay the ever rising rents had to

355

slave in the workhouses to pay back those who put them there. The poor were blamed as if they had chosen this hard life for themselves and punished for that choice. What little they had was taken from them and this broiling mass of mankind had no say in the world.

And women had no rights at all as such, twenty one or not twenty one.

It could be changed. It should be changed. It would... but the ends did not justify the means. She knew that.

But she was not responsible for the means.

But she could be for the ends.

But... and that was Mrs Frasier's point.

Earnestine gasped, winded, and needed to stretch out her hand to grasp a lamppost for support. She bent over and–

"Are you well, Miss?"

"Yes, I'm well," Earnestine replied without looking, "don't worry yourself, everything is going to be well."

If... only, but there was time yet.

No more 'buts': she would join Mrs Frasier and change the world. She was a member of the Derring-Do Club, after all – best foot forward and all that.

"Perhaps you should step this way, Miss."

"No, I have to–" but everything went dark. Something was over her head, a coat, a bag... something cloying and there were strong arms around her and her kicking feet came off the ground. Doors clattered and clunked and she was bundled into a carriage.

A deep voice shouted: "Move it."

The floor jolted under Earnestine as she struggled to extricate herself.

"Be still," said the voice, "if you know what's good for you."

Earnestine heard a revolver being cocked.

She went still, jolly still.

Mrs Arthur Merryweather

Outside, it had been suddenly ordinary and normal, a street like many, many others she knew and a complete shock after the future world.

"What do we do?" Charlotte asked as they ran.

"We go to the Club," Georgina replied. "The men will know what to do."

"The men!"

"Otherwise it's taking them all on single handed... Charlotte, come back at once."

Charlotte did so, but froze: "Peelers!"

There were a few appearing, searching, gradually spreading out as they assigned each other various routes.

Georgina and Charlotte shrank back to the wall, and worked their way down the street.

"Underground station," said Charlotte pointing. It was the City and South London Railway at Stockwell. "We can change at Bank."

"Unaccompanied young ladies don't go on the Underground," said Georgina.

"I'm accompanying you."

"That doesn't... but under the circumstances."

They made it to the station, handed over their two pence each and descended into the depths. The platform was full of men and accompanied ladies. Eventually, the train arrived, pushing a strong breeze before it, and they entered the 'padded cells'. It was claustrophobic, the only windows were mere slits at the top of the carriage, but then there was nothing to see in this underground tube. It snaked north-east and then went under the Thames. Georgina felt her stomach lurch as the slope took them down below the waters.

At Bank station they changed, the gate-man opening the barrier for them to disembark. They climbed the stairs and then, just as the fresh air began to revive Georgina, they descended again to catch Central London service to British Museum.

357

All this was so new, only opened properly in the July, and it was heralded as the future. Was this really preferable to Mrs Frasier's dream? Is that why her sister Earnestine hadn't followed them?

"If we keep getting involved in adventures," said Georgina, "one of us is going to get killed."

"Not me," said Charlotte.

Miss Charlotte

The Club, boasting members like Major Dan, Captain Caruthers, Lieutenant McKendry and so many others, was a good walk away from the British Museum. When they arrived, Georgina marched straight towards the staircase, but the Porter intercepted her.

"Miss?" the Porter began.

"Ma'am."

"Ma'am."

"Major Dan or Captain Caruthers please – *at once!*"

"They're not here, Ma'am."

Georgina took a step forward.

"I'll take a message," said the Porter quickly, before he beetled off.

As they waited, Lord Farthing arrived, noticed them with surprise and doffed his hat. He placed it down in the Porter's hatch along with his white scarf, gloves and cane.

A Junior Porter came over to collect them, but he interrupted by a strange ringing noise.

"My Lord, the Porter's gone to fetch Major Dan or Captain Caruthers," Georgina explained.

"I see," he replied. "Thank you, Miss."

"Ma'am."

"Ma'am... and Miss."

Finally, Charlotte thought, someone's noticed me.

The Junior Porter reappeared: "My Lord, you are wanted upon the telephone."

"Very well."

Lord Farthing took the apparatus: "Yes... I see... they are gathered upstairs... Splendid... I can't talk... I'll see to it... Good-bye."

Lord Farthing gave the device back: "Ladies," he said, and he went away, not up the stairs, but down a side passage.

"I wonder where he's going?" Charlotte asked.

"Never you mind, it's none of our business," Georgina said.

"Perhaps I could just go and get a lemonade."

"No."

Chapter XXV

Mrs Frasier

Mrs Frasier returned the ear piece to its resting position on the telephonic device. It rattled as the hook descended activating the switch to cut off the connection. She checked her gold watch.

"And Jerry?"

"I put him back in Cell 19," said Chief Examiner Lombard. "It seemed best."

"Then we'd best see this through to the end." Mrs Frasier snapped the watch cover shut.

"Are you sure, Ma'am?" Chief Examiner Lombard asked.

"I am sure."

Chief Examiner Lombard was appalled: "But, Ma'am, the Ultimate Sanction?"

After years of planning, the final hours were crowded with desperate improvisation.

"It is necessary," she said.

"Jones will find those girls."

"Lord Farthing is planning to move against us."

"We are not ready, we need–"

"There is no more time, Lombard. If one of those dratted sisters convinces them..."

"They won't believe them."

"They believed Miss Deering-Dolittle when she told our side," Mrs Frasier put her hands together to emphasise as if ten fingers pointing were needed to put the idea across. "The law is all that matters – what's written."

"The pen is mightier than the sword," said Chief Examiner Lombard. "But the Sanction?"

"We must."

"And the Conspiracy?"

361

"Farthing will deal with that, I've rung him. He thinks he needs to defeat us, but our part is to ensure that there's nothing to contradict him."

"But Farthing—"

"He'll be bound by the law," she replied. "He won't undermine what gave him his power and, without evidence, who can say what is real and what is not."

The tall man nodded: "We'll keep to the script, Ma'am."

"Thank you, and issue the firearms."

"I'll see that the preparations are made," he said.

"You are a good man."

"I take direction."

"We'll be in the West End soon enough."

The man laughed and Mrs Frasier smiled.

"It's been a good run," Lombard said.

"The curtain's not down yet."

Miss Deering-Dolittle

"Well, well, well," said Lord Farthing in an insufferably superior manner. He slicked his hair back and cupped his hand to his ear in a theatrical manner. "I don't hear any Temporal Peelers rushing to your aid."

Earnestine, blind beneath a bag over her head, said nothing.

"This must be an event you forgot," the young man continued. "No hint, when you were ordering me about on the Alexander Bell. Time is mutable; we are changing things, so certain matters are adjustable... like your own personal survival. You're not the controlling, know-it-all confident Mrs Frasier, are you?"

"No, I'm not," said Earnestine, truthfully, trying to gauge where the man was standing. She was covered in coarse hessian, but reckoned she was underground. Once bundled from the carriage, she'd been hustled down stairs. She'd heard drips and echoes. Her hands had been

362

handcuffed behind her back and her wrists caught when she tried to move.

She also heard the man walking as he talked, changing his position to disorientate her. There was another man present, some bruiser, standing still somewhere behind her, she thought.

"Your plan to hand over the reins of power to yourself, jolly clever, but those of us more suited to power, born to it, don't agree with that part of your scheme."

"I'm sure," Earnestine mumbled. Overturning these insufferable male bounders was another jolly good reason to join Mrs Frasier and her Chronological Committee.

"Take the hood off her."

The covering whipped away suddenly and the room wasn't dark as she expected, but lit with galvanic light. Cables coiled like serpents along the floor and then rose to glowing bulbs held in cages that were hung from hooks. Water dripped down from the ceiling to splash into an already full bucket. Clearly no-one had come down here in an absolute age.

"Can't have gas down here," said Lord Farthing.

"I suppose not," said Earnestine.

"On account of the explosives."

"Exp– Oh!"

There were barrels of gunpowder stacked against the far wall dwarfing the empty wine racks.

"Another of your little schemes."

"My schemes?" Earnestine said. She wracked her brains, but she had no idea what he meant.

"Once the law is passed, then the opposition, the conspiracy if you like, will meet here in the very rooms above. I've seen to that."

Earnestine looked up and saw the vaulted brick ceiling, stained on one side where the water seeped through. All that weight held up by crumbling bricks weighed on her mind briefly, but not as much as the explosives that dominated the far wall. Earnestine was no expert,

Charlotte would know, but they appeared to have stocked more with zeal than calculation.

"Well, serpent's egg, your kind won't grow mischievous for I shall kill her in the egg."

"I beg your pardon."

"Julius Caesar, Act 2, Scene 1."

"That's nothing like Julius Caesar."

"With you gone, and your future self with you, and all of the Chronological Committee's enemies blown to kingdom come, I shall take the controls."

"You're operating under a misconception."

"I think not," said Lord Farthing. "I intend to change the course of history. Tie her up properly!"

"What? No, just– arr-uum, mmmm..."

Rough hands yanked her head back and, as she opened her mouth to complain, a gag went between her teeth and pulled her cheeks back. She kicked, but they simply pushed her over, grabbed her legs and wrapped cord around her ankles. She struggled, but she was expertly trussed, and then dragged across to be dumped by the barrels.

"Here, all your exciting belongings," said Lord Farthing. He dropped her penknife, Kendal mint cake, a peg, the small sewing kit and so on, onto a barrel. He paused when he found the key. The fob dangled catching the weak galvanic light.

"The future," he said, "I think yours is over. Someone has to die."

"Mmm mm mm."

"What was that? This would be a more useful key," said Lord Farthing. He showed her the key to the handcuffs and then dropped both onto the barrel with the rest of her kit.

"Mmmmmmm!"

"Language, hardly the expression for a young lady. I suppose you expect to escape, crawl over here and get the keys to those handcuffs – the stuff of Derring-Do."

"Mmmm mmm."

"Tie the rope to the pipe, man!"

The thug did so, a midshipman's hitch, and Earnestine groaned when she realised that she'd never get that undone. Even so, Earnestine tugged with her feet, but both the rope and the pipe were secure.

"The Derring-Do Club, always ready for adventure–"

"Mmm mmmmmmmmm."

"Now, now, my dear. Derbies secure?"

The bludger man yanked her wrists, the handcuffs threatening to crush her wrist bones.

"Aye, boss."

Earnestine squirmed, managed to roll over to look at Lord Farthing, just as his servant cast black powder all over her and the floor.

"Goodbye, dearest Ness," said Lord Farthing. He strode away, laughing. The other man took his time, walking away backwards and leaving a trail of gunpowder behind.

Earnestine tried to spit, but couldn't because of the gag, and her curse was muffled too.

She pulled at the cord, but her ankles were completely secured. Far too far away, the keys on the barrel glinted in the weird galvanic illumination.

The lights went out.

It was pitch black.

"Mmmm mmmm mmm *mmmmmmm!*"

Mrs Arthur Merryweather

Georgina told Charlotte to stand to one side: she would do the talking. For once, Charlotte did as she was told.

Captain Caruthers arrived.

Georgina explained.

The Captain didn't believe her.

Neither did McKendry.

The Porter scoffed too until Caruthers gave him a sharp look.

"It is true, Captain," Georgina insisted.

Caruthers fished into his inside pocket and retrieved a set of much thumbed daguerreotype prints. He flicked through, selecting one, which he showed to Georgina. It was a double exposure of Earnestine and in the background... no, wait! It was a picture of Earnestine standing next to Mrs Frasier and behind them the panoply of a future city, complete with glass towers and flying machines with the Houses of Parliament in the distance.

"That's one of Miss Deering-Dolittle and Mrs Frasier together," said Caruthers. "She's due to grow into a remarkably beautiful woman, isn't she? A flawless face, if you don't mind my saying so."

"Yes," said Georgina, distracted.

"The camera doesn't lie," said Caruthers.

Georgina took the picture off him. Caruthers fanned out the others for her inspection. It was as if he were asking her to choose a card before showing her a trick.

"I do not know the process used, I confess, but this is faked."

"They've built that street outside like they do in the theatre," said Charlotte. "It isn't real. It's paint and canvas."

Caruthers shook his head: "Everyone is convinced."

"People used to think that it was impossible to travel faster than twenty five miles per hour," Georgina said.

"Which is an argument for the extraordinary wonders we see in these images," Caruthers said.

"Perhaps, or our gullibility to want these wonders, but this is some trick, a painting, scenery or some photographic illusion," Georgina said, handing the picture back to the Captain. "I am certain."

"And the disappearing and appearing?"

"A stage magician's trick, nothing more."

Caruthers looked at her and then the picture, weighing it up in his mind. Georgina waited, knowing that anything she said would weaken her argument. He had to decide between his eyes and his heart. He flicked through the images: Earnestine, Earnestine, Earnestine with Mrs Frasier...

"Porter?"

"Yes, Captain?" said the Porter.

"Get Major Dan on the... ringing box."

"Telephone, Sir."

"Major Dan on the Tele... how do you pronounce it?"

"'Telephone', Sir."

The Porter went to collect it.

"It might be quicker to send a boy?" Georgina said.

"It's the future," said Captain Caruthers.

"If the future is all telephonic contraptions, then I don't want it," Georgina said.

"Nonsense," said Caruthers. "Soon everyone will have these convenient contraptions."

"Sir," said the Porter. "I'm afraid the cord won't reach, you'll have come into the office."

Caruthers made his way into the Porter's room: "Major Dan... Major Dan... Can you hear me? Hear me? I said... yes... I'm at the Club... At the Club. It's one of the Deering-Dolittle sisters... No, the middle one."

"What's this?" Lord Farthing arrived from the side passageway.

"Lord Farthing," said Caruthers.

"You shall explain to me," said Lord Farthing.

"Of course, Sir," said Caruthers. He put the phone down, but he didn't place the earpiece on the hook. Georgina opened her mouth to remind him, but the Captain shook his head almost imperceptibly.

"Now," said Lord Farthing, "what's all this about?"

"It's about the Temporal Peelers and the Chronological Committee," Caruthers explained.

"What of it? The laws have been passed, the thing is done. I've just been assuring those meeting here, who disagree, that their fears are unfounded. All will be well. I'm just off to celebrate myself."

"My Lord, if you please," said Caruthers. "Mrs Merryweather."

"My Lord," Georgina responded, politely. "It appears that the Chronological Committee hasn't been telling us the complete truth."

"In what particular?"

Georgina thought for a moment: "In all particulars. Indeed, it is hard to think of any statement that has any truth."

"No truth!" said Lord Farthing, looking to Caruthers for explanation.

"My Lord," said Caruthers. "The suggestion is that this Chronological Committee has been pretending. There is no time travel and there is no future catastrophe to circumvent."

"Mrs Frasier assured me," said Lord Farthing. He glanced back down a passageway towards the cellars as if seeking an answer there.

"Mrs Frasier is a liar," Georgina said.

"How can you say that about such a woman? Your own sister?"

"She isn't my sister, my Lord, that's the point."

"Then all our laws, all the legislation is for nothing."

"Surely not for nothing," Caruthers said. "The worth of an idea should be for the idea's sake, not due to its source."

Lord Farthing stepped apart. He thought for a moment, rubbed his smooth chin. He glanced down the passageway again.

"I would be... we would be the laughing stock of the Empire," he said. "No. We simply cannot believe you and–"

"It is true, My Lord," Georgina said. "There is evidence."

"It is not that we don't believe you, but that we cannot believe you. As for evidence, I doubt that will survive for long. What's more we've gone too far to turn back now."

"In the blood so deep it's best go on than be mired here," said Georgina. "Or something like that. Mrs Frasier said it."

"Exactly my sentiments. We rule an Empire, we cannot be revealed as fools. It will not do," said Lord Farthing. "Caruthers, McKendry, Miss... I forbid you to discuss this matter, or to act independently upon this information. I forbid it absolutely."

"But my Lord–"

"Forbidden!"

"Yes, my Lord."

"Your word as a Gentleman."

"My word, Sir."

"McKendry!"

"My Lord," said McKendry.

"Miss?"

Georgina had to object: "But my Lord–"

"Miss!"

"Yes, my Lord."

"You are not to act unless you have orders and you are not allowed to seek alternative orders," said Lord Farthing and, after the young man had looked at each in turn to satisfy himself that they had understood, he went over to the Porter.

"My hat?" said Lord Farthing to the Porter. The young man, so confident, so important, kicked his heels as he waited.

Georgina was glad Charlotte was keeping quiet and, for once, looking down in a proper manner as if for once she'd realised her place. This was terrible news, but they would have to bear it.

The Porter went into his office, and, as he did so he tidied up, replacing the earpiece on the telephone's hook. He collected Lord Farthing's belongings.

"We will come out of this well," said Lord Farthing. He took back his hat, white scarf, gloves and cane. "Our good deeds today will go down in history and your silence will be rewarded in the next life, Caruthers."

As he left, he nodded towards the passageway. Georgina saw a servant there, nod back and then turn away.

Lord Farthing walked away with long strides.

"So, that's the end of it," Georgina said.

Caruthers smiled and pointed upwards. Georgina didn't understand the gesture, but McKendry did and raced up the stairs.

"But you're not allowed to act unless you have orders and you're not allowed to seek orders," said Georgina.

"He didn't say anything about making preparations in case we do receive new orders."

"You're not allowed to seek new orders," Georgina repeated.

"I'm not seeking new orders, but I—"

The telephone device rang.

The Porter answered and then offered it to Caruthers, who stepped into the office to speak into it.

"Caruthers here... I'm afraid, Sir, I'm not allowed to talk about it. I've been given very strict instructions," he said, and then after a pause, he continued: "If that's new orders, Sir?"

As Caruthers listened, McKendry returned down the wide staircase with a collection of young men from the rooms above. He looked to his Captain.

Caruthers shook his head in reply: "We need proof."

The men turned despondently and made their way back up the staircase.

"What sort of proof?" Georgina asked.

Caruthers just shrugged.

"Oh, honestly," said Georgina.

"Ted, see that they have a hansom back to Zebediah Row."

"Sir," said the Porter.

"I'll see if there's anything I can do," said Caruthers to Georgina. "I don't like this anymore than you do."

As Caruthers went upstairs to join the others and the Porter went outside to hail a cab, Georgina was suddenly left alone.

Where was Charlotte... oh! The girl was bent over on the floor!

"Charlotte, what are you doing?"

Miss Charlotte

Kneeling, Charlotte touched the dirt on the floor. The black grains stood out against the white marble. She licked her finger, dabbed a few grains to pick them up and then tasted them.

"Charlotte!"

It tasted very familiar.

"Charlotte," Georgina repeated, "Stop it at once, you'll catch cholera or influenza."

"This is gunpowder," Charlotte replied. "It came off Lord Farthing's shoes."

Her gaze followed the faint line of dirt from the Porter's hatch to the passageway. And then, with sudden purpose, she stood upright and made her way to the passageway.

"Charlotte, come back this instant."

Georgina went after her, but only caught up once Charlotte was through the door and into the long passageway beyond.

"Look," said Charlotte, "a gunpowder trail."

There was a black trail, much like the one Charlotte had made to blow up the door of the Temporal Peelers base, but this one was thicker.

371

"Oh my," said Georgina, "we'll have to get it all brushed up directly. I'll see if I can find a maid."

Charlotte knelt down, touching the trail with her hand.

"Charlotte, don't touch that, it's filthy. You'll get your dress... ruined further."

"This is soot."

"All the more reason–"

"The gunpowder! It's already been lit!"

"Well, it still needs–"

"Lummy!"

Charlotte leapt forward and sprinted along the line of soot.

"Lottie," Georgina shouted after her. "You'll need a light."

But she didn't.

Round the corner, fizzing loudly as it belted away from her, was a bursting, fiery living ball of light. She ran past the burning, turned and stamped down upon the fire. It spluttered, flaring around her shoes and she had to lift her skirts to see it spread under her and ignite the trail behind her.

She let out a yelp.

Georgina appeared in the passageway.

Charlotte realised that she needed to get well ahead, and make a gap too large for the conflagration to jump, otherwise her efforts would be in vain. It had turned a corner, twisting down a spiral staircase and the smoke was being drawn up as if it were a chimney.

She coughed as she went into the fumes, almost tumbled, running down after the firestorm, and leapt over the moving barrier again, but this time she went on.

It was a cellar.

She went a further ten paces, counting in her head and then, without looking back, Charlotte–

Barrels.

Barrels and barrels.

Weapons grade.

Enough for a barrage like no other.

A bound figure, writhing.

Earnestine.

Her eyes white and shining from the fire that was rushing into the room.

And then, without looking back, Charlotte selected a place and kicked the trail of gunpowder: kick, kick, kick.

The trail was broken, a little, perhaps a foot, maybe more and then the racing fire caught up with her, flared where the tight line had been scuffed away.

It fizzled, spluttered, thinning as it caught all the scattered grains.

"I did it," cried Charlotte.

At her feet, the dusting of gunpowder flared with one last effort, a brief burst like a match catching, and then Charlotte's undergarments, her camisole and petticoats – everything – burst into flames.

Chapter XXVI

Mrs Frasier

The ignition blazed and the match took.

Mrs Frasier lit her narrow cigar and inhaled.

Jones was trying to intercept the Derring-Do Club.

Lombard was preparing the Sanction in case they were discovered.

Farthing was going to dispose of any opposition to the Chronological Committee.

Soon, she thought – *bang!*

Miss Deering-Dolittle

"Mmmmmm!"

Charlotte was screaming in panic, and, as she did so, she stumbled around in the gunpowder dusted cellar.

Georgina nearly collided with her, nearly knocked her into the room beyond, the room full of barrels and barrels and barrels and barrels of gunpowder. Loose black powder was spread everywhere, all over the floor and all over a tied-up Earnestine.

"Mmmmmm mm mmmmm!"

Earnestine was having a fit, shaking her head like she was demented.

All around Charlotte, fireflies gathered, whirling around in the vortex of flame as the heat tried to find an escape.

"Lummy!" said Georgina.

Charlotte flapped, slapped her dress with her hand, sending spiralling wisps of burning material spinning upwards and around.

"Mmmmmm!"

375

"Roll!" Georgina shouted. She pushed Charlotte, who spun, flew away and down to crash on the floor sending soot everywhere.

Beyond the narrow kicked aside line, everything seemed to be on fire.

"Mmmmmm!!!"

Involuntarily, Georgina stepped back and her foot clanged against something. She looked down and saw a–

"Mmmmmm!!!"

Georgina grabbed the pail of water, turned, hesitated as she realised she'd have one shot, and then she cast the water. The ground fizzed and spluttered and a dark canopy of soot rose like a demon to envelope everything.

She stumbled back, and fell in the dry and expectant gunpowder.

Earnestine kicked her.

"Yes! What!" Georgina shouted. She reached out and tugged off Earnestine's gag.

"Mmcket! Water!"

"Yes, all jolly good," said Georgina, "I've done that."

"Keys!"

"Yes, after Charlotte."

Georgina crawled on her hands and knees to the gap that Charlotte had made. Beyond it, a creature like a demonic chimney sweep coughed and hacked.

"Stay – *ack* – there!" Charlotte commanded.

Georgina stopped.

Charlotte spat in a jolly, unladylike fashion.

"If I'm still hot, I could ignite the gunpowder."

"Gunpowder?"

"You're covered in it," Charlotte said. "You look a mess."

"You should talk," said Georgina. "You've ruined your dress."

"It just went up."

"Are you all right?"

"Of course not, I'm drenched!"

"And filthy," Georgina added.

"If you'd let me wear trousers," Charlotte said, "this wouldn't have happened."

"We will not have rampant bloomerism."

"KEYS!!!" screamed Earnestine. "Will you two stop blathering and get the keys!!"

"Where?"

"There," said Earnestine, her head jerking like an overwound clockwork toy.

Charlotte, having checked she wasn't alight anywhere, found them. There was very little left of her outer layers, her crinoline gone and her corset singed and blackened.

"Which one?" she asked.

"Bring them both!!!"

"Will you stop shouting," Georgina yelled.

Charlotte went over to Earnestine and fumbled behind her until she'd released the mechanism from the Sheffield steel restraints. Once free, Earnestine flung the handcuffs away.

"What's the other key for?" Charlotte asked. "It says *'The Future'*?"

"Gina!" Earnestine put out her hand: "At least you could help me up."

"Gladly," said Georgina, and she leant down and extended her hand to help her sister up.

Mrs Arthur Merryweather

At the reception desk, Ted the Porter looked upon their arrival with pure horror mixed with utter disbelief, when three filthy chimney sweeps came up from the cellar, a horror that intensified when he realised that the chimney sweeps were female.

"We need a dress," said Earnestine.

"Miss, I... dress, this is a Gentleman's Club."

"My sister needs a dress. Her current attire, as you can see, is somewhat ruined."

"We've spare dress for dinner."

"A dress, excellent."

The man fussed at the back and returned with a smart dinner jacket, trousers and shirt on a hanger.

"Thank you, now Charlotte, if... those are trousers."

"I don't mind," said Charlotte sweetly, showing her pearly white teeth in the middle of her blackened face.

"No, Charlotte, we will not have rampant bloomerism."

"Ness," said Georgina.

Earnestine lips tightened: "Just this once."

"Yippee!"

Earnestine must have said "oh, hurry up" a dozen times before Charlotte emerged from the Porter's office clad in a jacket that looked like a skirt and trousers that were rolled up at her ankles.

"That's..." said Earnestine. "Words fail me."

"Comfortable," Charlotte suggested.

"Unladylike."

"Excuse me," said Georgina to the Porter. "But you need to clean up in the cellar."

"Why, Miss?"

"It's Ma'am, and it's because your cellar is full of dangerous explosives."

"Now, Ma'am, how likely is that?" said the Porter. "I'm sure you've confused it with something else."

"Go and look, but I'd advise against taking a lighted flame."

Earnestine led them outside.

It was a lovely day, blue skies and the usual bustle of London went on despite the legal revolution that had occurred around them.

"Now," she said, "we have to–"

"Peelers!" Charlotte shouted.

Across the road, Scrutiniser Jones and other top hatted men heard her and reacted to their appearance.

"We'll just talk to them," said Earnestine.

"Not likely," said Charlotte, and she nipped along the pavement.

The traffic was heavy for the time of day, four wheelers, hansoms and growlers jostled with a landau and omnibus coming the other way.

"Back to the Club," Georgina suggested.

When an omnibus obscured the Peelers from view, Earnestine picked up her skirts and took to her heels. Georgina struggled to keep up.

Charlotte was talking to a cab driver.

"Would you mind fetching my trunk," Charlotte said. "There's a shiny silver sixpence in it for you."

The man got down, his posture complaining about a bad back, but he ambled towards them. Georgina and Earnestine slowed to a walk and passed him. Charlotte waved to them.

"Oh no," Georgina said.

"Come on," said Earnestine, and she sprinted to the hansom.

"No, no," Georgina said, even as she ran too.

Charlotte clambered on the top.

"Take it steady," said Earnestine as she stepped up and turned to hold a hand out to Georgina.

"Oi!"

The cab driver had turned, his bad back forgotten in his haste to intercept them. Behind him, Temporal Peelers were crossing the road.

Charlotte whipped the reins: "Yay!"

The hansom jumped as the horse lurched forward.

Georgina knew it was too far – she wasn't going to make it – and then a hand grabbed her and up she went.

A Peeler reached the cab too and clutched at her bustle, yanking her back, but somehow using the force to pitch himself up onto the platform. He fumbled for a gun, but Earnestine stabbed out with her umbrella. He fell back, his revolver clattering down onto the cab floor as he disappeared.

379

There were more men in front now, the cab driver and several Peelers, but they scattered as Charlotte drove the horse on. Georgina was half in the cab, half out and then on the floor at Earnestine's feet.

"Go slowly," Georgina shouted.

"Yay! Yay!" Charlotte yelled, flicking the reins.

When they turned the corner, it was Georgina's turn to grab Earnestine to stop her falling out.

"I'll drive," said Earnestine, pulling herself up onto the cab.

Georgina fell back as the hansom slalomed between one side of the street and the other as they bounced along at breakneck speed. Horses and carriages tried to get out of the way and only just succeeded. A four-wheeler cracked a spoke and, out of control, hit a lamppost.

Earnestine wasn't there anymore; she was up top with Charlotte precariously holding on.

Through the rectangular window at the back, Georgina saw others in pursuit, Peelers with their top hats long blown away by the wind.

"I'll take this," Charlotte said reaching down to grasp the fallen revolver.

No, no, thought Georgina, not Charlotte and guns!

Boom! Boom!

The percussion of Charlotte firing cracked even over the clatter of hooves on the cobbles.

Luckily, she'd missed.

The traffic behind them slewed, destined for one of those appalling pile-ups that left horses writhing on the floor, whinnying in agony, until some kindly gentleman arrived with a revolver.

Earnestine yanked the reins and the horse turned right, the hansom going up on a single wheel threatening all the time to tip over.

Georgina pulled herself into the cab properly and sat down. The small doors in front clattered and banged shut.

Charlotte's hair streamed behind her as she leaned out from the top of the hansom like a sailor tacking a boat. She took aim: *boom!*

Georgina had no idea where the bullet went. It was really irresponsible of them to let Charlotte have a gun.

Behind them, the Peelers scattered in their chase.

Charlotte's weight pulled their vehicle over... almost, yes, the wheel came down with an almighty smack sending sparks hither as the metal rim struck the stones.

Ahead was a tram, gentlemen talking in the street, a nanny crossing with a pram and a landau manoeuvring.

Earnestine pulled back, slowing, but not enough and so jigged the horse to the left. It jumped the pavement edge easily enough, but the shock of the hansom mounting the kerb was bone shaking. Passers-by dodged left and right as the horse galloped along the pavement smashing dropped belongings into fragments. They reached a crossroads, came down off the kerb and then right into another busier street.

This one was completely blocked: street vendors had positioned fruit and vegetable stalls across the road and there were barrels with burning coals at intervals. Men looked up from warming their hands in shock at the sound of their arrival.

Earnestine turned left.

There was no street left!

A set of ornate metal arches flickered past overhead – *Georgina just ducked in time* – and tore the top off the hansom as the vehicle entered a fashionable arcade. The clatter of hooves on marble, echoing back from the high, glass ceiling was percussive and overpowering. In front, those out for a stroll flung themselves into shop doorways as the horse and carriage hurtled past.

Georgina saw herself suddenly, here and there, reflected in the shop windows like some crazy moving stained glass image. Earnestine, leaning down behind the vehicle, tried to steer the horse she could no longer see.

381

Then, suddenly, they were outside again, turning, going across a bridge over the Thames.

Charlotte whooped.

There was no pursuit behind them now.

Earnestine had control of the vehicle, slowing the panting horse and turning again. Zebediah Row was over there, Captain Caruthers and Lieutenant McKendry's Club must be there, Georgina thought, but they were making for Queensbury Road.

The hansom jerked slightly as Earnestine brought them to a halt.

They each alighted: Georgina felt quite pale.

"I threw up," she admitted.

"Never mind," said Earnestine. "You! Boy!"

A young lad of about twelve was standing opposite, torn between the order and a desire to run for it.

"A shilling if you look after the hansom."

"Shillin'."

"Now and one when we come back."

Earnestine hooked her umbrella over her arm and checked her bag: "I've only got a sovereign."

"Oh, give it to him," Georgina said. She took the coin and flipped it through the air. The boy caught it expertly. He bit it and checked the lack of imprint, no lead in that.

"Right you are, Miss," he said. He took the exhausted horse and pulled it towards the kerb. It was sweating, moisture coming off its flanks like a pea-souper rolling up the Thames.

They went inside the Patent Pending Office, Earnestine depositing her umbrella by the coat stand.

"Oh!" said Earnestine. "We gave the boy that coin from the future."

"He can spend it when he's an adult," Georgina replied.

"I think more likely he'll have run off with our money, horse and cab," said Charlotte. "This is a daft place to hide."

"This is the Patent Pending Office," Earnestine said striding across the study to the shelves. "And we're not hiding."

"I've been here," said Georgina.

"And so have the Peelers," Charlotte reminded them.

Earnestine pulled at a particular book and a section of the wall opened.

"Through here," she said.

"I've been through there too," Georgina said.

"It's jolly exciting," said Charlotte.

Having marched along the small passage into the wide open warehouse full of machines, engines and mechanisms, Earnestine stopped, struck by indecision.

"I need to get back to the Chronological Committee's base," she said.

"Whatever for?" Georgina asked.

"If I can get Mrs Frasier to see sense," Earnestine said. "She's planning some Ultimate Sanction."

"What's that?"

"I don't know," Earnestine admitted. "But it's in case their plans fail, then... they might blow up Parliament."

Georgina asked the obvious: "How?"

"Gunpowder. Like in the rhyme."

"How are we going to get there? There are Peelers all over the place and they have agents in this time."

"This time?"

"I mean... well, yes, this time."

"What about us?" Charlotte said.

"You two can stay here and keep out of trouble," said Earnestine.

"You still have to get through the streets and across the river," Georgina said.

Earnestine pointed to the warehouse's central exhibit: "This is a modified hansom cab. There are controls inside to release a spray to make the road behind slippery, and the lanterns at the front swivel away to reveal shotguns, and the front seat comes up to show a map of London, and see this lever? Don't pull this lever, because if you do the whole top comes off and—"

"I'm not getting in that," Georgina said. "And it needs a horse."

"Ah."

They were defeated for want of a horse. Wait, they had one outside attached to the ordinary hansom cab, but Georgina decided not to mention that.

"Is there a horseless carriage?" Charlotte asked.

"A horse, a horse..." Earnestine said, absently.

"Can we order one using the telespeaking apparatus?"

"No, of course not," said Earnestine. She was still searching and her unconscious acted like a magnet guiding her to...

"The Haversham!"

"The what?" Georgina asked.

"Help me put it on."

Earnestine dragged a lot of brass cylinders and straps out from a crate of similar devices, and started to put it on.

"Well, help," she said.

"How can we help when we don't know what it is?" Georgina said.

"It's a haver-rocket," said Earnestine fiddling with the brass buckles.

"What's a haver-doodah?"

"'Haver' as in 'Haversham' and 'haversack'... these straps... It's like a haversack, but instead of a sack it has a rocket."

Charlotte went forward and took the weight of the brass cylinders, so that Earnestine could get her arms through the shoulder straps. It stopped being a strange metal and canvas spider and became a piece of luggage for hiking.

"Charlotte, get the welder's goggles," Earnestine said pointing.

Charlotte went over and unhooked them.

"And the rocket part?" Georgina asked insistently.

"The 'sack' is replaced by a rocket. Hence 'haver-rocket'."

"Yes, I can see that, it's stencilled on the side – what's a rocket?"

Charlotte jumped up and down and put her hand up: "Oh, oh, oh..."

Georgina knew Earnestine wasn't going to give her a straight answer, so: "Charlotte?"

"It's a Chinese military weapon. You light the end, fire shoots–"

"Fire!"

"Yes, out the back and it flies–"

"Flies!"

"Through the air and then it hits the enemy and explodes."

"Explodes!"

Georgina looked from Charlotte to Earnestine, back again and then ended up wide eyed looking at her elder sister.

"Ness, no, no, no..."

"Don't be a baby, Gina."

"Ness!"

Earnestine jiggled the straps and checked that the large apparatus was secure on her back.

"This is a firework," said Georgina suddenly. "You are strapped to a firework, a jolly big firework!"

"It's a lot more powerful than a firework," Earnestine said.

"Do these work?" Georgina demanded; she checked the stencilled letters, "The Haversham Mark III Haver-rocket?"

"He had some success according to his notes," Earnestine replied. "The Mark I didn't work at all, but the Mark II went twenty feet."

"And then what?"

"It hit the roof of his laboratory, exploded and the resulting fire burnt the building down."

"What about this one, the Mark III?"

"It was never tested."

"Why not?"

"Because he moved on to the Mark IV."

"And..."

"It exploded."

"Exploded!?"

"They found his hat."

"Ness, you're using the one between burning the laboratory down and the one that just blew up!"

Earnestine took the goggles from Charlotte and put them on, wiggling them until they felt comfortable. They made her eyes look wide and innocent.

"I'll be fine," said Earnestine. "I've done this before."

"No-one alive has done this before."

"I've flown."

"You plummeted out of a Zeppelin straight down and were saved only because you had an umbrella," said Georgina pointing down and then she indicated the sky. "This is up and attached to a portable volcano."

"Wait," said Charlotte. "You can't."

"Not you as well?" Earnestine complained. "What is it now?"

Charlotte pointed upwards towards the ceiling with all its girders and cross beams supporting a very solid looking pitched roof. There was a lantern section, a skylight letting in plenty of sunshine, crisscrossed with ironwork to hold the thick glass in place.

"Good point," Earnestine said, and she began to haul herself and the extra weight to the door. "Bring my brolly."

"Whatever for?"

"Insurance."

The two sisters went outside leaving Georgina alone with her awful worries. She went down the secret passageway and into the study.

Where would Earnestine put her stupid brolly?

Georgina wished she'd never bought it for her, although to be fair it had saved her life once before.

There! Propped up against the coat stand.

As she retrieved it, the door burst open.

For a moment, a brief glance, Georgina saw the top hat wearing Temporal Peelers piling into the room. She fled, through the secret door and across the warehouse – good grief, she was out of breath easily these days – and out into the yard.

"Ness!!!"

"I'll be fine," Earnestine repeated checking the sky. "We're not indoors and I'm not wearing a hat."

"Found it," said Charlotte. "Blue touch paper."

Georgina doubled over, panting: "Peelers... peelers... right behind me."

"Hold them off. I'll tell Mrs Frasier to call off her dogs," and then Earnestine commanded: "Light it!"

Charlotte opened her box of matches: "All gone!"

"There were three left," Georgina insisted.

"I used them on the gunpowder."

"Then that settles it," Georgina commanded, "take that dangerous thing off Ness."

"Wait!" said Earnestine, and she fished in her clothing and produced another box of matches. "Mrs Frasier gave them to me."

Georgina was adamant: "Ness, no!"

Charlotte struck a match and touched the burning Vesuvian to the blue paper. It shone orange, reluctantly at first, and then it took light and burnt away into a brass pipe. It seemed to have gone out and then it fizzed, showering sparks downwards.

"It's lit!"

387

"In that case," said Earnestine, "I suggest you start running."

"What? In case you blow yourself to smithereens!?" Georgina gasped.

"Yes," said Earnestine, "or, if it works, it shoots flame out of the end."

"In that case–"

"Oh lummy," said Charlotte, and she grabbed Georgina and they started to run.

Their shadows suddenly hardened and leapt out in front of them as a dreadful noise rent the air: a mix of thunder, steam engine and screaming.

Miss Charlotte

The warehouse room was full of Temporal Peelers, tall in their frock coats and top hats, swords by their sides, with their strange white eyes staring impassively. They talked in clipped voices.

"She took a Haversham."

"Are there any others?"

Charlotte's involuntary glance gave it away.

"Here."

Scrutiniser Jones took charge: "You four – after her!"

"Why not–"

"Because I'm far too heavy – quickly."

The four Peelers quickly grabbed the metal canisters from the crate and strapped them on as a fifth, thankful to have avoided selection, went from man to man tightening straps.

"Outside," Scrutiniser Jones ordered.

Georgina took a step forward: "Arthur!"

One of them paused: "You're not my mother."

"I know," said Georgina, concerned, "but be careful."

He gazed at her, then nodded, before he and the other men moved into the yard.

388

"Here," said Scrutiniser Jones and he flung a box of matches through the air. The man caught it and fumbled the matches loose.

Charlotte wondered whether they could make a run for it, but Scrutiniser Jones was such a brick wall of a man.

Outside, there was some brief scuttling as the Peeler went from man to man lighting their Havershams and then–

Woosh!

A column of flame appeared as the first man went aloft.

Another!

And another!

And finally–

The explosion threw them all to the ground. A sound like tinkling bells followed and–

"Down!"

The glass from the roof, blown out by the blast, cascaded down, shattering into bright, sharp fragments on the solid floor.

When Georgina and Scrutiniser Jones picked themselves off the floor, Charlotte had a Duelling Machine cutlass pointed at the man's throat.

"You don't know how to use that," said Scrutiniser Jones.

"Oh, I've had lessons."

"Who from?"

Charlotte pointed to one side: "From that machine."

The Temporal Peeler hesitated, weighing up his chances, when Georgina stepped in and took his revolver from its holster.

"You don't know how to use that either," he said.

"Oh, I took lessons too," said Georgina as she levelled the gun and cocked back the hammer.

"Who from?"

Georgina nodded towards her sister: "From her."

389

Chapter XXVII

Mrs Frasier

It was finished. Mrs Frasier stubbed out her thin cigar. It seemed to symbolise the situation.

She'd heard nothing.

Time had run out.

Miss Deering-Dolittle

Earnestine's hair, which had been in a tight bun, now streamed out behind her as the powerful rocket motor whooshed incessantly. A trail of smoke, rocket fuel and burnt skirt, spiralled and zigged all the way down to the wide and expanding ground, but all Earnestine could see through her goggles was the sky thundering towards her.

She no longer had her umbrella. It had been torn from her grip by the sudden acceleration, but then she'd needed both hands to hold the control levers.

She was no longer screaming. The air pressure forced into her lungs made sound impossible. She wouldn't have been heard, the noise from the machine was incredible.

Touching the controls, just the merest hint... and she careened sideways, down, up, buildings zipped underneath. She turned upwards, ascending, trying to ascertain the lie of the land. She saw the Thames lurch this way and that, its gentle curves distorted by the vibration that shook Earnestine like a rattle.

Where was Big Ben?

How did one land again?

She'd read the manual, but–

Arrghhh, concentrate – it jigged sickeningly.

There!

She saw the curve of the river, blinking, and then she realised that it was like looking down on a map folded out

391

on the kitchen table. There was the Isle of Dogs and so... there would be Queensbury Road.

She saw a flare, a suddenly bright light, followed by another and another. Three dots... no, one had exploded in a bright conflagration. The others hurtled upwards disturbing and brushing aside her own smoke trail. Another was aloft. The tiny shapes became odd doll-like objects and then–

The man fired a weapon at her, the report and zip sounding almost together.

Earnestine banked to one side and her pursuers did the same, erratically. She twisted the control lever and her Haversham flamed, roaring with noise and energy. She dipped down as two pursuers came up on either side. One aimed a gun and fired, the bullet zinged past.

Earnestine glanced the other way: no such luck.

All three were still with her.

She dived, rushing downwards until the Thames filled her view. She levelled, flew along the river and the Haversham's exhaust split and fizzed the water in her wake.

Behind her, two Peelers were following and another gaining height above and–

Woah!

Boats – everywhere.

She darted left and right, had to slow down between two tall sails and a Peeler came in behind her, closer, closer. Looking down Earnestine could see her dangling feet and the Peeler almost within arm's reach–

But the fire from her rocket engine caught him. As he put his hand up to protect his eyes, his control rod hoicked aside and his Haversham careened off. He hit the river, but instead of splashing underneath like a diver, the surface of the water seemed to go hard like ice. The man and Haversham broke into pieces and then exploded. Fire spewed out and the river itself ignited in a sudden conflagration. Shrapnel whizzed away, punching holes in canvas sails and clinker built ship hulls.

Gun shots!

Above, to her right... a bridge. Tower Bridge! The new construction that was so huge and made of steel, granite and Portland stone.

There wasn't time to turn and fly up and over, they'd bottled her into this dead end.

Earnestine panicked: threading a needle, she flew beneath the road. Her motors roared and echoed briefly as she zipped through.

She pulled back and arced up, over, juddering, turning in the air in a wide, vertical circle before it brought her plunging downwards, then further until she was approaching the bridge again.

Her pursuers' trails clearly showed their course around the bridge and she was behind them now.

As she completed the loop, going between the upper and lower spans this time, she was chasing them, rather than they chasing her... but she had no weapon, no revolver with which to take pot-shots. Indeed, she should be going away from them, not towards them.

And where was the other one!?

Up, down, left, right, buildings, towers, a panorama of solid shapes and she went up, clearing the danger.

And the Peeler appeared from nowhere, right behind her.

She twisted, turned, but he did the same, somehow cutting the corner of her turns and gaining, closer, ever closer, and the man was strong enough to guide the machine with one hand. With the other, his fingers like hooks, he reached out, his hand gripping her skirt, tearing it. Earnestine turned the controls to speed away and the spouting jets from her backpack swathed her pursuer in fire. He screamed, his hands coming up to protect his eyes causing him to lose control, but then–

393

The sudden explosion and wall of heat punched Earnestine forward.

Fragments hurtled away making bright arcs across the sky, smoke trails that led inexorably towards the ground to burst into tiny fires so far below.

Phut... phut...

For a moment Earnestine was falling, her stomach lurching within her, and then the engine hammered back into life. Taking a firm grip of the left hand control, she grabbed the fuel gauge. The movement caused the air flow to change around her, flapping her skirts sideways and causing her to lurch down appallingly. The needle jerked about, sometimes just in the red and sometimes... empty.

Downwards: the buildings looked small on the distant ground.

There, suddenly, she saw the Houses of Parliament, its spires sharp like a stockade, and just beyond was the glass tower.

If she could just fly a little further, if... if...

Phut... phut... put!

Earnestine felt suddenly deaf such was the silence and there was a peace as she completed a gentle arc up, hovered for a moment at the apex of the curve before she began to plummet.

Mrs Arthur Merryweather

It was a strange game to shuffle to get Scrutiniser Jones back along the secret passage, but they managed it. Charlotte now had the gun and Georgina was thankful for that. The younger sister had also armed herself with a sword strapped around her waist.

"Don't step in front of me," Charlotte warned.

"I'm going to ring Captain Caruthers, tell him we've bagged a Temporal Peeler and warn him about Lord Farthing."

Georgina found the telephone and fiddled with the unfamiliar nozzle and weight. The latter looked, for all the world, like the pull on an indoor convenience.

"Ear," said Charlotte, and then, "mouth, turn the handle and ask for the Operator."

Georgina did so and eerily a word floated out of the device: *"Operator."* She shuddered; the disembodied voice reminded her of voices from beyond the grave.

"You say 'hello'," Charlotte suggested.

"Hello," said Georgina.

An ethereal voice repeated what she'd said, before a louder voice said: *"What number please?"*

"I need to get a message to Major Dan."

There was more warbling at the end of the contraption: *"What number please?"*

"I don't know."

"Ask for his department," Charlotte said.

"What is his department?" Georgina asked.

Scrutiniser Jones shifted his impressive bulk from one leg to another: this would be his chance and they all knew it.

"Ask for his Club."

"Major Dan's Club?" Georgina replied, but she was interrupted by the distant voice.

"Putting you through now."

"Thank you," Georgina said as she moved the receiver from one ear to the other in an attempt to reduce the whooshing sounds of the seaside.

There was a distant cough.

"Hello," she said. "Hello, hello... it's a foolish word."

"Here, let me try," said Charlotte.

Miss Charlotte

Charlotte took the telephone off Georgina.

395

She said, loudly and clearly: "We need soldiers to attack the Chronological Committee and you need to arrest Lord Farthing!"

She listened.

"Well?" Georgina asked.

"I think he's deaf."

"Rather stupid to have a deaf man operating the telephonic apparatus."

There was a distant cough.

"Oh," said Charlotte, "it's the Club. He can't talk to women."

They both looked at Scrutiniser Jones.

Charlotte held her revolver out threatening: "Say 'we need soldiers to attack the Chronological Committee and you need to arrest Lord Farthing'."

"I will not," said Scrutiniser Jones.

Charlotte gave the communication device back to Georgina and stepped up to the big man.

"Do as I..."

But Charlotte heard a deep rasping noise behind her, and then a man's voice said: "Send Dan and Caruthers to raid the Chronological Committee at once, wot?"

Charlotte turned round, amazed.

"Inspector Jones, Scotland Yard," – it was Georgina with her best play-acting voice – "At once, do you hear? And arrest Lord Farthing. Yes, Farthing – at once!"

She hung up.

"Gina! That was–"

Scrutiniser Jones bolted for the door.

Charlotte fired after him.

Chapter XXVIII

Mrs Frasier

Mrs Frasier was supervising the unloading of the gunpowder from the carts. The future alleyway looked strange, a future of gleaming glass and strange signs, but ruined by all the present day horses and carts with all their dirt and industry.

A sound, a '*phut*' or a scream, made her look up.

The Zeppelin model suddenly jerked, folding in on itself, as a trail of smoke ran straight into it. At first, she thought they had been shelled, but, as it fragmented, a figure emerged and struggled to hold onto the ropes as the canvas ripped. The being changed, like a squat chrysalis turning into a butterfly, except that this was more like a flapping airship gasbag becoming a falling, wounded bird; screeching and squawking in pain.

Earnestine, complete with goggles, landed in the alleyway, the metamorphosis complete for she now appeared as a fiery, avenging angel. Smoke swirled around her, whipped up in eddies all the way to heaven it seemed. The destroyed artifice collapsed behind her bringing down the flats and artificial walls, stripping the illusion away to reveal the old brick walls beneath.

Mrs Frasier's hands came together automatically and she clapped: "What an entrance!"

"She's on fire!" Chief Examiner Lombard shouted.

"Yes, magnificent!"

"The gunpowder!"

Everyone scattered.

Earnestine unclipped her backpack, wrenched it off and then leapt forward. Her dress was indeed smouldering.

The girl cried out: "*Ah...* ah... ah..."

The men rushed about, some putting barrels on the carts to keep them safe, others taking them off, and others looking for another exit. Mrs Frasier herself blocked the doorway back to the underground complex and she was more frightening than three cart loads of gunpowder.

Lombard acted with competence and deposited a bucket of cold water over the struggling girl, turning the scene from an amazing spectacle into a damp farce.

"Enough!" Mrs Frasier shouted, clapping her hands now for attention. "Back to work! Bring her."

She turned and marched away.

Chief Examiner Lombard grabbed Earnestine by the scruff of her neck and hefted her up like a naughty child.

<u>Miss Deering-Dolittle</u>

Earnestine looked somewhat dishevelled, her skirts burnt and ripped, and she was bent double, but she was alive after flying into the sky. She tried pulling her dress into some shape in an attempt to restore her dignity. Her hair was a mess, scorched and soaked.

"You have to flee," Earnestine said.

"Why?"

"Mrs Frasier, you are about to be attacked."

"Cowards run."

"A wise man lives to fight another day."

"We can still win."

"How?"

"By writing the history," Mrs Frasier said. "There are rumours that this is fake, but no proof. We've won it in the courts and in parliament, it's law. If we remove all trace of the illusion, then it will stand."

"That's mad."

"We just need a little more time," said Mrs Frasier.

"You haven't got any more time."

"Are you with us? Once it's all gone, then neither friends nor foes can hurt me."

"If all men count with you," said Earnestine.

Mrs Frasier grinned, she clearly liked this sparring: "None too much."

Earnestine put out her hand, and Mrs Frasier took off her sword and handed it to her.

"Unus pro omnibus, omnes pro uno," said Earnestine, taking it.

Mrs Frasier laughed: "Un pour tous, tous pour un."

"You know it."

"I played Milady de Winter once," said Mrs Frasier. "Villains are always the best parts."

"It could be our Club motto."

"We'll make Dumas proud."

"Or Kipling: Mulvaney, Ortheris and Learoyd."

"Yes, Earnestine, you almost make me believe we can pull this back from the brink."

"We can try," said Earnestine as she held out her hand: "Welcome to the Derring-Do Club."

Mrs Frasier's grip was as strong as Earnestine's own.

"Thank you."

"You're welcome... what are your orders?"

"Get to the conveyor," said Mrs Frasier. "Stop anyone from finding out."

Earnestine saluted: "Aye, aye, Ma'am."

"Call me Charity."

"I'll call you Earnestine."

Mrs Arthur Merryweather

The boy had waited with the hansom cab and thankfully knew enough about horses to drive them back towards Battersea. They dropped Charlotte off nearby, although Georgina had contrived to keep her some distance away. The girl was still in men's clothing and wearing a sword belt, but she'd found a coat from somewhere.

"You'll just observe," Georgina told her.

"Yes."

"From a distance."

"Yes."

"Promise."

"Cross my heart," said Charlotte, "and hope to die."

Georgina asked the boy to take her across the river and on to Captain Caruthers's Club. It seemed a long journey, and then they were there.

"Do I get another sovereign, Miss?" he asked.

"It's probably worth sticking around," Georgina admitted. "These gentlemen can be very generous."

Georgina entered, and the Porter intercepted her.

"Captain Caruthers, please."

"Again?"

"Yes."

The Porter sent the Junior Porter running upstairs.

"You are becoming quite the regular, Ma'am."

"I'll have to take out a subscription."

"Not to a Gentleman's Club, Ma'am."

Captain Caruthers came running down the stairs, followed by the faithful McKendry. Others dressed in regimental red or evening black gathered at the top of the staircase.

"Mrs Merryweather," he said. "Any news?"

"There's gunpowder under this club."

"So the Porter told me, I didn't believe it–"

"It's there!"

"So I looked."

"Lord Farthing placed it there."

"Lord Farthing!"

"To kill you all."

"To help Mrs Frasier... that makes no sense."

"If he disposes of the dissenters here, you, me, Mac, Mrs Frasier, Ness, Lottie, Uncle Tom Cobbley and all, he can control the Chronological Committee. Whoever says what's in the future is the one who says what happens now."

"McKendry?"

The Lieutenant came to attention: "Sir."

"Let's raid this Chronological Committee."

"Surely, we need orders."

"In that case, I order you."

McKendry smiled: "Right ho, Sir."

Quickly, McKendry signalled to the others and they departed, hailing cabs as they went outside. The bustle was efficient and military.

"Good," said Caruthers. "We'll make this our base of operations, field hospital and so forth, if it comes to a fight."

"What about me?" Georgina demanded.

"You're to stay here. Ted, keep her here."

"Sir, this is a Gentleman's Club," complained the Porter.

"Then be gentlemanly."

"I suppose you can stay in the Ladies Drawing Room, Miss," the Porter said.

"Ma'am," Georgina said, before turning to Caruthers. "I can help."

"Bandages and so forth," said Caruthers. "I'm afraid a woman in your condition should stay at home."

"Oh, don't be ridiculous, Captain... what do you mean 'a woman in my condition'?"

"You're expecting."

"Expecting?"

"Do I need to spell it out?"

"Yes, I think you should."

"You're expecting," he said, and then he lowered his voice to a whisper. "That is to say, as in... you're pregnant."

Georgina laughed: "Don't be foolish! Or impertinent! That was all a ruse. I'm not pregnant. How can I be pregnant? I'm not married."

"You were married."

"Yes," said Georgina patiently. "But I'm not now, I'm widowed."

"But you did sleep with him."

"That one night... and we did more than sleep, we... oh my!"

And Georgina sat down, not because she was pregnant or from shock, but because she felt so utterly bewildered: pregnant, not pregnant and now pregnant again for sure. So she simply sat in the Gentlemen's Club, while the men went in carriages to save the day.

It was hardly the stuff of Derring-Do.

How could she have been so foolish as to not realise?

All those visits to the Natural History Museum, all that interest in the theories of evolution and Darwin's Natural Selection, and yet she had failed utterly to apply that knowledge to her own species and to herself. She still thought, ludicrously, of storks flying with bundles of joy and discoveries under gooseberry bushes.

Charles Darwin himself had written that light will be thrown on the origin of man and his history. Of course, man reproduced in the same manner.

Oh, how foolish, how utterly blind!

Arthur's watch felt solid in her hand, round and comforting, like an egg, and it seemed the only real thing in the world, so she held on to it tightly, missing him.

Miss Charlotte

Charlotte reached the factory at the same time that Captain Caruthers and Lieutenant McKendry arrived with five or six carriage loads of soldiers, some in uniform and others still in their dress suits. The hastily assembled militia formed up and there was a hurried negotiation between the officers to find out who was the more senior.

Caruthers went down the line: "Be ready for anything," he said.

Charlotte fell into step behind him.

"This is going to be jolly spiffing," she said.

"Perhaps," said Caruthers, "but no place for a child."

No, no, surely they weren't... but they were, and she wasn't going to cry, but it was so unfair, utterly unfair.

"But I helped with the Austro-Hungarian business," she said, conscious that her voice had gone up by an octave.

"And that was no place for a young lady either... Mac."

Lieutenant McKendry came over at the double.

"Where did you get that coat?" Caruthers asked.

"It was cold," said Charlotte, shifting her sword belt around to hide it beneath her jacket.

"What have you got inside?"

"Nothing."

He frowned: why did adults never believe her?

"Mac, make sure she's on her way," said Caruthers. "We'll move when the second group arrive."

"Come on, Lottie," said McKendry, and he led her away, and waited until she was all the way down the street and turning the corner. When Charlotte looked back, Captain Caruthers had led Major Dan's Boys along the wall towards the iron arch. They took up position just outside the gate to the factory yard.

Unfair – they had all the fun and she was sent home to kick her heels. Mrs Frasier had locked her in a store room, so she was entitled to her revenge – surely? But she had no choice, and turned the corner trudging as much as she could. She wasn't going to look back, she decided, she wasn't going to give McKendry the satisfaction, except... that was strange.

Behind her, set in the wall was a door.

On it was a small symbol, a sundial. She glanced up at the sun, then squinted past the bright, orange smudge in her eyesight at her own shadow. She had no real idea of the time, except that the sundial wasn't at anything like the right angle to work.

She fished into her pocket and took out the second key, the one that had been on the barrel in the cellar next

403

to the handcuff keys. There was a piece of string threaded through the loop end of the key to hold a fob. It said, simply '*The Future*'.

Oh, this was a side door.

This door must lead into the Chronological Committee's base.

And Charlotte had the key.

She should tell Caruthers about this way in, but he'd said to go home and he was busy and she'd found it and there wasn't time anyway.

Charlotte glanced right and left, and then–

She had to wait for an omnibus to clatter past, its horses fretting with their load.

Right and left again, and then she nipped across the road to the doorway. She listened, but the noise of the street was too loud and the door too solid.

Huddling in the recess, so no-one could see, she checked her revolver – empty. She shouldn't have fired all those bullets at Scrutiniser Jones when he was making a run for it. At least she had her sword.

Nothing ventured, she thought, and she pushed the key into the door. It turned, easily, and she went inside.

There was an office with oak panelling and a large desk with a green leather inlay. On the wall was an oil painting of Boadicea in a scene that was jolly stirring.

Charlotte went on and found herself somewhere near the Chronological Conveyor. She could see out of the windows of the corridor to the main entrance. Outside, in the central area, Peelers were busy unloading barrels off carts. They rolled them along and then down a chute.

Slipping around the glass wall of the Pepper's Ghost apparatus, she went along the other dilapidated corridor and past the identical control lectern. The view from these windows, although superficially the same, ended with a backcloth expertly painted with buildings and the sky.

Turning round, she saw the other dais room. It was an extraordinary contraption, but even so, now she knew how it worked, she was amazed that she had been taken in at all.

There were a few barrels placed against the wall. When she went over and examined them she found them full of gunpowder. The grain size suggested it was artillery grade.

If she could find more of it, she could blow the place up, she thought and sniggered. That would show Mrs Frasier and her Temporal Peelers.

She made her way through Temporal Engineering towards the Rotunda, sneaking down some stairs to get to the 'future' version of the building. The gunpowder must be stored somewhere there, she thought, and sure enough, she found some more stacked by a wall.

She split the top of a barrel with her sword, and then glanced around wondering what was the best method to go about this. She tried picking up the barrel, but this one was too big. She needed a priming charge like the one she'd used earlier on the door.

"Charlotte!"

It was Earnestine.

"Ness, help me here."

"I can't allow this," Earnestine said.

"We've got to stop them," said Charlotte. "And besides, it'll be such an explosion."

"What they are doing here is too important."

"Ness?"

"Charlotte, put that down."

"Ness?"

"Put that down *at once!*"

"No."

"Do as you are told."

"No."

"Charlotte Deering-Dolittle, you are going to be in a great deal of trouble when we get home."

"I don't care."

"Will you—"

"You've always told me to do what is right, and, surely, the Defence of the Realm is important."

"Then I will just have to teach you a lesson."

"No you won't."

"Yes, I will."

"Won't."

"Will."

"Won't."

"Wi–"

"Don't be childish, Ness."

"I am not!" Earnestine drew a sword: "How dare you talk to me like that? I'm your elder and better."

"Elder, but not better," said Charlotte. She backed away and raised the sword she'd used to open the barrel. "I dare."

The two sisters faced each other, weapons drawn.

"Did you use the duelling machine?" Earnestine said.

"Edgar, yes, every day, even when you were in the future."

"Edgar?"

"It looked like Uncle Edgar."

Earnestine laughed: "Oh, it does."

"Which proves that I applied myself."

"The proof of the pudding is in the eating. Did you get to the tenth level?"

"I did."

"The Deutsche Fechtschule?"

"Yes."

"The Fiore Furlano de Civida–"

"I did them all, Ness! I just didn't work out how to pronounce them."

"Well, Lottie, you clearly aren't the expert you claim to be."

"We'll see... en garde."

"No, Lottie, I cannot allow you to move on to practical aspects until you have a proper grounding in the academic side."

"You're only saying that because you know you'll lose."

"I most certainly am not."

"En garde."

"En garde."

They both brought their swords up in front of their faces. Charlotte imagined the dueling machine, Uncle Edgar, and then kept a watchful eye on Earnestine, so that Earnestine didn't take her by surprise and attack before she was ready. Earnestine had killed someone in a duel, she knew, so she was a formidable foe. But still she had to fight her elder sister. It was clear that Earnestine had been turned by the evil, but charismatic, Mrs Frasier.

So Charlotte attacked, a lunge, and Earnestine had to sidestep and parry to avoid it.

"Oh, you did apply yourself, Lottie," Earnestine said.

"Yes."

They cut and parried, moving sideways and then to-and-fro, each countering the other as if playing different Jacquard cards from their hand, one after another.

Snap!

Their swords clattered back and forth until–

"Ow!"

Earnestine leapt back, putting her left hand over her right where Charlotte had smacked it with the side of her blade. Charlotte realized just how much further she'd reached with the Dueling Machine than her sister.

"See... Ness, you can't beat me, so you'll just have–"

Earnestine slashed angrily catching Charlotte off guard. Her sword clattered to the ground, her left hand gripped over her right arm copying Earnestine's earlier gesture, but this time vivid red blood seeped between her fingers.

They glared at each other.

It wasn't a game anymore.

Earnestine leveled the point of her sword.

407

"Now, Charlotte, say sorry, put away this gunpowder and we'll say no more about it."

"Never!"

Charlotte leapt to one side, lurching into a cartwheel and as she went over, her heels and borrowed trousers uppermost, she picked up her fallen sword. When she landed, she was ready for a second bout.

They fought again with no love lost between them.

The stakes ever higher, Earnestine fought with renewed strength, but it wasn't brute force that counted. Although the machine had more power in its fully wound springs than any person, Charlotte could still beat it.

She parried, blow after blow, but each attack from her sister, despite her longer arms, was wilder and clumsier. Charlotte just needed to wait for the best opening as her older sister tired.

It came soon enough.

Earnestine's sword went down, strong and powerfully, going past Charlotte's in an arc. The edge of Charlotte's sword found its target and she drove the move home.

Earnestine's yelped, her sword clattered across the floor and she put her right hand to her face. Blood spurted and then oozed between her fingers, dripping down and splattered bright red flecks on the ground.

"That hurt!"

"Sorry Ness."

"I'm bleeding."

"I'm sorry, Ness, really I am, but I win: you have to give ground."

"No."

"Ness, you have to ask for quarter, because I can just run you through."

Earnestine lips tightened, but she had no choice: "Quarter?"

"Of course," said Charlotte, genuinely disturbed by the injury she'd inflicted.

"NO!"

It was Mrs Frasier.

The woman put the toe of her boot under Earnestine's sword and flicked it into the air. She caught it expertly.

"But I won," Charlotte complained. "It's two against one."

"Don't whine," said Earnestine and Mrs Frasier together.

"There's only one other person besides yourself here," said Mrs Frasier. "We can't help it if we came here twice. Ah ha! We can finally use the Royal 'we'."

"You aren't Ness!" Charlotte roared. "You're a fake. See! Ness will have a duelling scar and you don't."

Mrs Frasier put her sword to her cheek and pressed: when she took the blade away, a line of blood oozed and dripped.

"En garde!" she said.

She slashed forward, swiping at Charlotte, who parried giving ground.

"Don't kill her!" Earnestine shouted.

They fought, Charlotte and Mrs Frasier, swords clashing, but for Charlotte it was her second bout. She might have beaten Earnestine, but her skills didn't match those of Mrs Frasier. The older woman showed flair, a dramatic ability to cut and thrust, moving and skipping to change the angle of attack with confidence and aplomb.

Charlotte, used to a machine, couldn't cope with the changes of pace. The speed and agility required were beyond her. With each attack, she had to back away, a step here, a shuffle there.

In a flurry of cuts, Mrs Frasier trapped Charlotte against the glass wall and, with nowhere to go, Charlotte's defence was desperate, each parry more hopeless and more uncontrolled until, inevitably, she left herself open.

Mrs Frasier stabbed forward.

There were men running behind Mrs Frasier, hidden in the blur of tears and fear, but all Charlotte could see was

409

the steel point coming in, past her own sword, closer than an arm's length, striking her with utter conviction.

There was nothing Charlotte could have done.

Mrs Frasier let out a cry of triumph: "Ha!"

And Charlotte was still alive.

Charlotte wrenched her own arm around, twisting her wrist to bring her blade to bear, and then she stabbed with all her might. Her weapon went under Mrs Frasier's corset, somehow finding a way through the ribs of whalebone to penetrate deep into the woman's tightened internal organs.

Mrs Frasier let out an almighty bellow.

The woman punched Charlotte with her right fist, still encased in the cutlass hilt, and Charlotte felt the blow ring inside her skull. She toppled over, the darkness of unconsciousness rushing in just as she saw Earnestine on her feet, running towards her. Her sister was moving too slowly and Charlotte knew she wouldn't reach her in time.

Earnestine's mouth opened, a silent shout, words that Charlotte could not hear and then...

Charlotte hit the ground.

Chapter XXIX

Mrs Frasier

Mrs Frasier felt herself slipping from her body. She'd heard of that, a common description in séances, and for a moment she felt like she was looking down from above and that the candles were flickering.

Two figures stumbled down the corridor: one coughed, blood coming up, and the other pulled her upright. They made it to the court room. Everywhere else was chaos and confusion, clashes of metal, gunshots, the screech of ricocheting bullets and human screams.

There was no-one in the court room: the battle was in the Rotunda. Whoever held that, held the future.

Earnestine hauled Mrs Frasier towards the Judge's office.

"No," said Mrs Frasier. "I'm done for."

"Come on," said Earnestine, tears in her eyes. "We can make it."

"I had the chance to kill her, but instead I locked her up. I couldn't – she was like a sister – remember how she hugged me when she first arrived here? So sweet. She's done for me."

"Nonsense."

"Cowards die many times before their deaths. The valiant never taste of death but once."

Mrs Frasier slipped down and Earnestine, trying to hold on, went with her.

"I pulled the blow," Mrs Frasier explained. "Instinctive."

"You didn't want to kill our sister."

"No... it was... oh, this hurts so. Bloody stage combat... looks good, but useless in the end."

"Please..."

"Mother said acting would be the death of me."

411

"You're an actress?"

"An actress can be... you can... Ness. Be anyone."

"Me?"

"You were–" Mrs Frasier coughed, blood came up.

"Lie still," said Earnestine, her left hand raising the fallen woman's head and her right hand fluttering over the injuries as she agitated over what to do. Her own face must have stung and throbbed, but she ignored it.

"All those earrings to get my ear lobes to look like yours," Mrs Frasier said. "You were my best part. I see myself, the girl I could have been, in you."

"Lie still."

They were alone in the court. All the seats were empty: the judge's bench, the lawyers, jury and the Public Gallery. The paraphernalia of the drama, the grand set and the litter of props were just waiting to start up again for another act.

"My death scene..." Mrs Frasier laughed then, a cackle that slipped into a painful hacking. "And – typical – there's no bloody audience!"

"I can get help," said Earnestine, but Mrs Frasier could feel her lifeblood flowing out to make the stage slippery. She saw it now, a bright light above her, stronger even than limelight, but not as welcoming, and the edges of her vision were like a curtain slowly closing.

She gasped, clutched in her pocket: "Watches... Jerry gave them... I miss him... they're yours."

"No, I–"

"Silver is... the past and the other... the golden future."

"No... please."

"Take them."

"Thank you."

"I did it well, I convinced them all... for nothing. The dream, Ness, it will die with me. Ness... Ness... don't let it... end. Prom... ise... m..."

Mrs Frasier's eyes fluttered and then a most strange exhalation blew from her lips.

412

Miss Deering-Dolittle

"I promise you... Earnestine," said Earnestine, moving aside a loose lock of Mrs Frasier's dark red hair.

Earnestine was not sure how long she sat there with Mrs Frasier slipping from her arms and into her lap. When she looked up to find the source of a gasp, she saw a line of Temporal Peelers.

Scrutiniser Jones burst in, bleeding at the shoulder, full of energy and rage.

"They hold the north end, we must..." but then he saw the body before him. He stopped, deflated, the fight going out of him in an instant. He took off his top hat and held it in his big, meaty hands.

The others, one by one, took off their top hats too and held them to their chests with heads bowed.

"Not Mrs Frasier," he said, and then he added: "We're done for."

"She was an extraordinary woman," said Chief Examiner Lombard. "So bold, imaginative and she tried to change the world. She weaved this amazing story and we were taken in."

"I heard Doctor Deering tell it, but she made you believe it," said Checker Rogers.

Scrutiniser Jones leant down and, despite his great musculature, he acted with painstaking tenderness as he closed Mrs Frasier's eyes, then, so carefully, he arranged her body tidily.

Earnestine shuffled away, still sitting on the floor.

"Aye," Chief Examiner Lombard said, "she gave us a better script than you get on the number three tour."

Earnestine felt numb: "Number three?"

"We're all actors. *Were* actors. There just aren't the roles. Charity... Mrs Frasier gave us a future, literally a future."

Earnestine realised she was holding the pocket watches: gold and silver. They were slippery with blood.

413

They represented a choice. She opened the gold one and saw an engraving on the inside cover:-

'*For Our Future, J. J. D.*'.

"She treated me like a person and not just a boxer and strongman," said Scrutiniser Jones. "She didn't just promise a better future, she was going to deliver."

"But why can't we still create that future?" Earnestine pleaded. "Surely if everyone wants a better world, then it ought to be straight-forward."

"People need to believe. That was the plan: pretend it was real, argue it in the courts and then it would become real."

"It's not over," said Earnestine.

"She's dead, there's no-one else."

Earnestine stood, faced them: "There's me!"

"You?"

"If we can hold them off," Earnestine said, "and set off the gunpowder, then the laws can still stand. It won't be for nothing."

"You're just a child."

"If she could pretend to be me, then I can become her."

Earnestine brushed her dress down and held her head up, stretching, trying to become taller, to stand prouder, and to somehow fill the space vacated by Mrs Frasier's exit.

"Different actors play the same parts," she said.

The Scrutiniser shook his head: "You're not Mrs Frasier."

Earnestine rounded on him: "I'm not Mrs Frasier *yet!*"

Mrs Arthur Merryweather

Arthur Merryweather appeared before her.

Georgina saw his shoes first, singed trousers and damaged frock coat. He held his arm and winced.

"I thought you..." he began, but words failed him.

"Arthur?"

"I'm not."

"No."

The wounded were being brought in from the battle, a fleet of carriages pulling up outside the Club and stretcher bearers hurrying back and forth. Georgina had started to help, brought into it when someone practically dropped some poor young boy, not much older than herself, onto her lap. There were a few other women too, moving between the camp beds that had been set up in the hallway of the Club. There were screams from the billiard room, where an army surgeon worked on those who needed to be stitched up or sawn apart.

"Shame," the lad said. "I'd liked to have been."

"Your arm?"

"Broken."

"Here..." she said, leading him to one side.

"Miss, he's our prisoner!" Georgina noticed the two guards for the first time.

"It's Ma'am! And he's my patient."

She sat him down and took off his frock coat gingerly. He flinched but didn't cry out. She checked, frightened of hurting him, and then strapped his arm to his chest.

"How did you?" Georgina asked.

"That flying rucksack... tricky to land."

"I imagine."

"You said be careful."

"Did I?"

"You're the second person in my life who's shown me any concern."

Georgina fussed with the knot: "Surely not?"

"I had nothing and Mrs Frasier gave us hope: all the actors, pick pockets, con artists, the disenfranchised. She cared in her harsh way."

"Much like my sister."

"You know..."

"Yes."

415

"That one moment, even though I was your enemy, even though I'd deliberately hurt you."

Georgina said nothing, the pain was still too raw.

He met her gaze: "But you sounded as if you really cared." The young man shivered.

Georgina reached for his frock coat, but, instead, she picked up a khaki jacket and slipped it around her patient's shoulders.

The guards had moved away, standing tall with their arms folded to intimidate another Temporal Peeler, a prisoner too. There were shouts, another struggle as the fervour of battle spilled out again, even here amongst the wounded and dying.

"Head up, shoulders back, and just walk out," she said.

"What?"

"Make your mother proud."

"I will."

He stood above her and he could have been Arthur. He held out his uninjured hand: "Philip."

She shook it.

"My son will be called Philip," Georgina said, amazed.

"You don't have to do that."

"Arthur, my husband, wanted it."

"Then that's all well and good."

"Philip."

"Yes."

"Be careful."

"I will."

"Here," and Georgina gave him the watch.

"What's this?"

"Your father's watch."

"I never had a father."

"Now you do."

"Don't cry... Mother."

"I won't."

He went and she did feel proud. He walked towards the light and became a dark blurry shape in the bright

416

rectangle of the doorway, and then he stepped into the bright sunlight beyond and was gone.

Georgina rubbed her eyes, dried her hands on her dress and then went about her rounds.

Miss Charlotte

Charlotte wasn't sure when the clamouring in her head was drowned out by the clamour around her. She tried to stand, but stumbled against the wall. Her mouth tasted of iron, blood, and the side of her face where Mrs Frasier had struck her throbbed.

There was an explosion, a deep '*crump*' of a noise, distantly.

She made her way... her leg gave under her and she faltered, but kept going.

Nearing the Rotunda, she was suddenly surrounded by retreating soldiers mixed with gentlemen.

"They're putting up a hell of a fight!" said someone... McKendry. "Someone's given them a second wind."

Charlotte shook her head and winced. That woman had knocked her so hard, she was addled.

Suddenly, she was alone and standing in the Rotunda.

A gun cocked.

She saw, behind a makeshift barricade, a Temporal Peeler aiming a rifle at her. They'd made a redoubt to defend the Judiciary section. Her own revolver was in her pocket, the weight pulling on one side of the frock coat, but she'd never fish it out fast enough and she'd still not found any ammunition to load it.

So she raised her hands.

The man took two steps towards her.

Charlotte heard a woman's voice above the shouts and noise. It was Mrs Frasier's grating voice, shouting: "Fall back! Don't let them draw you out of the defensive position."

The man kept his aim, and then, hearing that woman shout again, he raised his gun and withdrew from the barricade.

Charlotte breathed again – that dreadful woman, Mrs Frasier, had saved her life.

The third body had ammunition for her revolver. Charlotte loaded, carefully filling each chamber with a round before closing the top break with a satisfying click. The cylinder spun without obstruction. She held the gun up and aimed, squinting along until the fore sight blade sat in the rear notch. She held it firm until the lanyard ring stopped swinging. It was big for her hand, but satisfying: a good gun, the Webley, Mk 1.

In saving her, Mrs Frasier had made a mistake; Charlotte would make sure of that. She had a score to settle.

She scuttled across, keeping her revolver at the ready, and disappeared into the Prison area. She zigzagged around the fallen bodies, until she reached the stairs, jarring herself badly on the second step when she skidded on some black powder spilt across the floor.

Down below was the cell block. The two desks were unmanned. The *Half-penny Marvel* with its Sexton Blake story lay crumpled on the floor.

At the end of the corridor, she found Number 19.

She knocked.

"Whatever it is, I won't," came a familiar voice.

"Uncle," Charlotte whispered. "I'm here to rescue you."

"Who's that?"

"Charlotte... Charlotte Deering-Do–"

"Lottie!"

"Yes."

"It's not safe here, run along home at once."

"Uncle!"

Charlotte didn't wait for a reply, but hurried back to the Warder's desk. She put her gun back in her pocket and searched the drawers until she found the keys. They were all big and heavy. The fourth one she tried unlocked her Uncle's cell door.

For a moment, they looked at each other and then she was not sure if she was hugging him or he was hugging her. It hurt and it was good at the same time.

"Are you in fancy dress," Uncle Jeremiah said, gentle mocking, "or is it this rampant bloomerism?"

"Oh, Uncle," she said. Her jaw felt strange, loose.

"Nasty knock there, Lottie," he said. "You've a big bruise forming. Did you fall out of the tree again?"

"No, Uncle, I fought Mrs Frasier."

He nodded.

"Let's get out of here," Charlotte said.

"Yes, my dear, good idea."

They made their way back to the Warder's desk.

"There's no-one on guard," Charlotte said, "but it might be jolly tricky upstairs."

"Filthy place, I'll be glad to go, look at the dirt."

"That's gunpowder, Uncle."

"Gunpowder?"

"Yes, it trails up the stairs and probably goes to wherever they've stored the gunpowder."

"The Ultimate Sanction!"

"Uncle?"

"It was Charity's... Mrs Frasier's plan to blow everything up, hide the evidence. Without evidence to the contrary, the new laws would stand. Perhaps it would be for the best. Why did you say it would be tricky upstairs?"

"There's a battle going on."

"What? Derring-Do Club to the rescue, eh? Our brave Earnestine fighting them single-handedly?"

"Hardly," said Charlotte, pulling out her revolver.

They went back up the stairs, Uncle Jeremiah having to take each step one at a time. Charlotte went back to help him and so was taken by surprise when a figure appeared at the top.

419

A gun cocked.

"Stay where you are!"

Standing silhouetted in the door was Mrs Frasier!

"Mrs Frasier, we—"

"What are you doing here?"

"Escaping."

"I should hope so too, I'm going to blow the place up."

Charlotte's eyes adjusted to the light: Mrs Frasier was still bleeding from the cut to her face, but even so she looked younger.

"Ness!?"

"So you'd better get a move on and escape," Earnestine said.

"But Ness, you'd never outrun gunpowder."

"I'm meeting Triumph and Disaster!"

"What?"

"Kipling."

"Now isn't the time for homework."

"Don't be impertinent."

"I'm not being impertinent."

"I haven't forgiven you for this!"

Earnestine showed her bloodied hand in reference to her face. In the moment that she did so, Charlotte drew her revolver.

Earnestine tensed her aim: they were ready to resume their battle. All those times before, when the elder had beaten the younger, told her off, locked her in the pantry.

"Girls."

So softly had Uncle Jeremiah spoken and yet his words silenced them quicker than any screeching governess.

Earnestine spoke as if she only just seen him: "Uncle?"

"Say you are sorry."

"Sorry for what?"

"To Lottie."

Earnestine lips went tight and then, in response to years of training given her by her elders and betters, she said: "Sorry."

"And Lottie."

"Sorry Ness," said Charlotte, and for once she meant it.

"I'd like to see Charity," said Uncle Jeremiah.

"Charity? Who's Charity?" Charlotte asked.

"Mrs Frasier," said Earnestine. "I'm... she's dead."

Uncle Jeremiah reacted as if he had been struck and grabbed the banister: "No... no."

Earnestine gave Charlotte a sharp look.

"It wasn't my fault," Charlotte whined.

There was gunfire again, distant.

Uncle Jeremiah collapsed until he was sitting on the cold steps: "Oh, no, no, please no."

"She died bravely," said Earnestine.

"She would," and the old man looked over his half-moon glasses at Earnestine. "She was so like your mother. How could I resist? How? And that's what drew me to her, you see. A chance to win her instead of my brother, damned Earnest – he had all the luck. And Charity was the spit of your mother, the very spit, and you..."

"It was your idea?"

"Just an idea, a tiny fancy, a thought... but she teased it out of me and I made such embellishments to entertain her, until we both believed in the impossible."

Earnestine nodded.

"It was a story," said Charlotte.

"Yes," said Uncle Jeremiah, "a story I started, so it's only fitting I should end it."

He had a box of matches and he was sitting on the trail of gunpowder. He lit one, letting it flare and then turning the match so that the wood caught. It was mesmerising.

Uncle Jeremiah looked at Earnestine: "What's the line of Kipling's '*If–*' after 'If all men count with you, but none too much'?"

421

Earnestine frowned: "If you can fill the unforgiving minute with sixty seconds' worth of distance... *RUN!*"

Earnestine grabbed Charlotte's hand and pulled. They were up, showing a good pair of heels, as they raced up the stairs, sprinted down the corridor and ran for their lives.

To anyone and everyone they passed, friend and foe whichever side they were now on, they shouted: "Out, everyone out!"

Earnestine was first to the Chronological Conveyor and hopped from one foot to another looking for the control.

"How does it work!?"

"Up here!"

"No, stand there," said Chief Examiner Lombard.

The two sisters stood on the dais as the gaunt man went to the control lectern. He yanked at a lever and the floor shot upwards with a hiss of hydraulics and a burst of light. Suddenly, the tawdry future corridor was replaced by the pristine paintwork of the past.

Captain Caruthers was there to greet them: "Lottie! Miss Deering-Do– You're injured."

"Never mind that, run for it."

"We're not beaten, we'll never retreat."

"They've lit the explosives!" Charlotte yelled. She grabbed Captain Caruthers by the hand and then they were all running for the exit.

"Clear! Fall back!" Caruthers shouted.

The soldiers and gentlemen scampered under the iron archway and scattered into the street.

"How far?" McKendry shouted.

Charlotte thought about the barrels and barrels of gunpowder: "How would I know, but I imagine we're nothing like far enough yet, because it'll be–"

The moment was etched on their memories by an overpowering flash like magnesium powder flaring above a camera. It seemed that they were frozen, held trapped in a picture already, as the colour leeched from the scene. Then, with savage abruptness, they were plucked from the ground, hurled sideways, and hammered by the noise of the explosion.

The future had been underground, so the blast went up. The walls of the factory held long enough to deflect the flying shrapnel upwards and then they failed, tumbling down...

... broken.

Epilogue

Mrs Frasier

Houses of Parliament,
St. Margaret's Street,
Westminster,
London.

Miss Deering-Dolittle,
12b Zebediah Row,
Kensington,
London.

My Dearest Earnestine,

If you are reading this, then I am dead. That does not matter. Hopefully we ~~will become~~ have become firm friends and allies over the many years to come. It is the work that is important. You must carry the torch into the future. You will undoubtedly discover our secrets: what was done and how. Please understand why. I am confident that you are pragmatic and possessing that abundant common sense needed to see our great work through to the end. It is for the greater good.

Yours with highest regard,

Earnestine Frasier

Mrs Marcus Frasier.

Miss Deering-Dolittle

Earnestine fought the impulse to scratch. The dueling scar on her face hurt so, especially when she was anxious. She was still angry with Charlotte. *I do not want to talk about it*, she'd insisted. She'd been tempted to put the daguerreotype without Charlotte up on the wall, but the original picture of them all at the theatre was back in its place in the drawing room.

There was a scream.

Everyone looked at the ceiling briefly.

"Shame about your party," said Captain Caruthers.

"I'll have other birthdays," Earnestine replied.

"But you only come of age once."

Another piercing scream ripped the very air.

"Any news of Lord Farthing?" Earnestine asked.

Caruthers shook his head: "He got clean away. There was a report that he'd been seen in Paris, but that came to nothing. It's not the sort of news you want as a birthday present, I know. They've declared all the laws null and void, so that's something."

"Yes, something."

"It was all very awkward for the powers-that-be," said Caruthers, smoothing down the chevron of his brown moustache with his free hand. The other held a package. "We're not exactly hushing it up, but everyone's too embarrassed to talk about it."

"It is extraordinary how so many Members of Parliament changed their tune."

"Have you any plans?" Caruthers asked by way of changing the conversation.

"I think we might take a holiday in Georgina's country house."

"It's in the middle of nowhere, isn't it?"

"Yes, Dartmoor."

"That's Devon, isn't it?" Caruthers said, and he turned to McKendry: "Mac, isn't that where those lights in the sky were reported?"

426

"Near Mag... sorry, *More Darling* – is that it? – Chase," said McKendry, "No, that was all just local superstition – absolutely nothing in it."

Charlotte piped in: "It's cold and horrid."

"Lottie!" said Earnestine. "It'll be a chance for some welcome peace and quiet."

"You deserve it," said Caruthers.

Earnestine checked her gold pocket watch, seeing the engraving under the cover about the future: the mechanism itself was running slow.

Captain Caruthers had been hovering with a package for far too long. He shuffled uneasily, so Earnestine prompted him: "Yes?"

"For you – birthday, and all that."

Earnestine took the proffered present. She carefully removed the ribbon and paper to reveal what she already knew was underneath by the feel of the rectangle. It was a framed picture... or rather a poem.

"Oh," she said, "'*If*–' by Rudyard Kipling."

"You know it! It's only been privately circulated in the club and regiment, based on that Jameson chap business; it's not been officially published."

Earnestine read it, remembering the lines: *Or watch the things you gave your life to, broken.*

"Foolish really," Caruthers continued, "but I think we should put it up on the wall in every cadet's room, a sort of motto, advice really, so I thought... that is... it's good advice."

"If you can keep your head..." she said. "Yes, thank you. Good advice indeed."

"That's what I thought," said Caruthers. "It's embroidery, you sew it, and when it's finished you can put it up in a nursery. That is, when you have a son."

Earnestine knew what she wanted to say to that, but instead she said, "Lovely."

"And a husband, obviously," Caruthers added quickly. "Anyway, many happy returns."

McKendry was even more embarrassed: he'd brought a posy of flowers.

"Beautiful," Earnestine said.

"Major Dan sends his apologies," Caruthers added. He'd also sent an envelope, but that ended up unopened upon the mantelpiece where the clock used to be.

"Your Father wanted sons, didn't he?" Caruthers said.

There was more screaming from upstairs followed by a stream of invective.

"Yes, he did... and Mother, probably for the peace and quiet," Earnestine said.

"Earnest Deering-Dolittle was a great man."

"Earnest George Charles Deering-Dolittle – he couldn't really have any more children, could he? You think he's dead?"

"Well... I don't know... There are expeditions that do disappear without a trace and then re-emerge many years later. Stanley, for example."

She looked at the embroidery pattern: 'Yours is the Earth and everything that's in it, and – which is more – you'll be a Man, my son!'

Birthdays!

Long awaited, always over too quickly.

However, she was a woman now.

Mrs Arthur Merryweather

"Oh, oh, bal– bal– bally hell – you watch your language, you stupid cow, I'm splitting apart!!!"

And Georgina went on in that vein, along with some ornament throwing.

Arthur had done this to her! Her Arthur. The utter–

"Oh! Oh!!!"

The younger midwife hovered by the bedroom door, much afraid.

Miss Charlotte

"Where did she learn words like that?" Charlotte asked, slightly horrified.

"She married," Earnestine said. "I expect there was a lesson."

It had been a wonderful birthday and there had been cake, and even more cake for Charlotte when Georgina had gone into labour, and Earnestine had looked lovely in her new burgundy dress. She wore her hair down to hide the scar, and her long, red curls jiggled when she turned her head. Charlotte was very thankful that Earnestine had forgiven her: they would never mention it again, her elder sister had assured her: *I do not want to talk about it.*

Captain Caruthers and Lieutenant McKendry eventually made their farewells, leaving Charlotte and Earnestine alone in the drawing room.

Earnestine lit a thin cigar, inhaling deeply and lost in her own thoughts.

The maid came in to clear up.

"Leave those, Jane," Earnestine said. "I'll gather everything up when we've finished. You and Mary can go out if you wish."

"Thank you, Miss," said the maid with a curtsey, "very much obliged, Miss."

Georgina yelled from upstairs: "I am blowing, you stupid—"

And more words, such words that made Charlotte snigger even though she had no idea what they meant.

"School for you," said Earnestine.

"Can I join a cadet college?"

"Hmmm."

There wasn't a Women's Cadet Academy for Charlotte to enrol in; perhaps there never would be, but it was good to dream.

Earnestine seemed withdrawn, staring at the Lincrusta wall covering while seeing some other vista.

"Are you going to find Marcus?" Charlotte asked.

429

"Marcus?"

"Mister Frasier, your future husb–"

"I most certainly am not."

"But it's destiny."

"I haven't forgotten that you should be married off as soon as possible."

Charlotte felt a certain horror at the idea and thought it best to change the subject: "Do you think Georgina will have a boy or a girl?"

"Either way, it'll be a Derring-Do."

Earnestine put the virgin embroidery, still in its frame, onto the mantelpiece, moving some envelope to one side.

"...or watch the things you gave your life to, broken, and stoop and build 'em up with worn-out tools," said Earnestine. She didn't look happy.

"What was that?"

"Kipling."

"It's gone now, isn't it?" said Charlotte with understanding. "That dream that Uncle Jeremiah and Mrs Frasier had."

"Not yet."

The End

The Derring-Do Club

will return in the

Invasion of the Grey

David Wake launched the first of the **Derring-Do Club** novels when he was Guest of Honour at ArmadaCon 25. This instalment was brought out for Loncon 3, Worldcon. He'll be picking another SF convention to release the next episode.

Thank you for buying and reading *The Derring-Do Club and the Year of the Chrononauts*. If you liked this novel, please take a few moments from your own adventures to write a review and help spread the word.

For more information, and to join the mailing list for news of forthcoming releases, see www.davidwake.com or www.derring-do.club.

Many thanks to:–

Dawn Abigail, Siân K Bradshaw, Richard Clay, Andy Conway, Pow-wow, Marion Pitman and Jessica Rydill.

Cover art by Smuzz: www.smuzz.org.uk.

A ripping yarn of cliff-hangers, desperate chases, romance and deadly danger.

Earnestine, Georgina and Charlotte are trapped in the Eden College for Young Ladies suffering deportment, etiquette and Latin. So, when the British Empire is threatened by an army of zombies, the Deering-Dolittle sisters are eager to save the day. Unfortunately, they are under strict instructions not to have any adventures...

...but when did that ever stop them?

"Think 'Indiana Jones pace'. It's fast and dangerous and does not involve embroidery!"

★ ★ ★ ★ ★

"A brilliant fast paced steampunk adventure, trains zombies and zeppelins, what more could you want?"

★ ★ ★ ★ ★

THE DERRING-DO CLUB

*Putting their best foot forward,
without showing an ankle, since 1896*

The first novel in the adventure series available as an ebook and a paperback.

A ripping yarn of strange creatures, aerial dog-fights, espionage and *pirates!*

Strange lights hover over Dartmoor and alien beings abduct the unwary as the plucky Deering-Dolittle sisters, Earnestine, Georgina and Charlotte, race to discover the truth before the conquest begins...

...but betrayal is never far away.

*"Well-written, fast-paced, and dangerously addictive
- but with some extra thinking in there, too,
should you choose to read it that way."*
★ ★ ★ ★ ★

"As with previous adventures I really enjoyed the imaginative scene setting, building intrigue into unexpected twists and a spectacular ending."
★ ★ ★ ★ ★

THE DERRING-DO CLUB

*Putting their best foot forward,
without showing an ankle, since 1896*

The third novel in the adventure series available as an ebook and a paperback.

Do you fear technology – we have an App for that.

I, Phone

DAVID WAKE

Your phone is your life. But what if it kept secrets from you? What if it accidentally framed you for murder? What if it was also the only thing that could save you?

In a world where phones are more intelligent than humans, but are still thrown away when they become obsolete, one particular piece of plastic lies helpless as its owner, Alice Wooster, is about to be murdered...

In this darkly comic near-future tale, a very smart phone tells its own story as events build to a climactic battle to decide the fate of virtual, augmented and real worlds... and whether it can order Alice some proper clothes.

"Excellent novel – by turns strikingly original, laugh-out-loud funny and thought provoking."
★★★★★

"Want to read it again soon..."
★★★★★

"A thoughtful, tense and funny look at a future that seems to be already upon us."
★★★★★

Available as an ebook and a paperback.

A tonic for the Xmas Spirit

Being Santa's daughter would be a dream come true for any child, but for Carol Christmas, the fairy tale is about to come to an end. Evil forces threaten the festive season, and only Carol can save the day...

A grim fairy tale told as a children's book, but perhaps not just for children at all.

"This starts out as a delightfully childlike modern take on the Christmas myth - the kind of Pixar-esque story that can play to the kids and give the adults a knowing wink or two, but it gets dark. Very dark."
★★★★★

Available as an ebook, paperback and audiobook.

Think *Black Mirror* with a Scandi-crime feel

In this alarming vision of the future, even your most spontaneous thoughts are shared on global social media. With privacy consigned to history, pre-mediated crime is dead and buried.

When Detective Oliver Braddon stumbles upon an unknown corpse, he's plunged into an investigation to track down a murderer who can kill without thinking.

A gritty, dystopian neo-noir that poses uncomfortable questions about our obsession with social media and presents a mind-bending picture of what life might be like when your very thoughts are no longer your own.

"Superb futuristic scenario – good story and touches of dark humour."
★★★★★

"Oh my God what a fantastic concept!"
★★★★★

"...and suddenly you need to tell everyone else to go away and let you finish this book!"
★★★★★

Book One of the Thinkersphere series available as an ebook and a paperback.

The dark sequel to *Hashtag*

Black Mirror meets Scandi-crime in a mind-bending dystopia where 'likes' matter more than lives.

Detective Oliver Braddon investigation into an apparent suicide leads him to a powerful media mogul and a mission into the unknown. Is he the killer?

In this alarming vision of the near-future, everyone's thoughts are shared on social media. With privacy consigned to history, a new breed of celebrity influences billions.

Just who controls who?

A gritty, neo-noir delving into a conflict between those connected and those who are not.

Book Two of the Thinkersphere series
available as an ebook and a paperback.

A bloke-lit tale of political intrigue and beer

CROSSING THE BRIDGE

DAVID WAKE

**Guy Wilson lives in the past.
Every year, he and his friends re-enact rebellion.
Every year, they celebrate the Jacobite's retreat.
Every year, they have a few drinks and go home...
...except this year, they go too far.**

An unstoppable boozing session meets an unbreakable wall of riot police in this satirical thriller. Guy struggles against corrupt politicians, murderous security forces and his own girlfriend in a desperate bid to stop a modern uprising.

And it's all his fault.

Will anyone survive to last orders?

"Witty, warm and well-written, "Crossing The Bridge" was so enjoyable that I didn't want to finish it."
★★★★★

"My sort of book. Couldn't put it down. Comedy, tension and an uncanny resemblance to the moral fibre of some of our elected representatives."
★★★★★

Available as an ebook and a paperback.

Printed in Poland
by Amazon Fulfillment
Poland Sp. z o.o., Wrocław